I0819279

BY MONIQUILL BLACKGOOSE

To Shape a Dragon's Breath
To Ride a Rising Storm

TO RIDE A RISING STORM

TO RIDE A RISING STORM

THE SECOND BOOK OF
NAMPESHIWEISIT

MONIQUILL BLACKGOOSE

NEW YORK

Del Rey
An imprint of Random House
A division of Penguin Random House LLC
1745 Broadway, New York, NY 10019
randomhousebooks.com
penguinrandomhouse.com

A Del Rey Trade Paperback Original

ISBN 978-0-593-49830-9
Ebook ISBN 978-0-593-49831-6

Printed in the United States of America

1st Printing

BOOK TEAM: Production editor: Cara DuBois • Managing editor: Paul Gilbert • Production manager: Angela McNally • Copy editor: Scott Heim • Proofreaders: Ethan Campbell, Liz Carbonell, Anya Getschel, Dan Goff

Book design by Alexis Flynn
Map and periodical chart illustration by Francesca Baerald
Dragon tack illustration by Crystal Sully copyright © 2026 by Crystal Sully

The authorized representative in the EU for product safety and compliance is Penguin Random House Ireland, Morrison Chambers, 32 Nassau Street, Dublin D02 YH68, Ireland. https://eu-contact.penguin.ie

THE BJALLADREKI
SADDLE
HINDCINCH
CRUPPER
CHEST
COLLAR
BREASTPLATE
FORE-
CINCH
III
I
II

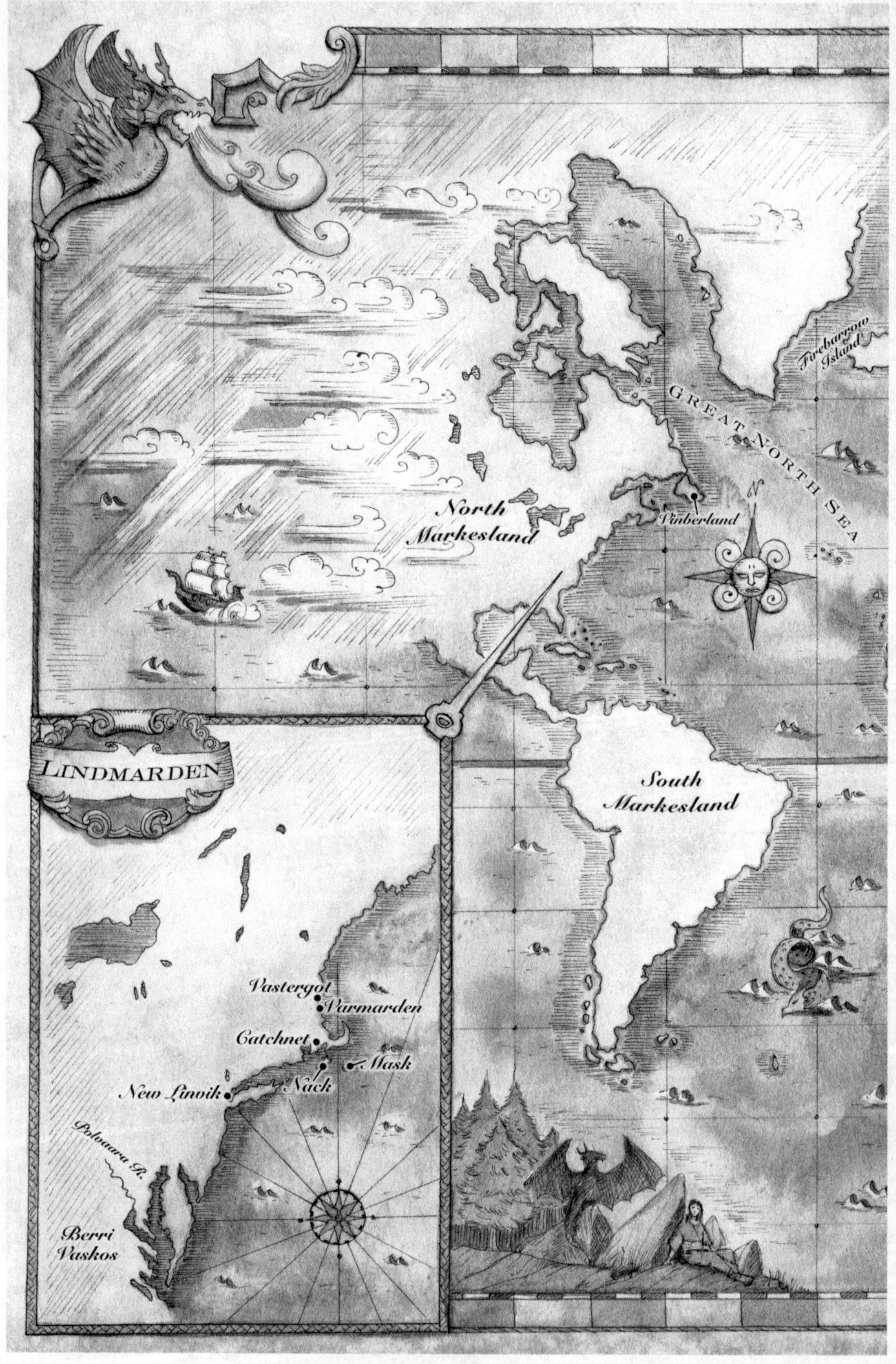
North Markesland
Vinberland
GREAT NORTH SEA
Firebarrow Island
South Markesland
LINDMARDEN
Vastergot
Varmarden
Catchnet
Mask
Nack
New Linvik
Polovaara R.
Berri Vaskos

Russland
Norsland
Finnland
Swedeland
NARROW SEA
BALT SEA
Anglesland
Celtsland
Tyskland
Polland
Frankland
Roveland
Tuscanland
BLACK SEA
Vaskosland
Turksland
MIDLAND SEA
Parshanland
Zhongu
Shiang-Gang
Zhippon
Farth
Widnes
Coptland
Kindah
Kedar
Indusland
Aprika
THE KNOWN WORLD

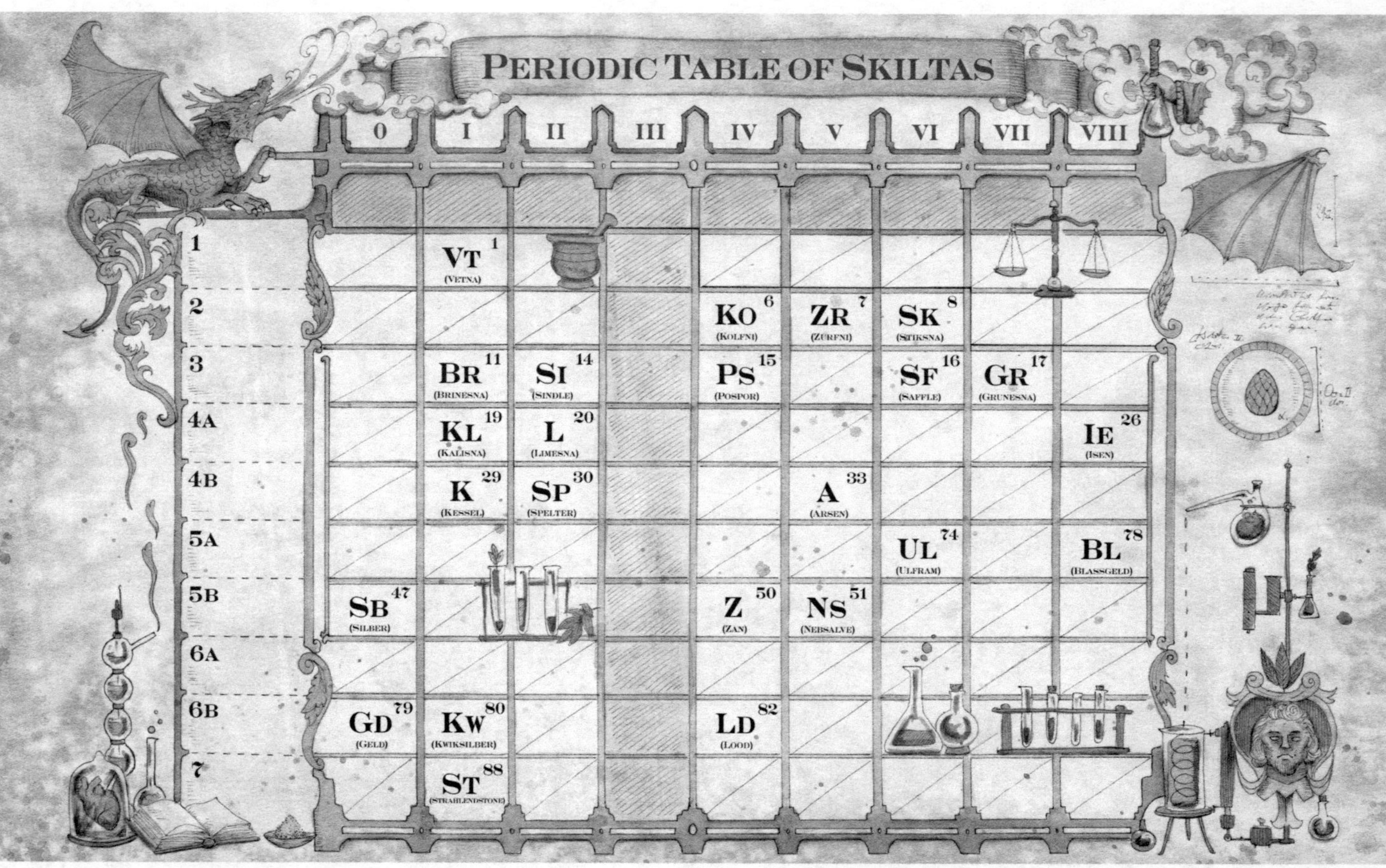

Periodic Table of Skiltas

	0	I	II	III	IV	V	VI	VII	VIII
1		VT 1 (VETNA)							
2					KO 6 (KOLFNI)	ZR 7 (ZURFNI)	SK 8 (STIKSNA)		
3		BR 11 (BRINESNA)	SI 14 (SINDLE)		PS 15 (POSPOR)		SF 16 (SAFFLE)	GR 17 (GRUNESNA)	
4A		KL 19 (KALISNA)	L 20 (LIMESNA)						IE 26 (ISEN)
4B		K 29 (KESSEL)	SP 30 (SPELTER)			A 33 (ARSEN)			
5A							UL 74 (ULFRAM)		BL 78 (BLASSGELD)
5B	SB 47 (SILBER)				Z 50 (ZAN)	NS 51 (NEBSALVE)			
6A									
6B	GD 79 (GELD)	Kw 80 (KWIKSILBER)			LD 82 (LOOD)				
7		ST 88 (STRAHLENDSTONE)							

PRONUNCIATION GUIDE

Akashneisit. . . . . ah-KASH-nay-ih-SIT
Akashnet. . . . . a-KASH-net
al-jabr .al-JAH-brr
Anequs. . . . . .ahn-eh-KOOS
Anglish. . . . . .AN-glish
Aponakwe . . . . app-on-ACK-way
Aponakwesdottir . . . . app-on-ACK-ways-dot-ter
Ashaquiat . . . . ash-AH-quee-at
ather . . . . AH-ther
bjalladreki . . . . BYA-la-DRAY-kee
Chagoma . . . . sha-GO-mah
Chequnnap . . . . .che-KOON-app
Eiriksthede. . . . . EYE-riks-THEED
Ekaitz . . . . eh-KITES

erelore . . . . EHR-lore
falterdrache . . . . FALL-ter-drack
Fyra . . . . FIE-ruh
Hekua . . . . HECK-oo-ah
Henkjan . . . . .HENK-yahn
Ivar Stafn . . . . EYE-var STAFF-in
jarl. . . . . YARL
Johan Einarsson . . . . YO-hahn EYN-ar-son
Jule . . . . YOOL
Karina Kuiper. . . . . .ca-REE-nah KY-per
Kasaqua . . . . ka-SAH-kwah
kesseldrache . . . . .KESS-el-drack
Kuhaukis . . . . koo-HOW-kiss
Leiknir Joervarsson . . . . . . .LEEK-near YORE-var-son
lichtbild . . . . LICHT-build
lichtbildmacher. . . . . .LICHT-build-mak-ker
machinakraft. . . . . MAHK-een-ah-craft
Mamisashquee . . . . MAH-mee-SASH-kwee
Marta Hagan . . . . MAR-tah HAY-gan
Masquapaug . . . . MASS-kwah-pog
Masquasup . . . . .MASS-kwah-sup
Masquisit . . . . MASS-kwis-it
Maswachuisit . . . . .mass-wah-CHOO-ih-sit
meddyglyn . . . . MED-DY-glin
Menukkis. . . . . men-OO-kiss
Mequeche . . . . meh-KWESH
Minanneka . . . . MEEN-ah-NECK-ah
Mishona . . . . mi-SHONE-ah
Motuckquas . . . . MOH-tuck-kwas
mupauanakausonat. . . moo-pow-AHN-a-COW-so-naht

musquetu .moos-KET-oo
Nampeshiwe . . . . nahm-PESH-ih-WAY
Nampeshiweisit. . . . . nahm-PESH-ih-WAY-ih-sit
Naquipaug . . . . .NAH-kwi-pog
Naquisit . . . . NAH-kwi-sit
Naregannisit . . . . nah-re-GAN-ih-sit
na'samp . . . . .nah-SAHMP
Nepinnae. neh-PIN-ay
Nikkomo . . . . ni-KO-mo
Niquiat. . . . . NICK-ee-aht
Noskeekwash. . . . . nos-KEEK-wash
Ommishqua . . . . .om-MISH-kwah
Peyaunatam . . . . pay-OW-nah-tam
sachem . . . . SAY-chem
Sakewa . . . . sah-KAY-wah
Sander Jansen . . . . SAND-er YAHN-sen
Seseque . . . . .seh-SEH-kway
Shanuckee . . . . SHA-noo-kee
Shiang-Gang . . . . .SHEE-ang-gang
Shulefrau Verbindung . . . .SHOOL-frow ver-BIND-ung
Sigoskwe . . . . .sih-GOSE-kway
silberdrache . . . . SIL-burr-drack
Sjokliffheim . . . . SYO-cliff-hime
skiltakraft . . . . SKILL-ta-craft
Strida . . . . STREE-dah
Tanaquish . . . . TAN-ah-kwish
Theod Knecht. . . . . THEE-ode NECKT
thynge. . . . . THING-ah; THING-eh
Valkyrja . . . . val-KEER-ya
Valkyrjafax. . . . . val-KEER-ya-fax

Valkyrjafaxnacht . . . . val-KEER-ya-fax-nockt
Vaskosish . . . . vas-KOH-sish
Vastergot . . . . VAS-ter-gaht
velikolepni . . . . vell-ih-KOH-lep-nee
Wampsikuk . . . . WAMP-see-kuk
witskraft . . . . WITZ-craft
Wompinottomak . . . . WOMP-ih-NOT-oh-mak
Wunnepan . . . . WUN-eh-pan
Wuskuwhani . . . . whu-SKOO-WAH-nee
Zhina . . . . ZHEE-nah
Zhippon . . . . ZHIP-on
Zhongu . . . . ZHON-goo

TO RIDE A RISING STORM

FIRST, ANEQUS CAME HOME

The first thing I saw, as Masquapaug became visible on the horizon, was the new Anglish encampment. The sight of it made my eyes sting and my breath catch. The Anglish were not supposed to be on Masquapaug—*home was supposed to be safe from them.*

I wanted to scream. I wanted to ask Kasaqua to loose her breath at it, shapeless and wild, reducing everything to ash and wind. I didn't just want the camp and its people gone; I wanted it to *never have been.*

The jarl and his people had hidden all of this from me until this morning.

On the ninth of May, a representative of the Ravens of Joden had made an attempt on the jarl's life, and had shot at Kasaqua and me in the process. Kasaqua had dispatched the would-be assassin. She wasn't yet one year of age and still could not fly, but she'd already killed a man in my defense—and in defense of the jarl, which made the act heroic rather than monstrous. At least to the jarl and his supporters.

It was the twenty-sixth of May today, and Theod and I had been informed just this morning that, in the wake of these events, the Ministry of Dragon Affairs had decided that Masquapaug—as a district of Lindmarden—ought to have an outpost of thanegards. Every other district had one, after all—even Naquipaug. Especially Naquipaug.

Whatever I might have expected them to do in seventeen days, it hadn't been this.

What had been the point of my going to the academy, in following all the rules that had been dictated to me, if the Anglish were going to be here anyway?

A neat row of white canvas tents stood along the road that led from the docks back to the village, and the skeletal timber frame of a building under construction loomed behind them. It was twice the size of the post and telegraph office, built in the Anglish style—a square base with a sharply sloping roof. It was not at all the kind of building that belonged on Masquapaug. I wondered, as we approached, if they'd sourced the timber locally—if trees that had grown on the island had been felled to make that monstrosity. And if they'd thought to plant new ones to replace the ones they'd killed.

"It's bigger than I thought it would be," I said, swallowing hard, gripping the rail so tightly that my fingers ached. I glanced at Theod. We were both leaning over the railing near the bow of a boat, gazing toward the island. He was staring at the tents, his face devoid of emotion. It couldn't be the same for him; he'd been raised among the Anglish. He wasn't *from* Masquapaug.

"Isn't it a provision of the treaty of 1757 that the Anglish can't even visit Masquapaug without special invitation?" he asked uncertainly, not looking away from the camp.

"It is," I said. "I wonder if Sachem Tanaquish signed an amendment, or if this is just a breach of the treaty. I wish someone had told us about this before."

Another thing they hadn't told us until after breakfast was that our travel plans from the academy had changed. We wouldn't be taking the train and the ferry as usual, but would instead be delivered by automotor to a private sailboat chartered by the office of the jarl. We'd be accompanied by a pair of handpicked guards armed with pistols. No one had been precisely clear on what we were being protected from. Or what was being protected from us.

Apart from "seeing to the safety of our journey from the academy to the island," the men in our company were here to ensure the seamless installation of the thanegards at their new outpost. They'd be staying on the island all summer and would be escorting us back to the security of the academy's grounds in September.

We had very little choice in the matter.

The worst of it was that the Anglish force was on Masquapaug because of me—because I was Nampeshiweisit.

I'd become Nampeshiweisit on the eighth of July last year, when a dragon of the kind native to this land—a Nampeshiwe—had been hatched in our meetinghouse on Masquapaug. Upon her hatching, Kasaqua had chosen *me* to be her lifelong companion.

The Anglish did not approve.

I had learned very soon after Kasaqua's hatching that the Anglish had innumerable laws concerning the keeping of dragons, particularly relating to who was and who wasn't allowed to pair with them. The indisputable fact that nothing, save death, could sever the bond shared by a dragon and its human companion meant that any dragon who chose a companion deemed unfit by Anglish authorities was at significant risk of being put to death. I had been expressly threatened with such a fate for Kasaqua, in the event that I did not prove myself fit—by Anglish standards—for the command of a dragon.

Because the Anglish did very much view it as *command*—not as a partnership or a way of relating.

By the Anglish way of thinking, dragons were weapons before anything else.

There were people in authority who believed that neither

Theod nor I should be allowed the command of dragons, because of our race. Theod's dragon, Copper, had only avoided being killed because he was held under the auspices of Frau Karina Kuiper, headmistress of Kuiper's Academy of Natural Philosophy and Skiltakraft. So long as Copper was housed in the school's dragonhall, his attachment to Theod had been . . . tolerated. That concession had made Theod something of a prisoner—a state of affairs that he had been willing to accept. The same fate had been intended for Kasaqua and me, but unlike Theod, I was not of a mind to endure separation from my family and my home.

So I'd become accomplished in the art of skiltakraft, and I'd dragged Theod along with me.

Having passed our examinations, we had the provisional permission given to all passing students of the academy: to travel home—with our dragons—for the duration of the summer recess.

Kasaqua thrust her nose into my armpit from behind in a demand for attention, pushing me with enough force that I had to steady myself against the handrail to keep on my feet. I could feel my connection with her in the cores of my bones; I was broadly aware of her wants and worries, and she of mine. At times of high emotion, it could seem that we were one creature.

She knew that I was angry and fraught, just now, and she didn't understand why.

Kasaqua made a chirping sound, and I turned to tousle the feathers at the crown of her head, right between her antlers. She'd gotten tall enough in these last weeks that she could comfortably rest her muzzle on my shoulder. She was still so slight in build that I hadn't tried her as a mount, but she was filling out quickly. Riding classes would certainly be on my schedule when I returned to the academy in September.

Theod's Copper was a year older than Kasaqua and nearing his adult size—six and half feet tall at the shoulder, twenty feet from nose to tail, thirty from wingtip to wingtip at full spread. He was an Akhari, of an excellent pedigree, bred across generations to be a long-distance flyer. He'd had his first flight in December, and while Theod could ride him over land, he couldn't bear Theod's weight in the air for more than fifteen or twenty minutes. Yet. He was sleeping on the sunniest part of the deck and seemed blissfully unaware of anything upsetting happening on the island.

Before I'd become Nampeshiweisit, the only person living on Masquapaug who wasn't a native of the islands had been Mister Aroztegui, the fastidious Vaskosman who ran the post and telegraph office. Naquipaug had had thanegards since the tragic events of 1825, but Masquapaug had been a place below Anglish notice of any kind.

Now, because I was Nampeshiweisit, we were subjects of great interest.

I stepped off the ferry and directly into my mother's arms. My siblings, Sigoskwe and Sakewa and especially Niquiat, had been able to visit me at school. I hadn't seen Mother or Grandma since Nikkomo—almost half a year. I'd been shot at, in the meantime.

"I've missed you *so* much," I said against her shoulder, hugging her as tightly as my tender ribs would allow. "I have so much to tell you about, and things I want to talk about, and—"

"Let's get you *home,*" Mother said, the warmth of her voice making my eyes sting.

There were introductions to be made, of course, and polite welcome made to our guards. They, thankfully, bid us goodbye and moved toward the encampment and building site. There was a whole carton of letters and telegrams waiting at the post office, some addressed to me and some addressed to Theod. We thanked Mister Aroztegui for them, and he welcomed us home.

My younger siblings were very keen to play with the dragons, marveling at how they'd both grown. That was just as well, because both Kasaqua and Copper were restless from general confinement, and having Kasaqua stretch her legs and wings was a point of pure relief among many different points of tension.

Nothing had ever tasted as good as the bowl of sobaheg that Mother put into my hands. It was a very green batch, as befitted springtime—made with ramps and sea rocket and cherrystone clams. It tasted like *home.*

I'd spent the last nine months, more or less, at Kuiper's Academy of Natural Philosophy and Skiltakraft in Varmarden. I'd studied many things there, but most importantly skiltakraft—the art of shaping a dragon's breath with witskrafty figures called skiltas. I'd successfully proven, under academic examination, that I was sufficiently skilled at skiltakraft to be allowed to pursue independent study—with the understanding that I'd return to the academy in September. Passing those examinations was the only reason that I had been allowed to take Kasaqua from the school grounds. Had I failed, Kasaqua would have been confined to the academy's dragonhall. I'd have been confined with her, because the idea of parting from Kasaqua was so abhorrent as to be immediately dismissed.

I hadn't particularly enjoyed leaving home to attend an Anglish academy, but I'd never have met Theod if I hadn't enrolled there. Theod's pairing with Copper had caused its own troubles with the Anglish, which my pairing with Kasaqua had redoubled. I had, in turn, redoubled Anglish troubles with Theod by reacquainting him with the family he'd been stolen from as an infant and giving him a reason to be something other than grateful and obedient. We were the only two nackie dragoneers, so we were seen as a natural pair—what either of us did reflected on the other, in the estimation of the Anglish. But we were both still very much outsiders.

Yet on the same day the jarl was shot, he'd made a declaration that *all* of the people residing on the outlying islands were citizens of Lindmarden—nackies included. The Anglish people settled on Naquipaug, in Nack Port, did not at all approve. The miners were on strike, and there'd been no shipments of coal since. It was something that would become a cause of concern to the mainland soon enough, when the coal stoppage impacted prices at market.

On the first afternoon and evening home, we relaxed and talked with everyone about the events of the last few months. I learned about events that had happened in the village since Nikkomo; none of it seemed terribly exciting in comparison to my last few months, but I was happy to hear it.

Theod and I unpacked some of our belongings; he was sleeping in Niquiat's old bed, as Niquiat was living in Vastergot, working at the cannery and studying machinakraft at his co-op.

We went down to the shore to gather mussels and enjoy the beach. Copper and Kasaqua had great fun splashing around the shallows, Copper taking short flights up and down the beach in pursuit of herring gulls. We made an early night of it, and my last thought as I lay on my bedroll staring up at the ceiling, listening to the crackling of the fire and the assorted breaths and murmurs of everyone else falling asleep, was that it was good to be home.

AND REACQUAINTED HERSELF WITH HER LOVED ONES

The next day, Theod and I were welcomed home like returning whalers. There'd been a feast prepared, and there was going to be a dance. It had all been planned in advance, and I was terribly glad that Mother had insisted on our behalf that we have a day to rest after our travels, before the celebration of our return.

We all pretended not to notice the Anglish men from the camp who came to quietly observe, and to ask the sachem why we were assembling. They seemed especially interested in the people who'd come across from Naquipaug in canoes, keeping a record of who was coming and going from the island.

They left without making friendly conversation.

Apart from the staples of any feast—baked beans, succotash, corn cakes, and steamed mussels—there were springtime foods on offer. It felt like an *age* since I'd eaten a green salad; vegetables at school had always been baked or stewed or pickled. At the feast my people had laid out, though, there was salad of fresh young spring leaves—sorrel, dock, greenbrier, rocket, and violet flowers. There was nettle soup with ramps and morel mushrooms, and steamed fiddleheads with roasted hazelnuts and maple syrup, and roasted cattail shoots. There was brook trout with saltwort shoots and bitter cress, and roasted eel with spruce-tip sauce. There were biscuits with cattail pollen, fried dandelion heads with honey, and locust-flower tea. All the best of springtime—none of which had been available at school, or even at the jarl's palace. The jarl's food had been a remarkable improvement from the school's bland and serviceable options, but it had still been Anglish food.

A circle was drawn; the four points were marked and blessed. Tobacco was offered.

The dancing began.

At first I sat out of the dances, too busy greeting friends and family—Theod's aunt Wampsikuk and her three children were among the visitors, as were my aunt Shanuckee and her children. I was a bit worried about the potential harm I could do to my ribs, which were still healing from the bullet wound. I did join in the young women's social with Hekua and Mishona, because it was a moderately paced dance that didn't require jumping or spinning.

Theod got pulled into the young men's promenade, despite protests of not knowing how to dance. The promenade was a simple two-step, and he managed it without much trouble. When the sachem announced the maiden's choice dance, Hekua swooped in and insisted that Theod dance with her. I came up to them as he was stammering, "I'm sorry, I don't know—"

"It's the maiden's choice dance, and I'm choosing you," Hekua said with a wild grin. "If you don't dance with me, that would be *rude.* And you'd owe me a boon."

Theod looked at me—begging for an explanation, or asking permission, or something like that. I couldn't help laughing, which felt mean because it only made him look more distressed.

"What kind of favor or boon?" he asked, looking from me to her and back.

Hekua crossed her arms and glared, because no able young man from Masquapaug would've even considered refusing something as simple as a dance with a girl who asked for one.

"If you don't dance with me," Hekua said, looking sly for a moment, "then you have to build me a house."

I whistled through my teeth, because that wasn't the kind of boon that anyone ever asked for. It was within the realm of things that *could* be asked for, of course, but it was outlandish. Brazen. Hekua was a third-born daughter with no prospect of ever being head of her mother's house, so she'd have to either build a new house someday or marry a man with no sisters.

Theod turned to me and asked, "Is she . . . serious?"

"*Dance* with her," I said, rolling my eyes. "It'll be fun."

Hekua took him by the hand and dragged him toward the dance circle.

I didn't ask anyone to dance for the maiden's choice—though I did notice several young men openly preening at me. Chequnnap, who'd asked my father if I was courting anyone. Seseque, who wasn't *formally* courting Hekua. I pretended great interest in teaching Kasaqua to catch thrown blueberries in midair until the choosing was over and I was safe.

The whole affair was awkward and hilarious to watch—Theod's stiff and mismatched steps, Hekua's mounting frustration, and Copper pawing the ground nervously as he looked on, momentarily unaware of being adored and celebrated. Kasaqua was not so distracted, and was shameless in her begging. It was mildly ridiculous now that she was so large, but she still managed to get bits and pieces from everyone's plates.

I rescued Theod from Hekua's attentions when the dance ended, and she seemed quite glad to leave him to me. He really was a hopeless dancer . . . at *our* dances. He'd been reasonably well accomplished at the Valkyrjafax ball, however, as I recalled. A waltz was a far simpler dance, in terms of rhythm and motion and footwork, than anything happening in this circle. It was also an altogether more *intimate* sort of dance.

"Well, that was certainly . . . something," Theod said as soon as Hekua was out of earshot.

"I don't expect Hekua will ask you to dance again," I said, stifling a giggle. "Which must have you absolutely devastated, I know."

"Hekua seems like a lovely girl," he said, tugging on the bottom edge of his shirt to smooth it, "but I don't want to give her the wrong idea about me."

"Oh, and what's the wrong idea?" I asked, unable to resist teasing a bit.

"There's only one girl I've got my eye on, Anequs," he said, fixing me with his gaze. I flushed, and found myself quite unable to take another breath, because there was such intensity in his warm brown eyes. There was something thrilling and disquieting about being fixed in a gaze like that. I swallowed, trying to think of what to say. Kasaqua butted her head into my shoulder, demanding my attention, saving me from having to say anything. A moment later, Seseque came over and invited Theod to play hoop-toss, and I encouraged him to go because it was important that he make friends with young men our age.

Late in the afternoon, Mishona managed to pull me aside. She was a first cousin, my uncle Mequeche's daughter, and we'd always been close—the same way my sister Sakewa and I were close—because I had no older sisters and Mishona had no younger ones. Her eyes were very bright and her voice a conspiratorial whisper when she said, looking around to make sure no one else was paying attention, "I've had no bleeding since the beginning of March."

My eyes widened, and I brought my hand up to cover my mouth and prevent myself from squealing in excitement.

"I've only told Mother, and Ashaquiat, and now you," she said. She didn't have to tell me not to tell anyone else, and I knew better than to offer congratulations. It could bring bad luck to mention a pregnancy before the baby quickened. We said nothing more on the topic, electing to visit the feasting tables for more fiddleheads.

I managed to get a few minutes with Sachem Tanaquish, and we talked about the presence of the Anglish on the island—how he'd first received a letter from the jarl himself that broadly praised Theod and me, and how he'd written about the possibility of proper representation in the law—and that for Masquapaug to be a district of Lindmarden, it would have to have thanegards. The sachem had written a letter in reply allowing them to build the outpost. He wasn't especially happy about it, but it was a pragmatic thing to concede to if it meant that we'd have our own torgar eventually.

Theod followed his family back to Naquipaug when they returned in the evening, with plans to come back for Strawberry Thanksgiving. I wasn't entirely sure how I felt about his departure. Part of me was glad to have a bit of time to spend alone with my family, but I found myself missing Theod from moment to moment; we hadn't really been apart since the meeting with the jarl. More than once I turned to see his reaction to something, only to remember that he *wasn't* standing quietly just to the side.

We hadn't talked about courting since December. I'd said then that we could talk about courting again after he'd passed his exam . . . and he had. I kissed him on the cheek before he mounted up on Copper to follow the canoes, and knew we'd have to talk about it properly when he returned. That I'd have to think about what I wanted to say, when we talked about it properly. That I'd have to tell him about my feelings for Liberty . . . which he might not understand at all, having been raised among the Anglish and their strange ideas about how people ought to arrange their households.

For the next week, I relaxed and enjoyed time with my loved ones. I sat with Mother and Grandma while we wove cattail mats and just talked for hours and hours. I gathered mussels with Sigoskwe and Sakewa, who played with Kasaqua in the surf in between telling me all the things I'd missed in the village while I'd been gone. I hilled up corn with Mishona and talked about her upcoming wedding feast. I slowly went through my stack of letters and telegrams.

There was a letter from Marta addressed jointly to Theod and me, about how we absolutely *must* come to visit her at Sjokliffheim for a garden party and bonfire that she was hosting on July eleventh. She said that Sander and Lisbet would be in attendance, and not to worry overmuch about attire because what we'd worn to the Fyrafax gathering would suffice.

Liberty sent me a letter detailing the relative quiet of the academy now that students weren't in attendance, and how she had more free time to do piecework—petticoats and shifts as well as gloves and handkerchiefs. She ended the letter with *all my love, Liberty*, and I felt a strange little thrill at reading those words, even though they were probably just pleasantry.

Most of the rest of the letters were either vitriolic condemnations—though none were specifically threatening harm to us or our dragons—or missives lauding us jointly, or me specifically, for having saved the jarl.

There was a letter from Ingrid Hakansdottir, whose father was one of the six men who'd been murdered in the anti-nackie riots after a series of newspaper articles both praising and condemning Theod and me had appeared. The murders were what had caused the jarl to hold the council we'd appeared at—the one immediately preceding his attempted assassination.

I felt a trepidation that was probably largely unwarranted as I broke the seal; Ingrid would certainly be within her rights to hate Theod and me for our indirect part in her father's murder.

Est. Miss Anequs,

I am very sad to tell you that my Father has been killed tho you might already know that because of the newspapers. My family has moved to Catchnet to live with my mother's cousin. Her children don't like Aksel and I very much Im afraid. I miss my father and I miss my old house.

I hope that you are quite well—I read in the newspaper that you were shot while defending the Jarl but that you are recovered. Mother and Auntie (she has told me to call her Auntie even though she's not my aunt she's my mother's counsin) have given me permission to invite you to come and have tea—please write me back with a time that is conveenent to you if you would like to. Mother would like to thank you for your kindness to Aksel and me at Fyrafax. I look forward to your reply,

With great admiration,
Ingrid Hakansdottir

I'd have to arrange to visit Ingrid as soon as possible to offer my condolences. I wondered if her family were at all involved with the first peoples group that Theod and I had met at midwinter last year, or if that group might be able to offer support to her family in their time of need.

I began penning a response immediately.

THEN SHE VISITED A FRIEND

I sent a reply to Ingrid on Tuesday the thirtieth, and she sent a reply on Friday the second. I sent a telegram to Theod the same day, and on the following Tuesday, he flew across the sound on Copper's back to meet me at the ferry office.

Copper could carry Theod for about fifteen minutes at a time without landing to rest, which meant that he could clear the three or so miles between the islands with ease, but getting to the mainland still required a ferry. I couldn't help but feel jealous of Theod for just how easily he was able to cross the channel—a ferry ran to and from Nack Port every day. By this time next year, Kasaqua would probably be capable of the same, and there would be no more bother about the ferry from Masquapaug to the mainland only running on Tuesday and Friday. Before I'd become Nampeshiweisit, I'd never imagined having any cause to visit the mainland more than a few times a year, so the infrequency of the ferry had never mattered.

I'd been dutifully putting Kasaqua to tack at least three times a week, as Professor Mesman had instructed, to keep myself practiced in putting it on her and her accustomed to the wearing of it. The professor had warned against trying to ride her over land without instruction, even if she grew large enough over the summer recess for that to be possible. Poor husbandry could result in injury to either or both of us.

Theod arrived at half past eight, landing Copper on the far side of our garden. The ferry was set to depart at nine.

"Did you have a good time with your family?" I asked as he was dismounting.

"I did, though things are even more fraught on Naquipaug than they were back in December," he said. "Nack Port has entirely closed itself to nackies, and there's rumors of dragoneers in town. They're building a dragonhall just outside the town wall."

"Well, we knew that they were planning to build a dragonhall," I said. "But I'd expected it to be somewhere near North Village, if Copper and Kasaqua are going to be quartered in it eventually—"

"I don't think this one is intended for us," he said, frowning.

I made a sound of worry and let that statement hang between us. Anglish dragons being quartered on Naquipaug couldn't mean anything good. After a long moment of silence, I said, "I missed you. While you were on Naquipaug, I mean."

"I missed you, too," he replied, sounding a bit flustered.

We walked together to the ferry office. Kasaqua was terribly excited to see Copper, bounding and prancing all around. She was out of tack, and Copper was fully tacked—and thus more restrained in his excitement and affection. Being in tack meant that he was on duty, and had much the same demeanor that Frau Kuiper's dragon had possessed the first time I'd seen him. I wondered, absently, if I should have put her into tack for this trip. I didn't have a saddle for her, but just putting her harness on communicated a certain discipline and purpose.

There was an Anglish man sitting in Mister Aroztegui's office when we arrived.

He was wearing the same kind of uniform that the thanegards in Vastergot wore: a double-breasted coat of gray canvas with a double line of bright brass buttons down the front, belted at the waist. He had a truncheon and a pistol hanging at the ready. He was reading a newspaper and looked up when Theod and I entered. He looked past us, out the door, where Copper and Kasaqua were standing. He frowned.

"Good morning," I said, more from surprise than out of any real desire to be congenial.

"You're the two dragoneers, eh?" he said, folding the newspaper and tucking it away before standing. "Come to check for more letters?"

"We're visiting a friend on the mainland, actually," I said, stepping toward the counter. Mister Aroztegui appeared from the room behind the office, carrying a stack of papers.

"Ah, well, if that's your intention, I'm very glad that I happened to be here," the thanegard said. "My name is Captain Trov Johansen, and I'm the seniormost officer of the Mask Island outpost. Henceforth, we're going to require anyone who comes or goes on the ferry to sign a guestbook, so we can keep a record of any and all travelers to and from the mainland."

He gestured toward a large volume that was sitting on the counter, beside the cash register. Mister Aroztegui, standing behind the register now, offered a thin smile. There was apology in his eyes.

"We've never had to do such a thing before," I said, warily approaching the book. At the door, Kasaqua made an inquiring noise and nosed the doorknob.

"Yes, it's quite clear to the jarl and his council that all record-keeping regarding the activities of citizens on Mask Island has been shockingly lax," Captain Johansen said, looking to the door and frowning. "One of our chief goals with the new outpost is to better integrate you islanders into society at large. Catchnet Thede has clearly been in need of attention for quite some time, and Jarl Joervarsson is seeing it to rights. We'd like to do everything in our power to avoid another unfortunate incident like the one in 1825."

Incident? The Anglish considered the massacre of fully half the population of Naquipaug an "incident"? I set my teeth and took a breath. On the other side of the door, Kasaqua made a louder and obviously complaining noise. She was fully capable of knocking the door down, and I tried to convey through our bond that she should *not* do that . . . which was harder than it ought to have been, because I couldn't stop thinking about how amusing that could be.

"Is Sachem Tanaquish aware of this?" I asked, glaring at the guestbook. Was this another concession he'd made to keep the peace, in hopes that we'd be treated fairly if we behaved "civilly"?

"If that's the name of the elderly gentleman who's been acting as a representative, then yes, everything has been approved by local governance. Any dispute can be brought up at the thynge in August."

In the guestbook, there were fields for our names, the time of our departure, the time of our intended return, and what business we were about. I could see, on the lines above, the names of people who'd come from the mainland when the ferry had arrived at seven-thirty. All of them were Anglish men, claiming some involvement in the construction and manning of the outpost. Most of them declared intentions to return to the mainland with the evening ferry.

Theod put his hand on my shoulder, his voice quiet and terribly precise when he said, "It's not unreasonable for someone to be keeping track of who's coming and going. It's a safeguard against mainlanders arriving uninvited and unannounced."

"If they come by ferry," I said. "Anyone with command of a fully adult dragon could turn up without being accounted for, at any time of the day or night. Frau Kuiper rode Gerhard here last summer, and she hadn't been expressly invited. You rode here on Copper just now, and no one had anything to say about it."

"Actually, the young man's passage was recorded in the watch log," Captain Johansen said. "Both he and his dragon are quite distinctive and easy to identify at distance with a spyglass."

"It won't hurt anything to have a record, especially with so many more people coming and going than there were before," Theod said.

I turned to look at him then, wondering how I could make him understand. Masquapaug had managed to avoid having any dealings with Anglish governance at all, beyond the annual visit in November when they collected taxes and took folkreckoning. Now they had an outpost of thanegards. How long would it be before there were mainlanders looking to build docks or farmsteads?

Theod and I signed the book and paid our fares, then boarded the ferry with our dragons. I spent a long time caressing Kasaqua behind the ears and running my fingers through her hackles—more to calm myself than her. She crooned softly and leaned into it, understanding that I was upset.

"Do you know anything at all about Quoquinna's War?" I asked Theod, when the island had slipped out of view.

"Can't say that I do," he said. "Erelore lessons weren't exactly a part of my upbringing. I know a bit about Stafn Whitebeard and a bit about Fyra Eiriksdottir, but I don't know if I've ever heard the name Quoquinna."

"Quoquinna's War ended in 1757, with the signing of a treaty," I said, leaning against the rail and looking out across the water. "Quoquinna was the sachem of the Naregannisit—the one that's supposed to be Ingrid's ancestor. The Naregannisit people lived all around Gannet Cove, and west of the Gannet River, and points inland, back when the Anglish arrived to settle Catchnet in the 1730s. The Akashneisit people lived east of the Gannet River and along the south coast, all the way up the Fishhook Headland. The

Maswachuisit people lived farther north, where Vastergot is now. The Anglish brought them to ruin first, in Vaster's War, in the 1650s."

"Nobody's ever told me *any* of this," Theod said, bitterness creeping into his voice.

"You'd have been told if you'd grown up among your own people," I said. "The Anglish like to pretend that erelore in Markesland started when Thorvald Eiriksson found Vinberland, but people have always been here. After Vaster's War, the remainders of the Maswachuisit people fled south, into Akashneisit lands. Quoquinna put aside the old enmity to form an alliance between the Naregannisit, the Akashneisit, and Maswachuisit. The Naquisit and Masquisit remained largely uninvolved; the Anglish were a mainlander problem until the founding of Nack Port."

"Which was when?" Theod asked.

"In the 1740s; I'm not sure exactly. Emanuel Nordlund visited the Naquisit from 1746 through 1750, I know that. He was one of the first Anglish settlers on Naquipaug. If the Maswachuisit hadn't been so kind and hospitable to Stafn Whitebeard and his shipthede back in 1626, they might have avoided all manner of problems with the Anglish in the long run. I wish there were a way to go back in time and warn them about what was to come."

"If there was a way to go back in time, I'm sure there's a lot of things that a lot of people would wish to change," Theod said.

I didn't know what to say to that, so we were quiet for a while, just watching the water. I wanted to talk to him about courting, wanted to be holding his hand right now . . . but the ferry was too conspicuous a place for that kind of thing. No one seemed to be paying very much attention to us, but there were Anglish men on the boat—and any of them might begin rumors that could cast doubt on our "correct and honorable behavior." Dragoneers declared "morally unfit" by the Ministry of Dragon Affairs could have their dragons seized and killed, under Anglish law.

We arrived at the Catchnet docks at half past ten. No one there asked us to sign anything indicating our passage, though everyone at the docks paid attention to the presence of dragons. Ingrid and her brother, Aksel, were waiting for us, and Ingrid rushed forward to hug me practically as soon as we'd stepped off the boat. I sucked a sharp breath through my teeth, because my ribs still weren't entirely all right.

"Careful," I squeaked. Kasaqua made a chuffing sound of complaint, stepping forward to nudge Ingrid with her head until she pulled away from me and focused her attention on petting Kasaqua instead. Kasaqua dropped to the ground, her tail thumping on the cobblestones, presenting herself for adoration. Copper's attitude was cooler, and he edged forward to put himself between Theod and the children.

"I'm so glad you came!" Ingrid said, bouncing on her toes. "Everything has been awful since our father was killed. We had to move, and now I live far away from all my friends, and Aksel can't go to school anymore, and we couldn't even bring most of our things with us."

As we walked from the docks, Ingrid gave an unceasing commentary about her family's recent move, and the disposition of her aunt and uncle and cousins, and everything she'd learned about Catchnet so far. Aksel, by contrast, was silent and dejected, with his hands shoved in his pockets and his gaze firmly on the ground.

There were people watching our passage through the streets—staring openly, pointing, whispering to one another. We were four nackies with two dragons walking through downtown Catchnet. Theod and I had appeared in several different newspaper articles, besides, with lichtbilds of us and the dragons. Anonymity wasn't really open to us anymore.

Kasaqua was four feet tall at the shoulder now, and Copper more than six. Theod and I walked side by side, the dragons flanking us, with Ingrid taking the lead and Aksel tagging behind. There was a certain confidence that came from being bracketed between two such formidable creatures; it made the glares and murmurs seem inconsequential.

I realized after a bit of walking that we were headed in the same general direction that we'd come at midwinter: a district of Catchnet north of Merchant Street and its shops. Until last year, I'd only ever come to Catchnet for our annual shopping trip when Father came back from the sea with his whaling shares. We passed by the warehouses, including the one where the dance had been held, and to the residences beyond. This part of Catchnet reminded me of the cannery district in Vastergot: tall brick walls and narrow alleys, the whitewash dingy with soot. The air had a slightly oily quality, and the smell of coal smoke and scorched lard penetrated everything.

The faces became markedly friendlier, though, as we got farther from Merchant Street. More people were visibly of nackie heritage; I thought I recognized a few from the midwinter feast, in fact. People were less likely to stare and more likely to smile and wave and call their children to come look at the dragons as we passed.

The building we arrived at was one of a row of three-story brick edifices, the whitewash flaking off to reveal the brick beneath. It was immediately apparent that the dragons were too large to comfortably follow us inside. Kasaqua was, with vocal and obvious disapproval, becoming used to bedding in the three-sided structure we'd built beside the house for the dragons—though she still draped herself across the doorway from time to time, or stuck her head in to make complaining noises if she felt neglected. She whined and huffed when she realized that she'd be staying outside, but joined Copper in flanking the front door without more fuss than dramatically lying down to sulk.

My very first thought, upon meeting Ingrid and Aksel's mother, was that she seemed entirely too young to have a twelve-year-old son and a ten-year-old daughter. She was a small, neat, tired-looking woman older than twenty but younger than thirty, a bit lighter skinned than Theod or me, with dark hair braided back and liquid black eyes like a deer.

"Hello!" she said, standing aside from the door to let us in. "It's so good of you to come. I'm Wigdis, and of course you already know Ingrid and Aksel. My cousin and her children have stepped out for the day, so we have the flat to ourselves. Come in, have a seat. What's that you're carrying?"

"Oh, we've brought corn cakes and blueberry jam," I said. "As thanks for inviting us."

"That's terribly kind of you," Wigdis said, standing aside and gesturing for us to enter.

The interior of the flat was a single room, one corner divided off by a set of curtains. There was a cast-iron stove in another corner, and Wigdis fetched a kettle from it. The table was a couple of planks set on bricks. Folded blankets served as chairs. Bedrolls were lined up against both interior walls, and the singular window, set in the back wall, was covered in greased brown paper that let in a weak and sallow light. It was a strange combination of familiar and unfamiliar. My house back on the island was only one room, really, and not much larger than this. We didn't have chairs and a table in the Anglish style, and mostly took meals sitting around the fire or—weather permitting—outside. But there was something that felt pinched and shabby about this place. There were no deerskins or woven hangings on the walls. The coal fire smelled wrong. It felt more like Niquiat's flat in Vastergot than like home.

Wigdis offered us tea in chipped, worn clay mugs. There was no sugar. If it weren't for the cakes and jam we'd brought, there wouldn't have been any food.

Once we were all situated, Wigdis said, "My given name was Weeweeshas." Her voice was very soft, as if it were secret or shameful. Ingrid looked at her then with absolutely fervent curiosity, but didn't ask any of the questions she obviously had. "I've gone by Wigdis for years now—the whole time I lived in Vastergot, really. My grandmother, Sautaashsqua, was one of Quoquinna's daughters. I was quite young when she passed, and didn't learn as much from her as I should have. I'm not sure how much you know about Quoquinna's War, and the way the Anglish took the Narry-gannet lands, but . . ."

"I don't know many Naregannisit people, I'm afraid," I said. "I know that there was war in the 1750s, and that the treaty of 1757 was when the lands held in common by the Naregannisit were formally ceded to the Anglish. This past winter, we met briefly with Mokumannit Aestridsson—I think he's also known as Machman Aestridsson? He's a representative of the Confederation of the First People of Akashnet, along with Lise Nokehick and Alrik Mowashuck."

"I don't know anything about those people, except having heard their names a few times. Ardis, my cousin, says that we do not associate with people like that. People who want to make trouble."

"What kind of trouble have they made, exactly?" Theod asked. "The headmistress of Kuiper's Academy was very angry with us this past midwinter for having appeared together with them in a lichtbild in the newspaper."

"They form illegal assemblies," Wigdis said. "They print and distribute subversive writings and encourage people to write angry letters to the thane, and things like that. A lot of them have been arrested and imprisoned. They want to overthrow Thane Jespersen and replace him with a nackie thane."

It hadn't occurred to me that it might be possible for a thane to be a nackie; thanes were chosen by the landowners of each thede, with any business concerning smallfolk represented to the thanes by torgars. The torgar responsible for both Naquipaug and Masquapaug had never even visited Masquapaug. The thane responsible for Catchnet Thede at large had never been to either island, as far as I knew. What Anglish landowner would ever vote for a nackie?

"Well, I'm not sure what makes an assembly legal or illegal; on Naquipaug, we frequently bring the whole community together in the meetinghouse. We'll be doing it on the fifteenth, for Strawberry Thanksgiving."

"Oh, my grandmother used to talk about Strawberry Thanksgiving," Wigdis said, an edge of longing in her voice. "Strawberries are so dear, though, we're not often able to justify the expense. Certainly not this year."

The idea that strawberries could be anything but a gift was foreign and wrong in a way that made me frown. Strawberries weren't meant to be bought or sold. But then, this wasn't the kind of place where the land offered up gifts. Every part of Catchnet I'd ever seen was paved in cobblestones or gravel or crushed shells. Nothing *grew* in Catchnet, unless it was in window boxes.

"You should come to the island for our feast, then," I said. "The three of you. We'd love to have you."

"Oh, I couldn't possibly. The ferry fare—"

I reached into my pocket and took out three marka coins. Fare for the ferry to Masquapaug was a halfmarka, so three marka would pay for all three of them both ways. I had the money because Niquiat had sent extra home. When I was at the academy, I'd had an allowance of five marka per week, because "It would reflect badly on the school for anyone to think me a penniless ragamuffin." Before Niquiat had started working at the cannery and sending money home, our family had only had Anglish money from my father's whaling shares—around five hundred marka for the year. Three marka would have been a considerable expense.

"The fifteenth is a Thursday, though, and the ferry to Mask Island only runs on Tuesday and Friday," Wigdis said, looking at the coins in her hand as if she weren't sure they were real.

"Then come on Tuesday and stay until Friday," I said. "You could stay at the meetinghouse, with the people who come visiting from Naquipaug."

"That's . . . that's very kind of you," Wigdis said, sounding plainly astonished. "I had meant to ask you—and please let me know if this is an inappropriate thing to ask, and I won't mention it again—but how does a person petition to come and live on Masquapaug?"

"I don't know that anyone's ever asked, apart from marrying into someone's household," I said, considering. "But I'm sure that Sachem Tanaquish has the authority to allow such a thing. I'll introduce you at the feast, and you can talk with him about it."

"I'd be very grateful," she said, smiling. "I've felt terrible imposing on my cousin's hospitality. She and her husband already have three mouths to feed, and I haven't been able to find wage work here in Catchnet yet. I took in washing, in Vastergot, but there's a plunderbund of public laundries here that are all run by the same Vaskosish family and . . . well. Work isn't easy to find, and without work, I can't afford rent, so here we are."

"I'll talk to the sachem when we return on the evening ferry," I said. "And you can talk to him when you come for Strawberry Thanksgiving."

We spent part of the afternoon playing card games; I didn't know the rules to Linger Longer, but Theod did, so the two of us played as a team until I'd gotten the knack of it. At Ingrid's suggestion, we took a walk to the community garden—an empty lot paved with crushed shells that housed at least a dozen raised beds. They'd all been recently tilled, and in a few of them I could see seedlings starting. Kasaqua was immediately happy to chase Ingrid through the maze of knee-high boxes, which involved a lot of crouching and peeking around corners. Copper watched without joining in, instead stretching and yawning hugely and settling himself at Theod's feet; Theod was in conversation with Aksel, and I didn't want to interrupt.

"The lot belongs to the same landlord who owns this whole block of flats—there was a building here, but it burned down," Ingrid told me, gesturing broadly to the row of flats we'd come from. "We don't have a box; they're rented just like flats are. But it's as nice a place to come walk as anywhere in the north end."

"What's growing here?" I asked. Upon closer inspection, all of the boxes seemed to be laid out in rows in the Anglish style; nothing looked interplanted.

"Potatoes and summer squash, mostly, according to my cousin," Wigdis answered. "Some of the people who can afford box rents sell produce when the harvest comes. Fresh produce is very dear at market."

I had to wonder if that was as true for the Anglish as it was for anyone else; food at the school was seldom fresh and seemed to center heavily on oats, potatoes, cabbage, and sausages. There wasn't nearly the kind of variety I was used to at home. I had a feeling that Wigdis and Ingrid and Aksel hadn't enjoyed that kind of variety at any time in their lives, but I didn't want to ask.

Theod and I returned home on the four o'clock ferry, arriving at half past five. After dinner, we visited with Sachem Tanaquish at his house and talked about the day over coffee. He said that he'd ask around some of the other homesteads to see if anyone might be willing to host Wigdis and her children until a new homestead could be built—which reminded me that I ought to be thinking about the building of my *own* future homestead and dragonhall.

In all, it felt like a very important day—like our visit to the mainland had set something new into motion. Masquapaug had, in the distant past, been much more peopled. Before the great dying, there'd been a city here as great as Catchnet or even Vastergot.

There was no reason to think that such a thing couldn't be achieved again.

AND CELEBRATED STRAWBERRY THANKSGIVING

Theod went back to Naquipaug after our conversation with the sachem, and we still hadn't made time to talk about . . . us. There hadn't been a comfortable time to bring it up; we hadn't been alone together.

In the first half of June, quite a lot of my spare time was devoted to picking strawberries—from the gardens, of course, but also from farther afield. Like gathering nuts in autumn, it was an occasion for the whole family to go into the forest together in search of the gifts of the season—though Father was always at sea for strawberry season. The ripening of strawberries marked the first breath of summer, with the promise of blueberries and blackberries and brambleberries to follow, and summer squash and green corn and fresh beans, and the bluefish run.

Strawberries in household gardens tended to be larger, from being kept carefully and fed on fish meal and leafmold—and from generation after generation of gardeners choosing which runners to nurture and which to pinch off to give the others room. Strawberries in the forest were smaller—no bigger than the tip of a little finger—but they were sweeter and more brightly flavored. Mid-morning was the best time to hunt for wild strawberry patches, the sun burning off the dew and carrying the fragrance of the ripe berries into the air along with the smell of new grass and wildflowers. It was the smell of June on Masquapaug.

We dried some of the berries, made some into jam, and pickled some others. The majority, though, were dedicated to the feast of Strawberry Thanksgiving. It was a time to put aside any quarrels and strife, to be thankful for the gifts of the land and the return of vigorous life after spare winter and tentative spring.

On the morning of Tuesday the thirteenth, Theod and I went to the docks to wait for the ferry from Catchnet, which arrived at half past seven. Sachem Tanaquish met us on the way; he was coming to welcome our guests, too. The boat arrived at the dock, and Wigdis was standing on the deck with Ingrid on her right arm and Aksel on the left. They were noticeably distanced from the rest of the passengers: a gang of Anglish builders and day laborers coming to work on the thanegards' outpost.

"Good morning," the sachem said, as Wigdis and her children stepped off the boat, well behind all the other passengers. "My name is Tanaquish, sachem of the Masquisit—you might understand me best as a kind of torgar of the island. I've talked to many different households, and Chansompsqua is willing to host you until Friday. She says her house feels empty since her youngest son married. She doesn't move as well as she once did, which is why she didn't join us to greet you—you'll meet her at the meetinghouse."

"Thank you so much for having us," Wigdis said, as we walked to the office so she could sign the guestbook. There was a thanegard at the ferry office—not Captain Johansen—who barely looked up from the sheaf of papers he was reading and said nothing to us. It seemed that there was going to be a thanegard posted here in perpetuity.

We left the office and the Anglish compound behind, heading

for the meetinghouse. Even on days with no planned gathering, there were always people at the meetinghouse; today it was a group of elders drinking coffee. Grandma was among them, and I greeted her and kissed her cheek. The sachem introduced Wigdis and the children to Chansompsqua, who was one of Grandma's contemporaries, but not someone I knew especially well; her sons were all much older than me. Wigdis gladly accepted coffee and joined the circle of elders, saying to her children, "This will probably be very boring for you. Why don't you join Anequs and Theod? Anequs, you have siblings my children's ages, don't you?"

"A little younger," I said. "Sakewa became nine in November, and Sigoskwe became eleven in March."

"I'll be eleven in September!" Ingrid said. "And Aksel will be thirteen in October."

"Close enough," Wigdis said with a small, brittle laugh. "Go on, have fun."

"When in September?" Theod asked, looking to Ingrid. "My birthday is the sixteenth."

"Mine is the twenty-eighth, and Aksel's is the third of October, and since they're so close, usually we have cake together in the middle. How old are you going to be?"

"Eighteen, this year," Theod said. Ingrid nodded, looking thoughtful.

We returned home, where Sakewa was sitting in front of the house, working on some finger weaving. Mother was at the fire, making corn cakes.

"Hello, Ingrid!" Sakewa said brightly as soon as she noticed us, her greeting gaining Mother's attention, too. Ingrid immediately fell into conversation about finger weaving with Sakewa, and Theod was still talking with Aksel, which left me free to talk to Mother about Wigdis and her installation at Chansompsqua's house. Mother quietly made enough corn cakes to share with Ingrid and Aksel. Half an hour later, Sigoskwe returned from the forest with a basket of strawberries freshly ripe that morning and inserted himself into Aksel and Theod's conversation.

We spent all of Tuesday and Wednesday acquainting our visitors with the island. Ingrid fell in quite naturally with Sakewa's friends, and Aksel only a bit less well with Sigoskwe's. We showed them the ruins at Beachy Hill, and took them to Great Sweet Pond, and gathered mussels by the shore. Ingrid learned more about finger weaving, and Aksel about fishing. Wigdis spent most of her time with Chansompsqua, who introduced her to women her own age—her sons' wives, and their sisters and cousins.

On Thursday morning, Mother spent the early hours boiling rounds of dense, sweet strawberry bread. Grandma went early to the meetinghouse to talk with other elders and help arrange dishes as people brought them. Sigoskwe and Sakewa took Ingrid and Aksel into the woods to hunt for newly ripe berries and came back with two baskets full. When the boiled bread was done, we all headed to the meetinghouse.

By the time we got there, people were arriving from across the channel—including Aunt Shanuckee's household. Great-Aunt Mamisashquee hadn't been over from Naquipaug since Nikkomo, and Auntie Shanuckee and my cousins hadn't been since the whalers' departing dance, which I'd missed because I'd been at school. There was a lot of greeting and hugging and marveling about how everyone had grown—especially the dragons. Theod's family—his grandmother and aunt and little cousins from Naquipaug—had also arrived, and he left our party to visit with them.

Once everyone had assembled, all of the best dishes of Strawberry Thanksgiving were on offer—smoked turkey with strawberry-mint sauce, green salad with pickled strawberries, strawberry-elderflower shrub, boiled strawberry bread with strawberry sauce, and strawberry corn cakes. Strawberry Thanksgiving wasn't the kind of gathering where a circle was drawn and blessed, and there were no formal dances. That didn't mean that dancing wouldn't happen, though.

Kasaqua had tired herself out playing with the children and was sleeping in the sunshine just outside the meetinghouse. Theod had put his little cousins on Copper's back and taken them on a walk in a circle around the meetinghouse, and now other children were begging for a chance to ride a dragon. Copper seemed to be enjoying the attention very much.

I spent a while talking to Auntie Shanuckee and Great-Auntie Mamisashquee, catching them up on recent events—the installation of the thanegards chief among them.

"Has anyone told you yet that there are six dragons on Naquipaug?" Mamisashquee said, looking dramatically scandalized and indignant.

"Theod heard rumors about that," I said. "We only got back to the island on the twenty-sixth, and I've been catching up this whole time. No one told us about the thanegards, either, until we'd arrived."

Mamisashquee sucked her teeth and nodded sagely before saying, "They say they were sent by the jarl to keep the peace. They've built a dragonhall just outside of Nack Port, and you *have* to pass by it if you want to get into the city from anywhere else on the island. Not that nackies can, generally; the port is closed to us, save access to the ferry. There's a new road to the docks, outside the town wall. Two of the dragoneers visited North Village. Not dragons like yours, but thorny silver-white monsters eight foot tall at the shoulder."

"Silberdraches," I said, nodding. Eight feet at the shoulder was probably an exaggeration, but not by much. "They're a favored breed in the dragonthede, along with kesseldraches. Most of the jarlsgards who are dragoneers are bonded to silberdraches, I think."

Mamisashquee hummed agreement, then said, "There's a lot of talk about the choosing of new torgars, too, whatever that may be."

"They're an office of governance; they're supposed to report the needs and wants of the common people—anyone who doesn't own land—to their thane. I have no idea how they're chosen, but I think it has something to do with the thynge that the jarl is having in August."

"The two dragonriders who visited said something like that. They also said that they expect the jarl to announce that Masquapaug should have its own torgar, independent from Naquipaug."

"Really, if I've understood how the ranks work, we ought to have a thane of our own and not just a torgar; we're the principal landowners! But I suppose any representation would be better than none. We've been paying taxes for how many generations now?"

"At least since my grandparents' time," Mamisashquee said, thoughtfully. "Wompinottomak is having a meeting in North Village soon. You and Theod ought to come. With your dragons."

"Maybe we should," I said, glancing out the door of the meetinghouse. Theod was still leading Copper in circles. "I'm going to see how Wigdis and her family are getting on. They're guests that I invited, after all."

"There's a good girl, always thinking of others," she said with a motherly smile, reaching out to smooth my hair.

Ingrid found me before I found Wigdis; she was sitting in a circle with Sakewa and some other girls of that age, but she jumped up when she saw me and told the others she'd be back in a moment. She seemed to have something very important to say, taking me by the hand and leading me away from the general commotion of the gathering. She looked around to make sure no one was listening when she asked, her voice just above a whisper, "Anequs, who's that man, and why is he dressed like a woman?"

She looked over her shoulder at Mamisashquee, who was sitting with the other elders again. Someone had said something that made her laugh. Great-Auntie had a laugh like a seagull's, unapologetically loud and sharp.

"That's my great-aunt, Mamisashquee—my father's mother's sister. She's not a man. She's a mupauanakausonat—she has a woman's spirit and is regarded in every way as a woman. When she was a little child, everyone thought she was a boy—but she grew up to be a woman."

"But she looks and sounds like a man!" Ingrid said, sounding a bit distressed.

"Well, she's not. And I'm glad you asked me instead of making a fuss about it. I don't think the Anglish have mupauanakausonat people—or at least I've never met any Anglish person who is. But there are mupauanakausonat people living on the islands, and there always have been since the first people."

Ingrid nodded, biting her lip and looking thoughtful.

"You know, Great-Auntie Mamisashquee is an excellent storyteller. I bet she'd tell a story to you and all your new friends if you asked her nicely."

"Would . . . would you come with me? To ask?"

"I'd be delighted," I said, then, turning to where Mamisashquee was sitting, called, "Auntie, Ingrid has a question for you!"

My great-aunt rose and moved toward us, like a goose floating across water. I tossed my head to indicate the whole group of girls, and we all convened there. Ingrid took a deep breath, as if she needed to steel herself before asking, "Can you tell us a story? Anequs says you're a very good storyteller."

"Oh, well, if Anequs says so, then it must be true," Mamisashquee said, smiling broadly, lowering herself to the floor with unhurried grace, smoothing her skirts just so. She immediately became the head of their circle and the center of their attention. Sakewa grinned, glancing at me for a moment before looking back to Mamisashquee.

"Everyone listen well, because this is an important story," Mamisashquee began.

THIS IS THE STORY THAT MAMISASHQUEE TOLD

Now, I'm sure that you already know, my lovelies, that Masquasup the Giant created the islands of Masquapaug and Naquipaug while he was building a fishing weir; you can still see the remains of the weir that make up the fishhook cape. He and his wife, Sequannit, the sea woman, gathered sand and stones from the bottom of the bay and threw them over their shoulders into the sea behind them. Soon enough the coast of the mainland was hollowed out into a hook shape, and the two islands and all their little islets had been built up on the other side. Seeing the new islands, Masquasup thought of his friends, the first people, who then were living along the south coast of the narrow land.

The first people had many sons and daughters who were clever and adventuresome, and they filled their canoes with good things from the mainland and paddled across to the islands. The first people named the islands for the fresh water that could be found on them, because an island with no fresh water is no place for a settlement. The northeast island, they named Masquapaug—the sweet-flag pond. The southwest island they named Naquipaug—the cliff-cove pond. They called themselves Masquisit and Naquisit, and on the islands they built fine cities and prospered greatly. They were very thankful to Masquasup and to Sequannit for having pulled such lovely islands up from the bottom of the sea, and offered them gifts of fine cornmeal, and tobacco, and for each of them a beautiful carved pipe with a bowl of soapstone and a stem of juniper wood.

Now, I'm sure that you already know, my lovelies, that all of our relations are elder to us. The creatures of the waters—fish and crabs, clams and mussels, turtles and frogs, mighty Whale. The creeping and crawling creatures—the singing crickets, the bees and ants, many-legged centipedes, Spider the weaver. The winged creatures—the birds of the sky, heron and snipe, eagle and thrush, Crow who brought us fire from the sun. The four-legged people—deer and rabbit, bear and puma, fisher and chipmunk, the awesome dragon Nampeshiwe's Mother. All around us and eldest, the green and growing creatures—every kind of plant and tree, root and mushroom. Sacred tobacco and juniper. The three sisters—corn, squash, and beans—who Crow tucked under his wing in the land west of the sunset to bring to the first people. Human people are the youngest kind of people in the world; that's why it's important for us to listen and learn from every other kind of creature, because they're all more experienced than we are, and they all know things that we don't know. We are not, as it might seem, the only thinking and talking people. There are others, elder and queer, who we have kinship and quarrel with.

Now, if you don't know them—for they aren't so common now as they once were—the pukwadjisuk are a kind of little people. Even fully grown, they're never more than waist-high to a human person. From behind, it's easy to mistake a pukwadji for a large porcupine, because they have a coat of pointed quills instead of hair—but if you see them from the front, they have faces and arms and hands like human people. Their skin is gray and mottled like sycamore bark, their ears are very large, and their fingers are very long. They can turn into animals, if they take a mind to, and can become invisible, too.

The pukwadjisuk were once friends of human people, but when they saw that human people had become the favorites of Masquasup and his wife, and how much the human people loved Masquasup and his wife in return, they became jealous and angry. Masquasup spent much of his time, in those early days, teaching human people all the things they needed to know to live in a good way—how to hunt and fish and dig for clams, how to build canoes, how to tan hides and make clothes, how to make medicine. Now I'm sure, my lovelies, that some of you have younger siblings. I'm sure some of you might feel jealous and angry sometimes, when your little siblings get more attention than you do from the people you love, so you know that this story is true.

The pukwadjisuk took to playing tricks on the first people. They would blow sharp notes on their bone flutes at the moment a hunter loosed his arrow, to make him miss his shot. They would unweave nets, and steal from snares. When the time came to put food by for winter, to smoke meat and dry squash, they would call up storms and fogs to spoil everything with wet. They would turn into fireflies and lure anyone walking at night away into the deep woods, and even off cliffs or into swamps.

The first people tried to be good neighbors to the pukwadjisuk at first, but by and by, as they proved themselves jealous and greedy, lazy and cruel, the first people determined that they should be made to leave. They called upon Sequannit, who spoke to Masquasup, who was very angry when he heard about how the pukwadjisuk were behaving. He took up his gathering basket and walked all across one island and then the other, picking up every pukwadji and stuffing them inside. When they became invisible, he blew smoke from his pipe on them and was able to see them well enough to stuff them into his basket. When they took the shapes of animals, he was able to recognize them by their all-black eyes, and into the basket they went. The pukwadjisuk screamed and cried and railed, but they were no match for Masquasup the Giant. When he'd gathered all of them up, he swung his basket around and around and around and around and finally threw it high into the sky! It was caught by the four winds and tossed all around, scattering the pukwadjisuk widely across the mainland—to the shores of the deep lakes to the northwest, to the shores of the narrow island to the southwest, even to the shores of the river now called Polvaara.

Many of the pukwadjisuk died from their rough treatment, but many didn't. The survivors declared war on humankind—and even now, sometimes, a person may be shot by one of their invisible poison arrows and die very suddenly. A baby's warmth may be stolen as they lay upon their cradleboard. It is a bitter, bitter thing, the hatred that the pukwadjisuk feel for human people.

If you ever catch sight of a pukwadji, it is very important not to anger it, or bother it, or let it know that you've seen it—or it will surely do you a terrible mischief. So now you know, my lovelies, why the pukwadjisuk are as they are today, and what you should do if ever you see one.

ANEQUS AND THEOD DISCUSSED THE TOPIC OF COURTING

Theod stayed with us after Strawberry Thanksgiving, because the celebration went well into the evening. That meant that in the blue hours of dawn on Friday, when he and I were both awake before anyone else, I was able to invite him for a morning walk.

I took him to the weeping beech that overlooked the pond, where we'd spoken in December. He seemed to understand the significance immediately, looking flushed and uncomfortable as we sat down. Copper followed us into the shelter formed by the branches, laying his head in Theod's lap and crooning softly—which was more nuisance than anything, because Copper was bigger than a horse. Kasaqua was preoccupied with chasing after grasshoppers, only looking back over her shoulder at me occasionally, eyeing Copper with curious speculation.

"Do you remember back during the winter recess—" I began, not sure how to broach the topic I'd brought him here to discuss.

"Yes," he said, cutting me off, catching me with a painfully intense gaze that had me looking away. All right, then. He remembered.

I took a breath and asked, "Do you still think that you're in love with me? You've passed your exam, and come to spend summer on the islands, and we've had Strawberry Thanksgiving—"

"Yes," he said, quietly. "I'm still in love with you."

"Well," I said, feeling myself flush, biting my lip to keep myself from grinning at such an admission, "what would you like to do about that?"

I turned to meet his gaze again, his dark eyes burning, searching.

"You're teasing me," he said, frowning. I couldn't keep myself from laughing, even though it wasn't funny; he just looked so perfectly *serious.*

"I'm not!" I insisted, hiding my mouth with my hand, then hiding my face entirely and making a frustrated sound. I composed myself and took a breath before continuing,

"I'm ready to talk more seriously about courting, now. I want you to know that any overtures you might choose to make would . . . not be unwelcome. I'm very fond of you, and I can certainly see that growing into love. It's just that I don't know much about how courting happens among the Anglish, except what I've gleaned in novels and magazines and from Marta's observations on the subject."

"And I know nothing at all about the proper way to court here," he said, nodding. "I said as much to your father."

"Well," I asked, "what would you have done if you were still a servant and had met some Anglish girl of your own class who you wanted to court?"

"I wouldn't have been allowed to," Theod said resolutely, staring down at Copper. "Not an Anglish girl, at any rate—because of my race. I was told in no uncertain terms that I would be the absolute ruin of any young woman who chose to engage with me in any kind of impropriety. That I'd be turned out of the household without so much as a good recommendation if there was even a *rumor* of such things."

"Anglish society seems to be incredibly concerned with impropriety," I said by way of agreement. "The claims made by Arjan Stafn and his ilk that we are, as a people, universally guilty of *sexual immorality* seem to be rooted in the fact that marriages among us are soluble, and can be plural. Among other things. Did you have a chance to meet Auntie Mamisashquee yesterday?"

"The man who—"

"She's not a man," I said, rather more sharply than was polite. "My great-aunt is a mupauanakausonat, which seems to be a category of person absent from Anglish society."

Theod made a sound of understanding, or agreement, or something like that. I did not believe that he understood.

"Anyway," I said with a sigh, "I wanted you to know that two young people exploring perfectly natural feelings toward one another isn't regarded, among us, as something ruinous. I think we're much more free than the Anglish are regarding love and affection and all that comes with it. There are no laws or conventions that forbid congress outside of marriage, as long as all parties are agreed. I've never done anything of this kind with anyone at all, before, so I'd like to take my time and find out where the natural course of affairs leads—though I certainly don't want to do anything just yet that might get me with child—"

Theod flushed and choked and coughed into his fist. Copper raised his head and made a concerned noise, and Kasaqua bounded over and stuck her head between the branches, alarmed, wondering what had Copper upset. I sighed and pushed the heels of my hands into my eyes. I hadn't pictured the conversation going quite this badly when I'd practiced it in my mind.

When Theod composed himself, he asked, "If . . . the sort of activities that could possibly put a woman into a delicate condition—"

"Physical love. It's all right to call things what they are," I said, and Theod looked *very* distressed.

"If such things aren't confined to marriage," he asked, "what becomes of children that naturally result?"

"I'm not sure that I understand the question," I said, frowning. "A woman who gets with child generally becomes a mother, unless something goes wrong. A woman's choice to raise children doesn't have much at all to do with her marriage—though *traditionally* a woman who's proven that she can bear children is more desirable as a wife than one who hasn't. It's very lucky if a woman is with child during her wedding, in fact—a good sign for the strength of the union. Is having children outside of marriage another of those things that's shameful among the Anglish, like dissolving a marriage is? Because it's not, here. Auntie Shanuckee has three children, but she's never felt inclined to marry."

Theod looked mildly shocked at that revelation, saying, "I'd presumed that she was a widow. No one ever spoke of her children's father . . ."

"Fathers," I said. "She knows who fathered each of her children, I'm sure. I don't know, nor do I particularly care. She decided that she didn't want to set up a household with any of them or have their help in raising her children. It's *different,* here. A man may have more than one wife, or a woman more than one husband. Men may marry men, and women may marry women. I've been informed already that these things are unlawful among the Anglish, and that under Anglish law, such households could be brought before a moot and charged with immoral behavior. But that's how our people have been conducting themselves since the beginning of time—and I honestly think it's the more responsible way to go about such things, really! You said, at the dance, that there's only one girl you've got your eye on. I want to be totally honest with you—you're not the only person I've got *my* eye on."

"Who else—" he asked, looking confused, hurt.

"Liberty," I said. "Though she's made it very clear to me that she and I *cannot* court while she's still indentured. She said that you're a much more suitable target for my affections, but seemed more curious than appalled when I pointed out that among my people, there's no reason that I couldn't pursue both of you so long as both of you agreed."

Theod was silent for a while after that, looking at me and looking away several times.

"Is that what you'd want? To court me and Liberty both?" he asked.

"If I could have everything go my own way, yes," I said. "I'd like you and Liberty to meet properly, and for all of us to talk about the subject of courting and perhaps eventually setting up a household together."

Theod took a long breath and blew it out, wavering.

"I do hope you'll forgive me, Anequs, if all of this is a bit much for me to turn over in my mind. I'm going to need to . . . think about . . . everything."

He stood, and Copper stood, too. Theod pressed his hand against Copper's shoulder and was quiet for a long moment before saying, "I'm going to take Copper for a walk. Alone. To think. I might go back to the house and put him in tack and go visit with my grandmother and her family. I'll . . . I'll let you know when I've given thought to everything you've said."

"Theod, I—"

"I'll talk to you later, Anequs," he said, not looking at me. He pushed the branches aside and led Copper away, leaving me sitting there under the tree with only Kasaqua for company.

SACHEM WOMPINOTTOMAK CALLED A MEETING

Theod did as he'd said, and Mother was *very* curious about what had happened that made him return to Naquipaug so soon, but I wasn't in any mood to talk about it with her . . . not yet. I didn't entirely understand why he needed so much time to think instead of just talking about it until it was solved; it was frustrating in the way that everything about his Anglish upbringing was.

Wigdis and her children went back to the mainland later that morning, and returned to Masquapaug on the following Tuesday carrying everything they owned—which was distressingly little, really. Chansompsqua was very happy to have her house full of people again, calling Wigdis the daughter she'd always meant to have, and Aksel and Ingrid her grandchildren. Ingrid was especially enthused to have me as a neighbor, and to be able to see Kasaqua every day.

The new thanegards, however, were absolutely *incensed* by this turn of events.

I wasn't there to see it, but by the end of day on Tuesday, everyone knew that Captain Johansen had been to Sachem Tanaquish's house, demanding to know the meaning of three people signing in as new residents with intent to stay indefinitely. The sachem charged the captain with proving what law, if any, the people of Masquapaug were collectively in breach of. When he couldn't cite any such law, he stormed off back to the outpost camp with promises that the jarl and the council would be informed of this.

To compound matters, upon learning that Wigdis and her children had been so easily accepted as new residents of Masquapaug, her cousin's family was in communication with Sachem Tanaquish to see about coming over, as well.

The meeting that Sachem Wompinottomak was holding, the one that Great-Auntie Mamisashquee had mentioned, was on Friday the twenty-third.

Sachem Tanaquish and I went by canoe, Kasaqua standing in the prow with her wings outstretched—which was more hindrance than help, really. I couldn't fault her for the action, though, because the feeling of wind against her wings was absolutely elating. We hadn't announced our departure to the authorities at the thanegards' outpost. They didn't like the fact that we weren't *entirely* reliant on the ferry and its attendant guestbook to come and go from the island, and would certainly have had *opinions* about the sachem and I attending any kind of assembly happening in North Village. I wasn't sure how to feel about this smallest bit of subterfuge, or the fact that it had been the sachem's idea.

It felt dangerous, defying Anglish will. But it felt important, too.

Naquipaug was close enough to Masquapaug that it could be seen from Beachy Hill on any day the weather was clear, but I'd only been there a few times in all my life. Our only family there was Auntie Shanuckee's household—Great-Auntie Mamisashquee and her husband, Auntie Shanuckee and her children. Shanuckee was Father's younger sister, and they'd been the only ones of their generation in the family to have survived the massacre in 1825. Shanuckee's family came to Masquapaug for dances and feasts and such more often than we went to Naquipaug for the same, because Naquipaug was a place steeped in pain in a way that Masquapaug wasn't. The Anglish were an ever-present threat there, a promise that the events of 1825 could easily be repeated.

Now Masquapaug had an office of thanegards, an ever-present Anglish threat of our own.

We'd invited Aunt Shanuckee's family to come and live with us on Masquapaug, but Great-Auntie Mamisashquee was *very* firm on staying on Naquipaug; she wouldn't let the Anglish take the farmstead that her family had been working since the beginning of time. The Anglish had, since 1825, been in the habit of claiming any land that they declared to be "in disuse" for "improvement in the public good." None of the land was in disuse, not really, but the Anglish didn't seem to see much value in forest, in hunting and foraging. Land was "improved," in their estimation, when it was clear cut. Then it could be paved over for houses and shops and factories, or turned into crop fields or grazing meadows.

Masquapaug had been lucky, because it didn't have anything the Anglish wanted. Naquipaug had been the same, mostly, until the Anglish had discovered the coal seam. Before, they'd been content to use only the east coast of the island and its sheltered cove as a port stop between New Linvik and Vastergot. It had once been a whaling port, when whales had been commonly found this far south. But they'd taken too many whales too quickly, and whales had changed their habits. For a few generations, there'd been an uneasy peace between the Naquisit people and the Anglish, with the Naquisit keeping to the interior and the west coast while the Anglish stayed in the city they'd built and the farms around it, grazing sheep on the land they'd cleared for timber. That peace had been strained when the Anglish had discovered coal, and had shattered entirely in 1825.

We made landfall on the west coast, near North Village. There was a party there waiting to meet us—Theod with Copper, two of his younger cousins, and Sachem Wompinottomak.

I hadn't ever been formally introduced to the sachem of Naquipaug; I'd only seen him at a distance when we visited family. He was younger than Sachem Tanaquish, closer to my parents' generation; he'd been fourteen years old during the 1825 massacre. His left arm was lame, and the whole left side of his face badly scarred. He was wearing an eyepatch on that side, as well, red felt with a beaded dogwood blossom at the center. Kasaqua bounded off to greet Copper as soon as we struck sand. I pulled the canoe up past the strand line while Sachem Tanaquish went to make a formal greeting. Sachem Wompinottomak was staring at Kasaqua, his good eye bright with pure awe.

"It's one thing to see a lichtbild," he said, "but to see a Nampeshiwe in the flesh—"

"Sachem Wompinottomak," Sachem Tanaquish said, "this is Anequs, daughter of Chagoma and Aponakwe, and her dragon, Kasaqua. I see you've already met young Mister Knecht."

"Wuskuwhani introduced us," Wompinottomak agreed. "It's good to have both of you here. Come, I'll show you the meetinghouse."

The two sachems took the lead, and Kasaqua and I fell neatly into step beside Theod and Copper. Theod's cousins alternately tagged behind and ran ahead.

"How've you been?" I asked, quietly, mindful not to intrude on the sachems' conversation.

"I've been well enough," he said, keeping his gaze resolutely forward. "Now isn't a good time to talk."

I frowned and sighed through my nose. He was probably right, there were more important things happening than the state of our shared affections, but still.

The most immediate difference I noticed between our village on Masquapaug and North Village on Naquipaug was the stockade. The whole village was surrounded by a wall of stripped, sharpened tree trunks packed tightly side by side; we had to pass through a long, narrow corridor to reach the village proper, with watchtowers perched every ten or fifteen feet. Half a dozen men armed with rifles could have held a group of any size back at this chokepoint.

The meetinghouse itself, at the center of the village, was very like our own: a large oblong building with stone walls and a domed roof of bent sapling wood covered in woven matting and bark shingles. Inside was an assembly chamber with a central firepit and low tables against the walls. As I led Kasaqua in, I noted that the assembly was mostly elders, with a few younger men. I seemed to be the only woman younger than fifty in attendance. The mood was entirely different from the kind of friendly village gathering I was used to. I noticed all three representatives of the Confederation of the First People of Akashnet—Alrik Mowashuck, Lise Nokehick, and Mokumannit Aestridsson. Something about their presence felt thrilling, forbidden, and most of all, important. I was glad that they'd been invited. That we'd been invited to join *them*.

Theod and I were the youngest people in the room by at least a generation, so it wasn't hard to work out that we'd only been invited because of our dragons. Because of what the presence of dragons might mean in any coming conflict with the Anglish in Nack Port.

Because Kasaqua was a Nampeshiwe.

Mamisashquee was one of the elders gathered, and she beckoned us over to take a seat near her. Kasaqua was curious about this new place and all the new people, wanting very much to smell and greet everyone, so I had to encourage her rather strongly to lie down at my side. Theod didn't seem to be having the same trouble with Copper. When we were situated, Sachem Wompinottomak took up a position at the center of the circle, by the firepit.

"I want to thank you all for coming here today, especially those of you who've come from elsewhere." He nodded toward Theod and me, and then to the representatives from the mainland.

"I fear that we stand on the precipice of a great struggle. Our land, our people, and our way of life are under threat from those who seek to take all that is ours for their own. For too long, our people have sought to be gracious hosts and welcoming neighbors to the people who arrived on our shores some hundred years ago. My grandfather's uncle, the sachem Nahomequin, welcomed Emanuel Nordlund as a friend because he was an honorable man—one who only wanted to know our ways. But those that followed him seek to plunder our lands and destroy our way of life."

Someone at the other side of the circle gave an affirmative shout, and the sachem nodded toward them before continuing.

"Who was it that hunted the whales so harshly that they changed their habits and moved north? Who felled the forests? Who brought sheep and cattle and horses that devour everything to bare soil? Who has laid the land itself open to dig out its hearthstones, hollowing it of coal and shipping it to the mainland? I know better than many the danger in opposing these newcomers, in the price it might exact." He gestured broadly with his right arm to the whole left side of his body. "Everyone here has felt the loss of the 1825 massacre—sons and daughters, brothers and sisters. We've watched the ruins of South Village be divided by Anglish farmers, watched our homesteads and hunting grounds be reshaped under their hands. No more can we stand and watch as they try to impose their will upon us. We must resist, with all the strength and courage that we possess."

There were more affirmative noises from the gathered crowd.

"This past year has brought us two great blessings—Anequs of Masquapaug was chosen by the dragon Kasaqua, a Nampeshiwe of legend come to us like Crow from the land west of the sunset. And Theod, son of Nepinnae, grandson of Wuskuwhani, has returned to us with a dragon of his own. This can be nothing less than a sign that it is time for us to wake, to see what has been done to our people here on the islands and to our cousins on the mainland. We have, like cowards, ignored the plight of the mainlanders for too long. Where, today, are the Mohocannisit people? Where are the Pokumtuckisit, the Nauhaisit, the Nepmetuckisit? What has become of the Maswachuisit people? The Akashneisit, the Naregannisit? They are scattered like ashes on the wind, forgetting the tongues of their ancestors. They're left scrabbling in squalid corners and alleys of Anglish cities that are built from the very stones that were once their great temples and monuments. How many of our people have, in despair, crawled into bottles of hard spirit and drowned there? The Anglish have moved at every turn to divide us, to turn brother against brother, to silence the teachings of elders to children. I say no more! I say we know better now!"

There were whoops and trills of agreement now, and I found myself clapping and nodding along. My mind flashed to Mamisashquee's story, and how satisfying it would be to pluck up the thanegards into a basket and fling them away into the sky.

"We know that our struggle is just, that our cause is right. This land is ours and always has been, since the sun caught fire and Crow stole the first firebrand to give to the first people! Remember, our ancestors fought and *died* to preserve that which we hold dear. They refused to be cowed by pale men with dragons and guns, ledgers and coins, maps with lines drawn on them. It is our turn, now, to carry on their legacy! We will stand together, Naquisit and Masquisit, Akashneisit and Naregannisit and Maswachuisit, united in our determination to defend our land and our people—to take back what has been stolen from us! We will resist the Anglish, no matter what the cost. We will fight for our dignity, our right to determine our own future. I call upon all of you to join me in the coming fight. Let us stand together, shoulder to shoulder, and show the Anglish that we will not be felled like the trees of the forest or picked apart like the stones of our ancestors' homes. Let us take back the land that is ours!"

Kasaqua stood up, wings flaring, at the cheer that filled the meetinghouse. She understood that something very important and exciting was happening, but not more than that. Still, she was very pleased to be involved . . . and was aware that something had gone very wrong a moment before I was, turning her head sharply and fluffing the feathers of her mane.

Outside, there came the sounds of wings, of dragons touching down. I was on my feet even before the shrill blast of a thanegard's brass whistle cut through the air.

Kasaqua flared and hissed, moving to put herself between me and the door.

Many other people were on their feet now. I followed Kasaqua's gaze to find a thanegard standing at the entrance of the meetinghouse, with another behind him. Outside, I could hear dragons breathing and pawing.

The thanegard's gaze swept balefully across everyone present, pausing at the dragons, landing on Sachem Wompinottomak. The thanegard had one hand on the pistol at his belt when he shouted, in a sharp, clear voice, "By the authority of Wilhelm Hasenjager, Torgar of Nack Island, under the authority of Svend Jespersen, Thane of Catchnet, under the authority of Leiknir Joervarsson, Jarl of Vaster Hold, under the authority of Yngvarr Silvertooth, High King of Lindmarden: I declare this assembly unlawful! If two or more persons assemble together to do an unlawful act, or do any act in a violent, boisterous, or tumultuous way, such assembly is an unlawful assembly. So says the law. Every person who participates in any rout or unlawful assembly is guilty of a misdeed. The name of each and every person present at this assembly will be recorded and reported to Torgar Hasenjager and Thane Jespersen. You are to disperse and return to your homes, under penalty of arrest."

"What unlawful act do we stand accused of?" Sachem Wompinottomak said, raising his hands a bit in a gesture of peace.

"This assembly is clearly a prelude to acts of violence against the common peace of Nack Island, and of the city of Catchnet at large. There are people among you who are known, by the city of

Catchnet, to be agitators. There can be no innocent explanation for the presence of nackie separatists—"

"We *live* here," someone in the circle said—one of the elder women. "You have come into our *home,* without invitation, and you dare to tell us that we can't have a gathering with guests? These people are our cousins. We came here to celebrate the young dragoneers."

The thanegard took a little paperbound notebook from his pocket, his gaze fixed on the woman who'd spoken. He stared hard at her for a few seconds, as if trying to memorize her face.

The other thanegard called for the sachems, who joined the pair of them by the door. They spoke together in harsh tones for a while, too quietly for me to pick out more than a word or two here and there.

After a few minutes of terse negotiation with the sachems, the thanegards began going to each and every person in the meetinghouse, recording their names and where they lived and how they'd come to today's meeting. Anyone who might have decided to leave without giving a name thought better of it when they saw the two silberdraches that were posted on either side of the door. We were forced to pass between them to leave the meetinghouse; Kasaqua's hackles stayed up the whole time.

After the full accounting, everyone was instructed to disperse to our homes and stay there.

Sachem Tanaquish was very grim as we paddled back to Masquapaug.

ANEQUS AND THEOD VISITED THE MAINLAND

Marta's garden party was on Tuesday, July eleventh. Attending it was a great deal more trouble than it might have been before the meeting on Naquipaug, because the thanegards there were in communication with the thanegards at home, and all of them were in agreement that no one—or at least no *nackie*—should come or go from the islands at all. Not between islands, and not to the mainland. The ferry office on Masquapaug was effectively shuttered, only delivering mail and sending and receiving telegrams. A thanegard, armed with a brace of pistols, was always at the door.

I sent a letter to Jarl Joervarsson explaining the situation, but I did not get an answer, so I very much doubted that the letter was actually conveyed to him. Instead, I sent a letter to Sander containing instructions for him to deliver a message to Frau Kuiper, who I *knew* had the jarl's ear. I imagined that whoever was intercepting the jarl's letters wasn't paying any attention at all to Sander

Jansen's correspondence. That message did manage to reach the jarl, and in response he sent official letters of permission—stamped and signed and everything—for Theod and me to carry and present to anyone who gave us challenge. He also sent a telegram to the office on Masquapaug detailing the rights of all citizens of Lindmarden—including the right to travel within Vaster's Hold: Catchnet, Estervall, Skaldstead, Varmarden, and Vastergot. Mister Aroztegui nailed the telegram to the wall beside the guestbook. When the thanegard posted made disapproving noises about Theod and me buying tickets to visit the mainland, he glared and pointed at the sign.

I rather liked Mister Aroztegui.

Marta had informed us in the original invitation that the gathering was expected to go well into the night, so we'd be guests in her home until Friday. The arranging of that had necessitated an absolutely *tiresome* series of letters and telegrams, because I was on Masquapaug and Theod on Naquipaug, and neither of us had the ready coin for telegrams (not if we were going to pay ferry fare two ways), so when we received her telegrams, we had to reply in letters. I'd run through most of my remaining allowance money from school helping Ingrid and her family.

There were so many things happening now that were more important than Marta's garden party that the fuss hardly seemed worth it. Still, party arrangements gave me a ready excuse to visit Mister Aroztegui's office every day, showing the thanegards that I was not afraid of them.

In the most recent telegram, Marta had announced that Miss Dynah Wozniakowa and her younger sister would be visiting to join the festivities. Dynah was a former student of Kuiper's, and her sister would be joining Marta and me this year. If nothing else, meeting her was a reason to attend the party—getting a feel for another roommate around whom I might well have to negotiate socially. It could make meeting with Liberty that much harder this coming year. Marta frequently went home on the weekends, but I couldn't imagine someone coming all the way from Runestung Hold doing so.

The only dress I had that was at all appropriate to an Anglish garden party was the yellow satin one Marta had gifted me at Fyrafax; it was carefully folded in my pack along with its crinoline. Working out how to fold a crinoline into a small circle had been a trial unto itself, when packing.

Theod met me at the ferry dock just a bit before nine. I was wearing the dress that Liberty made for me, to travel, because it was the smartest *practical* dress that I owned. Theod was dressed to match me, in corduroys and a calico shirt. We looked like ourselves—like islanders, like nackies. We'd have to change into our party attire when we reached Marta's home.

I asked Theod if he wanted to talk more about . . . what we'd last spoken about. He said no.

So we didn't talk about that.

Instead we talked about the changes to village life in light of the Anglish mandate against certain kinds of assembly. The thanegards on Masquapaug hadn't tried to disperse the village meeting that Sachem Tanaquish had called, but they had turned up to observe it. The thanegards on both islands were visiting the village daily. After a long silence, I changed the subject, and we talked about Theod's younger cousins and their interests, and about how his aunt's husband had taken Theod fishing and hunting—though it was Copper who did most of the actual hunting, bringing back three fat rabbits. His grandmother had made stew. We talked about how Ingrid and Aksel were getting on, which led to how Sigoskwe and Sakewa were.

Theod and I arrived in Catchnet around ten-thirty in the morning. Marta's father had arranged for his assistant, Mister Otterlo, to collect us at the docks and take us to Sjokliffheim by private automotor. The estate wasn't particularly close to any train stations, and even if it had been, our dragons were large enough that taking them on a train was very bothersome and costly. Even

Kasaqua needed a horse stall now, and Copper was quickly outgrowing such conveniences entirely; he was very cramped in a typical horse trailer. Theod could have flown Copper to Estervall, stopping to rest as needed, but Kasaqua couldn't fly at all yet, much less take a rider.

The journey to Estervall from Catchnet wasn't as long as the journey from the academy, along a road that hugged the coast and offered exceedingly lovely views. The automotor moved at the speed of a galloping horse, and did so constantly without any need to rest, so we were able to cover the twenty miles from the ferry docks to Marta's home in less than an hour. Sjokliffheim was perched on a cliff above a stony beach, a grand edifice of gray stone and blindingly white brick. Theod and I had been here once before, at Marta's invitation, at the beginning of October last year. I hadn't noticed, then, that there were climbing roses growing all around the front door; they hadn't been in bloom. The flowers were white with pale yellow centers, and the scent of them drifted on the wind across the wide lawn to mingle with the scent of freshly cut grass.

Marta came to meet us as Mister Otterlo was seeing the dragons out of the trailer. She was wearing a pale blue afternoon dress that I'd never seen before—one that was intensely fashionable. It had a bodice styled like a jacket with delicate mother-of-pearl buttons, lace at the wrists and throat, and the kind of voluminous skirt that required a crinoline. Marta liked to keep on the very cusp of fashion, and her father had the kind of money that let her indulge such habits. Apart from her uniforms at school, I couldn't recall ever having seen her in the same dress twice.

"Anequs! Theod! I'm so glad you were able to come, and look how big your dragons have gotten! Oh, just wait until you see Magnus! He's grown, too. I'm sure you'll want to wash and change, after your journey. Dynah and Jadzia arrived half an hour ago. You're just in time for luncheon, or you will be once you've gotten ready. Most of the other guests won't arrive until later—Bergitte,

Saskia, and Annetta are all coming, and of course Lisbet and Sander."

"Thank you for having us, Miss Hagan," Theod said, dipping his head a bit. I wondered if I was supposed to have dropped a curtsy, but it felt too late to do so now. Theod knew all the little unspoken rules of Anglish society in ways that I didn't. Then again, despite knowing that it was quite uncharitable to think such things, I didn't particularly care about impressing Marta with perfect Anglish manners.

"Anequs, if you'd please follow me, I'll show you to the guest room where you'll be staying," Marta said, "and Theod, if you'd follow Mister Otterlo, he'll get you situated. We'll reconvene in the back garden shortly, and I'll introduce you to Dynah and Jadzia. The roses are at their very best this time of year, and our cook has absolutely outdone herself . . ."

Marta's house had interminable rooms, and I wasn't at all surprised to learn that the guest room had its own attached washroom with running water. I changed into my yellow dress and braided my hair up in the Anglish style, turning to the huge mirror Marta had provided to inspect the results. It was strange. When I was younger and would visit Catchnet with my family for shopping, I used to look at the plates in magazines depicting the latest fashions and feel a sense of longing—a desire to be fashionable, sophisticated, and beautiful. Now that I had dresses like that—the yellow satin I had on and the bronze taffeta that I'd worn to the Valkyrjafax ball, which was now packed away in camphor paper in the rafters—I always felt ridiculous, false, when dressed up in fashionable Anglish attire. Both dresses had been gifts from Marta. She had a keen interest in making me into a proper lady of Anglish society, a peer to Anglish dragoneers who came almost exclusively from moneyed families. That wasn't the kind of woman I was, nor the kind I wanted to be. But it had taken trying it on to know that.

I returned to Marta, and after a brief inspection, she declared me presentable and led me to the back garden. I could tell, in the interim, that something very exciting was happening to Kasaqua. She was curious and joyful about it, and I very much wanted to join her.

We followed a cobbled path that wound around the house, with Marta pointing out varieties of roses every so often; they each had particular names. It was quite an impressive sight, the gathering of so many flowers of the same kind, each with a slightly different hue or shape or habit of growth. The scent of them was pronounced, but not overpowering.

At the back of the house was a paved courtyard, where a large table was situated under a white cloth canopy, though nothing was on it, at present. There was a large pile of firewood neatly arranged on a bed of sand in the middle of the wide lawn beyond the garden, and bunches of lupines and oxeyes and poppies and roses gathered at its margin. The dragons were gathered on the grass: Copper and Kasaqua, Marta's dragon Magnus, and two dragons that I didn't know at all, seemingly of the same unfamiliar breed. One was the largest dragon present, the other the smallest. They were both green and gold, narrow-faced, with long, slender necks. The small dragon was covered in a pattern of dark green dapples, and the large dragon had a pair of curving horns like a ram. It was lying in the grass, watching with mild interest as the younger dragons flared their wings and bowed and feinted at each other in friendly greeting. The smallest dragon was no bigger than a cat, clearly hatched very recently, and it hung by the large dragon's side.

Magnus had grown nearly as large as Copper; with the quills of his mane extended, he seemed taller, and he'd put on a great deal of muscle through the chest and shoulders. Kasaqua was very excited to meet the new dragons, particularly the hatchling, but had been waylaid by Magnus's demand for attention and was exchanging pleasantries in the fashion of dragons, which involved a lot of sniffing and feinting.

A filigreed table of wrought-isen stood a ways apart from the firewood pile, and two young women were seated at it, sipping from porcelain cups. Theod returned from wherever Mister Otterlo had taken him, and the two strangers stood as Marta swept forward to make formal introductions.

"Mister Theod Knecht and Miss Anequs," she said with smooth flourish, "I'd like to present you to my esteemed guests, Misses Dynah and Jadzia Wozniakowa of Runestung Hold. Anequs and Theod join us from the outlying islands, Mask and Nack. Dynah is a former student of Kuiper's Academy, and Jadzia will be joining us in the coming year."

Dynah Wozniakowa seemed to be twenty or so years of age, and Jadzia was quite young—thirteen or fourteen, perhaps. The sisters looked very alike—both had dark, curling hair and round, earnest faces. Dynah's eyes were brown, and Jadzia's paler, more hazel. Both of them were dressed in a style just *slightly* unlike the common Anglish mode. Their blouses were white, with high collars of cut lace, and they were both wearing black felt vests richly embroidered with silk ribbon. Their skirts were very full, with vertical stripes in many colors—Dynah's were red and orange and pink, Jadzia's blue and yellow and green.

"Pleased to meet you!" Dynah said, offering a hand to Theod. From her bearing, it seemed that she was offering a handshake, but Theod responded in the correct Anglish fashion and touched her hand while making a bow. She responded with a musical little laugh. "The two of you are the ones we've read about in the papers, yeah?"

"I can only presume so," I said, "as I know of no other nackie dragoneers in Vastergot besides Theod and myself."

"You saved your jarl though, right?" Jadzia said, her eyes very wide and eager. "You were *shot,* and you ordered your dragon to dispatch the assassin, and Jarl Joervarsson was saved?"

"That's a reasonably accurate account, yes," I said. It was strange to have the events laid out like that, especially in light of all the recent troubles with the thanegards. "I didn't know that the news had gotten as far as Runestung Hold."

"Well, an attempt on a jarl's life is no small thing," Dynah said with a frown. "Jarl Rikkert Halfhand—that's our jarl in Runestung Hold—already made an official declaration against the Ravens of Joden. They're not allowed to assemble in our hold at all, and Sveni Audulfsson will be arrested if he tries to go there."

"I can only hope that he decides to visit your hold sometime soon, then," I said. Both sisters laughed, and Theod smiled with a speculative look in his eye. Sveni Audulfsson was wroughtthane of the Ravens of Joden, and the father of Birning Svenisson—the man who'd attempted to assassinate the jarl. The man Kasaqua had killed.

"You'll be rooming with me in the coming year, won't you?" Jadzia said, catching my attention back. "I've never been away from home before, and I expect there'll be few enough friendly faces. You and Marta and I will all be sharing a room, if the school is still the way it was when Dynah attended. Oh, and you *must* call me Jadi, if we're going to be rooming together. Yours is the Misigennebeg dragon?"

"That *what* dragon?" I asked, puzzled.

"Are they called something else here?" Jadi asked. "The dragon with the feathery mane and the antlers. Our neighbors call that kind of dragon Misigennebeg, which I might be saying wrong."

"Oh, Kasaqua," I said, glancing over and smiling fondly. Kasaqua was, at present, rolling on her back in the grass in front of the two green-gold dragons. "She's bonded to me. Her breed is called Nampeshiwe, by my people."

"Forgive me my sister," Dynah said, looking at Jadi with a wry smile. "Her mouth runs away with her because she thinks faster than she can talk, and it all happens at once."

"No one needs to forgive you or me anything," Jadi insisted, crossing her arms. "I talk as I talk, and if people can't keep up, that's hardly my problem, now, is it?"

Dynah said something back to her in a language that I couldn't follow at all. It reminded me of the Tysklandish that I'd picked up to better understand skiltakraft and natural philosophy, but I didn't recognize the words individually. Jadi replied in kind, and they went back and forth for a moment in what might have been an argument. Neither seemed particularly upset, though.

"If it's not rude to ask, how is it that you're familiar with Kasaqua's breed?" I asked. "Everyone I've met until now has said they've never seen anything like her."

"Our neighbors north and west of us—the Howden-noshawnee, which I might also be saying wrong, I'm sorry—they're the same kind of people that you and Theod are. Well, not the same-same kind, but the same the way that Anglish people and Norse people are the same, if that makes sense? They're original people."

"Our jarl and our minister of dragon affairs have both mentioned the Hudden-seeonnee Rikesband—" Theod began, only to be interrupted by Jadzia.

"That just sounds like they're saying it even worse than I am!"

"Jadi!" Dynah scolded.

"Well, they are! The Anglish can't ever say words the correct way! That's why they call Lake Oswego 'Oxwagon' and Lake Kitchi Kami 'Catch-It-Coming.' I expect it's because they only speak one language, and it's not even a very good one. Anglish is just what happens when you take Tysklandish and Norse and Frankish and smash them together with whatever the Angles and Sachsens were speaking, like kippers in a tin."

"Which languages do you speak?" I asked.

"Well, we speak Anglish, of course, because you *have* to, because God forbid they ever learn any others, and we speak Polszczyzna, because that's the common language of Polland, which is where our grandparents are from, and we speak Zhidish because we're Zhidi, and I know some L'shon Hakodesh for the same reason, but I wouldn't call myself a good scholar. Dynah is better at it, and Hiram is best of the three of us. I know some phrases of Kanienkeha, but I wouldn't say I really know it. Anyway," she said, pointing to Kasaqua, "that's the kind of dragon our neighbors have, that they call Misigennebeg. Or at least that's what our *closest* neighbors call them. They have a lot of little nations who each have their own languages and all."

"Kasaqua's mother came to us from someplace west, and continued east after laying her egg," I said. "We don't actually know anything about her history or motivations, only that she laid an egg in the ruins of the temple on Slipstone Island. What sort of dragons are yours?"

"My dragon's name is Gikka," Dynah said. "Well, Gikhkayt, really, but she's called Gikka. It means 'speed' in Zhidish. Gikka is a Złocisty; Papa had her egg imported from back in Polland. Jadi's dragon is Dreyst, and he's Gikka's son. His name means 'bold,' more or less. He's some kind of cross, but we don't know anything about his father. Gikka chose a mate that pleased her—probably one of the soldiers' dragons from Verzlavatten. We come from Katshketeykh, which is twenty miles from anywhere, on purpose. Verzlavatten is the nearest city. It's not as big as Vastergot."

"I'm afraid I don't know much about Runestung Hold," I admitted. "Before I bonded with Kasaqua, I'd never been anywhere but the islands and Catchnet."

"I've never been anyplace farther than Verzlavatten," Jadi said brightly, "so I'm terribly excited to see Vastergot and attend the academy."

"It's always exciting when another girl takes up dragoneering," Marta said. "If it hadn't been for Anequs, I'd have been the only girl at the academy last year; can you imagine?"

"Just you?" Dynah asked, frowning. "What happened to Kersti? She was in her first year when I was in my last, so she should still be there—"

"Miss Kerstin Linna transferred to a school abroad," Marta supplied. "One of the old Tysklandish schools, I think."

"Oh, her father must've finally come into his inheritance," Dynah said with a sage nod. "Well, at least Jadi will have the two of you for company. The boys can be so standoffish if they don't think that you're a marriage prospect—no disrespect to present company, of course," she amended, nodding to Theod.

"None taken," Theod said. "I quite agree with the assessment that the ranks of the young men at Kuiper's are . . . largely closed."

Before Dynah could say more, a maid appeared to let us know that luncheon was being served, and Marta led us to the table to dine.

TO SPEND TIME WITH NEW ACQUAINTANCES AND OLD ONES

The other guests began arriving in the middle of the afternoon—Sander and Lisbet Jansen first. They were *not* accompanied by their mother, much to my relief. As a point of fact, aside from the intermittent presence of Mister Otterlo and of a pair of women I presumed to be servants of some kind (Marta had not made introductions), there were no chaperones at all at this gathering. Marta's father was away on business; she'd explained that in the series of letters arranging this gathering. There had been chaperones at both the Valkyrjafax ball and the Fyrafax garden party, which were the only formal Anglish events I'd previously been to, and both had taken place at the academy. I'd have to ask Theod about the ins and outs of chaperones later; I didn't want to embarrass myself.

Sander's dragon, Inga, had grown enormously since I'd last seen her. She was now the size of a pony, and her triple set of golden horns had grown out to three or four inches in length. She was more shy and reserved than either Copper or Kasaqua had been in greeting Dynah's and Jadzia's dragons.

Sander had gotten taller, too, and he looked remarkably *well* in a way I couldn't precisely qualify—less subdued and uncertain in his general demeanor. Having met Sander and Lisbet's mother on several occasions, I could imagine that being out of her auspices was an enormous relief. Sander had been staying in his quarters at the academy through the recess, rather than returning home.

Marta made polite introductions, and we sat and sipped tea and caught one another up on all the most recent happenings. Neither Dynah nor Jadzia made any comment at all upon the fact that Sander communicated by writing on a mechanical wax tablet. He was explaining his current situation as a summer resident of the academy. Lisbet took up the task of reading his words aloud for the rest of the party.

"Frau Brinkerhoff joined me as a character witness, when I appeared before the moot," she read. "They ruled that, because I'm sixteen now, I am within my rights to refuse Mother's attempt to disenroll me. Her claim that I am some species of simpleton and should be treated as a child was very soundly struck down after five minutes of questioning from a lawyer. Once we were able to explain that I am functionally mute but of entirely sound mind, the judge declared me unconditionally adult. Father's legal will was very clear, though, that I am to inherit what remains of the family fortune at the age of twenty. Mother has flatly refused to pay my tuition for the coming year, but Frau Kuiper is very understanding of the situation and is willing to allow me to complete my education with promise of payment when I inherit."

"But why would your mother want you to leave Kuiper's?" Dynah asked, frowning.

"Because a number of other students withdrew," I said. "Thane Stafn withdrew his son Ivar, and many other families who align with the Ravens of Joden and even the Eiriksthede followed suit. Kuiper's is now, functionally, an expressly Freemansthede institution."

"Well, it always was, at least a little," Dynah said, frowning. "The Ravens never approved of Frau Kuiper in the first place, but the only other academy for skiltakraft in all of Markesland that I know is the one in New Linvik, and I can't remember what it's called. Are all the Ravens in Vastergot sending their children there?"

"I don't know," I said. "That bit didn't particularly concern me."

"Well, I suppose it wouldn't, with everything else you've said about what's been happening in Vaster's Hold," Dynah said, frowning. "Things are done differently, here in the south."

"Where exactly is the border between Vaster's Hold and Runestung Hold?" Theod asked. "I've never bothered to closely examine a map."

"I don't know where the hard border is, but everything this side of the green mountains is Vaster's Hold, and everything west is Runestung," Dynah said. "Folks from the old country in Runestung Hold mostly came down the Runestung River—" She looked to Sander and asked, "May I borrow your little tablet for a minute to make a map?"

Sander nodded, sliding his tablet across the table. Dynah took it up and began sketching; I watched the familiar coast of Lindmarden take shape, then she began marking water courses and mountains.

"So here's the Runestung River, and Lake Catch-It-Coming, and Lake Oxwagon," she said, pointing with the tip of the needle. "As far as I know, there are only original people—people like you two—north of the Runestung. Maybe some fur trappers and woodsmen, but no cities. So here's Osheaga Island, where there's a big city—I've never been, but our neighbors talk about it. South of there is Lake Bitawbagok, and south of *that* is the Shademuck River. It's carved a valley right through the green mountains, and if you follow it all the way south, you'll end up in New Linvik. We followed the river south, camped last night at Fort Witswood, and proceeded east from there. Everything is much more peopled east of the fort, and we could follow roads and train tracks toward Vastergot. There's no easy way besides dragonback to get from Verzlavatten to anywhere in Vaster's Hold. It takes days and days of camping in the wilderness if you're on horseback."

She marked *Verzlavatten* on the map, just a bit north from Vastergot and very deep inland—farther west than I'd ever considered going for any reason. The two of them had come from there, across mountains and valleys and rivers, in little more than a day of travel.

I was still considering that when Mister Otterlo came to inform Marta that another of the guests had arrived, and she excused herself to make an appropriate welcome. Saskia Britsch arrived with a woman she identified as her "poise instructor" as a chaperone. Then Bergitte Ravnsdottir and her older brother Hartvig, who was also a former student of Kuiper's, arrived in a carriage drawn by a sizable male kesseldrache. The dragon didn't seem particularly interested in socializing with our gang of younger dragons, sitting well apart and glowering at all proceedings with the air of an offended cat. Annetta Virtanen and her cousin Mira arrived a bit later, which completed the party. The maids began bringing refreshments—rose-flavored ice cream, sparkling honeyed-wine punch, little sandwiches, cakes, and cookies. Nothing that called for sitting down at a table to eat.

Conversation was lively, mostly centered on Vastergot society—who was hosting parties, who was invited, who attended which ones, and who was seen speaking to whom. Much speculation was made about courting prospects. Marta, Bergitte, Saskia, and Annetta all dropped names that I was passingly familiar with: other students and young men of high society. It was rumored that Ivar Stafn had asked for Dagny Sørensen's hand. No one could properly substantiate the rumor, though. I tried a few times to bring the conversation around to politics, and the upcoming thynge in August, but both Marta and Theod gave me stern glances, and I resigned myself to talking about polite nonsense.

A string quartet arrived just before six o'clock and situated themselves on the paved area just behind the house. They began the kind of pleasantly looping music that was meant to be only half listened to, nothing that imposed on conversation or invited dancing. Theod hung by my side until he was cornered by Hartvig Ravnsson and invited to take brandy and talk about dragon husbandry. I pushed him to talk to Hartvig, because having friends among the dragoneers of Vastergot could only be a benefit. Theod hadn't been wrong in his assessment that the ranks of our classmates at Kuiper's were largely closed to him; he should have been grabbing this opportunity. Everyone had spent all of last year telling me that it was important to make social connections among other dragoneers, after all.

I'd stepped aside for a moment to pay Kasaqua a bit of attention when Jadi's dragon bounded up, with Jadi herself not far behind. She was pink-cheeked and grinning, coming to a halt as Kasaqua dropped into a play-bow before Dreyst. A year ago, she'd been as small as that, able to ride on my shoulder and sit in my lap. A year from now, she'd likely be as large as her mother had been.

"How old is she?" Jadi asked, looking at Kasaqua with open speculation.

"Kasaqua will be a year old in the first week of July," I answered. "I'm afraid I don't know much about the development or conformation of her breed. You might know more than me, in fact. You mentioned neighbors?"

"The Howden-noshawnee," Jadi said, nodding. "They're a confederation of little nations. The only person I really know anything about is Pinedog; he's a trader who sells pelts to my papa and uncle. He's a dragoneer, and his dragon's a Misigennebeg like yours, but bigger and older and a buck. I don't remember his name. He's less gold than your dragon and more red, and his mane of feathers is more full, and they sort of shine in a different way—like rooster tail feathers? Pinedog visits on his dragon two or three times a year and, until Gikka, his was the only dragon I'd ever seen closely."

I looked over to where Dynah was standing with Marta, evidently deeply engaged in telling a story that Marta was politely listening to.

"What made your family decide to . . . acquire a dragon egg?" I asked carefully, knowing that in the Anglish tradition, dragons' eggs were bought and sold and speculated on as much as dogs or horses.

"It was supposed to be my brother, Hiram, both times," Jadi said. "He wanted to be a dragoneer, and everyone agreed that it would be good for the business to have a dragon—the courier kind. But then when Gikka hatched, she only wanted Dynah! She's the oldest. She was sixteen when Gikka hatched. Hiram was fourteen, and I was ten. So there was so much *geruder* about that, that Gikka chose Dynah, and what it meant for a *girl* to be a dragoneer. But anyway, it was done, and Dynah enrolled at Kuiper's, and for four years she was gone between September and May with just letters and telegrams. Then Dynah finished her education, passed her examinations, and got a license and all, so she came home to stay. Gikka's all grown, and Dynah's flying off to Verzlavatten every second day, doing the kinds of jobs that Hiram would have if he'd been the dragoneer of the family. Then back in January, Gikka laid an egg! Hiram was so excited, thinking he had a second chance to be a dragoneer, but he's eighteen now and that's a bit old for a dragon to pick usually, but no one wanted to jinx it by telling him so. Dreyst hatched at the beginning of May, and picked *me* instead of Hiram, and Papa lamented that clearly it was not meant to be for Hiram, and now he's got two dragoneer daughters."

She was laughing, and I laughed, too, more to be polite than because anything about that story seemed especially funny. It was worth knowing that her people—who were evidently something other than Anglish in a way I hadn't fully worked out yet—were of a similar mind in finding it odd and noteworthy for a woman to be a dragoneer.

"What did your family think of Kasaqua choosing you?" Jadi

asked, glancing over her shoulder at Dynah again before looking back to me.

"Well, my mother was terribly worried, and my father didn't even find out until I'd been at school for three months, because he's a whaler and is at sea every year from April to November. Our customs are a bit different, though, regarding dragons' eggs. The egg stayed in our meetinghouse, and everyone in the village visited with it and sang songs and told stories. It wasn't any kind of sure thing that I'd be the one the hatchling chose. Our people haven't had the company of dragons for two hundred years—"

"Why not?" Jadi asked, interrupting.

I gave her a pointed look, but she didn't seem to understand, so I just continued. "Two hundred years ago, something happened that we called the great dying. It was a plague that killed seven people in ten, and every single dragon. People then thought the world was coming to an end. But it didn't. Things were very different before the great dying, and before the Anglish came to Markesland. We only have stories about it now, but it's said that the islands weren't as remote when there were many dragons on Masquapaug and Naquipaug. There were trade routes between different nations from here to South Markesland, back then."

"Is this erelore, or just lore?" Jadi asked, looking suddenly sly. Dreyst came bounding over to her and jumped up, bracing his front feet against her skirts, demanding to be picked up. She gathered him into her arms, and I smiled, looking to where Kasaqua was carefully approaching the big kesseldrache, nosing at his tail, like a raven bothering a wolf.

"Both. Either. Neither," I said, shrugging. "I have no reason not to believe that our stories are true."

Jadi made a humming noise of speculation at that, stroking Dreyst under the chin in a way that made him tilt his head back and croon softly. The sun was just beginning to set, and Marta called for everyone to assemble for the lighting of the bonfire, so we moved to join her and the others.

ANEQUS AND THEOD SPOKE AT LENGTH, PRIVATELY

The garden party and bonfire went on well past midnight, as predicted. Most of the guests left when the musicians did, and not long after that, those who were staying proceeded to bed in our various guest rooms. The bed was much too soft, even more than the bed at school was, and the pillow smelled overwhelmingly of lavender and rose water. After an interminable period of tossing and turning in an attempt to find a comfortable position, I stripped the bed of its covers and slept on the floor instead.

I woke in the blue hour before dawn, despite having been up late into the night. The house was unsettlingly quiet in the same way that school was on nights I slept alone there. I didn't know anything at all about Dynah or Jadi's morning habits, nor Sander or Lisbet's, but Marta probably wouldn't be up for another hour at least. Kasaqua was awake, though not in any particular hurry to do anything about it. I washed and dressed, braided my hair, and proceeded out to the stable that was currently serving as Marta's dragonhall. It had clearly been built with horses in mind, and was barely serviceable for our half-grown dragons. Dynah's Gikka was curled up on the lawn, too large to enter the stable at all. I moved past her quietly, and she didn't stir.

Theod was already inside, brushing down Copper. Kasaqua was standing in her stall, resting her chin on the gate, watching the proceedings with mild interest. She looked at me as I entered, ears perking. Theod was facing away and didn't notice immediately.

"Good morning," I said, my voice seeming very loud in the quiet. Theod startled, freezing in place.

There was an uncomfortably long moment of silence before he turned and said, "Good morning. You're up early."

"So are you," I countered. I walked over to let Kasaqua out of her stall. She stepped out and stretched languidly, moving to touch her nose to Copper's. "I feel like it's been a while since we talked about anything of substance."

Theod took a breath and said, "Since last time we talked . . . since we talked about . . . us . . . I had a few different long talks with my uncle Kuhaukis, and with Askaski and Mamunapit—"

"Who?" I asked.

"Young men close to my age, on Naquipaug . . . the only ones, really, because there's a gap after 1825. They were both infants, at the time. My little cousins introduced me," he rambled, shrugging. "Anyway, I've been talking to them about . . . us? That sounds terrible, when I say it that way; I don't mean that I went telling tales or anything! I was just . . . I wanted advice from people who know better how this sort of thing works. Among islanders."

"Oh," I said, trying not to laugh at how absolutely *earnest* he was, because I didn't want him to feel ridiculous. "And what did they have to say about . . . us?"

"They said that I'd be an absolute *ass* to refuse any offer that you made to me regarding . . . personal affections. That it's entirely sensible to pursue a woman who loves other women, and that it's a good way to turn out with a household with two or more women in it, which to their opinion is the best of all possible situations in life. Never mind that we'd be allying the only two dragoneers on the islands if we married—"

"Oh, are we talking about *marriage*?" I asked, unable to resist teasing just a little. "That's rather forward. I'm much too young to consider marriage! But if we're simply talking about physical love . . ."

"Anequs, please," he said, sounding pained enough that I felt bad for teasing. I reached out and took his hand, and he . . . allowed it. Though he didn't precisely hold my hand in return.

"In absolute seriousness, Theod . . . I'm not at all experienced in love of the romantic kind," I confessed. "I've never really understood how characters in novels can gaze at one another across a room and be instantly swept away, and moved to take all sorts of mad actions that complicate the lives of everyone around them. Those kinds of books have always seemed a bit silly to me, though Hekua seems to enjoy them a lot; she's especially fond of the sort where one of the pair of lovers is dying of consumption or something. I've never understood the appeal."

"I confess that I've never read any romance novels at all," Theod said, fixing me with his gaze. "I didn't expect there to be much romance in my life. Not until I met you."

"See, you say that sort of thing, and it brings me up short—I don't know what to say, what to think, what to do." I looked away, my gaze finding Kasaqua, who was standing and staring at me with her head tilted, as if trying to work something out. "Maybe something is wrong with me," I said. "Maybe most girls are capable of that sort of thing—the kind of frantic love that overcomes everything else. But I don't think I am. I can't help but approach things pragmatically, Theod. I liked dancing with you at the ball. I liked it when you kissed me, back in December. I like the way your hand feels in mine right now, and I'd very much like to feel your arms around me. I know that I'm not overwhelmingly in love with you—in that there's no fervent madness or long sleepless nights—but I'm *fond* of you. I'm comfortable with you, and I can imagine building a life with you. But I don't really know what I *want* yet, and I *can't* know without trying things on! I'm very interested in exploring . . . certain things . . . and in exploring them with *you,* specifically. Though that doesn't make me any less interested in trying out those sorts of things with Liberty. My affection for her doesn't diminish my affection for you, or the other way around."

Theod's hand gripped mine a little more firmly, and for all my talk of pragmatism, I *did* feel a thrill go through me at just that bit of encouragement.

"Anequs, you have become the lodestone around which my life revolves," he said, his voice sounding thick and labored. "A year ago, I was both convinced of and contented with the evident fact that Kuiper's Academy would be my place of residence for the rest of my life. I was a penniless orphan with no prospects, and incalculably lucky to have Frau Kuiper bestow charity upon me. Then suddenly, there you were. I met you, and my whole life changed. Irrevocably. You made me believe that I could be something other than Kuiper's ward, that I could properly learn skiltakraft; I'd never have learned it under Professor Ezel. You introduced me to *my family.* If you never spoke to me again, I would go on loving you for the rest of my life. I speak of marriage, Anequs, because I cannot imagine a life in which you are not the center of my world. I'm muddling through what it means to be a nackie, what it means to be a man, and what it would mean to be yours. But that's what I want, in whatever capacity you'll have me. As a husband, a lover, a friend—whatever you want of me, so long as I know that you want me. Even if I'm not the only one that you want."

I met his gaze, my hand moving to the side of his face, to stroke his cheek as I searched his eyes. There was something frightening in the kind of devotion he was talking about. I didn't doubt his sincerity at all, but we'd never done anything more intimate than kissing! How could he be so sure?

"May I kiss you?" I asked, swallowing hard. He took a stuttering breath, and nodded fractionally. His arms moved to the small of my back, pulling me closer, enclosing me in the warmth and presence of him.

I leaned in and kissed Theod Knecht. And kissed him. And kissed him. And *kissed* him.

Magnus made a chuffing noise from inside his stall, then a greeting call.

Theod and I pulled away from each other just as Marta walked into the barn. She was wearing a stylish wrapper, her hair tucked up under a little white cap, and she was fiercely scowling at us.

"What are you two *doing* out here?" she demanded, sounding annoyed. "You woke Magnus, and he woke me, and it's entirely too early for anyone to be up. I've called for tea and breakfast already. There's no reason to be out here at this hour; Mister Otterlo will see that the dragons are fed. Come back to the house. We clearly need to talk about the proper behavior of houseguests."

I looked over at Theod, who was wearing his perfectly blank, stoic face, and I bit my lip to stop myself from saying anything at all as I guided Kasaqua back to her stall.

We followed Marta back to the house.

SUMMER CAME

Marta had a lecture for us about the correct behavior of guests and hosts that only ended when Lisbet came to join us. Still, if Marta had seen Theod and me *doing* anything, when she'd found us in the barn, she elected to say nothing about it—and Marta did not generally turn a blind eye to anything she considered improper.

Dynah and Jadzia departed after breakfast to visit cousins of theirs in Vastergot, but Sander and Lisbet stayed. We played card games, promenaded around the grounds, played with the dragons, read novels to one another aloud, and generally had a fine time. No other ready opportunity arose for Theod and me to talk privately, which was incredibly frustrating. We returned to Masquapaug on Friday morning, the ferry crowded with builders and thanegards, who eyed us suspiciously.

Sigoskwe and Sakewa were waiting for us at the dock, demanding to know all about the garden party. Sakewa especially wanted details, to know if it had been like the garden parties in magazine plates. Theod and I didn't have a chance to talk alone before he took Copper back to Naquipaug. I wanted very much to scream about it, because I still didn't know whether or not we were *officially* courting now, whether I could *tell* people that.

He'd just run away, again, leaving me wondering.

Wigdis's cousin, her husband, and their three children all came to live on Masquapaug. Her husband was Blackfolkish, which visibly set him and their children apart from everyone else. The thanegards were again loudly upset, and made that known to Sachem Tanaquish and anyone else in earshot. There seemed to be some consensus among them that the children weren't *properly* nackies, because their father was Blackfolkish. That was strange, because no one had implied in any way that Ingrid and Aksel weren't nackies, and their father had been Anglish.

The family stayed at the meetinghouse while a new homestead was being built, which only took a couple of weeks; it was the right time of year for green saplings, and there were many people willing to lend a hand. I'd never seen anyone build a house *defiantly* before.

Mishona and Ashaquiat's wedding was on the twenty-second of July.

Her mother's family came from Naquipaug to attend, and some of her mother's cousins from the mainland. The thanegards insisted on marking down the names of everyone who visited—even those who'd come by canoe. Theod came, riding Copper, and they made note of that, too.

We danced together. I didn't dance with any other young men, and Theod didn't dance with any other young women, and I knew that others *noticed* that. I spent most of the social dances trying to work out some way of dragging him off where the two of us could talk, without it being rude or gaining anyone's attention. I did not succeed.

Niquiat also came, with Zhina. Mother sidled up to her while

Niquiat was dancing the young men's promenade, and they spoke at length; from afar, it seemed rather like Mother was interrogating her. I made it my business not to get involved. If Mother was fishing for answers about Zhina and Niquiat's possible courtship, she'd certainly do the same regarding Theod and me.

We had as lovely a time as could be managed, ignoring the thanegards. Mishona announced at the wedding feast that her baby had quickened a few days ago, and there were congratulations, gifts, blessings, and rejoicing.

Mishona and Ashaquiat formally departed from the feast together in the middle of the afternoon, to be alone together newly wedded in her mother's home. Everyone else in the household had made arrangements to spend the night elsewhere. The festivities continued in the happy couple's absence, people slowly departing in ones and twos as afternoon became evening. It didn't escape my notice that Hekua left with Seseque; she'd absolutely want to compare notes with me tomorrow. She'd want to know if I'd made any progress with Theod. But I didn't *know* if I'd made any progress with Theod, not really.

"You look like you're thinking too hard, Chipmunk," Niquiat said from just behind my shoulder. I startled a bit; I hadn't noticed him approaching. My gaze had been on Theod, who was talking with Aksel.

"Maybe I am," I replied, sighing through my nose. "Theod is . . . frustrating. He declared love to me last winter, and I told him then that we needed to focus on our studies. It wasn't even a sure thing then that he'd be allowed to take Copper away from the school's dragonhall. Everything with the threatening letters and the jarl happened, and our exams . . ."

"Not exactly the proper setting to strike up a romance?" Niquiat offered.

"No, definitely not," I said. "We talked about courting again at Strawberry Thanksgiving. I told him that I want to try things out with him, but that I've also got an eye on a girl at the school—

Liberty. You haven't met her, but you'd like her. I was entirely ready to proceed with Theod, having told him that, but he was all prickly and morose about my wanting to court both of them, and he left."

"He was brought up by the Anglish; he's obviously absorbed a lot of their foolish ideas on the subject," Niquiat said. "I expect he'd have been even more affronted if you had several young men you wanted to try things on with—it's a different sort of jealous, knowing that a woman you fancy is courting other women as opposed to knowing that she's courting other men. If two men are interested in the same woman and can't get along about it, they can have a shouting and shoving match if they need to. The Anglish take that sort of thing entirely too far, and might even holmgang over it, but the principle's the same. Theod can't very well confront this other girl you're talking about like that, and he's probably never given a second thought to the idea of a woman courting another woman."

"I know! Liberty and I talked about this—Anglish ideas of courtship, I mean. They've got *laws* against women loving women and men loving men. According to Liberty, it's serious enough that the Ministry could declare me morally unfit to be a dragoneer if I courted her and they came to know! I've been very careful in what I write in our letters, because I'm reasonably certain that someone associated with the thanegards is intercepting my correspondence. I had to make three left turns to make a right, getting a letter to Jarl Joervarsson."

"I don't like this whole business of a thanegard outpost any more than you do," Niquiat agreed grimly. "I wonder what the whalers will have to say about it, when they come home in November."

"Nothing good, I'm sure," I said. I hadn't even considered what Father might think of the thanegards, but I ought to have. So much was happening all at once. "Anyway, Theod and I talked again at Marta's, when we visited last month. He said he'd confided in his uncle and some young men on Naquipaug, and he declared love for me again, and we kissed . . . and then he left *again*!"

"Do you want me to talk to him, man-to-man, and set him straight about the way things are on Masquapaug?"

"No. Yes. Augh, I don't know! I don't know if that would make anything better or worse, frankly. I have been trying very hard to be entirely honest about my feelings and how I'd like to pursue things with him and with Liberty, and he's so absolutely closemouthed and standoffish about the whole affair! He says that he's in love with me, but he won't *do* anything about it! Every time I try to talk to him about courting, he immediately wants to talk about marriage."

"Proper and good Anglish folks don't *do* physical love outside of marriage," Niquiat said, with a mocking tone of severe seriousness. "They regard it as especially ruinous to women, so a young man is expected to become familiar with the particulars of physical love by engaging professional women. Jorgen and Ekaitz brought me to a place for drinks and dice once . . . never mind. A young *woman,* according to the Anglish, is meant to neither know nor care about the subject *at all* until she's married."

"How are they even people?" I groaned, covering my face with my hands in frustration. "How can they so thoroughly ruin the most basic things about love and family and not be completely miserable all the time?"

"Oh, a good number of them *are* completely miserable all the time, especially the rich. I mean, you've read the same pennik novels I have."

"I didn't think they were serious," I said.

"Neither did I, until I went to Vastergot and lived among the Anglish. And I've been among the poor people, who are more sensible about the facts of life than the rich ones. The toffs at your school are exactly the kind of people that those novels are about. I'd bet money that your friend Marta has never seen a naked man."

My brain rebelled at such a thing, and I had to consider for a moment . . . Marta's book on perfect comportment indicated that a young woman should never, ever be alone in the company of a young man without a suitable chaperone present. Any time it mentioned courting, it proceeded immediately to marriage, the same way that Theod did. It made a certain kind of horrible sense.

Had Theod ever seen a naked woman? I'd have to ask him.

I noticed one of the thanegards watching Niquiat and me, writing something down in a little notebook. I locked my gaze with his when he looked up again and held it for a long moment. He looked away first, and went back to writing.

If I wanted to pursue Theod, I'd have to find a way to do so away from prying eyes.

ANEQUS AND THEOD WERE FINALLY ABLE TO HAVE A MOMENT APART

It had gotten dark enough that the fireflies were coming out when I spotted Theod slipping away from a conversation with my uncle Mequeche. I'd been watching him all evening—the way his eyes would find me across the room and then quickly dart away; how he'd adjust his shirt collar whenever I came near. This was my chance, and I was going to take it. I sidled up to him, my fingers brushing his elbow just enough to feel him tense at my touch.

"There's something I want to show you," I said. He hesitated, looking just slightly alarmed—but nodded and followed.

The night air hung heavy with summer warmth and the scents of blooming bee balm and hummingbird mint as we walked side by side down a narrow path, not quite touching. My heart was beating faster than I wanted to admit. For all my pragmatism about love and courtship, something about Theod made me feel less certain than I liked to appear.

"You've been avoiding me," I said, breaking the silence between us. The statement came out more accusatory than I'd intended.

"I haven't been avoiding you," he replied, staring down at his boots. "I danced with you several times today!"

"Before that," I said, stopping to turn and face him. A firefly flashed beside his face, briefly illuminating the tension in his features. I wondered if he could see the frustration in mine.

"I've been . . . considering," he said carefully. "Everything you told me. About courting. About Liberty." The way he said her name made my stomach twist slightly—not from guilt, exactly, but an awareness of the complexity I'd introduced. Everything would be simpler if I loved him and him alone.

I sighed. "And here I thought we'd made progress at Marta's." I reached for his hand. He stiffened but didn't pull away, which I counted as a small victory. "Theod, look at me."

When he finally raised his eyes to meet mine, something caught in my throat. For all his reserved nature, his eyes always betrayed him—dark and expressive, full of a yearning he seemed determined to keep contained. I wondered what he saw in mine, and tried to project confidence I didn't entirely feel.

"There's no one watching us now," I said softly, tugging him toward a thicket of blueberry bushes that I knew had a clearing in the middle. Tall pines formed a canopy overhead, and their needles carpeted the ground. "No thanegards taking notes, no dragons butting in. Just us."

"That's what concerns me," he muttered, but followed nonetheless.

Inside the ring of bushes, with moonlight filtering through in silver patches, I released his hand and stepped back against the trunk of a pine tree. I needed the support more than I cared to admit.

"You've said that you love me," I said, aiming for directness. "Did you mean it?"

"Of course I meant it." His voice was low, but *certain* in a way that made my heart flutter. "I wouldn't say such a thing lightly."

"Then why do you keep running away whenever we get close to . . . anything?" The question came from somewhere raw within me—a place that wondered if I was the problem, if my pragmatic approach to love was somehow . . . lacking.

Theod began pacing a small circle, hands clasped behind his back like he was giving a recitation at school. "It's not that simple, Anequs. Where I was raised—"

"You're not there anymore," I interrupted, pushing away from the tree. My patience was wearing thin. I'd spent so many nights thinking about him, about us, trying to understand why this had to be so difficult. "You're here. With me. With your family on Naquipaug. You don't have to live by their rules."

"It's not just rules," he said, dragging a hand through his hair. "It's . . . everything I was taught to believe about what's proper, what's right. What it means to be honorable. To protect someone you . . ." He trailed off.

"Love?" I finished for him, moving closer until I could smell the woodsmoke and sweat of him, feel the warmth of his skin. Despite my frustration, I couldn't help but soften at the genuine conflict in his expression. "Is it protection to deny us both what we want?"

Theod swallowed visibly. "And what is it that you want, Anequs?"

I considered the question carefully. What *did* I want? Liberty's face flashed in my mind briefly, but she was far away at school. Here, now, among the blueberries with the moon painting silver light across Theod's serious face, I knew exactly what I wanted.

"Right now?" I smiled, tilting my head. "I want you to stop thinking so much. To stop worrying about what's proper according to people who aren't here. I want you to kiss me like you did at Marta's, before we were interrupted."

His eyes widened slightly. "And Liberty?"

"Liberty isn't here, either," I said plainly, though my heart twisted slightly at the reminder of my complicated affections. "This moment is only about you and me."

I reached up, my fingers trembling slightly as they brushed along the side of his face, tracing the curve of his cheekbone. His skin was warm beneath my touch, and I felt him trembling, too—a shared vulnerability that made me braver.

"You make everything sound so simple," he whispered.

"Some things *are* simple," I replied, surprised by how steady my voice sounded when my heart was racing. "Like this."

I looped my arms around his waist, closed the gap between us, and pressed my lips to his. For a terrible moment, he remained still, and doubt crashed through me—then, with a soft sound that made my heart soar, his arms encircled my waist in return, pulling me against him. The kiss deepened, and I felt a thrill course through me that was nothing like the frantic passion described in Hekua's romance novels. This was warmer, more real, more grounding—like coming home to a place I hadn't known I was missing.

When we finally broke apart, both breathing a little faster, I felt oddly shy despite my earlier boldness. "See?" I said, grinning. "Simple."

Theod's expression was dazed, but I could see the conflict still lurking behind his eyes. His hands lingered at my waist for a moment before he stepped back, creating distance that felt colder than it should have on such a warm night.

"I should go," he said, his voice hoarse.

I sighed, disappointment settling heavy in my chest. "You always do."

"I need time, Anequs." He ran a hand through his hair again, disarranging it in a way that made him look younger, more vulnerable. "This isn't just about a kiss. It's about what comes after. What it all means."

"It means we care for each other," I said, trying to keep frustration from my voice. Why couldn't we just . . . let everything develop naturally? "The rest, we can figure out together."

He nodded slowly. "Together," he echoed, as if testing the word. Then he leaned forward and placed a gentle kiss on my forehead that felt both tender and like a retreat. "I promise I won't keep running. But tonight . . . I need to think. When we're back at school, we won't be able to . . . I don't know if I could stand that, if we started something and then had to stop."

Before I could respond, he slipped through the bushes and back toward the distant lights of the celebration. I watched him go, touching my lips where the warmth of his kiss still lingered. A complicated mix of satisfaction and frustration swirled within me.

At least he'd stopped saying he wanted to marry me before trying anything.

Yet despite my frustration at his departure, something had changed tonight—I could feel it. The ground beneath us had shifted, ever so slightly. For the first time, I truly believed that Theod and I might find our way to each other on terms that we could both accept.

With that thought warming me, I followed the path back to the wedding celebration, already wondering when I might corner him again. After all, if there was one thing I'd learned tonight, it was that Theod Knecht was worth being patient for.

ANEQUS AND THEOD ATTENDED THE THYNGE

The rest of July proceeded with a kind of quiet tension, a sense of *wrongness* on the island. The thanegards were . . . present. At the beach, at the meetinghouse, at the docks. Watching. Judging. They seemed especially interested in Kasaqua, and thus in me and my family.

On Friday the twenty-eighth, I received a letter formally inviting me (and Kasaqua) to the thynge being held at town hall in Nack Port on August first. Jarl Joervarsson was stopping at Masquapaug to collect us, and Sachem Tanaquish, so we'd be *members of his party* when he arrived at Nack Port. I was very glad of that forethought, because I had no doubt that if we turned up at the gates of Nack Port without him, we'd have been flatly denied entry. I hoped that he'd arranged similar protections for Theod and Sachem Wompinottomak.

Before I'd become Nampeshiweisit, I hadn't known anything at all about the details of Anglish governance. I'd been aware that a jarl existed, abstractly, and that we paid taxes to the office of the jarl every November. I hadn't known anything at all about thanes or torgars. It was only at the jarl's moot in May that I'd learned who the torgar was supposed to be for the islands: Wilhelm Hasenjager. I'd never met or even seen him. He'd never been to Masquapaug, despite supposedly being our representative to Thane Jespersen, who was in turn Catchnet's representative to the jarl.

I took Kasaqua to wait at the dock at a quarter before nine on August first; the jarl's letter said he'd be arriving then. I'd tacked her up for this, because she behaved more calmly when she was in tack. It also gave me an excuse to keep my hand at the brass ring near her shoulder—a reason to stay in arm's length at all times. I was wearing the dress Liberty had made for me again, because it was the smartest thing I had that I still looked and felt like *myself* in. The thanegard stationed at the office stared at me coldly, but said nothing. Sachem Tanaquish came to join me in waiting, and we exchanged pleasantries . . . but he seemed grim and concerned.

The jarl's sailboat didn't arrive until nearly ten.

Jarl Joervarsson was as impressive a figure as he'd been at the moot in May—tall and broad-shouldered, dressed in blue-and-gold silk, his golden hair and beard braided with beads and charms. The jarl dressed in a manner markedly different from the common mode of Anglish fashion—clothing that must have been ceremonial or traditional or something like that; I'd never asked anyone about the specifics. He was flanked by a pair of guards who walked half a step behind him.

"You know, I think this is the first time I've ever come to this island," he said as he stepped off the boat and surveyed the ferry office and the new thanegards' outpost beyond. "I should come back some other time when things are less pressing and have you give me a tour!"

"I'm sure something like that could be arranged," the sachem said diplomatically, dipping his head a bit in deference to the jarl. Something about that rankled; Sachem Tanaquish was much older than Jarl Joervarsson, and in my estimation, not of a particularly different rank or class.

"You're not having trouble with the ferry anymore, are you?" the jarl asked, his gaze still on the outpost, which was in the last stages of construction.

"We've been allowed to traverse, if that's what you're asking," the sachem said. "They're still keeping records of every person who comes or goes by any means at all, including canoe travel and dragon flight."

"Good, good, all to plan then," the jarl said with a grin, as if we should have been *happy* about the thanegards watching us every moment. "Come aboard; I'm sure they're already waiting for us at town hall. I know I'm late, but one of the benefits of being jarl is that nothing starts until I arrive."

Crossing the channel was faster on the jarl's boat than it would have been by canoe, and we arrived at Naquipaug in half an hour. Nack Port reminded me of Catchnet more than anything else—buildings in the Anglish style with whitewashed walls, cobbled streets, and Anglish people milling about the dockside. Kasaqua was very interested, because this was someplace new and different—someplace that had its own smell. She wanted to *explore.*

"Walk next to me," the jarl said, beckoning me over as the gangplank was lowered. The jarl's personal guards walked directly behind us; I couldn't help noticing that they were armed with pistols. I resisted the urge to glance back at them as we descended, telling myself that they were here to protect us.

There were lots of Anglish people staring, pointing, and talking to one another as we made a procession down the main thoroughfare toward the town hall. I caught movement from the corner of my eye and felt something fly just shy of my face as I turned; it had almost hit me. There was a wet slapping sound, and I looked to where a half-rotten peach had struck the pavement. Kasaqua flared her wings and bent to sniff at it, not understanding at all that it wasn't an offering; people often threw food to her at home. The jarl was already pointing in the direction the peach had come from. Some other guards than the pair following us went that way, and there was a commotion. We didn't stop.

I wondered what, if anything, would happen to the person who'd thrown the peach.

Town Hall was a two-story building made of gray stone, not at all as grand as the jarl's palace but clearly built on the same model. It had the same kind of intricate reliefs, all knots and whorls, laid out in little bits of mortared stone and tile that flanked each side of the huge double doors. There was also a pair of thanegards mounted on silberdraches to either side of the main entrance; we would have to walk between them. I wondered if they were the same guards, the same dragons, that had brought an abrupt end to the assembly in North Village. I very carefully avoided looking at them as we passed. I kept my shoulders squared and my face stony, trying to seem wholly unaffected. But Kasaqua's hackles went up, and she hissed very softly, glaring at the dragon to our left as we passed.

The main entrance was made to the kind of proportions that would allow someone to ride through on horseback if need be, so it was quite large enough for Kasaqua. I had to wonder when this building had been constructed. The Anglish had been on Naquipaug for something like a hundred years, but I wouldn't have thought that Nack Port was the kind of place that warranted a building like this. What was it even used for when there wasn't an assembly?

The room we arrived at, after passing through an impressive marble-and-granite corridor, was very like the school's lecture hall. Without the breeze from the ocean, the air was stiflingly hot. The room was absolutely full of people—not just Anglish people, but folks from North Village, as well, which was heartening. I hadn't expected them to be allowed. Many of them were women of my parents' generation; Aunt Shanuckee was there, but I didn't see Mamisashquee.

The Anglish probably wouldn't have been kind to Mamisashquee.

At the center of the room there was a long, narrow table on a short stage with chairs behind it that faced the rows of seats arranged in tiers around the other three sides of the room. Theod was seated in a front row to the far side of the stage, beside Sachem Wompinottomak. Copper was lying down in front of them, head resting on his crossed forelegs. His tail thumped the ground once when he noticed Kasaqua, but he was otherwise obediently still. Kasaqua pulled a little bit, intent on heading that way, but stopped when I held firm on the brass ring at her shoulder. She gave a little huffing sigh of frustration, which I absolutely sympathized with. There was an empty seat to Theod's left, at the very end of the row, and another empty chair to Wompinottomak's right. The jarl turned to Sachem Tanaquish and me, broadly gesturing at them, which I took as instruction to go sit. Kasaqua dropped dramatically to the floor as soon as I allowed her to, rolling onto her side and stretching her forelegs, canting her head backward to touch noses with Copper.

The jarl proceeded to the table on the stage and took a seat at the chair in the middle. I recognized some of the other men who were already seated; they were the thanes who'd been at the moot in May. The front and center row of seats, opposite the table, were all occupied by similarly dressed men who all wore blue and gold sashes from right shoulder to left hip. They were obviously some kind of ranking mark, but I didn't know what they meant; I'd never seen anyone else wearing them.

There were four very obvious empty seats at the end of that row, farthest from us.

Once we were seated, the jarl loudly cleared his throat, and the quiet murmurs among the gathered crowd stopped.

"I'd like to thank everyone for being here today," he began. "I know it can be troublesome to take time from your work to do your civic duty. For those who have never been introduced to me, I am Leiknir Joervarsson, Jarl of Vaster Hold—which encompasses the thedes of Catchnet, Estervall, Skaldstead, Varmarden, and Vastergot. Those thedes are each represented by a thane." He gestured to the men seated at the table with him in turn. "Svend Jespersen of Catchnet. Havard Authunsson of Estervall. Gustav Lindgren of Skaldstead. Jorborg Eidsson of Varmarden. Arjan Stafn of Vastergot. I am here to say, before all witnesses, that after careful investigation, Svend Jespersen has been found derelict in his duty as thane. Likewise his torgar, Wilhelm Hasenjager, has been derelict in his duty to the people of the outlying islands. As of this moment, I declare—by my powers as jarl—that they are both released from their duties—"

"You have no right to remove a people-chosen torgar or thane!" someone shouted from the audience, making me turn to look. I couldn't tell who it had been; a lot of the Anglish people looked very angry.

"That would be true if the men in question had fulfilled the duties of their office!" the jarl shouted, smacking the table hard with the flat of his hand. The murmuring took longer to die down this time, and sounded more angry and jeering than before.

"According to the most recent folkreckoning," the jarl practically snarled, "there are one thousand and twenty-five citizens of Lindmarden living on Mask Island. I've gotten reports from the new thanegards' outpost that there've been half a dozen or so new residents since then, moved from the mainland to live with family, and the thanegards are so terribly worried about it." He turned his gaze to one of the men in the first row who was wearing a sash. "Have *you* heard? How often do you go to Mask Island, Herr Hasenjager, to take account from the citizens there regarding their opinions on the laws and ways of our nation?"

The man stood with obvious reluctance. Wilhelm Hasenjager was a solid-looking man, probably between fifty and sixty years of age, with a scraggly beard and long white hair held in a neat tail at his nape. He was dressed in a tidy but somewhat old-fashioned gray suit. He did not look at all pleased.

"I have never been to Mask Island," Herr Hasenjager answered, his voice weary and annoyed. "There are no relevant people there to take account from."

"No relevant people?" the jarl asked, leaning forward, baring his teeth in a way that was not a smile. "What is it about the one thousand and twenty-five citizens of Lindmarden who reside on Mask Island that makes them somehow *not relevant*? They pay taxes. They're citizens, according to the 1757 Treaty of New Linvik. So go ahead and say it—*say* what makes them not relevant."

Wilhelm Hasenjager didn't say anything. He just stared at the jarl coldly. After a moment of brittle silence, the jarl continued.

"Sit down, Herr Hasenjager." He raised his gaze to the audience at large and asked, "Who here knows what the point of a torgar is? What a torgar's *duty* is?" There was an uncomfortable silence while he waited for someone, anyone, to answer. No one did, and the jarl turned his gaze back to Herr Hasenjager, then to Thane Jespersen. His voice rose to a shout when he continued, "A torgar's duty is to listen to the smallfolk and bring their concerns to the thane! Svend Jespersen, how long have you been thane of Catchnet Thede and the outlying islands?"

"It has been my honor to serve as thane for forty-one years, Jarl Joervarsson. The landowners of Catchnet Thede have, thynge on thynge, elected me to report their wants and needs to you. My torgars throughout the thede have regularly come to me, or sent letters, detailing the wants and needs of the smallfolk in their districts. I helped restore peace to the islands after the events of 1825—"

"What peace?" someone in the Naquisit part of the audience spat. "We've had no peace since the townspeople of Nack Port murdered everyone in South Village! Your people hanged two dozen of our people for having the audacity to fight back and push squatters off of land they didn't own, and *didn't* hang a single one of the murderers who poisoned children and elders! When will we have justice for those you killed?"

"The past cannot be undone," the jarl said, his voice clear and even, "but I intend to see to it that the future is more just for *all* citizens of Lindmarden. That is why I have arranged this thynge—and why we are all here today. I have asked for a representative for *every single household on Nack Island* to be present at this thynge. Does anyone here know of any household that has not sent a representative? I ask this because it has come to my attention that for the past however many years, quite a few households on this island have not had representatives at assemblies like this."

Sachem Wompinottomak stood, turning to nod at the gathered Naquisit folks before looking back to the jarl.

"Yes, Jarl Joervarsson. There are two hundred and eighty-two households represented here from North Village and the surrounding lands."

There was a loud and complaining murmur from the Anglish crowd then, until the jarl smacked the table hard with the flat of his hand. He nodded to Sachem Wompinottomak, who sat back down.

"We are here today," the jarl continued, "to see to the appointment of torgars, who will then cast their votes for thane of Catchnet Thede—"

"A thane ought to be chosen by the landowners!" someone shouted.

"And a thane *will* be chosen by the landowners in January of 1845. But at this moment, Catchnet Thede is without a thane. There is precedent for a provisional thane to be chosen by a thede's torgars; that's how it was done when Thane Fretheim of Varmarden died suddenly in the middle of his term. All of the torgars for each district of Catchnet were invited—by personal letter from my own hand—to attend this thynge. Those who have not made the time to be here have the people of their own district to answer to.

"Now, according to the most recent folkreckoning, there are two thousand two hundred and thirty-four landless citizens living in the city of Nack Port. In his great wisdom, High King Thrand Thorvaldsson—the first king of Lindmarden—wrote the Great Charter with the help of his advisors. It is stated in the charter that there shall be a torgar for every thousand landless folk living in any hold. I do not think, when King Thorvaldsson wrote the charter in 1628, that he could have imagined that the city of Vastergot would be home to one hundred and thirty-six thousand and more people. Still, the charter is sound! There are more than a hundred torgars, who report to the thanes, who report to me! As there are more than two thousand folk living in Nack Port, the city ought to have two torgars. I am appointing Eldert Garsensaar and Arnvid Svartbrandsson. Gentlemen, if you would kindly rise and join the other torgars in the front row?"

"You can't just remove Herr Hasenjager and replace him with a pair of lickspittle boys who'll smile and nod and sign off on everything that the Freemansthede suggests!" a man in the audience shouted, rising to his feet. There was an echo of agreement from the people around him.

Jarl Joervarsson snarled, leaning over the table. "They are the men that I am appointing to the position of torgar. If you, the people of Nack Port, wish to choose new torgars in three months' time, you'll have every right to have a community thynge about it. Until then, Mister Garsensaar and Mister Svartbrandsson are the men to whom you can report your grievances, and they in turn will report to your thane—who will be also chosen today. Svend Jespersen has proven himself unequal to the role by ignoring the needs of half the people on Nack and all the people on Mask. There are one thousand six hundred and fifty-five citizens of Lindmarden on Nack Island residing outside of Nack Port—principally in the settlement called North Village, along the northwest coast. I am declaring that settlement a district of its own, and appointing Wompinottomak—chief of the Nack Islanders—as its torgar. There are also better than a thousand people living on Mask Island. That means, in accordance with the charter, that they're a district in their own right, as well. I therefore, by my power as Jarl of Vastergot, appoint Tanaquish—chief of the Mask Islanders—as torgar of Mask Island. Gentlemen, if you would please come and join the rest of the torgars?" The sachems, and the two Anglishmen the jarl had named, all rose and proceeded to the center row.

A voice called out from the audience, loud and clear and coldly precise in a way that reminded me of Professor Ezel. My gaze found the speaker—a tall, broad, ginger-haired man in an immaculate black suit with very square shoulders. He was wearing a brooch on each lapel—a pair of silver-colored ravens facing each other.

"It is terribly suspicious, I think, that the Jarl of Vastergot should come to install four new torgars—all of whom are presumably allied to a greater or lesser extent with the Freemansthede—when he has just removed from office a torgar and a thane who are respectively aligned with the Ravens of Joden and the Eiriksthede. One might think that you were leveraging your power to silence the voices of those who disagree with you politically."

"Unless I'm mistaken," the jarl said, making a small gesture with his hand that seemed to mean something to the guards standing behind him, by the way they suddenly shifted their attention, "you are Sveni Audulfsson, wroughtthane of the Ravens of Joden."

"You're not mistaken, Jarl Joervarsson," he said with a smile that might have been charming in some other context. "As Herr Hasenjager is a member of my party, I thought it prudent to come and see these proceedings for myself. I came here because I am a concerned citizen of Vastergot, interested in the preservation of the ways of our ancestors. I also came here because I have, several times now, been denied passage to Mask Island to address a grievance. That young woman"—he pointed at me, and I suddenly felt every gaze in the room on me—"killed my firstborn son."

AND ENCOUNTERED A POWERFUL ENEMY

"I'm sorry," I said, more from reflex than any real feeling of remorse. *I* hadn't killed Birning Svenisson, exactly—Kasaqua had, without being instructed to. Because he'd shot me, and her, and Jarl Joervarsson. He hadn't managed to kill any of us, which made him a very poor assassin.

"I don't believe that for a moment," he said, his voice cold and precise, "but even if you were truly sorry, my son Birning—a torgar of Vastergot reporting to Arjan Stafn, a young husband with a child on the way—would still be dead. His wife is a widow, and his child will be born fatherless."

"He *shot* me," I said, still rather at a loss that this man should be here, confronting me, in front of the jarl and his thanes and torgars and all the people of Naquipaug. What did he hope to accomplish?

Herr Audulfsson's face tightened slightly, forming a narrow, mirthless smile. His suit was the same kind of black that Captain

Einarsson's was; something about the weave of the fabric seemed to absorb light. It made the ravens on his lapels stand out starkly.

"My son was not a patient man, and in his impatience thought to take very rash action, and came to ruin because of it," he said. "Traditionally, it would be within my rights to extract a weregild from you for the killing of my firstborn. However, the lawmakers currently in authority have declared my late son a criminal, and thus not worthy of recompense."

"Your son attempted to murder me," the jarl said, rising to his feet in an unhurried, implacable way. "Miss Anequs heroically put herself between the gunman and me, and then her dragon dispatched him."

"That is the series of events that was reported to the newspapermen, I'm sure," Herr Audulfsson said. "I didn't come here looking for justice; I know that I will never achieve it. I came here in the name of the Ravens of Joden, because I have watched this nation deteriorate more and more each year under the weak and insipid leadership of the Freemansthede. The council of thanes made a grave error in the year 1836 when they elected to depose Kjeld Niklasson. It has not gone unnoticed that in the years since, Leiknir Joervarsson has replaced three of the five thanes of Vastergot—and he seeks to replace a fourth today. He has gutted the Ministry of Dragon Affairs, replacing two ministers—Levi van Brackle back in 1838, and Aleksanteri Turunen quite recently. It is a very disconcerting pattern, this elimination of any dissenting voices with no regard given to the choices of the people—"

"The men that I removed from office did not fulfill their duties!" Jarl Joervarsson interrupted. "Alek Turunen was the lieutenant minister overseeing Catchnet and the outlying islands. He ought to have been aware of a dragon egg on Mask Island, and should have reported it to Captain Einarsson."

"The savages were deceitful about the whole affair," Thane—or rather *former* Thane—Jespersen spat, his face very red. "Absolutely no one was informed of the presence of the egg until after its hatching and bonding!"

"And how often did any sort of representative—a torgar, a minister, a thane—visit Mask Island to take account of happenings there? I think we've already established that those responsible have been lax in their duties, which is why new men are being posted to those positions. I am not here to entertain accusations made by would-be despots who claim to care about the will of the people with one breath, but ignore the voices of thousands of citizens with the next!"

"Which brings us to the real meat of the problem, doesn't it?" Herr Audulfsson said with a sneer. "Why should these or any savages be considered citizens of Lindmarden?"

A murmur of agreement went up from the Anglish portion of the audience, answered by jeers and complaints from the Naquisit side.

Herr Audulfsson paused, waiting for quiet again before continuing, "We know well enough why *you* want them to be represented, Jarl Joervarsson; it's an excuse to install torgars and thanes of your choosing, who will be loyal to you and your Enkiwroughten party! You want a body of unintelligent, uneducated, biddable Hnefatafl pieces! The Freemansthede has always courted the attention and sympathy of the smallfolk—the landless and impoverished, the idlers and drunks, the morally bereft masses who do nothing to preserve or improve society—"

"As an impoverished, landless, idle, drunkard," someone in the Anglish part of the audience shouted, "I, for one, am terribly pleased to have *someone* courting my attention!"

"Who do you think you are—" said Herr Audulfsson, turning his gaze toward the person who'd stood.

"Anyone can speak at a thynge!" the other man shouted back, cutting Herr Audulfsson off. He was a very stout Anglishman, and I couldn't gauge his age other than "older than thirty but younger than sixty." He had yellow hair in a pair of braids, and his face was clean-shaven. He was wearing a suit cut in the typical style, but it was chicory-flower blue and stood out starkly among the other men, who were all dressed in subdued colors—black, brown, gray, tan. He was holding some kind of wooden tool—a stick about a yard long with an ornately carved head. He was using it to gesture broadly as he spoke.

"As to who I think I am," he continued, "I'm reasonably sure that I'm Eskil Gerdasson—professional bastard, occasional seitherman, champion of the smallfolk, and generally disreputable troublemaker! Since no one else seems to be willing to tell you to shut your mouth, I volunteer!"

Herr Audulfsson pinched the bridge of his nose and sighed audibly. "Jarl Joervarsson, surely we can agree that this man cannot possibly—" he began, casting Herr Gerdasson a withering glare.

"No, he's right," the jarl interrupted with a sly grin. "Anyone can speak at a thynge."

"Thank you!" Herr Gerdasson said, taking a bow and flourishing with his stick. He straightened up, looked back to Herr Audulfsson, and said, "So often do you Ravens call the men of the Freemansthede 'Enkiwroughten'—as if it would be some great shame to have been wrought by Enki! Who is Enki if he is not the solver of problems, eh? Who does Joden turn to, again and again, when things are at their worst? Enki is wit, and cleverness, and cunning. He serves as an inspiration for us to approach life's troubles with open minds—to seek *untraditional* solutions. Enki is curiosity. He is ever unquiet, having insatiable thirst for knowledge, always seeking to unravel the mysteries, questioning and needling and dissenting. Isn't it curiosity that leads to discoveries, advancements, innovations? Enki is change. He shifts his shape, always able to adapt himself to any situation he's thrown into. Is it not through change that we find growth and progress? Enki shows us that even in our lowest times, we have the power to reinvent ourselves and rise above our circumstances. He serves as a reminder that redemption is possible for those who seek it earnestly. You claim to speak in Joden's name—what would Joden have to say about your wrath toward his brother, eh? You asked me who I think I am, but I ask you, who do you think *you* are to disparage a god by using his name to insult us?"

"You are a childish halfwit who should have stayed home," Herr Audulfsson said, turning his attention back to the jarl but speaking in a way that clearly addressed the whole audience. "Vastergot was founded by Vaster Stafn and his shipthede—men of Norse stock, seafarers and overthrowers. It is our duty to honor the memory of these great men by shaping a society that they'd be proud of. All human achievement descends from Norsland, Swedeland, Daneland, and Finnland—the original home of mankind. It was the Norse overthrow of the savages of Tyskland, all along the river Elva, that allowed the great civilizations of the ancient world to flourish. The Angles—for whom Anglesland is named—were savages living in huts made of sticks and mud and dung before the men of the enlightened north brought them properly in line. It was only possible for our Norse forefathers to tame and teach the Anglish because they are fundamentally the same species of mankind. The savages of New Anglesland, who are *still* living in huts cobbled together from bark and stone, just as they were when Stafn Whitebeard arrived in the year 1626, are of a different kind entirely—no more like the Norse and Anglish than Kindahs or Aprikans or Shangs. Anyone who's studied phylogeny even in passing, the work of van den Ouden or Nootkamp—"

"You are boring everyone here *and* wasting all of our time," Herr Gerdasson called, his voice almost singsong. "This thynge is being held to depose useless paper Vikings and install diligent public servants in their place. I, for one, came here to find out who the new torgars of Nack Port were going to be. None of us came here to listen to *you,* and especially not to listen to you bluster on about the greatness and glory of the Norse people. If

Norsland and Swedeland and Daneland and Finnland are such good and great places, why did so many of the bravest and strongest and most intrepid men decide to leave there, eh? What's stopping you from going back there, if that's the kind of society you want to live in?"

"The founders of Vastergot clearly never intended—"

"The founders are DEAD!" Herr Gerdasson shouted. "Why should we give a feathering fuck what they intended, eh?"

I felt my face flush at his crass language, but it was delightful that someone in the Anglish camp should be on our side in any capacity at all. Herr Gerdasson was quite possibly the least serious Anglishman I'd ever met. He reminded me of Professor Ulfar, somehow. They were nothing alike, but I was reminded regardless.

"Because the Freemansthede and those of their ilk would have us all believe the very obvious untruth that all species of mankind are equal in their capacities. They are not, and it does a disservice to all to pretend that they are. The savages here cannot be civilized, and it is folly to call them citizens."

"The citizenship of the nackie people is not something open for debate in this forum at this time, Herr Audulfsson," Jarl Joervarsson said curtly. "We've heard your statements about my appointments of torgars. Does anyone else have actually relevant statements concerning the vote that's about to take place for the new thane of Catchnet Thede?" He paused, his gaze sweeping across the audience. "If not, I think we should proceed. Gentlemen, if you'd kindly write down who you'd like to see in the thane's chair—"

He gestured to one of the thanegards, who gave each of the torgars—both sachems included—little slips of paper and pencils. I didn't know when or how the sachems had been informed of procedures, or who the candidates were, but neither of them seemed at all uncertain or confused. After a minute or so, he collected them again and delivered them to the jarl.

"Now, I understand that there are some people here who might think me partial, so I call upon the rest of my thanes to confirm as I read each vote," the jarl said, unfolding the first bit of paper.

"We have one vote for Isak Lingstadt," he called, then handed the paper to Thane Authunsson, who said, "Confirmed—Isak Lingstadt," and then handed the paper to Thane Lindgren. It proceeded through all four thanes who weren't Thane Jespersen; then, the jarl unfolded a second paper and said, "Another vote for Isak Lingstadt."

It proceeded in that fashion through fourteen votes—the four torgars who'd been named today and the ten who represented the people of the mainland. I hadn't the slightest idea who Isak Lingstadt was, but six of the torgars had voted for him. Three voted for someone named Oddfrye Leonardsson, three for Brikka Ingvaldsdottir, and two for Anders Avardsson. I had to presume that the sachems had been informed earlier which person stood for which position, politically. I trusted them to make the best choice for our people.

"It would seem that Isak Lingstadt will be Thane of Catchnet Thede until the althynge of January 1845—unless, of course, the people of Vastergot decide to rally an althynge sooner than that," the jarl announced. "I'd like to thank everyone who took the time to come here—particularly those of you who will be reporting back to newspapers and suchlike. Please report any of your concerns to your local torgar. If no one else has anything to say"—he paused for what seemed an uncomfortable amount of time—"then I conclude this thynge and ask that all parties go in peace."

People began rising from their seats—the Anglish first, because they seemed to have a much better understanding of these proceedings than anyone from the Naquisit party. There were a lot of quiet, resentful comments about jarls overstepping their powers and how they really ought to rally an althynge.

I wasn't entirely sure what we'd accomplished here. I didn't know who Isak Lingstadt was, or what his positions were, or what that would mean for the islands in the next couple of years. The jarl seemed generally pleased, though, smiling and clapping some man I didn't know on the back, gesturing to sachems Tanaquish and Wompinottomak. I turned my gaze back to the audience, wanting to keep apprised of Herr Audulfsson, but he'd already moved.

I didn't particularly want to meet or speak with him.

BUT ALSO AN UNEXPECTED ALLY

After the thynge, we were formally escorted back outside with the jarl's party; he arranged for Theod and me to walk beside him again on the way out. The jarl's party included all of the thanes and torgars, and I was sure that I could feel angry and hateful gazes at my back.

We were led out a different door than the one we'd come in—a back entrance separate from the one that the audience was filing out of. It opened to a pavilion of white marble bracketed by waist-high walls. Along the walls were tables laid with bowls of punch and little glass cups. Above, the doorway we were going out of had a balcony. Guards with rifles were posted there.

Beyond the courtyard was a wide lawn of close-cut grass shaded by a pair of oak trees. At the far end of the lawn, facing away from us, another pair of guards mounted on silberdraches kept watch. A dragon was lazing under one of the trees—quite the largest dragon I'd ever seen, even bigger than Frau Kuiper's

Gerhard. It looked very much like a silberdrache in conformation, but rather than white with gray markings, this dragon was cream colored and rust red. It was wearing strange, colorful tack—worn and much mended, but with more decoration than I was used to seeing. The leather was stained many bright colors and looked embroidered or painted or something; I couldn't tell at this distance. I'd never seen a dragon lying down while wearing tack.

Kasaqua was *very* interested in meeting this dragon, which seemed imprudent given the circumstances. I kept a firm hold of the ring at her shoulder, and she chuffed in frustration. Between having the breeze again and being in the shade, it was markedly cooler outside than it had been inside. Kasaqua spread her wings a bit, fanning them in the cooler air.

There were lichtbildmachers and other newspapermen assembled outside, and we were compelled to stand for a whole series of pictures—the jarl presenting blue-and-gold sashes to each of the four new torgars; the jarl flanked by both sachems, with Theod and me and our dragons posed in the background; Theod and me and the dragons, posed together. I wondered what Frau Kuiper's opinion would be of us appearing in the newspapers again; she'd been very angry with us for appearing in lichtbilds with the Confederation of the First People of Akashnet.

None of the people in the Naquisit part of the audience had, to my knowledge, been representatives of the confederation. Had they been excluded deliberately?

The jarl invited us to take refreshment and "enjoy conversation" with the people who started to appear from the far end of the lawn by ones and twos. I could not help noticing that Herr Audulfsson was being detained at the margin of the lawn and not allowed to approach us. I was glad of that.

Theod was pulled away by Sachem Wompinottomak to talk to some newspaperman or other, so I moved to help myself to refreshment, as I saw some others doing. I kept Kasaqua within arm's length the whole time. When I looked again, Herr Audulfsson had gone.

I was just finishing my cup when Sachem Tanaquish appeared, the outspoken man in the chicory-blue suit in his company.

"Anequs, I've been asked—if you'll permit it—to introduce Herr Eskil Gerdasson," the sachem said, the corners of his eyes crinkling in a smile that his mouth didn't match.

"I'll permit it," I said, and it sounded more like a question than an answer. Herr Gerdasson took a deep, flourishing bow.

"Enchanted, my lady," he said as he straightened back up. This close, I could see that his suit was not only a cheerfully bright blue, it was also embroidered on the lapels with an assortment of floss and ribbon flowers.

"Pleased to meet you, Herr Gerdasson," I said, dipping a curtsy in return. "If it's not rude for me to ask—"

"Oh, things that are rude to ask are always the most interesting questions!" he interrupted with a grin. I couldn't help but giggle at that, and brought my hand in front of my mouth to hide my smile. Kasaqua leaned over my shoulder, sniffing at Herr Gerdasson with interest. She rested her chin on my shoulder and kept it there as I reached around to stroke her neck.

"Ask me anything," he said, when I'd composed myself. "Even the rudest question on your mind."

"You don't look at all like any of the other Anglish men I've met," I said, hesitating. "Your hair, and the color of your suit, and your . . . tool?"

"It's a distaff!" he said cheerfully, holding the stick out for me to examine more closely. It was about a yard long, made of finely polished blond wood. The top of it was a small round knob, and from it, several carved snakes stretched down to form an oblong or egg-shaped cage with a horizontal disk at the widest point. It seemed to be carved all from one piece of wood, and it couldn't have been very heavy from the way he handled it.

"I'm afraid I don't know what that is," I said, glancing to the sachem. He was looking away, and I followed his gaze to the jarl, who was gesturing him over.

"Will you be well if I leave you to talk?" Sachem Tanaquish

asked, looking back to me, meeting my eyes. I let my gaze flick to Kasaqua and back.

"Yes," I said. Herr Gerdasson didn't seem like someone I should be immediately *wary* of. The sachem nodded, then moved to join the jarl at the other side of the pavilion.

"A distaff is a spinning tool," Herr Gerdasson explained, catching my attention back. "It holds the carded wool for you, and you can stick it in your armpit like so"—he demonstrated—"and then you have both hands free for your drop spindle! I haven't got one of those with me, though. The distaff is more for identifying me as a seitherman to passersby. In case it wasn't otherwise obvious."

"You have me at a loss, I'm afraid," I said, still smiling. "I don't know what *that* means, either."

"Seither is a very old kind of witskraft—older than skiltakraft, maybe the oldest of all. It's the witskraft of the Norns, and of the Wanes—Fyra's original people."

"I've only recently started learning about Anglish gods and spirits and such," I confessed. "I haven't been an especially diligent scholar of lore, because I spent so much of my time studying skiltakraft. I have only the broadest idea of who the principal characters are. What do you do, as a seitherman?"

"I make trouble!" he crowed with a bark of laughter. "I am first and last a devotee of Enki, the champion of outcasts and misfits. Tamsyn and me, we travel. I gather stories and ideas, stuff them all into my head together, and make them fight. Now, I won't make presumptions about you and your meaning, because in my limited experience, your people are refreshingly different in their philosophies, but when an Anglishman asks, 'What do you do,' he usually means 'How do you make your living?' The answer to *that* question is that I am a shameless freeloader. I live by the hospitality of great and good men who keep me because they find me fascinating. When one of my friends gets tired of me, I pack my things, and Tamsyn and I seek another's hospitality. Right now we're guests in the home of Esben Vilhelmsen, who you might know as the wroughtthane of the Freemansthede."

"I hadn't known that, actually," I said. "The longer I spend among the Anglish, the more aware I am of just how little I know of the world."

"It speaks of a sharp mind that you've figured that out so young!" Herr Gerdasson said with a grin. "So many young people are convinced that they know everything there is to be known. Tamsyn wants to meet your dragon, if she's not scared."

"Who's Tamsyn?" I asked.

"That great layabout over there," he said, gesturing with his distaff toward the reddish dragon.

She got up and stretched like a cat, yawning hugely. The inside of her mouth wasn't black, like a silberdrache's, but blood red. She sat on her haunches and waited patiently for us to approach.

"I fear that I suffer among my peers for not having had a primary school education at all; I'm hopeless in lore lessons, because I never learned the erelore of the eastern world," I said as we walked toward Tamsyn. Kasaqua was very excited—the same kind of curious excitement she'd had the first time she'd seen Gerhard.

"I don't think I've ever heard anyone call Anglesland 'the eastern world,'" Herr Gerdasson mused, looking thoughtful, "but that would entirely make sense for you and your people, wouldn't it? It's east of you! When Anglishmen say 'the eastern world,' they mostly mean anything east of the midland sea. If they say 'the far east,' they mean Shiang-Gang and Zhippon."

"When does it roll around and become west again, I wonder?"

"I'm sure that depends entirely on who you ask," Herr Gerdasson said, and chuckled. "For the last few years, Tamsyn and I have been moving from stead to stead in New Anglesland, but we come from *Old* Anglesland, originally. We've been to Norseland, and Swedeland, and Daneland, and Celtsland—even Tyskland and Frankland, for a bit. I wanted to be Myrddin, you see, when I was a little boy. I couldn't find a three-legged dragon, though, so I had to settle for just being a skolde."

"What's a 'Myrddin,' and how does it involve a three-legged

dragon?" I asked, shifting a little to encourage Kasaqua to pick her head up. The pressure on my shoulder was becoming a nuisance.

"You've had lore lessons, but no one has ever told you about the Myrddin the allskolde, the wisest witskrafter? Come, sit, and I'll tell you the story. It's a shame that no one has yet, but I'm lucky that it gets to be me!"

THIS IS THE STORY THAT HERR GERDASSON TOLD

Be silent now, and listen well,
For truth I speak, of times foregone.

I'll tell you of a mighty king,
How he was born, and how he learned,
Son of Uthyr Pendrachen,
Arthes, strong of heart.

Upon the horn of Anglesland,
A mighty heath on headland stood,
Gwyrlass the Unworthy ruled,
Dull of mind and form.

He had a wife, of milkish skin,
Of star-bright eyes, and spun-gold hair,
And her name was Eigrynn,
And she loved him not.

From distant north, a-viking came,
With many kin, and sword in hand,
On dragonback a-riding,
Uthyr Pendrachen.

Well fierce his steed, and silver-white
And shined she like moonlight on snow,
And her name was Ydraigwynn,
She of isen tooth.

At Uthyr's side, a sage well wise,
Myrddin his name, the one eye-ed,
He too rode on dragonback,
His steed as red as blood.

Fell crippled he, on three legs ran,
Though sound of wing, and mighty breath'd,
And his name was Draiggarrig,
He through shadows saw.

Myrddin could see, both fore and back,
Deeds long foregone, deeds yet undone,
His foretellings all were true,
All-seer Myrddin.

Some say that he was Enki's son,
Or mayhap of Valkyre born,
And raised was he, by three wise Norns,
Verthandi, Skald, and Wyrd.

Their ways they taught, among the roots
of the great world-tree Ygdraysl,
Upon the teats of Ylva,
She-wolf was he nursed.

Uthyr bold came, like a snowstorm;
Upon Gwyrlass's heath he fell.
For many days siege did hold,
And many foes slain.

Myrddin seeing deeds all afore,
said unto Uthyr as his king,
Stand here in my weavings, man,
A skilta I craft.

Uthyr was changed in face and form,
and voice and mean, to Gwyrlass's twin.
Gwyrlass's men, unknowing,
Uthyr did welcome.

So did Uthyr steal into
The tower high where rested she,
Among her maids a-weaving,
Sweet fair Eigrynn.

In Gwyrlass's guise, with her he lay,
And sported they, all through the night,
Till Eigrynn slept well pleas-ed,
Her husband drowned in mead.

Come morning sun, Uthyr reveal'd,
To Gwyrlass called, for all to hear,
Last night I laid with your wife,
And Gwyrlass was shamed.

Gwyrlass roared then, in a fury
Called he out for Uthyr's blood,
Both did draw swords of good steel,
Man-to-man they fought.

Gwyrlass's men all stood watching;
Not one of them would lift his sword.
Gwyrlass fumbled, Uthyr struck
And cleaved his head off.

Uthyr called then to the tower,
where waited fair Eigrynn.
Said he, *I'd make you my wife*
Fairest of them all.

And so Uthyr held the heath fast,
And when nine months did pass away,
Eigrynn bore a boy-child,
Fair as she and more.

But Uthyr was discontented,
Saw not himself in Arthes's face.
Jealousy took Uthyr's wits;
he cast the boy off.

In a coracle of goatskin,
Arthes was cast upon the sea,
To live or die, by whim of Rune;
And Myrddin took him up.

Wise Myrddin seeing all afore,
did rebuke Uthyr as a fool,
And departed from that king.
Who scorned his wisdom.

Fair Eigrynn in grief did pine,
for the babe snatch-ed from her breast,
Her comely skin now waxen,
In her bed she died.

And wise Myrddin with one keen eye,
From the waters sav-ed the child.
To the lowlands he bore Arthes,
To good Sir Hector.

Good Sir Hector and his good wife
Rais-ed the child as were their own,
And Uthyr in folly died,
To Saxish axes.

While Arthes grew a sturdy youth,
Sharp-eyed was he, and stead of hand,
Oaken-strong and broad of back:
Arthes noble-heart.

He could pluck from sky the sparrow,
And faster than a hare could run;
Myrddin taught him secret things,
Of all gods and men.

When thirteen years had gone and passed,
Myrddin took Arthes on his knee.
To him said: *Arthes, go now*
Your trials must begin.

For I have seen in the Norns' threads,
That you will be the king of all.
Eager Arthes, untested,
Myrddin bore away.

Within the cold lake of Glasslynn,
High on the mountain Yir Widfye,
The lake-maid Nynue did dwell,
a daughter of Rune.

On shining shore did Nynue wait,
Fairer than clear water she,
And bade young Arthes to swim,
To sport in sunlight.

But Arthes, heeding Myrddin's words,
Refused the maiden of the lake.
She rag-ed at his spurning,
Arthes fair and strong.

Nynue she called up a dragon,
From the waters of the Glasslynn.
Arthes did the dragon fight,
By night and by day.

Arthes carried him a good sword,
Sharp and keen of isen forg-ed,
But shattered on dragon hide,
Arthes was unarmed.

A pity unto me maiden,
Arthes called her where she did stand.
I cannot, without a sword,
Defeat this dragon.

Cruel Rune's fair and fickle daughter,
Well-pleased at Arthes's mastery,
Called forth the sword Caliburn,
From the water deep.

Arthes slayed the dragon with it,
And from its body took an egg.
Down the mountain Arthes walked,
Treasures all in hand.

At the feet of wizened Myrddin,
Arthes lay his prizes shining.
smiled, one eye bright,
And his proving praised.

Hatched a dragon of poured silber,
And tame it was to Arthes's hand,
A fine steed grew for Arthes,
Hengreon his name.

So a-dragonback came riding,
with Caliburn in his right hand,
Mighty Arthes, Uthyr's son,
King of Anglesland.

ANEQUS AND THEOD RETURNED TO THE ACADEMY

The month of August seemed to pass very quickly. In the wake of the thynge, every newspaper published articles about the new torgar appointments. Some of the papers, like the *Catchnet Daily Local* and the *Estervall Gazette,* simply reported the events and listed the names of the new thane and torgars. Some, like the *Vastergot Gazette,* were quite glowing in their praise for Jarl Joervarsson—his uncompromising insistence on the letter of Thrand's Charter and the rights of the smallfolk to have representation. The *Vastergot Weekly Review,* however—the same newspaper that had published Thane Stafn's scathing letter about Theod and me last year—published an article upbraiding Jarl Joervarsson as some kind of scheming autocrat determined to dismiss or destroy any political opposition. It included a letter to the editor by Herr Audulfsson that said much of what he'd said at the thynge—but without the benefit of Eskil Gerdasson's commentary, it made a very dull lecture.

We hadn't gotten newspapers on Masquapaug, generally, before I'd gone to the academy. Mainlanders' daily news hadn't impacted us much. I'd appeared in several different articles and one interview last year, though, so the sachem and the elder council had decided that it would be prudent for the island to subscribe to the weeklies at least. They'd taken up a collection about it, and everyone in the village had given what they were able. The newspapers were kept in the meetinghouse's library for anyone who wanted to read them.

In the second week of August, Niquiat visited and brought several copies of the *New Linvik Gazette* from newsstands in the city. The first, from the day after the thynge, had a blandly factual article about the replacement of Catchnet's thane and the appointments of torgars. The other three copies were from the following days, and included four strongly opinionated editorials on the subject, two of which mentioned Theod and me with speculation about how the presence of nackie dragoneers might influence future governance and the likelihood of "nackie uprisings." There was a *terribly* interesting letter to the editor in the most recent edition from a woman named Kawiya, who identified herself as an elder of Lennilenape—one in which she expressed gratitude and hopefulness for her people in the future, given that "original persons" of the islands off Vastergot were granted representatives to the jarl. I rather liked the term "original persons." It was something that Jadi had said, too, of her neighbors.

Move-in day for Kuiper's Academy of Natural Philosophy and Skiltakraft was Monday, the fourth of September. Frau Kuiper sent a telegram telling me to be waiting at the Masquapaug dock at seven o'clock in the morning. It wouldn't *do* to have me parade Kasaqua through Catchnet, to take the train into Vastergot and thence into Varmarden, so a sailboat had been chartered, and an automotor would collect us from the docks. This time last year, Kasaqua had been small enough to curl around my shoulders and sit in my lap. This time next year, I'd very likely be able to ride her across the channel—and I'd *certainly* be able to fly between Catchnet and Varmarden overland, with Kasaqua able to stop and rest as she needed. Theod could probably have gotten to the mainland on Copper now, given his maturation over the summer. In a good wind, or on a ship with an engine, it took about an hour to get from either island to the mainland, and half an hour to cross the channel between them. It could take significantly longer in a canoe, depending on the strength of the paddlers and the direction of the currents. Theod had proven that Copper was able to fly between the islands in fifteen minutes, in fair weather.

If I was being honest with myself, I wasn't sure that I'd be attending Kuiper's Academy for a third year. I understood the principles of skiltakraft reasonably well—enough that studying on my own was more useful to me than listening to Professor Ezel's lectures. Once I'd learned everything I needed to become a competent rider and flyer from Professor Mesman, I'd know everything necessary to pass the Ministry of Dragon Affairs' licensure examination. Once Theod and I were both fully licensed dragoneers, there'd be no reason to keep attending the academy.

I certainly wasn't making the kind of social connections and lifelong friendships that my classmates were making with one another, which Sander had told me was one of the principal functions of academies—even above education. Schools were the sort of places where people like Niklas Sørensen met and became good friends with people like Ivar Stafn. Places where girls like Marta could find socially appropriate husbands.

I reflected, as I was packing my trunk, about just how much I hadn't known last year. No one had told me what to expect, what I might need or want, what would be provided and what wouldn't. Not to mention how many things I'd been expected to already be familiar with.

I packed my trunk with everything I needed to make the bed at school tolerable—a couple of cattail mats to firm up the too-soft mattress, and my familiar calico quilt that smelled like home.

I packed the school uniforms that I'd received last year, except the one that I intended to wear for the journey. I packed my lovely ball gowns, my best day dresses—including the one Liberty had made for me—and woolen underskirts for winter. I packed the sealskin cape Grandma had made for me last year. I had a feeling that traveling home for weekends and holiday visits would pose a greater problem this year than last, unless I was willing to leave Kasaqua at the dragonhall. I certainly couldn't casually walk into Haddir's or Niquiat's tinker co-op with her now, as I had when she was small. I couldn't take her on the train in the passenger car. A lot of the other students left their dragons, when they wanted to go away for a short time, but the idea felt *repellent* to me.

I reserved a small section of the "one standard military sea chest" that I was allowed for personal effects for canning jars—honey and candied hickory nuts, eel paste and smoked mussels and tautog fillets packed in oil, dried squash braids and beans, samp corn to make na'samp, dried spruce tips and juniper berries and sage and sumac. The food at school was *dull*.

I packed a medicine bundle of tobacco and juniper, just to have near me—to smell when I needed to be reminded of home. I hadn't smoke-cleansed at all during my stay at the academy last year, and I'd probably have suffered less if I had. I'd have to talk to Marta and Jadi about throwing the windows open and sweeping our shared room with sweet tobacco. It hadn't occurred to me that it was a thing I could do, among the Anglish, but I was less uncertain and wrongfooted about this whole undertaking now than I had been then.

I hadn't *apologized,* last year, for who I was and who my people were—despite quite a few people seeming to expect that from me. I'd been reserved, and quite game about learning Anglish ways. Only I'd learned that Anglish ways were very often convoluted, burdensome, and utterly foolish. So I was going to show anyone who'd listen how to live in a good way, this year, with Anglish customs given exactly the regard they deserved.

On the morning of September fourth, I dressed in my blue-

and-gray school uniform, put Kasaqua in her tack, loaded my trunk into a wheelbarrow, and reported to the docks as ordered. Mother and Sigoskwe and Sakewa came with me to see me off; I had to say my goodbyes to Grandma at home, because she wasn't feeling up to the walk.

The chartered sailboat pulled up to the dock opposite the ferry. Theod was already standing on the deck, with Copper at his side. They'd evidently visited Naquipaug before coming here.

Mother held my face, and ran her thumbs across my cheeks, and kissed me on the forehead.

"Come home when you can. We'll keep the fire burning for you," she said. "See if you can't get that brother of yours to come visit more often, too."

They were the same words she'd said last year, but it was different now. I'd done this before, with less experience and preparation, and I'd come through it. I could do it again.

"I will," I said, and hugged my little siblings goodbye. I led Kasaqua up onto the boat as soon as the gangplank was lowered. I didn't look back until I was on deck and situated, waving to my family as the boat pulled away. I might not see them again until December; no knowing if I could manage to come home for the whaler's return dance again, as I had last year. That had only happened because my father had come to collect me.

"It's good to see you," Theod said, once we were far enough away that I'd stopped waving. "I missed you."

"I missed you, too," I said, turning to him. He was dressed in his school uniform, like I was, making us a matched pair. His hair was slicked back with some kind of wax or pomade, but I could see that it was significantly longer than it had been. I hadn't noticed that at the thynge; there'd been too many more pressing matters.

I noticed it now, and couldn't help envisioning Theod with his hair grown out long enough to braid. Couldn't help envisioning braiding his hair for him.

I very much wanted to talk to Theod about his feelings toward me, and the particulars of courting, but a ferry full of Anglish builders and thanegards wasn't the place for such things.

We talked about the newspaper articles, and about our families, and the coming school year.

It was Hallmaster Henkjan himself who was waiting for us at the dock, driving an automotor with a trailer for the dragons. Theod's face absolutely lit up when he saw him—in a way it very seldom did, because Theod was commonly so reserved. Theod immediately fell into telling him everything that had happened over the summer recess. I didn't feel motivated to insert myself into that conversation, so I just listened and watched the scenery roll by.

Arriving at the academy was rather different, this year. This time, we were arriving at the same time as all of the other students. Last year, I'd been asked to come and install myself ahead of time, and Theod had already been in residence over the summer recess.

At the end of last year, quite a few students had withdrawn from Kuiper's Academy following a scathing editorial in the *Vastergot Weekly Review*. I knew that Ivar Stafn and Niklas Sørensen were among them, and that Frau Jansen had tried and failed to withdraw Sander; that had been the impetus for him to seek legal separation. I also knew that the majority of students in their fourth year and beyond had completed their educations. I knew that Jadzia Wozniakowa would be coming to the academy for the first time, and that she'd be rooming with Marta and me. It hadn't followed in my mind, somehow, that there would be an entirely new group of first-year students—between twenty and thirty new faces, each with a hatchling dragon of their own. Many students had family with them; move-in day was something of a social event. Last year, Marta had introduced me to Bergitte, Saskia, and Annetta—all of whom had brothers in attendance. Bergitte's brother Hartvig was one of the fourth-year students who'd completed his education last year, and I didn't know what that would mean regarding Bergitte's attendance at school functions. I'd come to consider those three young women as something of a set, all associated with Marta.

"We should get the dragons situated," Theod said, tossing his head toward the nearest entrance of the dragonhall. I immediately shook my head, repelled at the idea. Kasaqua wanted to meet and greet all of the other dragons, especially the hatchlings. She was exerting a great deal of effort to *be good* and stay at heel, however, the way she knew she was supposed to when she was wearing tack.

"No, Kasaqua needs to stretch herself out a bit after being crammed into the trailer. I can't possibly put her into a *stall* just now," I said.

"She's going to have to get used to being stabled a great deal more than she was last year," Hallmaster Henkjan said, closing up the now-empty trailer. "She's a proper dragon now, not a little hatchling that can follow you at heel."

I frowned at that, knowing objectively that he was correct . . . but it felt wrong. At home, there was no dragonhall, and Kasaqua was never stabled. She slept in the three-sided shelter we'd built for her beside the house, and she waited impatiently at the door for me whenever I was inside, but at all other times, she was at my side.

I understood, immediately, why Theod spent so much of his time at the dragonhall. I'd be following suit this year, it seemed.

"Well, I'm at least going to take her for a promenade around the grounds first," I said firmly. "You can join me or not, as you like, but I'm sure Copper would appreciate a chance to stretch his legs, too. I'm going to see if I can find Marta, and find out if Jadi has arrived yet."

"Copper wants out of his tack more than anything," Theod said. "I'm going to keep catching up with Henkjan, if you don't mind terribly." His face had gone blank and stony, the way it did whenever he was uncomfortable. "It's not as if you need a chaperone here on the school grounds."

"You're right," I said, frowning again. "Kasaqua and I will manage quite well on our own, I'm sure."

Theod offered a short bow and turned his attention back to Henkjan, and something about that felt wrong in a way I couldn't put words to. I tried not to be bothered by it as I led Kasaqua in the opposite direction.

SHE REACQUAINTED HERSELF WITH THE SCHOOL AND ITS PEOPLE

Kasaqua was exceedingly pleased to run and to roll in the grass, and I couldn't help but feel markedly better for having allowed her to do so. She was lying on her back, her forefeet kneading the air while her wings spread fully extended on the ground to soak up the sunshine, when someone called my name.

"Miss Anequs!"

I turned to see Jadzia Wozniakowa approaching at a quite unladylike trot, Dreyst scrambling along at her heel. Behind me, I heard Kasaqua rolling over and standing up.

"Hello!" I called back, waiting for her to reach me before asking, "How've you been? Theod and I only just arrived a few minutes ago; he's inside the dragonhall, talking with Hallmaster Henkjan."

"I've been well," Jadi answered, arriving in front of me with her cheeks a bit flushed. "Dynah's still here, talking with her old professors—she introduced me and everything already. We've been up to our room with my trunk, but I haven't unpacked anything yet or had time to change into a uniform."

Jadi was wearing a different outfit than the one she'd worn at Marta's party, less fancy but still quite smart, consisting of a crisply starched white blouse and a skirt of green calico.

Kasaqua dropped into a play-bow, her wings flared and her tail waving, as Dreyst approached her, and they touched noses. I couldn't help but be reminded of Kasaqua's first meeting with another dragon—Frau Kuiper's Gerhard—who at the time had paid her no mind at all and stood stoically at attention. Which was what a "well-trained" dragon *ought* to have been doing in the presence of an unruly hatchling. Professor Mesman would probably have had words for me if he saw how Kasaqua wiggled with excitement at the prospect of playing with Dreyst, how they pranced around each other, but I didn't care. Laughter bubbled up out of my throat, and I didn't even try to stifle it.

"There's a pair of *trousers* in my wardrobe, even though I won't be riding until next year at the earliest!" Jadi said. "Dynah said there would be, because they gave her trousers right from the start, too, but I didn't really believe it."

"You'll want to be wearing trousers any time you're in a class with Professor Mesman; they take place on the flight field, and the grass will get the hem of your skirt absolutely sodden in a morning class. Kasaqua was feeling restless after the journey, so I let her run for a bit, but I'll have to put her in the dragonhall before going inside."

"Dynah often complained about Gikka hating trailers and such, and how much better it was once she was big enough to just fly anywhere. Dreyst might be big enough by the winter recess that Gikka won't be able to carry all of us, so I suppose I'll find out then what his opinions of trailers and train cars are. Do you know if Miss Hagan's here yet?"

"I haven't been inside, or into the dragonhall; I probably ought to put Kasaqua up and go make my own introductions to the professors. Have you seen the dragonhall yet?"

"I haven't! Dynah was supposed to show me, but then she ran into the professor with the articulated chair. I can't remember his name even though she just told me a few minutes ago . . ." Jadi said brightly.

"Professor Ulfar," I supplied. "He teaches natural philosophy."

"Yes, Dynah said that, and that he was her favorite professor. Can you show me the dragonhall, since you've got to put Kasaqua up anyway?"

Kasaqua wasn't particularly upset at being put into her assigned stall, especially given the meaty bone that was waiting for her there, and I gave Jadi a brief tour of the dragonhall and the professors' dragons, which were of many different breeds. Professor Mesman's falterdrache, Kostbar, was a smallish black dragon with brilliant red patches on his wings reminiscent of a butterfly. Professor Ibarra's Arin, Abiadura, looked like an especially lean and lanky bjalladreki with shorter and stouter quills. Frau Kuiper's Gerhard, an enormous dark green kesseldrache, was built like a bear. Captain Einarsson's ill-tempered silberdrache, whose name I'd never learned, was white and gray—though her tongue and gums were black. Professor Nazari's jirada, named Zati, was dusty brown with especially long and narrow wings. I pointed out Copper as we passed by his stall; he was curled up asleep and apparently quite content. Jadzia had already met him at the garden party.

Having gotten Kasaqua settled, Jadi and I proceeded to the school proper with Dreyst at Jadi's heel.

Kuiper's Academy was a three-story edifice of dark beams and plaster, with little ornamentation compared to other "official" Anglish buildings. It had a wooden dragon figure above the main entrance, but it lacked the reliefs and inlays of the jarl's palace or the Town Hall in Nack Port. The main entrance opened into a foreroom, then the main hall with its grand staircase. From there, the dining hall was to the right and the great lecture hall to the left. The kitchen was behind the dining hall, with the laundry beneath it. Professor Ulfar's laboratory and the skiltakraft laboratory were behind the lecture hall, with the servants' quarters beneath. Student quarters were on the second floor, as was the library and the professors' meeting room. The third floor held professors' quarters and offices—save Professor Ulfar, who had a suite of rooms adjacent to his laboratory, owing to his inability to climb stairs in his crablike chair.

There were people milling around in the foreroom and the main hall—students and their families, some with hatchling dragons. The majority of people were gathered in the main hall and the dining hall. In the main hall, near the stairs, Frau Kuiper was standing in full dress uniform with Professor Ulfar in his articulated chair and a woman I didn't know—presumably some student's sister or mother. Dynah Wozniakowa was standing by Professor Ulfar, apparently in close conversation, both of them smiling. Dynah was wearing quite unmistakably masculine clothes—gray trousers tucked into polished black boots that came halfway to the knee, and a white collared shirt. Her hair was pulled back into a single plait, curls straying from it here and there. Her only concession to femininity was her vest—black felt with lavish embroidery depicting stylized dragons, flames, and clouds. It was cut with the sort of curving seams that made her womanly silhouette obvious.

Just behind me, Jadi called, "Dynah, look, I found Anequs! She showed me the dragonhall!"

Everyone in the group looked toward us then, Dynah looking slightly chagrined and Frau Kuiper looking quite stern. Some part of me wanted to challenge that. Jadi *had* been rude, shouting across the room like that, but what right did Frau Kuiper have to offer that kind of look in return? Jadi was clearly just excited, and why shouldn't she be, in all this commotion?

I stepped forward with all the confidence I could project and said, "Good morning, Frau Kuiper, Professor Ulfar, Miss Wozniakowa. I do hope all of you are well?"

"Miss Anequs," Frau Kuiper said by way of greeting, inclining her head slightly. "I see you've already made the acquaintance of the younger Miss Wozniakowa."

"I've met Dynah, as well, actually," I said, nodding. "We all attended a garden party that Miss Hagan hosted in July."

"Ah, excellent," Frau Kuiper said. "Since you're here, please let me introduce you to Frau Natascha Schreiber, our new professor of skiltakraft."

"What happened to Professor Ezel?" I asked, raising my eyebrows. I was immediately aware that it wasn't the correct, polite response. I turned my attention quickly to Professor Schreiber—the woman I'd presumed to be someone's sister or mother—in an attempt to recover. Dipping a curtsy, I said, "Very pleased to make your acquaintance, ma'am."

"The same, I'm sure," she said, smiling brightly. She was a great deal younger than any of the other professors—not yet thirty, if my capacity to gauge the ages of Anglish people was worth anything. She was tall and stocky in an athletic sort of way, pale and pink-faced. She had middling brown hair bleached to yellow on top, held back in a braided knot. Her eyes were brightly blue, almost perfectly matching the ruffle-fronted blouse she was wearing.

"Professor Schreiber, I present to you Miss Anequs, who is joining us for her second year, and Miss Jadzia Wozniakowa—the younger sister of Miss Dynah Wozniakowa—who is joining us for the first time. Miss Anequs has the distinction of being second of her class in skiltakraft last year, exceeded only by Mister Sander Jansen."

"Jansen—he's the one you told me about, the quiet young man with the velikolepni?" Professor Schreiber asked.

"The same, yes," Frau Kuiper answered. Looking to us, she said, "Professor Schreiber's dragon is also a velikolepni. Did you see him in your tour of the dragonhall?"

"I'm afraid I didn't," I said, "though I didn't poke my head into every stall, either."

"I shouldn't have expected you to," Frau Kuiper said. Then, turning back to Frau Schreiber, she said, "You'll find that Miss Anequs is a very diligent scholar, and I hope that the younger Miss Wozniakowa is able to follow her example."

"Thank you, ma'am," I said, dipping another curtsy. It felt strange to be praised for scholarship, considering how hard a time I'd had in many of my classes. My term under Professor Ezel last fall had been abominable, all my papers coming back to me covered in red-inked corrections and castigations. I'd absolutely neglected my studies of erelore and folklore to focus on skiltakraft and anglereckoning, and I had no doubt that Professor Ibarra thought me a *terrible* scholar because of it.

"Miss Hagan will be arriving later in the day; her father sent a telegram ahead about some minor inconvenience of travel," Frau Kuiper said. "I trust that someone from the dragonhall was able to help you with your trunk? I wouldn't expect a young lady to carry such an encumbrance up a flight of stairs."

"Hallmaster Henkjan said he'd see that Theod's trunk and mine each got to our rooms safely, after he'd put the automotor away," I answered, "though I wouldn't have had particular difficulty in taking it myself. It's not terribly heavy, just cumbersome."

"I carried Jadi's trunk up," Dynah said, something challenging in her gaze, though her tone was all mild sweetness. I could easily imagine Dynah carrying a sea chest. I couldn't imagine the same of Marta Hagan, though.

"Well . . . I'm glad that it's been sorted," Frau Kuiper said. She looked like she was about to say something more, but her gaze shifted, and she looked past us. I followed it to find Frau Brinkerhoff—the school's house matron—standing by the door to the foreroom. She gave a little nod, and Frau Kuiper said, "I'm afraid you'll have to excuse me; please help yourself to refreshments and make the acquaintance of the new first-year classmen, if you can. Several of them have expressed a desire to be introduced to you in particular, Miss Anequs."

There was a moment of awkward silence as she took her leave, crossing the room with purposeful strides to join Frau Brinkerhoff.

Professor Ulfar broke it by saying, "Miss Schreiber is one of ours, you know—a graduate of this very academy. She was the first female student to ever attend."

"*Professor* Schreiber, sir," she admonished, looking down at Professor Ulfar fondly. "And you say that like it's fargone eretide! It was only ten years ago that I completed my education here."

"Must have just missed me, then," Dynah said. "I started here in fall of '35 and finished in spring of '40."

"I attended from fall '28 until spring '33," Frau Schreiber said. "It's lovely to be back, and so very heartening to see more young women taking up the mantle of dragoneer. We make up half of all people, after all, so there is no good reason that we shouldn't be half of all dragoneers."

"I heartily concur," Professor Ulfar said. "We had one hundred and four students last year, two of them female. We have ninety-seven students this year, *three* of them female. I do hope that it continues as a trend."

"For the first two years that I attended, I was the only female student," Frau Schreiber said. "It was . . . lonely. I'm so glad you girls and Miss Hagan will have one another for company."

"As to your earlier question, Miss Anequs," Professor Ulfar said, "Professor Ezel was offered a position at the High King's Academy in New Linvik, so he has elected to leave us and pursue his career there. Luckily, *Professor* Schreiber has spent the last several years in Tyskland, earning her professorship in skiltakraft. We are exceedingly lucky to have her return to us."

"To be absolutely fair, I can't imagine what other academy would have a woman as a professor of skiltakraft, not unless I wanted to take a position at some far-flung new nation in Aprika or Shiang-Gang or someplace like that. The High King's Academy in New Linvik informed me flatly that they would not be offering positions to female professors within my lifetime. I'm rather glad that they offered one to Professor Ezel, though; I understand that he casts quite a long shadow. I will endeavor to be as informative and exacting as he was when he taught me."

I couldn't suppress a snort of laughter at the idea of Professor Ezel being "informative"—though "exacting" was a reasonable enough description.

Professor Schreiber frowned slightly, pausing for a bit longer than was comfortable before saying, "In any case, I was very glad to learn that we have three ladies among the student body this year. If all of you don't mind, though, there is something that I've been meaning to ask Frau Brinkerhoff before the student body is called to the lecture hall for class assignments. I look forward to seeing you in class!"

"As do I," I said, meaning it genuinely, because she couldn't possibly help but be an improvement on Professor Ezel. She nodded to us, then took her leave. This year was already proving itself more palatable than the last, and classes hadn't even been assigned yet.

AND LEARNED A BIT MORE ABOUT THE EXPECTATIONS OF EDUCATION

It was strange, how there seemed to simultaneously be more and less staring and whispering from my classmates and their families, compared to last year. All of the returning students recognized me, this year—but so did a number of the first-years, because my lichtbild had been in several different newspapers. I had once again become a different kind of person because I was Nampeshiweisit—not just "some nackie girl" with a dragonet, not even "the new nackie student of Kuiper's Academy," but "the girl who'd saved the jarl."

I got the distinct sense that several students wanted to speak to me—which Frau Kuiper had confirmed—but they were prevented by the rules of Anglish society. A young man could not approach a young woman without first being formally introduced by some third party—to secure the general safety and honor of young women, according to the books on comportment that I'd read. As if the sort of young men who'd make a young woman unsafe or dishonored would be concerned with following rules of social comportment. Ivar Stafn certainly hadn't, last year, when he'd accosted me with wholly inappropriate questions. I had been obliged to slap him to make him stop.

The polite thing to do would probably have been to stay attached to Professor Ulfar and allow him to formally introduce to me any and all of my classmates who had the courage to approach. Frau Brinkerhoff had taken it upon herself to formally introduce Sander and me, last year, and he'd quickly become one of the few people at school whom I counted as a friend. I had not enjoyed meeting his mother at all, though, and I didn't especially want to find myself pulled into conversation with anyone's parents. So I turned to Dynah and Jadzia and asked, "Would you like to join me in getting something to eat? I haven't had anything since breakfast back at home."

"That sounds lovely," Dynah said, looking back to Professor Ulfar and adding, "It's been wonderful catching up with you, Professor, but Jadi and I haven't had anything since breakfast either, and that was back at Fort Witswood."

"By all means; don't let me keep you. It was lovely to see you again, Miss Wozniakowa—and I look forward to seeing you in class, Miss Wozniakowa and Miss Anequs."

There was a smörgåsbord laid out for students and their families to take from, with a much wider assortment of foods than was generally offered to students—hot dishes and cold, potatoes and sausages and slices of meat, bread and butter, pickled vegetables and relishes, smoked and pickled fish, cold salads with vinegary sauces, hard-boiled eggs, and fish roe in little cut-glass dishes. I especially helped myself to the things that I knew wouldn't be on offer later.

"Do you not like sausages?" I asked, glancing at Jadi's plate. She'd taken bread and cheese and vegetables, but no meat. "They serve them often, here."

Jadi wrinkled her nose a bit and said, "Anglish sausages almost always have pork in them, and pigs are unclean animals."

"Ah, I think I understand," I said. "My brother's friend Zhina said something like that, once, but didn't want to go into detail. Her people are from Kindah."

"Oh, is she zarthustradi?" Jadi asked.

"I'm not completely sure what 'zarthustradi' means, but she has mentioned a prophet named Zarthu. She called what she follows something else, though. Masda-something, I think?"

"Masadayassa!" Jadi said with some excitement, as we took seats at the table that Dynah had claimed while we were still picking over the smörgåsbord. "Yes, that's zarthustradi, that's the word for it in Kindah, I think? We—Zhidi people—were neighbors of theirs in fargone eretide."

"Can we not have lore lessons at the table?" Dynah said with a short sigh. "For once?"

Jadi replied to her in another language, and they went back and forth for a moment. Dynah said something sharp, and Jadi frowned. The silence that followed was . . . awkward.

I broke it after a moment by looking to Dynah and asking, "If you don't mind, you're practically the only person I've talked to who's attended Kuiper's past a second year. I only know Marta and Theod, ahead of me, and they're each going into their third year now. Can you tell me a bit about classes in the third and fourth year? What's . . . *worthwhile* about them?"

Dynah looked at me for a moment, openly speculating, then grinned and laughed quietly. "Learning is worthwhile for and of itself," she said, "but I expect what you really want to know about is passing the licensure exam, yeah? With the ministry of Anglish *schmegegge*?"

"I . . . do not know that word," I said.

She laughed again and said, "Of course you don't; it's Zhidish! I'm sorry, I can't switch as easily as Jadi can; I'm out of practice. It means . . . puff and nonsense and suchlike." She paused, spreading a piece of bread with herby white cheese. "Anyway, when you apply to take the examination, they'll want to know where you've schooled, what classes you've taken, what tests you've been put to, and what your marks were. If you're not a good enough scholar, they won't even let you *try*."

"I think that's terribly unfair, myself," Jadi said, stabbing a chunk of potato with her fork. "Anyone who got picked by a dragon ought to be allowed to take the test at any time. I've read a lot of Dynah's books from school since Dreyst picked me, and I bet I could pass an examination of skiltakraft right now, given the chance!"

"Oh, of course you *think* you could," Dynah said, offering Jadi a pointed look. She looked back to me and said, "I think a lot of what's in the examination is held over from the kind of tests they do for the dragonthede? The jarl and his thanes need to know they can call up dragoneers in their thede to fight, if the need arises—though God forbid it ever does."

The thought was alarming and repellent, that I could be called on by the jarl to make Kasaqua fight for the Anglish cause in some war or other. Dragons had been turned on the people of Naquipaug in the year 1825. How many of their riders had attended this very academy?

"I wouldn't—" I began, unsure of how to politely say that I'd never be a soldier or make Kasaqua be one.

"Well, they wouldn't call *you* up, specifically; you're a girl," Jadi said. "Battlemaidens like Frau Kuiper are rare; most women are too tender for that kind of thing. I wouldn't have thought you too tender to be a warrior, though, not after you got shot protecting the jarl!"

"Having been shot, I'd rather not be shot again," I said.

Dynah made a humming noise of approval and said, "Sensible. To your earlier question, I took the test in spring of '39 and failed it, so I stayed on at the academy for another year and took two directed studies of skiltakraft. When I took the test again in spring of '40, I passed."

"So you can take the examination more than once?" I asked.

"Did someone tell you that you couldn't?" Dynah countered, frowning.

"Not precisely," I said, thinking a bit. "There was quite a lot of bother about Theod being allowed to bring Copper back to the islands for the summer recess, because he can fly now, and he wouldn't have been allowed if he hadn't passed the end-of-term examinations—"

"There's a lot of little bylaws about rearing dragons and what can and can't be done about dragons that are too young to be tested," Dynah said. "When they first made laws about dragons back in the 1620s and '30s, only the dragonthede were allowed to have dragons at all. I'm supposed to know what year it was that they expanded the rules to allow for the academy in New Linvik to be built, and who the jarl was who signed it, but it's one of those things that went out of my head the second I finished writing it on the erelore exam. It's never been important again."

"You're starting your second year, right?" Jadi asked, looking puzzled. "Didn't you learn all about this in your erelore studies last year?"

"No," I said, declining to elaborate just now.

"Anyway, back to classes and their worthwhileness," Dynah said. "Skiltakraft was never my strongest subject, but I managed to pass the examination. The ministry cares mostly that your dragon will obey you—that it won't go haring off frightening people, or eating someone's cows, or whatever. They care that you can make your dragon breathe at a particular target and nothing else nearby. They care that you can do normal sorts of skiltakraft—be able to make all of the principle athers, and know what the athers do, and know their uses and such. They especially care that you know what kind of dangerous things *not* to do in regard to skiltakraft. If you make a big cloud of smothering air, it will smother anything in the cloud. If you make pure kalisna and then get it wet, it will catch fire and explode. If you make strahlendstone, you have to keep it inside a lood or loodglas container, because it's radiant and will give you bonerot just from touching it. That kind of thing. They also want to be sure you can fly a course, and that you know enough about husbandry to keep your dragon healthy—

and a lot of that is riding form and how to use the tack correctly. You need to know how tight to cinch the girth and where the chest collar should sit and that kind of thing. For me, that part was just having a man with a notebook watch me tack Gikka up and then come check all the straps and slides and rings and all."

"I already know how to do riding tack," Jadi said brightly. "Dynah let me practice on Gikka."

"You might find it's very different on Dreyst, once he's big enough for it to matter," Dynah warned. "We don't know what his conformation's going to be like, and he's got shorter, rounder wings than Gikka did at his age."

Jadi looked like she had a ready reply, but we were interrupted by Frau Kuiper's reappearance at the doors separating the dining hall from the main hall. She cleared her throat loudly, and a hush fell over the room.

"We welcome and thank the families of our students, and wish them a prosperous year," Frau Kuiper said, and there was something mildly eerie about it, because she said it *exactly* the way she had last year; it was something practiced. "At this time, students may proceed to Lecture Hall One to receive their class assignments. Families are, of course, invited to finish luncheon at their leisure."

After a bit of bustle with students bidding their families goodbye—including Dynah's goodbyes to Jadi and admonishments to stay safe and be good—we proceeded across the main hall to the great lecture hall.

I hadn't been assigned any classes that took place in this room, last year. It was my understanding that Lecture Hall One was primarily Professor Ibarra's domain, and I'd had directed studies with him last year because I was so woefully unaware of Anglish lore. I wondered absently if I'd been accomplished enough in my directed studies last year to be in the general class this term.

"Auer, Henrich," Frau Kuiper began, and a young man rose to take the offered card before returning to his seat.

"Bidasolo, Luzio," she continued.

There were exactly thirty first-year students this year, where there'd been twenty-eight last year. Jadzia Wozniakowa was the second to last to be called, followed only by "Egon Zeigler." Frau Kuiper then proceeded to the second-year students, starting with:

"Alvenholm, Josef."

And, immediately after:

"Anequs."

She didn't call me Aponakwesdottir! I locked eyes with her for a moment as I took my card from her, and she offered just the hint of a smile. I nodded minutely in response. It was a small thing, really, calling me by my name and not by the surname that the Anglish had assigned me last year, but it didn't *feel* small.

"What classes are you in?" Jadi asked as soon as I'd returned to my seat. At our feet, Dreyst was wiggling with excitement. I felt a pang, because Kasaqua had been able to sit at my feet like that last year, and this year she was relegated to the dragonhall, because she'd grown too large to comfortably be indoors. She was bigger now than Magnus had been at this time last year.

When *was* Marta going to arrive? She was missing class assignments, after all. I rather wished Frau Kuiper had been more detailed, earlier. Still, I read the narrow letters printed on the card:

ANEQUS. SECOND YEAR, AUTUMN.

Directed Study: Al-Jabr. Professor Nazari. Library, Monday and Wednesday morning

Free Period. Monday and Wednesday afternoon

Dragon Husbandry Two—Riding. Professor Mesman. Flight Field, Tuesday and Thursday morning

Skiltakraft Two. Professor Schreiber. Skiltakraft Laboratory, Tuesday and Thursday afternoon

Lore One, Professor Ibarra. Lecture Hall One. Friday morning

Natural Philosophy Two. Professor Ulfar. Professor Ulfar's Laboratory, Friday afternoon

I was glad to see that I'd become sufficiently learned in Anglish lore to join the first-year class, if only because it meant no more directed studies with Professor Ibarra. No idea why I was in a directed study of al-jabr, though; I'd thought myself quite accomplished in Professor Nazari's classes last year. I hadn't had a free period last year, either, but then I'd had two different directed studies.

"Oh, we're going to be in lore together!" Jadi said, reading over my shoulder. "I'm in Lore One, as well! Why are you in first-year classes, though, if this is your second year?"

"Last year I was in directed studies for folklore and erelore," I said. "I wasn't brought up listening to Anglish lore at all."

"Oh, that makes sense," Jadi said, looking thoughtful. "I know a lot of lore that I don't think most Anglish people know, because I'm Zhidi and we have a whole lore of our own, but I know a lot of Anglish lore, too, because Papa says that Markesland is an Anglish country, mostly, and we should know the lore of our neighbors."

"Do you know much lore from your other neighbors, the ones you call 'original people'?"

"I know more than none but less than I'd like to," Jadi answered. "After we're dismissed from class assignments, when we go back to our room, I'll tell you a story if you tell me one. Does that sound fair?"

"It does," I said with a smile.

I paid a bit more attention to the rest of the class assignments than I had last year, listening for names that I recognized and trying to piece out which names were missing—which students had elected to seek educations elsewhere. Sander glanced at me and nodded after taking his card but before returning to his seat, and I smiled. I tried to meet Theod's eye when he was called with the other third-year students, but he was all stiff formality and proper comportment and didn't acknowledge anyone or anything other than Frau Kuiper.

I'd had very little to do with most of the young men in attendance at Kuiper's Academy last year. I'd only really talked to them in Professor Ulfar's class, and that only because Professor Ulfar's lessons often required us to work together to make discoveries or solve problems. If we'd had one hundred and four students last year, but only ninety-seven students this year, and thirty of those were first-years, that meant that we'd lost thirty-seven students. Some of them had surely completed their educations—I didn't know how many of last year's students were in their fourth year or beyond—but some had certainly left for social and political reasons. It would be good if I could work out which ones those were, and make inquiries about their families and affiliations. Knowing who opposed the Freemansthede and who supported it might well be important for the coming year, if I was going to be out and about in the city at all. I glanced over at Jadi, and smiled at the thought of bringing her to Haddir's, and to Niquiat's tinker co-op. She was using the edge of her skirt to play with Dreyst, who was pouncing at every movement.

I'd need to go and visit with Kasaqua again before going to our room. We'd been apart for a couple of hours now, and I already missed her terribly.

SHE INTRODUCED AN OLD FRIEND TO A NEW ONE

Jadi chose to join me in returning to the dragonhall; she seemed to have attached herself to me quite firmly, and I could hardly blame her, because there were so few people here known to her—and, save as-yet absent Marta, I was the only woman. Jadi talked a lot about not much, commenting on the food and the building and the grounds, and Dynah's opinions of all of that, as well. She didn't seem to desire any particular response from me, so I just made encouraging sorts of noises to let her know that I was listening, even when I wasn't.

Kasaqua was asleep when I arrived, but she opened her eyes and yawned hugely as I approached, her tail thumping on the ground. She was very happy to see me, because she had been very bored; there was nothing at all worth seeing or doing in her stall, and she wanted to *chase* something. So she was very excited to play touch-and-chase with Dreyst as we walked along the road that led from the school to the train station and back. Hallmaster Henkjan gave me a very pointed look when we returned, and I looked right back to him as if to dare him to say anything. None of the other students in their second year and beyond seemed to have taken their dragons out. Kasaqua didn't want to go back to her stall; she wanted to come inside with me. It felt wrong to put her up again and join Jadi and Dreyst in heading to our shared room. Kasaqua was betrayed, imprisoned, languishing in boredom and loneliness and *very* cross about it. I was being *monstrous,* leaving her here.

Were other dragons simply not as upset about being in their stalls? If they all felt like this, how was everyone else coping so well?

The suite of rooms that served as the women's quarters held a low table and four stuffed leather chairs, bookshelf-lined walls, a window seat, and a standing clock that chimed the hour softly. The window overlooked the flight field. This year, there were three beds, three wardrobes, and three changing screens—two sets on the left of the room, one on the right.

Liberty was changing the sheets on the nearest bed—or rather, she was *pretending* to change the sheets, tucking in a corner that had clearly already been tucked in—when we entered. She stopped immediately when she saw me.

"Welcome back, Miss Anequs!" she said brightly, offering a sweet smile that made my heart stop for just a second. Liberty was the kind of beautiful that people wrote songs about, with her glowing dark brown skin, her plump lips, her clever eyes, and her crafty hands. I hadn't seen her at all since the second week of May, though we'd exchanged careful letters. I found myself terribly affected, and wanted very much to close the distance between us and embrace her. That would have been difficult to explain to Jadi, though.

"I'm so glad to see you again!" I said, because it was far more honest than saying that I was glad to be back. "Jadi, this is Liberty.

She's one of my dearest friends here at the academy. Liberty, this is Jadzia Wozniakowa and her dragon, Dreyst. She's new this year."

"I was wondering about the third bed," Liberty said, folding her hands primly in front of her. "Has Miss Hagan arrived yet?"

"No, Marta's been delayed by something or other; I'm sure she'll tell us all about it when she does arrive. Are you able to stay and talk a bit?"

She met my eyes, then looked past me to Jadi, then back to me. "I don't know . . . am I?"

"Yes," I said firmly. "If you haven't any pressing work, I'd love for you to join us. I agreed to tell Jadi one of my people's stories if she'd do the same, and you're very welcome to listen, or to join us in telling a story of your own."

"I don't think I've got enough time to tell a story, but I can probably manage listening," she said, her smile turning conspiratorial. "If anyone comes asking after me, though, I've been changing the sheets."

"Of course," I said. Then, to Jadi, "Last year, Liberty and I had quite reasonable concerns that pursuing a friendship might get one or both of us in trouble; the Anglish can be very particular about social rank and class and that sort of thing. But I believe that everyone who might matter, the staff and professors and all, have come to terms with the fact that I have no intention of becoming a lady of high society. After the attempt on Jarl Joervarsson's life, I doubt that anyone will have the audacity to reprimand me for being congenial with the help."

Liberty giggled, and quickly covered her mouth with her hand, looking at me like I'd said something terribly wicked, and we each looked to Jadi to see her response.

Jadi looked confused and thoughtful in equal measure, and after a moment said, "Well, if you haven't the time to tell a story today, then maybe some other time? I've never had the chance to learn Blackfolkish lore, if that's a special, different kind of lore? I wouldn't know."

"Oh, I think I *like* her," Liberty said, her hand still hovering close to her face. She glanced at the tall clock and said, "All right, who's going first?"

"Can I?" Jadi asked eagerly. "I have a story in mind already!"

THIS IS THE STORY THAT JADZIA TOLD

Once, not so very long ago in the land of Anatol, there was a very old man of great wealth and wisdom. His dear wife had passed away some years ago, and he had just one son, named Eitan, who was grown and married to a beautiful and clever woman named Alma. One day this man sent a messenger for Eitan, telling him that he must come at once. Eitan, of course, obeyed, and when he arrived at his father's house, he found the old man lying abed, ill.

"My son," the old man said, "I know that I am soon to die. Do not grieve overmuch, for I have lived a good and a long life, filled with much love. You will mourn for the customary seven days, and they will end on the eve of the festival of the Passover. On that day, you must go forth into the market, and you must purchase the first thing that is offered to you by the first merchant you meet—whatever it might be and whatever price is asked. It will bring you good fortune, in due course. If you obey me in this, all will be well for you and your family forever after."

Eitan promised to obey his father, and just as the old man had predicted, he died seven days before the festival of the Passover. The old man was buried beside his wife, and after the seven days of mourning—on the day before the evening of Passover—Eitan went forth into the marketplace, determined to honor his father's dying wish.

He was not ten steps inside the market when an old Kindah man approached him, carrying an ornate box inlaid with beautiful shapes and patterns of wood in many colors. The old man said, "If you purchase this, good sir, it will bring you good fortune for all of your days."

"What does this box contain?" Eitan asked the merchant.

"I may not tell you that," the merchant replied, "because I do not myself know. This box can only be opened by its purchaser, and only on the Zhidi feast of Passover. When this box passed to me, I was told that I must sell it to the first Zhid I met in the marketplace this very day—and here you are, and here I am."

Eitan was very impressed by the merchant's words, and understood that this most fortuitous meeting must have been foreseen by his dear father. He asked, "What is the price of this wonderful box?"

The merchant replied, "I cannot possibly part with it for less than one thousand pieces of gold."

One thousand pieces of gold was an enormous sum—the whole of Eitan's savings. Eitan whistled through his teeth at the cost but, remembering his promise to his father, quickly agreed. He went with the merchant to his banker, and before witnesses, the bargain was made. Eitan took the box home and placed it on the table that night when the Passover feast had begun. On being opened, the box revealed a strange egg—not much bigger than a goose egg, blue-green and speckled. No sooner had Eitan looked upon the egg than it began to hatch, and out sprang the smallest dragon that anyone in this world had ever seen. It was green and gilt and very beautiful, though much too small to be of any use to anyone. Eitan and his wife were sorely disappointed to have given over all of their savings for such a thing, but they offered their strange guest the best hospitality they could regardless. The little dragon ate so much that when the eight days of Passover were done, it had grown enormously. First, Eitan was obliged to build a bed for the creature, but it soon outgrew this, so Eitan was obliged to build a stable.

The dragon ate so hungrily that Eitan and his wife could spare very little food for themselves, but they made no complaint about their strange guest. They were compelled to sell many of their belongings to keep the dragon fed—their fine silverware and crockery, Alma's jewelry, their good linens, and every lovely and useful thing from their home. Soon enough, they found themselves in a state of great poverty. When Eitan's wife went to the pantry one morning to make their daily kasha, she found it bare. Her courage finally failed her, and she began to weep, wondering what would become of them.

To her astonishment, the dragon, which by this time had grown to twice the size of a fine ox, spoke to her in the voice of a man. It said to her, "Listen to me, faithful wife of Eitan. You and your husband have treated me well, even unto your own ruin. So ask of me now anything that you wish, and I will see all of your wishes fulfilled."

"We have no more food," said Eitan's wife, drying her tears.

"I shall see it set right," said the dragon, and at once it leaped into the air and flew away so fast that Alma couldn't see where it had gone.

When Eitan returned that day from his labors, he found Alma pacing and biting at her fingernails. She said to him, "The dragon left this morning, very early. He spoke to me in the voice of a man, and said he would fulfill all of our wishes, and he left. There is no more kasha in the pantry. I know not what to do."

Eitan consoled his wife, and was thinking on what to do next, when there was a great flapping of wings and a knock at the door.

"Come out, Eitan and Alma, and see," a booming voice called.

The dragon had returned, and he was pulling a great wagon laden with every good thing to eat: bags of kasha and barley, beans and lentils, figs and apples and pomegranates, onions and leeks, pistachios and sesame seeds, jars of honey, loaves of sugar, packets of every kind of spice and herb, and many other things.

"I hope that this fulfills your wish, dear Alma, who is like unto a mother to me. I ask you now, kind Eitan, like unto my father, what would you ask of me? I shall see any wish of yours fulfilled."

"A dragon that can speak in the tongue of men must be very wise and learned," Eitan said, thoughtfully. "I wish that you would teach me all the lore of mankind."

"It will be so," the dragon said, and took up an apple from the wagon. With a delicate claw, he inscribed upon the skin of the apple all of The Law, and the seventy known languages, and all the secrets of skiltakraft, and many other things. When he was finished, he bade Eitan eat the apple. Eitan did so, and immediately became acquainted with everything—even the language of the beasts and the birds. Soon enough, all men regarded him as the most learned sage of his time.

Both Eitan and his wife were well pleased, and they made a great feast for all their friends and neighbors of the bounty that the dragon had brought them.

The next day, the dragon said to Eitan and his wife, "The time has come for me to fully repay you for all the kindness that you've shown me. Climb upon my back and come with me into the forest, and you shall see marvels done."

Eitan and Alma showed only small hesitation before mounting up on the dragon, who leaped into the air and flew with great swiftness across hills and valleys and forests and rivers until they came to a secret place known only to dragonkind.

Here, he landed, and as Eitan and Alma were setting their feet on the earth again, he called, "Come to me all you birds of the air, all you beasts of the land, all you fish of the sea, and bring forth every precious stone and root and herb to this good man and his good wife."

Then began the strangest and most wonderful procession. Thousands of birds came twittering through the trees; thousands of bugs came crawling from holes in the ground; and all the animals in the woods, from the smallest mouse to the greatest gryphon, came to answer the dragon's call. Each brought some gift and laid it at the feet of Eitan and Alma. Soon a great pile of precious stones and herbs was heaped before them like some king's treasure trove.

"All of this is for you," said the dragon, gesturing to the shining jewels and bits of silver and gold. "With these herbs and roots, you may cure all diseases and ailments. Because you obeyed the wishes of the dying, and offered me hospitality while expecting nothing in return, now you are rewarded. My thanks to you, and may you be happy and fruitful all of your days."

And with that, the dragon took to the air again, and all the creatures departed back to their burrows and dens and nests and hollows. Eitan and Alma made their way home with their innumerable treasures. They became famous for their wealth, their wisdom, and their charity, and they lived in happiness with all peoples for many, many years.

MARTA RETURNED, WITH SOME UNEXPECTED NEWS

When Jadi finished her story, I told the story of how Nampeshiwe came among the people on Masquapaug. Liberty excused herself after that, but not before telling me that her salon—which was usually held on the first Saturday of each month—had been postponed last week and would thus be meeting this coming Saturday. She'd be leaving on the morning train. The way her gaze locked with mine when she said that made it clear that it was an invitation.

I spent the next hour unpacking my things—fixing the bed, putting up wall hangings, putting clothes into the wardrobe alongside my uniforms.

Marta arrived in the middle of the afternoon, carrying a satchel, looking windswept and fraught. Her hair was disarranged, her cheeks red, her eyes bloodshot. She practically slammed the door and immediately fell onto one of the leather chairs at the front of the room, dropping her bag on the floor at her feet, covering her face with her hands. She was wearing the version of the school's uniform with trousers; I couldn't recall ever having seen Marta in trousers before.

"Marta?" I asked, carefully, watching as she looked up like a startled deer. As if she hadn't noticed that Jadi or I were present at all.

"Oh, Anequs . . . and . . . Miss Wozniakowa . . . oh, no, I must look an absolute fright; I'm sorry!"

"Marta, what *happened*?" I asked, sitting down in the chair next to her, putting my hand on the arm of the chair she was sitting in. Jadi came and sat in one of the others, opposite both of us, eyes wide.

"My father is getting married!" Marta practically wailed.

"I'm not sure I understand," I said carefully. "Why would your father getting married have you so terribly upset?"

She looked up at me then with a sort of angry incomprehension, as if I were being deliberately cruel. "Because it means that I'm going to have a *stepmother* and, worse than that, *stepsiblings* who are already older than me! The young man is starting out in the same business as Papa, and that's how Papa met Frau Morris in the first place. It means that I'll never get to be the mistress of Sjokliffheim!"

"Have you been turned out of your home?" I asked, baffled, because the few times I'd met Marta's father, he seemed a jovial and affectionate sort of man. I couldn't imagine him turning Marta out of Sjokliffheim, which easily had enough empty rooms to accommodate a dozen people.

"We had the most awful fight, Papa and me, when he told me that Frau Morris is coming and that they're to be married," Marta said, which wasn't exactly an answer to my question. "He told me that it's a foregone conclusion that someday soon I'm going to meet a nice young man, and that I'll fall in love and get married, and then I'll leave Papa to be the mistress of my own household. He said that he'll be left all alone in Sjokliffheim, and that I ought to be *happy* for him that he's found someone to give him companionship!"

"And you're not happy for him," I said, half question and half statement of the obvious.

"Of course I'm not! I've spent my whole life thinking that I was going to become the mistress of Sjokliffheim someday, and now that's all being ripped away from me by some stranger—"

"Forgive me, I think I've misunderstood something," I said, halting her because she seemed to be working herself into a frenzy. Her dragon, Magnus, was presumably already installed at the dragonhall, and he would know that Marta was terribly upset. He might be moved to take drastic action, if he felt she was in danger. "I thought that among the Anglish, property and wealth passed father to son rather than mother to daughter?"

"Is it some other way with your people?" Jadi asked, catching my attention; I'd quite forgotten that she was even there. "It's Zhidi law that property passes from father to son, unless he has no sons; then it goes to his daughters, and if he's got no daughters, it goes to his brothers, and if he's got no brothers, it gets complicated. But it's usually the oldest son who gets the family home."

"It's the opposite among my people," I said. "Homesteads pass from mother to daughter. Given that I'll need to build a new homestead that accommodates Kasaqua, the house that was my grandmother's and my mother's will be my sister Sakewa's one day. That doesn't matter terribly much, though—there's no question in my mind that I'd be allowed to keep on living there, if I wanted to. If I'd never been chosen by Kasaqua, and the house passed to me as usual, I'd never turn out my sister."

"Property does, generally, pass from father to son—which is exactly the problem!" Marta said, sniffing slightly. "I'm Papa's only child, making me a presumed heiress, which is the sort of social position that allows a young woman certain liberties."

"Such as?" I asked.

"Well," she said, taking a hiccupping breath, "I've always been somewhat shielded from the practicalities of planning a marriage. As heiress of Sjokliffheim, I could have chosen not to marry at all, if I'd fancied it! I could have made a love-match with any man, without having to worry whether or not he had the means to support us and any children that might come of the union."

"And that's different now?" Jadi asked.

"Papa told me quite plainly that he and Frau Morris are to join their fortunes, and that when I marry, my portion is to be a third of his new shared estate. The other two-thirds will go to young miss Morris and young mister Morris, respectively."

"I'm still not really understanding the problem, I don't think," I said. "So long as your father is alive, he's still master of Sjokliffheim, isn't he?"

"Legally, yes," Marta said, wiping at her eyes with the back of her hand. "But in practice, it's usually the mistress of a house who decides who does and does not live there—and now that won't ever be me. It will be Papa's new wife and, eventually, her son's wife."

"And you think that they'll turn you out? And that you won't be able to make a life for yourself on however much a third of the estate is?"

"That isn't the point, Anequs!" Marta huffed. "Papa didn't even tell me that he was corresponding with this woman, and the trip he was on while I was hosting the garden party in July? He took several extra days to meet her in person for the first time—and I knew nothing at all about it!"

"Well, I can understand being angry that he was secretive about the whole affair," I said, "but have you asked him why he didn't tell you?"

"No, of course not. We had a fight!"

"Have you met them?" I asked. "This woman and her children?"

"No," Marta confessed, pausing to fumble in her satchel for a handkerchief. "She's from the far north of Anglesland, and she's a widow, and Papa's *very* taken with her. My mother's only been dead for five years, and this just feels like such an insult to her memory! What will become of her rose garden? What's even the point of building a dragonhall for Magnus? I told Papa this morning that he mightn't bother, and I packed a bag and left. I came here on Magnus, which is the longest distance I've ever asked him to fly, and he's confused and his wings are sore, which I swear I can feel in my own shoulders! I feel absolutely awful, and I look an absolute mess, and everyone thinks that I'm in the wrong for being upset!"

She paused, red-faced and panting, as if she'd been running. If she'd been one of my friends back home, I'd have hugged her. But that wasn't the kind of friend I was to Marta.

"I wouldn't say you're in the wrong for being upset," I said. "But I think that perhaps you're running away with all the worst things that might happen, and not thinking about the good that might come of it. Last year, in your garden, you seemed quite wistful when you pointed out that I've got something of a large family. Now you'll have siblings of your own."

"Not really, though," Marta said. "Frau Janet Morris is a widow with two children—a son of twenty named Iain and a daughter of eighteen named Mathilda. We know absolutely nothing of one another, have no shared history . . . it's not like having siblings at all. They're strangers, both coming along with their mother to Markesland. They're all to live at Sjokliffheim, and I'm sure that Mathilda is going to need me to introduce her to society, and I'm woefully equipped for such a task! I'm a scholar, and a dragoneer, and I've come to accept that I've been entirely cut out of Dagny Sørensen's social circle; Niklas has very certainly lost all interest in me since he left the school. I know so few people, now, and they're coming just as everything's becoming so terribly fraught with the Freemansthede and the Ravens of Joden and all this political pish-tosh."

"It's rather more than pish-tosh," I said, frowning. "But I know that you're not terribly interested in politics, because you've told me that extraordinary interest in politics is not an attractive quality in a lady. Niklas Sørensen would have been a poor match for you, Marta, on the basis that he's a good friend of Ivar Stafn alone. Further, Dagny Sørensen's opinion is only worth anything at all because others have decided that it is. Why do you even *care* about being invited to her garden parties or tea gatherings or whatever?"

"Because Dagny Sørensen's good opinion determines the social position of young women in Vastergot. I thought we'd established that already," Marta huffed.

"Why do you care about the social position of young women in Vastergot? You're not just some young socialite—you're a dragoneer."

"I am, but Mathilda won't be!"

"And why is that your problem to solve, Marta?" I asked, folding my arms. "You chose to be a dragoneer. You chose to dedicate yourself to schooling for a number of years. You and Mathilda will not occupy the same position in Anglish society because of choices that you made long ago. There's nothing wrong with being upset, with having a good cry about the whole thing, but when that's done, you've got to brush yourself off and look at where you're going to go from here. I know that it's rude among the Anglish to talk about the specifics of money, but I'll remind you that for the better part of my life, the only money my family had was my father's whaling shares—about five hundred marka each year. On that, we fed and clothed and housed Grandmother, Grandfather until he passed, Mother, Niquiat, Sigoskwe, Sakewa, myself, and for part of the year, Father, as well. Are you going to have less than that to work with?"

"Your circumstances are entirely different from my own," Marta said coldly. "I shouldn't have expected you to understand."

"Perhaps you shouldn't have," I said. "I'm sure that I'm a poor comfort, because I don't understand the problem. You're about to gain a stepmother and stepsiblings, people who are likely to love and support you—"

"How can you possibly know that?" Marta demanded, practically snarling at me.

"I can't," I admitted. "Neither can you. But isn't it better to be hopeful than to presume the worst possible outcome?"

"I don't want to talk about this anymore," Marta said. "You don't understand. No one understands. Leave me alone."

Well, that, at least, was entirely clear to me. I nodded and got up, leaving Marta to mire in her misery, if that's what she wanted to do.

"I'm going to see if I can't find Sander," I said over my shoulder as I opened the door. "Shall I give him your regards if I do?"

Marta's only reply was a sort of strangled sob, followed immediately by the sound of the door closing behind me.

ANEQUS LEARNED ABOUT THE RIDING OF DRAGONS

I did not find Sander at all on Monday. He was presumably in his room in the young men's quarters, which I'd been specifically forbidden from visiting on the basis of my sex. I returned instead to the dragonhall and let Kasaqua out for another walk around the grounds, deliberately avoiding anyone. I returned her to her stall just before dinner, and by then, I felt markedly better. I didn't much feel like eating, and certainly didn't feel like talking to Marta or Jadi or anyone else who would demand social niceties from me. I proceeded instead to the library and selected a volume on the principles and practice of dragon husbandry and riding. I sat reading it by the light of one of the gas-fed wall sconces until a maid—not one that I knew—came to turn the lights off. She seemed very startled to find me there, and was rather abrasive in dismissing me.

I woke very early the following morning, before Jadi or Marta, and quietly dressed in my uniform with trousers. Having been deliberately tripped last year by one of my classmates, I would never again make the mistake of wearing a skirt onto the flight field. I never had found out who'd tripped me, and rather hoped that it was one of the students who'd left to seek education elsewhere.

I took Kasaqua out and drilled with her on whistle commands for a bit—asking her to stand at attention, to lie down, to sit, to fetch a knotted rope, to run to a specified location and back. I put her up again when the hall lads arrived to feed the dragons, and went inside to bolt down my own breakfast of porridge and boiled eggs. As soon as I'd finished eating, I went right back to the dragonhall. I wondered if this was what it had felt like for Theod, last year.

I wondered why he wasn't at the dining hall or the dragonhall just now; Copper wasn't in his stall, when I checked, and his tack wasn't on the wall.

I proceeded to put Kasaqua into her tack, which began with a brush-down that she enjoyed immensely. I could hear my classmates arriving in stalls nearby, going through the same process with their own dragons, and felt an unaccustomed sense of camaraderie. I had so little in common with most of my classmates, but we all shared bonds to our dragons. Listening to others brush down their dragons and speak to them in fond voices was . . . novel.

After the brushing came the underlay, a sort of blanket made from several layers of quilted felt. I wondered, not for the first time, who had quilted the series of blankets that Kasaqua had gone through last year as she grew. Who had fashioned the standard adjustable tack that we all shared in common? Kasaqua's first set of tack had been 00, assigned to her by Professor Mesman. She'd outgrown it by the end of September, and Professor Mesman had taken it back—presumably to be assigned to some new hatchling—and assigned me a set of 02 tack. The tack I was putting on her now was size 12, and I was already using the last set of holes in most of the straps. It was likely that I'd be giving the 12 back in favor of a set of 14 sometime quite soon. Eventually, when Kasaqua had reached her adult size, I'd have to commission a dedicated set of tack for her, made specifically to her measurements.

Kasaqua hadn't been fitted for a saddle yet, but she had a training frame—a piece of leather with the correct points of attachment—that attached with a forecinch and a hindcinch, the way a saddle would. The forecinch attached to rings on the saddle frame, slung underneath her chest just behind her forelegs, and threaded through the bottom of the leather plate at the center of the chest collar, which sat flush against her keel bone. The chest collar itself was roughly triangular or y-shaped, the two top straps looping around each side of her neck to fix onto the same brass rings on the frame, just ahead of the joint where her wing met her shoulder. At the back, the hindcinch looped underneath her belly just in front of her hips, attaching to rings at the rear corners of the saddle frame. A crupper looped around the muscular base of her tail, preventing the saddle frame from sliding forward just as the chest collar prevented it from sliding back. The purpose so far had been for her to become accustomed to the feeling of tack, and to learn that being put into tack meant that she was "on duty" and needed to be attentive and reserved, ready to obey commands.

I double-checked all of the buckles and made sure that everything was fitted snugly, with just enough space to put one or two fingers beneath the straps, then grasped the ring at Kasaqua's shoulder and led her out to the flight field. Several students had gotten there ahead of me, all with bjalladrekis at their sides. Bjalladrekis were far and away the most common breed in the academy's dragonhall, probably because the breed was famously even-tempered and versatile. And also because bjalladrekis begat more bjalladrekis, so their being popular meant more of their eggs were available. Marta's dragon, Magnus, was a bjalladreki. The breed was ruddy brown and gray, with a mane of quills like a porcupine's, and teal-green markings on the face and the backs of the wings. Silberdraches and kesseldraches followed in commonality. They were slower-growing than bjalladrekis, which meant that this class had several third-year students in it. Other breeds made up only a small percentage of students' dragons. Most dragons from the other side of the north sea were rather doglike in conformation, I'd noticed, long-legged and straight-backed. Silberdraches put me in mind of wolves, and kesseldraches recalled bears because of their low-slung heads and hugely muscled shoulders and forelegs.

Kasaqua was the only Nampeshiwe at the academy.

I'd seen exactly two examples of Nampeshiwe in the flesh—Kasaqua's mother, and Kasaqua herself. Descriptions of the breed were practically absent in Anglish lore. There was a pair of sketches in one of the natural philosophy texts that Professor Ulfar had assigned last year, a volume penned by a scholar who'd traveled with Fyra Eiriksdottir on her journey along the Runestung River and the deep lakes. The plate had been labeled *Dreki Markeslandi, buck and doe*. I didn't trust the artist's skill very well, though. The other sketches in the same text that depicted other animals—possums and skunks, porcupines and beavers, coyotes and moose—were all somewhat distorted and uncanny.

If Anglish dragons could be compared to dogs, Kasaqua could be compared to a wolverine—her legs were shorter and her body longer. She didn't carry her head low like a wolverine, though, because her neck was longer and recurved. When she was standing at attention, her back formed a gentle arch that peaked just ahead of her hips. At her hatching, she'd been a dull yellowish color with dark brown speckles. Those markings had remained on her face, along with a dark band across her eyes, but they'd faded elsewhere as she grew. Now she was a markless golden yellow across most of her body, and her wingleather shaded through all the colors of sunset, scarlet along the edge. The feathers of her mane, which had first grown in ruddy brown, had been replaced with brilliant red, as well—each one black at the tip and down the quill.

The row of chairs lined up against the rear wall of the dragonhall were spaced to accommodate grown dragons between them, and beside each chair was a wooden crate. Like last year, each chair had a small card on it with a student's name. The crates were similarly labeled this year, but included the names of each student's dragon, as well. Annoyingly, the card on my chair read *Aponakwesdottir, Anequs*. Evidently Frau Kuiper's dropping of the surname assigned to me was not universal. Last year, I'd been between Frederik Anderssen and Edvin Bjorn. This year, I was between Josef Alvenholm and Torstan Bach.

By the time the rest of the class had assembled, there were twenty-four students and their dragons; there had been twenty-eight students in my previous dragon husbandry classes. Our assigned places in line were arranged alphabetically, so I wasn't anywhere near Sander, but I'd at least be able to talk to him after class. I wanted to warn him about Marta and her apparently ruinous news before luncheon.

Sander and I were the only students in this class whose dragons weren't of the three commonest breeds. Sander's Inga was a velikolepni, white and buff-gold in color, with a wide, almost wedge-shaped head crowned with three pairs of golden-brown horns, each set larger than the one in front of it. Her rearmost set of horns were at least six inches long now, and beginning to show the kind of curves I'd seen in illustrations. She had barbles above her eyes and around her mouth that put me in mind of a catfish. Inga was nearly as tall as Kasaqua now—a bit over four feet at the shoulder. Sander had mentioned several times that his father had gone through no small amount of trouble to secure a velikolepni egg for him to stand before, because he was aiming at a career as an athermacher, and velikolepnis had been bred for powerful breath more than speed or strength.

Professor Mesman appeared from the other side of the dragonhall, leading his dragon, Kostbar. He was black and red, with striking butterflylike markings on the leathery skin of his wings. In full sun, I could see that he was a brown sort of black, rather than a gray sort of black. He was not, I noticed, wearing a saddle, but the same kind of saddle frame that the students' dragons had on. The professor led Kostbar past the line that we'd formed, and several of the students' dragons sniffed in his direction. Professor Mesman's eyes flicked to the side each time a dragon moved out of form—not saying anything, but obviously taking note. When he reached the end of the field, he stopped and turned, commanding Kostbar to sit at attention with a few sharp notes on his whistle. Several of the other dragons stood to attention at the sounds, but Kasaqua just looked to me and stayed sitting as I'd commanded. I hoped that Professor Mesman noted that, too.

"I'd like to welcome you all back to another scholarly year," the professor said crisply, his voice ringing out across the field. "We will soon see whether or not you've each been keeping up with your dragon's training during the summer recess. If you are in this class, it's because your dragons have grown sufficiently as to be able to bear the weight of a rider over land. It is crucial that you master trail riding before proceeding to the far more complicated task of riding a dragon into the air. I'd like to remind all of you that riding, even on the ground, is a rigorous athletic pursuit. If you think that the dragon will be doing all of the work, you will soon be disabused of this notion. You, as a rider, will have to maintain balance and coordination while directing your dragon in where to go and what to do. How many of you are experienced in riding horses?"

More than half of the young men raised their hands. Sander didn't, I noticed.

"*Your* first task is to put anything and everything about horse riding out of your mind, for the time being. Riding a dragon is absolutely nothing like riding a horse. In the first place, dragons are a great deal larger and far more varied in bodily conformation. They're less easily startled than horses, and a good deal more loyal under stressful or frightening conditions. They are, however, much more willful than most horses, and their bond with you will allow you awareness of their whims and fancies. It is important not to allow yourself to be swayed by your dragon. *You* are the rider, the leader, the one who makes critical decisions."

He blew a few more notes on his whistle, and Kostbar stood in "tacking" position.

"It is absolutely inevitable that you will make mistakes as you learn to ride. When you do, it's critically important that you *apologize* to your dragon. Not necessarily in words, mind you, but through touch and gesture and conveyed intent. Now, I'm sure that some of you have fathers or brothers who are dragoneers, and I'm equally sure some of them have been taught in the school of dragoneering, which holds that dragons ought to be *mastered*. In my experience, that approach leads only to dull, dispirited beasts with little drive of their own. It is better by far to understand your dragon as a partner; you must work in concert. A dragon that obeys its dragoneer out of fear, in submission, is a pathetic and fawning creature ever desperate for approval and affection. A dragon that obeys out of respect and trust, in collaboration, is a bright and confident creature—able to make decisions for itself at critical moments. While it is my greatest hope that none of you will ever be called into battle, it is important that you have the skills needed for such eventualities.

"Now, you will note that to the left of your seat, there's a crate with your name as well as your dragon's. Inside, you will find a basic ground saddle and also a helmet. I will brook absolutely no complaints or disagreements about the necessity of helmets for beginning riders. You will wear it every time you mount your dragon, anywhere on the grounds of this institution. The saddles being provided to you are of the sort favored by the dragonthede. It has not been made specifically to your dragon's measurements, because most of your dragons are still growing. Because the saddles are of standard sizes, you've been provided with pads and straps to perfect the imperfect fit. Today's lesson will be accurately fitting a saddle onto your dragon's saddle frame. If time permits, we'll work on mounting and dismounting at the end of the period."

I had rather hoped that there would be some actual trail riding today, but there was certainly practicality in doing something correctly from the beginning, rather than trying to muddle through it. I put the helmet on—it was just slightly too big, and felt like someone had put an overturned bowl onto my head.

The saddle itself, when I took it from the box, was roughly boat-shaped. It had a high, curved back and a pair of horns at the front. It wasn't especially heavy, and I allowed Kasaqua to sniff at it before placing it on her back. Her ears went backward when I did, and I was immediately aware that it was a curious and not especially welcome sensation for her. I threaded the billets on the saddle frame through the obvious hardware on the saddle itself, and cinched and buckled everything into place as well as I could—but the saddle did not sit correctly at all. It was entirely the wrong shape for Kasaqua's back, and she wanted it off.

I'd seen many saddled dragons, now, and knew that the saddle ought to set at the withers, about a handspan behind the crest of the shoulder blade. But Kasaqua's back wasn't flat there the way that Anglish dragons' backs were. She had a very distinct dip where her shoulder joints and wing joints came together, her spine rising at a sharp angle toward her hips; her hind legs were longer than her front ones. The saddle did not account for the dip at all, and so pressed against her spine at the front and the back while being wholly unsupported in the middle. She needed something with a deeper curve, or a joint in the middle. I was wondering if padding could achieve the desired effect when Professor Mesman walked up to me, watching with a critical eye.

"I must say, Miss Anequs, that I did not expect you to be in this class; I expected to have you in riding this coming spring. Your dragon has an uncommonly fast habit of growth. She also has quite an unusual conformation."

"I don't think that this saddle fits her, sir," I said, frowning.

"No, it doesn't," he said. "I'd been afraid of that when I first saw your dragon, but I'd hoped that it was a quirk of hatchling conformation that would sort itself out as she grew. This is a bit out of the ordinary, but I'd like to ask you to mount up without a saddle—I want to see how you'd naturally position yourself."

I couldn't help but notice that several of my classmates were watching now, and I was abruptly conscious of how exposed the trousers made me feel. I tried to put that thought out of my mind entirely as I took the saddle back off her and put it away in its box. I used my whistle to ask Kasaqua to lie down; no saddle meant no stirrup to step into. She seemed to understand my meaning well enough, and folded her wings down at her sides to expose her back.

Kasaqua's back was wide and well-muscled, and climbing onto her was rather like straddling a barrel. I was sure that I did not look at all ladylike doing it. I found that my rear fit quite naturally into the dip just behind her withers, my knees settling just ahead of her wing joints. I felt obliged to lean forward a bit, resting my hands at the base of her feathery mane, feeling the curving bones of her shoulder blades beneath the skin. Without prompting, she stood, testing my weight curiously, moving her wings and shifting her weight from foot to foot. I was a great deal heavier than the saddle, but also a great deal more comfortable in Kasaqua's estimation. She didn't want me off the way she'd wanted the saddle off.

I looked to Professor Mesman, who was frowning.

"Have her walk on, just a dozen paces or so," he instructed. I patted Kasaqua's withers and whistled—not with my whistle, just through my teeth. She understood and took several steps forward, exploring how it felt to have me sitting on her back. I had a sudden vivid memory of her just a year ago, when she'd been small enough to sit on my shoulders or in my lap, and I smiled.

"In correct riding form, your shoulder, hip, and ankle should fall in line; at present your knee is turned too far out, which turns your ankle and toes out, as well," Professor Mesman said thoughtfully. "Stirrups would go a long way to helping that, I think. You do seem to have an uncommonly strong accord with your dragon, which I've also noted with young Mister Knecht and his dragon. I've heard theories that peoples who live closer to nature often have a greater affinity for animals than those from civilized societies, and this might be an example of that. In any case, it's clear that we'll need to have a saddler in to take specific measurements and devise a saddle shape more suited to your dragon's conformation. For now, dismount and return to your seat. Riding without a saddle is to be discouraged, generally, as it can inspire bad form and bad habits and can put undo stresses on your dragon's back."

I guided Kasaqua to come back around and lay down again so I could dismount. Everyone in the class was looking at me . . . but it was a different kind of looking. They were looking at me as a part of the lesson, as an example. It was a strange feeling. I was quite glad to sit down again, and to have Kasaqua lay down beside me. She was terribly pleased with herself, utterly convinced that she had done very well, and I couldn't find it in me to disagree with her at all.

AND ENTERTAINED NEW ALLIANCES

At the end of the lesson, I took Kasaqua's tack off and put it away properly, brought her for a walk around the grounds, and gave her a second brushing down, because she deserved it for having been very good. The morning class ran from eight o'clock to ten o'clock, according to the schedule, but it was half past eleven by the time I'd finished with Kasaqua.

Sander was waiting for me at the entrance of the dragonhall, and half a dozen other young men were with him. That felt foreboding; Sander Jansen was not, in my experience, a particularly sociable young man. I recognized a couple of the gang as fellow classmates of the riding class that had just finished. Judging by the hatchling kesseldrache that was standing at one young man's heel, he was a first-year. I knew nothing at all about the other three; they all seemed to be older.

"Hello, Sander," I said carefully, looking to him for clues as to what this group of young men might be about. Sander handed me his tablet as soon as I'd gotten close enough, and I read it without prompting.

Anequs, may I introduce several people to you? I don't know most of them very well, but none of them are terrible.

"Oh, yes, of course," I said, handing the tablet back. Sander closed his eyes and took a breath, then, in a very careful and obviously practiced voice, said, "Osvald Gram was my classmate in primary school." He gestured toward the young man with the hatchling. I'd met a number of Anglish people whose hair could be described as "ginger" or "copper" or "rust" or what have you . . . but Osvald's hair was *orange.* Like the flesh of a pumpkin. I made a point of not staring as Sander went on.

"Ernst Gram is his brother." Ernst was the tallest of them, with more subdued ginger hair. "Their friends are Vinzent Wilder, Nils Hautle, Kam Hagelin, Evind Skovgaard."

I could not tell, from that introduction, which of the other four young men were which.

"Everyone, this is Anequs."

He finished with a smile and a little bark of strangled laughter. Words could be very difficult for Sander, and he'd obviously put quite a lot of effort into getting that introduction right.

"Very pleased to meet all of you," I said, still not sure what this was about.

"If you don't mind my taking over with the talking," Ernst said—asking deference to Sander, who responded with a vigorous nod—"we represent the academy's branch of the Disorder of the Grinning Teeth. We'd love for you to join us at our table at luncheon."

I glanced to Sander, who was looking at me with very eager and earnest eyes. I trusted his judgment rather more than I trusted anything about these other classmates of mine.

"I'd be delighted," I said. "I'll meet you at noon?"

Everyone seemed to find that agreeable. I spent the half hour freshening up and changing clothes, swapping my trousers for a skirt. As much as it was practical to wear trousers on the flight field, I didn't like the feel of them. Or rather, I didn't like the way I felt in them when a crowd of young men might be staring at my backside. I felt *exposed* in trousers.

The whole gang of young men was waiting for me at the bottom of the stairs, Sander with them.

Luncheon was already proceeding when we arrived. Jadi had commanded a table of her own, and clearly noticed me as I entered with Sander and his group of followers. It felt mean to leave her sitting all by herself; Marta was nowhere in sight. I acknowledged her with a polite nod, but continued following Ernst as he led the lot of us to one of the tables farthest from the entrance.

"I'd like to thank you very much for entertaining us," Ernst said, pulling out a chair for me. I did not immediately sit at the obvious invitation. "If I could have had things my own way, we'd have approached you last year, but I wasn't captain of the chapter last year, and it was out of my hands. That, and none of our number were at liberty to approach you, having not been formally introduced. But since you're friends with Sander here, and he's friends with Ozzie—"

"Don't call me Ozzie," Osvald interrupted, sounding weary. The hatchling at his feet stood up, bracing its front legs against his knees and making a little chirping sound of concern. He bent to pet it.

"Well, here we are!" Ernst finished, not acknowledging Osvald's interruption at all.

"If anyone had asked me, I'd have told you that I think the rules which prevent young men from speaking to young women politely and as equals are the height of nonsense," I said. "Now that I know where the table is, would you mind terribly if I got a plate before we continue?"

"By all means," Ernst said, gesturing toward the serving table. I helped myself and returned to the table, sitting beside Sander, because he was the only person I really knew. It was not the chair that Ernst had pulled out for me.

"So, what's this all about?" I asked.

"We'd like to invite you to join our ranks, of course!" Ernst said with a well-practiced and ostensibly charming smile. "Are you at all familiar with the DGT?"

"Not in the slightest, I'm afraid."

"Well, as you might have guessed by the name, the Disorder of the Grinning Teeth are devotees of the teachings of Enki. Our goal is to always introduce the unquiet thought, to disrupt and overturn systems of power. There are chapters of the disorganization in every city in every hold in Lindmarden! We gather to discuss philosophy and politics, and we contribute to a monthly newsletter with essays and book recommendations and that sort of thing. I've brought a copy of our articles for you to read and reflect on, before asking you to make a decision."

He slid a narrow booklet across the table to me. It was bound in plain brown cardstock, with no text or images of any kind on the face.

"Why is it that you think I'd be suited to . . . join you?" I asked, picking the booklet up. "And what would that mean?"

"It means that we'd like to have your thoughts and your voice in our meetings. Our chapter gathers weekly, on Wednesday evenings after dinner. We usually meet in the library, but occasionally at other places if the need arises. As to why *you* . . . well, you've proven yourself a very staunch ally of the cause of Freemen, given your defense of Jarl Joervarsson, and your appearance at the thynge on Nack Island this past August."

"I wasn't aware that anyone outside of Catchnet Hold was paying any attention at all to that thynge, or to the choosing of thanes," I said.

"The choosing of thanes is always of great interest to anyone who cares about the lot of the smallfolk," another of the young men said, sounding very eager. I still hadn't worked out which names matched which faces.

"We've been deliberating in letters for weeks about whether or not to approach you," Ernst said. "It was put to a vote yesterday.

We are very much a voting thede—every member gets a vote, and there's no ranks or titles or anything."

"But you just said something about being the captain of the chapter," I said, frowning.

"It's not a position of power over any other member of the disorganization; it just means that I'm the member of this chapter who's been involved longest, and that makes it my responsibility to educate new joiners about our ways and organize meetings and things like that. My vote isn't worth more than anyone else's."

"'Captain' is still a title, though," I said.

"I think you're missing the principle of the thing," Ernst said, his smile faltering just a bit. "We stand for equality, freedom, and justice between all people—between men and women, between young and old, between rich and poor, between every race and creed of mankind. In a more perfect world, there wouldn't need to be torgars or thanes or jarls or kings. Every person would have an equal vote in all of society's decisions!"

"And how would you manage that?" I asked, thinking on it. "That's rather close to how we've managed on the islands since the beginning of time, but there are few enough of us that everyone knows everyone else. It's a grand idea, but how does one practice such a system in a city as peopled as Vastergot?"

"With universal literacy, for one," another of the young men said fiercely. "It's absolutely criminal in a society as advanced as ours that we don't have comprehensive public schools and libraries. That's the kind of thing that our taxes ought to pay for, not lining the pockets of torgars.

"The whole purpose of torgars is to be representatives to the smallfolk; there's supposed to be a torgar for every thousand citizens, and folkreckoning is supposed to be done every ten years, but when was the last time a new torgar has been appointed? Not a replacement for one dying or stepping down or being voted out—a properly *new* one. Besides the ones appointed at this latest thynge, I mean. It's good that Jarl Joervarsson's finally doing something about the problem, but it's not enough! Do you think any of Thane Stafn's torgars have ever set foot into the cannery district or the mill district to take reckoning of the will of the people there? So many people crank on about Thrand's Charter as if it's perfect and accounts for everything forever and ever, but King Thrand wrote it when there were only ten thousand people living in all of Lindmarden. It's just as Anequs was saying, a matter of failing to scale appropriately!"

Well, *that* certainly had my interest. If there was some kind of action that these classmates of mine were taking to help push forward fair representation of the smallfolk, I wanted to help.

"When you say that you gather to discuss philosophy, what does that mean?" I asked. "I've only heard the word as part of 'natural philosophy'—which is a subject that I quite enjoy. I'm not sure how it relates to politics, though."

"Philosophy means 'love of wisdom' in Old Ellanic, which is what they spoke in Ellasland long ago," one of the young men said.

"I'm afraid you'll have to forgive my ignorance on matters of geography. Where is Ellasland?" I asked, trying to recall Professor Ibarra's map.

"It juts into the midland sea, between Turksland and Vaskosland," another of the young men supplied. "It's one of the first seats of civilization, with influences all around the midland sea."

"Konrad the Magnificent overthrew it, and that's what led to the rise of Tyskland as the greatest civilization of the old world. We know it from the writings of Baldram, who was one of Konrad's advisors," the first one finished. Something about his tone implied that I ought to have known that already.

"Have you read any of the translated works of the philosopher Broadman Aristonson?" Ernst asked, looking back to me.

"I'm afraid I haven't," I said. One of the other young men looked at him as if to say "I told you so," and Ernst levelly held his gaze until he looked away. I got the distinct impression that Ernst's vote *was* worth rather more than anyone else's.

"Broadman wrote a treatise called *Politeia* that's all about the best way to run a nation," Ernst said, once he'd finished staring down the other young man. "We've got a translated copy of it in the library here, but it's a copy that was translated from old Tysklandish. I've read a copy that was translated straight out of Old Ellanic, and there are interesting differences. But never mind that. The point is that he wrote a lot of wise things about the nature of mankind and of justice."

"I, for one, think too much is made of Tyskland's supposed enlightenment," another young man—the same one that Ernst had just stared down—said with unflagging confidence. "Tyskland did a lot of philosophy of all kinds, but they were still overthrown by the Anglish in the end, because the Anglish were fiercer warriors and better seafarers. We're not speaking Tysklandish right now, any more than we're speaking Ellanish."

"Ellan*ic*!"

"You know what I meant!"

"We're speaking Anglish because the founders of Lindmarden were from Anglesland," Ernst said, something in his tone exasperated, as if this were a well-trodden but still unsolved disagreement. "The majority of people in Tyskland still speak Tysklandish, even if they speak Anglish, as well."

"*Toh a quompi kittinnemonchemnekit*?" I asked, offering a pointed look.

"What?"

"*Toh a quom-pi kit-tin-nem-on-chem-ne-kit,*" I said, enunciating each syllable carefully. "When are you going home?"

There was silence for a moment, all of them staring at me. Then Ernst laughed, and the others cautiously followed suit.

"See, that's exactly why we'd like you to join our ranks," he said, grinning in a way that showed all of his teeth. "No one else would have said something like that, asked something like that.

Anequs has a point: The founders of Lindmarden were overthrowers just as much as the Anglish who overthrew Tyskland. We might have as much to learn about philosophy from Anequs's people as our ancestors did from the Tysklandish, as much as the Tysklandish learned from the Ellaslanders."

"You said that you meet on Wednesday evenings, in the library?" I asked.

"Yes," Ernst said.

"I'll read your articles," I said, picking up the booklet. "If I think that they're worthwhile, I'll see you there."

"Then we'll see you there," Ersnt said with absolute confidence.

"If you'll excuse me, I have skiltakraft for the afternoon session."

"Oh, I do, too!" one of the young men said eagerly. "May I have the honor of walking you there?"

"I'd be delighted, Mister . . ."

"Wilder. Vinzent Wilder."

"I'd be delighted, Mister Wilder," I said, because it was the polite thing to say, and Vinzent hadn't been egregiously impolite in any way.

He stood, offering his arm, and I took it. Sander followed us closely, standing at my other side. As we walked toward the skiltakraft laboratory, Vinzent launched into an animated lecture on the brilliance of Broadman's *Politeia* while I made polite noises of feigned interest.

SHE LEARNED MORE ABOUT SKILTAKRAFT

The skiltakraft laboratory, when we arrived, looked very different than it had last year. The twelve desks, which had been in two rows before, were now arranged in a circle. The professor's desk was still at the head of the room, but it was just another part of the circle. The chalkboard was gone entirely. In the middle of the room was a shallow container made of silver metal—a circle a couple of inches deep and a couple of yards across, half filled with sand. Professor Schreiber was seated at her desk, writing something.

Theod was sitting at one of the desks nearest the door, farthest from the professor.

As we entered, Professor Schreiber looked up from whatever she'd been writing to smile brightly at us and say, "Please have a seat anywhere you like. You can even sit three to a desk, if you prefer; move the chairs as needed."

Well, *that* was certainly a departure from the way Professor

Ezel had greeted me last year. I immediately moved to sit beside Theod. Sander sat on my other side, and Vinzent looked mildly annoyed that our desk was quite obviously at capacity. He and Evind claimed a spot at the next desk over, opposite Sander.

Other students arrived in groups of two and three, and Professor Schreiber repeated her cheerful instructions to each of them. When everyone had arrived, she stood and walked around her desk to stand in front of it, facing the circle.

"I'd like to welcome you all to Skiltakraft Three. Everyone in this class has passed Skiltakraft One and Two, including a practical test. In today's class, I will be handing out an assessment—it is *not* a test. The purpose of this assessment is for me to best understand what this class, as a whole, has and hasn't learned in Skiltakraft One and Two. You will note that there's no place to put your name, at the top of the paper; that is deliberate. For this exercise, it's not important for me to know which student is giving which answer. There is an unfortunate attitude among many instructors of skiltakraft that the point of initial introduction to the subject is to 'weed out' students who are not immediately promising—what a cruel and heartless thing to do to young dragoneers and their charges! I'm instead taking a page from Professor Ulfar. We all share the same goal of producing a group of competent, knowledgeable skiltakraft practitioners. To that end, it suits us far more to behave in cooperation with one another than in competition."

She turned and picked up a stack of papers from her desk, walking around the circle and giving one to each student. It was a path that brought her neatly back to her own desk, which she leaned against while saying, "Skiltakraft is, at its root, a branch of natural philosophy. It's practical application of atherlore—a realm of studies including minglinglore, the philosophy of materials, and several other related subjects. Athers, and the combinations thereof, are the fundamental stuff of the world—the building blocks from which all things are made! For example, your own body and the bodies of all living things are made principally of kolfni, vetna, zurfni, stiksna, pospor, and saffle. You'll find that most athers behave very predictably, once you've learned the laws that govern them and what their arrangements mean.

"Today, your task is fill out those assessments. I will study them, and our lesson on Thursday will be based on the strengths and weaknesses in knowledge that I notice. You may talk to one another, but I would appreciate it if you answered the assessment based on your own knowledge, not that of your canniest classmates. When you've finished, put the page face down on my desk, after which you may be dismissed. You may begin."

The paper both was and wasn't like the test that Professor Ezel had given me on my very first day at the academy last year. It asked: *List the twenty-four known athers in order by their number of motes* and *Draw the classical figures for Kolfni, Vetna, Zurfni, Stiksna, Pospor, and Saffle.* But it didn't ask me to number the motes. It instead asked for me to draw the circle-and-line models of each, and then to draw a skilta that would produce those athers, and what stocks would best feed such skiltas. I knew that kolfni was abundant in coal and charcoal and wood ash. I knew that vetna and stiksna could easily be pulled from water, including water suspended in the air. Zurfni was also abundant in the air.

I didn't know a rich source of saffle, but thinking on the corn-planting dance and how it translated as a skilta, I surmised that pospor must have something to do with the sun-bleached bone that one ring of dancers traditionally carried in baskets. In the modern version of the corn-planting dance, those bones and mussels and ashes were all pounded finely and tilled into the soil of the field being blessed after the dance, but if the dance was a skilta, it was very likely that in the time when my people had been friends of dragons, the process was achieved with much less labor and time.

Beside me, Theod was scowling down at his paper, obviously struggling. I wrote, on a scrap of paper that I had no intention of showing to the professor:

Corn planting. zurfni pospor kalisna, mussels bones ashes.

I slid the paper over to Theod, who looked quickly from me to the professor and back, then tucked the paper away in his jacket pocket as if it were something forbidden. He didn't seem to understand the hint I was giving him, based on the answers he was giving on the page. Professor Ezel hadn't gone into much detail about the materials fed to skiltas, last year. He'd said that we'd learn that later, when it was more relevant to us as practitioners. If we'd done more practical work, I might have felt confident enough to try implementing the principles of the corn-planting dance's transformative powers—to perform versuchs and observe the results.

Sander was first to finish his assessment, then me. We met in the hallway, and he was still writing whatever it was he wanted to say to me when Vinzent and Evind came out and joined us.

"What's on your schedule next?" Vinzent asked, turning to me and pinning me with an off-putting, too-eager gaze.

"I was going to go to the dragonhall; I'm waiting for Theod to see if he'd like to join me. You're welcome to come too if you like, I suppose," I said, feeling rather reluctant about that. There was no polite way for me to dismiss them, but I didn't want a whole crowd; I *wanted* to find a quiet place for Theod and me to talk.

"Whatever for?" Evind asked, frowning. "You've just had riding this morning, and you spent an hour and a half fussing over your dragon after that while we waited to talk to you. Your dragon will become quite spoiled if you spend too much time with her; she's got to learn to get used to being stabled."

"I don't share that opinion, regarding the rearing of dragons," I said. "At home, Kasaqua seldom leaves my side."

"How?" Vinzent asked, looking baffled and slightly appalled. "Jaeger started being stabled as soon as he was tall enough to knock things off of tables; Mother insisted. Yours is going to be a midsize, right? About the size of a bjalladreki? Even half-grown, a dragon's an absolute menace indoors."

"I don't spend a great deal of time indoors, at home," I said.

"And we don't have a dragonhall. When I *must* be in a building that doesn't suit Kasaqua's size, she waits for me at the door."

Theod finally came out of the classroom, the last student to leave. He seemed surprised to see the lot of us waiting for him. I turned to him and, before anyone else could say anything, asked, "Would you like to join me at the dragonhall?"

"I'd be delighted," he said, looking past me to the three other young men.

"You too, then, huh?" Evind said, narrowing his eyes a bit. "Is it a thing with nackies, spoiling dragons?"

Theod frowned, then looked to me with a question in his eyes.

"Vinzent wanted to know what I was doing after class. I declared my intention to go to the dragonhall," I said, running my tongue over my teeth. "Both Vinzent and Evind have opinions on this, despite not having been asked."

"Ah," Theod replied, looking coldly at Vinzent and Evind. Sander took the opportunity to catch my attention, handing his tablet to me to read.

Do you mind if I follow you two? I'd like to talk to you about the DGT.

"Yes, Sander, you're more than welcome," I said, handing the tablet back to him. Looking to Theod, I said, "The three of us could walk the grounds with our dragons, before dinner?"

"That sounds lovely," Theod replied. He looked at Vinzent and Evind in a way that indicated that they were absolutely *not* invited to join our party. He turned to me, offering his arm in a quite gentlemanly fashion, and I took it and allowed myself to be led away, with Sander following just behind us.

SANDER EXPLAINED THE TERRIBLE IMPORTANCE OF SECRET SOCIETIES

"What was that about?" Theod asked, once we were well out of earshot of Evind and Vinzent.

"Sander introduced me to some of our other classmates this morning, and I sat at their table during luncheon. They've got a club that they want me to join."

Sander made a frustrated noise and opened his tablet, writing very quickly, all of his movements sharp. He thrust it at me and said, "Read it, Anequs."

I frowned, because Sander seldom got upset—not like this. We all stopped, standing still in the corridor. Sander drummed his hands on his thighs as I read.

You are not taking this invitation at all seriously, and you ought to be! You didn't attend the kind of primary school that most of our classmates have. Even Marta attended a girls' school, which is a different kind of thing. But I did come from a boys' primary school—the same one that Osvald and Ernst came from—and I understand how these things work. Ivar Stafn and Niklas Sørensen were the central figures among the social ranks last year, and their chief rival was Lennerd Tepperik. Ernst Gram and Kam Hagelin were close associates of Lennerd. This year, because Lennerd has completed his education and Ivar and Niklas have gone, the balance of social power at the academy has shifted very significantly. Ernst Gram is almost certainly going to be the leader in all social machinations this year. Kam will be vying for that position, but Ernst will get it because the Gram family is much more established in Vastergot.

I paused, frowning, and said, "None of that seems either interesting or relevant to me. Why should I associate myself with Ernst and his gang? None of them paid me the least bit of mind last year."

Sander took the tablet back from me. He kept on writing as I summarized what I'd just read for Theod. Sander thrust the tablet back at me again.

Ernst Gram's friendship, and the network of associates and acquaintances that it will provide you, will serve you long after you've left the Academy. He's almost certainly going to become a torgar and a thane and might even be Jarl someday.

"He's not Jarl *now,*" I said, handing the tablet back to Sander. "When I complete my education, I'm going back to Masquapaug and leaving all of this political nonsense behind me! I don't expect I'll have anything to say to Ernst or Osvald or any of the rest of them that they'll especially want to hear. They seem keen on having me join them, and as far as I can see, it's just to have bragging rights—to be able to say that they recruited me. I have nothing in common with any of them."

Sander took the tablet back and spent a while writing. He was quite able to walk and write at the same time, and we proceeded to the dragonhall while he wrote. The fourth-year husbandry class had let out, and those students were still attending their dragons in their stalls, taking off tack and brushing them down. They were all at the far end of the dragonhall, opposite the professors' dragons, separated from us by the bank of second- and third-year dragons' stalls. Sander handed the tablet to me again.

I think that your not having anything in common with them is rather the point. Of course the chapter at the academy is going to be a very uniform selection; almost everyone here is a young man who comes from the kind of family that can afford a dragon egg. In the wider world, the Disorder of the Grinning Teeth is exactly the kind of organization that welcomes the unseen and unheard people of society. Eskil Gerdasson is the captain of the chapter in Vastergot, I think? One of the articles I read said that he was at the thynge. Did you have a chance to meet him?

"I did!" I said, raising my eyebrows. "He's a very interesting sort of man. Knowing that Eskil Gerdasson is a member is a better endorsement than anything that anyone has told me yet—they might have led with that!"

"Herr Gerdasson was the man who shouted down Sveni Audulfsson, wasn't he?" Theod asked.

"Yes," I said. "He mentioned that he's currently a guest in the home of the wroughtthane of the Freemansthede, but I can't remember his name—"

"Esben Vilhelmsen is the wroughtthane of the Freemansthede," Sander said, all in a rush.

He wrote furiously on his tablet: *I know that there are essays by Gerdasson in the DGT's monthly newsletter. It's only supposed to be available to members, but Osvald's always able to nick copies from Ernst—at least for the last few years.*

"What's the point of a secret society?" I asked. "If they want people to listen to and be interested in their ideas, why is their newsletter only available to members? I still don't see how my joining should make any great difference to them or provide any great benefit to me."

Sander cleared his tablet, then wrote: *If for no other reason, will you consider joining for my sake? I'm already regarded as some species of idiot by much of society, owing to my personal oddities, and the Jansen family has no particular sway in Vastergot. My mother is of smallfolkish birth, my father's fortune has been largely spent, and I have no living grandparents. Frau Brinkerhoff's position largely owes to her friendship with Frau Kuiper, she has no great fortune or influence of her own. The DGT has nothing particularly to gain from inviting me in. You and I both have a great deal to gain, in terms of social connections, by joining.*

"My concern, I think, is why they want me in particular," I said, frowning. "Why me and not Theod? Why not Marta, or Jadi? If they're really concerned about welcoming the unseen and unheard people of society, why aren't there any members from the serving staff? Lots of the maids in the laundry and the kitchen are the same age as the students, as are a lot of the young men who work in the dragonhall. I'm sure they'd each have things to say to whatever topic is at hand that would never occur to Ernst and his."

That's exactly the kind of thing that you can bring up if you join them! Sander wrote.

I couldn't help but sigh and roll my eyes, because I felt like we were going in circles.

"All right, how about this: Propose a meeting of minds," I said. "Tonight at dinner, all of us will join Ernst and his cronies—Jadi and Marta, as well, if they want; we might be obliged to push two tables together. If they want me to come to their meeting, they'll need to let *all of us* come, because we are all in some way or another generally pushed out of the society of the rest of the school. I won't join if they won't open their ranks to anyone who wants to be part of their group. No group that would exclude you is worth joining."

That answer seemed to satisfy, as Sander finally relaxed. We parted, briefly, to gather our dragons. Kasaqua was impatiently pawing at the door to her stall, wanting out and wondering why I was taking so long.

Walking the trails eased tension that I hadn't known I was holding. Neither Theod nor Sander said very much, and we simply enjoyed the air and the grounds together. Inga seemed to enjoy Copper and Kasaqua's company, though she was a somewhat shy and reserved creature in most settings— at least compared to Kasaqua's bold enthusiasm for everything. She was a bit smaller than Kasaqua, despite being older. Kasaqua had hatched at the beginning of July last year, where Inga had hatched in April. Professor Mesman had remarked on Kasaqua having an uncommonly quick habit of growth, compared to other breeds—I could have been riding her, if she had a saddle that fit. Sander wouldn't be riding Inga until the spring term, given the rate she was growing, so it was more equitable that we all walk. We made two full loops of the trails, and I parted from Sander and Theod after we put the dragons back in their stalls to freshen up before dinner.

I walked up the stairs feeling like I was preparing for a battle.

ANEQUS CONVERSED WITH MARTA

When I arrived at my room, Marta was sitting at the little vanity where she usually powdered her face and put up her hair. She was wearing her uniform skirt and blouse, her jacket tossed carelessly onto her bed. I had to admit that I'd been rather deliberately avoiding Marta since her dramatic and tearful arrival last night, and seeing her now in full afternoon light . . . she looked not at all well. She was pale and drawn, with dark circles beneath her eyes. She was holding a letter in her hands, which rested listlessly on the table's surface. Jadi was not present; I had no idea where she was.

"Marta?" I asked, closing the door behind me.

"Father wants me to come home for the weekend," she said, looking at the letter. "He sent a telegram. He wants to make up with me. I sent a telegram to Lisbet last night, explaining everything, but there's not much she can do for me now that she's back at school. She wrote back this morning and suggested . . ." Marta drew a shuddering breath before continuing, "She suggested that I might yet be mistress of Sjokliffheim if I consider marrying Iain Morris."

"The son of the woman your father's marrying? Who you've never even *met*?" I asked, slightly incredulous at the very idea.

"It makes a certain sort of sense," Marta said, setting the letter down and picking up a handkerchief to dab at her eyes. "If he's to be the eventual master of Sjokliffheim, marrying him would make me its mistress for the rest of my life. It *is* rather expected that a young woman of means will naturally marry someone who is her father's equal, and Papa seems to be folding Mister Morris quite happily into his shipping business. He owns majority shares in a few merchant ships that Papa wants to add to his fleet. Lisbet is being frightfully sensible about the whole thing, but then she's never been an heiress. She's been considering suitable marriage prospects since she was fourteen. She will necessarily have to marry to an advantage, given her family's small fortune; she cannot afford to be a burden to her mother."

"From what I've seen, the burden runs the other way in that family. Frau Jansen does not strike me as a loving support to either of her children," I said. "I'm sorry that I don't understand the intricacies of this situation. I think I must have tripped over some part of Anglish society that's so far outside of my own experience that I'm just not comprehending it. What will it mean for you, not being mistress of Sjokliffheim?"

She was silent for a long moment, then answered my question with one of her own.

"What do you think your life will look like ten years from now?" Marta asked, turning to fix me with an arresting gaze. There was anger there, and confusion, and perhaps actual curiosity. As if it were just occurring to her that I was not, in fact, being deliberately obtuse or cruel or whatever else.

"That's a strange question to ask, Marta," I answered carefully, frowning. "I'm not sure how to honestly answer it without falling afoul of Anglish customs regarding courting and marriage and all that."

Marta frowned, and sighed, and looked back at the letter. "I've found myself wondering if I haven't made some horrible mistake, becoming a dragoneer. I love Magnus dearly; I cannot imagine a life without him. But I chose to become a dragoneer thinking that I was secure in the position of an heiress—that Sjokliffheim would always be my home. The reality for girls of my station is that, in most cases—in dear Lisbet's case, for example—one's place in society will be almost entirely determined by the man one marries. I . . . have you read any of Johanna Lindemann's novels? I'm thinking especially of *Kolbrandtheim* and *The Sisters Baumgärtner.*"

"I've read part of *The Sisters Baumgärtner,* but I never finished it, because I got bored. I've never read *Kolbrandtheim,* but I've heard of it. They're both romances, after a fashion, aren't they?"

"Only in the broadest sense could *The Sisters Baumgärtner* be considered a romance," Marta said with a frown. "It's a serious and profound novel about the dangers of injudicious pairings and how they can lead to ruin. Have you ever read any novel at all in which an advantageous marriage is *not* the chief aim of any heroine older than sixteen and younger than forty? Sybille Stosch neatly avoids the question of marriage and suitors by never aging beyond fifteen years, which is a luxury that real people don't have."

"Anglish novels with women characters *do* seem to be terribly preoccupied with romance and marriage, yes," I agreed.

"How far did you read into *The Sisters Baumgärtner* before you put it down?"

"The part where Annalise agrees to Torsten's proposal and everyone congratulates her on what a fine match it is," I said, wondering what Marta was getting at and wishing she'd just speak plainly. "At that point, I decided that all of the characters were too stupid for me to care what became of them."

"Then you skipped the third act entirely and missed the whole point of the story!" Marta said, sounding appalled. "All of the couples in the book are object lessons. Annalise's mother married below her station, passion without thought, and she came to ruin because of it. She left her daughter with no fortune of her own and no prospects, forcing her to live on her sister's charity. Meanwhile Dorothea Baumgärtner married a stupid and insipid man for money and status and was miserable because of it. Torsten is very charming and wealthy, but he's an impulsive spendthrift and a rake! Annalise is canny enough to see that, but allows herself to be convinced of the match by her family—"

"They all treat her horribly, aside from Rasmus," I interrupted. "I could not understand at all why she stayed."

"What do you mean? Where else could she have gone?" Marta asked.

"Anywhere? She wasn't indentured or anything like that, unless I missed it somehow," I said. "What prevented her from leaving her family to find work in the city or something? I think I remember there being talk of her becoming a governess—"

Marta went pale, gazing at me with uncomprehending horror.

"Annalise was born to a great house," she murmured. "The idea that she should be forced into a vocation, should have to *earn wages*—"

"Oh, how terrible," I said, rolling my eyes. Marta scowled at me.

"Anyway, if you'd bothered to finish the book, you'd know that Torsten runs off with Dorothea and they have an illicit affair, and her husband divorces her, and the shame is so great that she does away with herself. Annalise, of course, breaks the engagement, and Torsten swans off to Frankland, unrepentant and having learned nothing. Rasmus finally sees how good and sweet and kind Annalise is, and marries her, and Jannik is killed in a holmgang, which leaves Rasmus as the heir to Nederbæk Hall and Annalise its mistress."

"Well, how lovely for all the characters who survived," I said.

"But I don't see how that story is especially relevant to you or your current concerns."

"It's relevant because I'm at the point of my life where I need to consider marriage and future and all of that, and Lisbet isn't wrong in seeing that if I marry Iain, I'd secure my future—"

"I think you ought to talk at length with your father about exactly why his marriage plans have you so upset. His wanting to make up with you can only be a good thing, in the balance."

"I suppose I'll find out over the weekend, however I arrange transport," Marta said miserably. "The dragonhall master actually *shouted* at me yesterday about pushing Magnus to fly here from Estervall, and it was *awful*."

"Is Magnus all right?" I asked.

"He's about as well as I am," Marta answered. "He's angry with me. I can *feel* it."

"Then you ought to go make up to him as soon as you can," I said firmly. "I didn't see you at luncheon. Have you eaten today?"

"No," Marta admitted.

I offered a hand to help her stand up. There was a long, brittle moment before she took it and allowed me to pull her to her feet.

"We'll go have dinner, and then we'll go to the dragonhall," I said. "You'll feel better."

Marta didn't look entirely convinced, but she nodded, biting at her bottom lip pensively.

As we made our way to the dining hall, I told her about Ernst, and the DGT, and Sander's opinions regarding both.

"It sounds like the sort of thing that you're lucky to be invited to join," Marta said.

"Would you like to join, too?" I asked.

"I haven't been invited," she said uncertainly. "I'm not sure that I'm the kind of person that they're looking for, not . . ."

"Not what?"

"I'm not scholarly. I'm not political. Having paired with Magnus is the most interesting thing about me, and it's not something that will be of particular interest to the kind of politically motivated young men who became dragoneers largely because of the social inroads it would make for them."

"How do you know their motivations for becoming dragoneers?" I asked.

"Well, it's rather obvious, given the standing of the Gram family in Vastergot. They're one of the oldest families, along with the Stafns, the Wilders, the Sørensens, the Lindgrens—all the people descended from the greatfathers that came here with Stafn Whitebeard and his sons. The Gram family seat at Seeblick is northwest of here, just far enough outside the city to not be crowded or bothered. I've never been invited to any occasion there. I've been to the Sørensen estate, though. The Grams are quite famous breeders of kesseldraches; most dragons of that breed can trace their ancestry to Gram lines sooner or later, especially the dragonthede's stock."

"I've never heard anything about any of this, or of those families or the people in them. None of it has ever been relevant to me in the last sixteen years, and I don't really understand why it suddenly should be," I confessed. "You and Sander both seem to think that there's something to this, some advantage to be gained by becoming friends with Ernst Gram, but I'm not sure that such things apply to me. I'm a nackie, and my father is a whaler. I'm never going to live in a house grand enough to have its own name."

"You could if you wanted to," Marta said. "You're very intelligent, and pretty in an unconventional sort of way, and *singular* in your accomplishments. You're a dragoneer, and now a person of some note, given your heroics with Jarl Joervarsson. You could marry into a great family, if you tried. I'm certain that there are classmates of ours who'd court you, if they thought you were open to such a thing."

"I'm *not,*" I said, trying not to pull a face at how utterly distasteful such a notion was. "When I complete my education, I'm going to go *home*. I'm going to live in a house very like every other house on Masquapaug, built by the hands of my neighbors and friends from field stone and bentwood and bark—the same way my people have been building houses since the beginning of time."

"And what happens to the next nackie dragoneer, then?" Marta asked, looking at me sidelong. "In just a few years, Kasaqua will be old enough to produce an egg. When she does, the Ministry of Dragon Affairs will certainly have a very keen interest in who's allowed to stand before it. I don't know the names of the individuals under Captain Einarsson, or who the minister in charge of Catchnet and the islands is, but it's someone. Someone you'd do well to establish a connection with, I think. Finding out which of our classmates is related to them and how would seem to be a canny way to do that."

"If it's a good idea for me to join the DGT, then isn't it the same for you? You've complained that your place in society is impacted somehow by Dagny Sørensen snubbing you. Why should you be beholden to her good opinion if you can make a name for yourself as a dragoneer and a peer of people like Ernst Gram?"

"Because I haven't been invited into the society!" Marta huffed.

"Sander has, I think," I said. "I have. I'm going to tell them tonight at dinner that I'm only interested in joining if they'll open their ranks. They claim to welcome the unseen and unheard people of society. There are exactly three young women currently in attendance at Kuipers. All three of us ought to be considered, if the society is actually concerned with equality. I'll ask Jadi, if she's at dinner—do you know where she is? Never mind. I'd ask Liberty, too, if I could find her! I presume she's in the laundry or otherwise downstairs, and she's told me that it's bad manners to seek her out there."

Marta stopped still and looked at me, her face turning quite pink.

"You're absolutely serious, aren't you?" she asked after a long moment.

"Is there a reason I shouldn't be?"

"You think that Ernst ought to open his society to one of the *servants*?"

"I think that any organization whose first article is *'All human beings are born free and equal, alike in dignity and natural rights'* ought to be held to that standard," I said. "If the school's chapter of the DGT isn't willing to embrace all of us, it shouldn't have any of us. Will you join me to speak to them?"

"I wonder if you're not half-mad, to be honest," Marta said, shaking her head slightly. "But yes. I'll join you."

I just smiled in return, and we proceeded to the dining hall.

THEY ALL MET WITH ERNST AT DINNER

There was a strange sort of tension in the dining hall—or perhaps that was just something that *I* felt. Jadi was already sitting at our usual table when Marta and I arrived, Dreyst sitting on the floor at her feet, staring up at her with an air of concern.

"Oh, good, I was worried that I'd have to eat all alone again," Jadi said as we joined her, a sharp edge in her voice.

"Would you like to join a secret society with me?" I asked. "It's what all the nonsense at luncheon was about."

"Nonsense at luncheon?" Theod asked, arriving at the table.

"The DGT," I said, glancing over to the table at the far side of the room, where Ernst was sitting with Evind and Vinzent. Ernst was staring at us. Sander arrived with Osvald, Osvald's dragon bounding along at his heel. That made six of us, all together—me and Theod, Osvald and Sander, Marta and Jadi. Jadi and Osvald's hatchlings rounded out the group. I briefly explained the plan. We'd approach Ernst with our "all or none" ultimatum and see what he and his gang had to say about it.

I really hadn't intended for us to look like a war band on the march as we crossed the dining room to Ernst and his fellows, but the fact was that the six of us moving together seemed to draw the attention of everyone else in the room.

Ernst was already holding court, flanked by the two who I presumed were third-year students, with Vinzent and Evind on the margins. He saw us coming, and several different emotions flickered across his features at our approach.

"Good evening, Mister Gram," I said, setting down the booklet of articles that he'd given me. "I believe that you wanted to speak to me?"

His gaze flicked to the booklet, and then to me, and then to either side. He looked mildly panicked. It was unkind of me to feel so good about that.

"You seem to have brought a crowd," he replied, his face settling on a wry smile that didn't reach his eyes.

"So I have," I said. "Think of us as a coalition. The articles mention solidarity, don't they? Would you rather talk to all of us, or none of us?"

"The invitation was for you, specifically, Miss Anequs," Ernst said, frowning.

"Oh, I understand that, and I'm giving very serious consideration to accepting the invitation. But if I do—if you really do want my thoughts and voice in your meetings—then you'll have to include my close associates, as well. As Sander so cleverly pointed out earlier, there are exactly four students currently enrolled at Kuiper's who are not young Anglish men descended from great families: myself, Miss Hagan, Miss Wozniakowa, and Mister Knecht. We all have experiences, and thus thoughts and opinions, that differ from the common experience of the 'young Anglish man of means who attended a good boys' school and decided to become a dragoneer.' I think you might find our disparate outlooks rather refreshing."

"You can't honestly expect our chapter, which only has five members at present, to happily include six more."

"Why can't I? A group of eleven people isn't unmanageable, I don't think. We could all be seated at the large table in the library without trouble. You can't care very much for disorder or the teachings of Enki if you're unable to contend with a few more people, and if that's not what you're about, then what *are* you about?"

"In discussions of philosophy—"

"Mister Gram, if you had to arrange a garden party on behalf of your sister, would you even begin to know how?" Marta asked. "Who to invite, who not to invite, what the social consequences might be either way?"

"That's not the sort of thing that—"

"Have you ever skinned a rabbit, Ernst?" I asked. "Or plucked a turkey?"

"Of course not! What does that have to do with—"

"Have you ever spent a whole day hauling coal, wood, and water?" Theod asked.

Ernst remained silent, frowning.

"How many languages can you speak?" Jadi asked. *"Czy możesz mówić po polsku? Tsi ir visn vos Zhidish iz?"*

"You've taken classes with Professor Ulfar," I said. "Did he ever have the lesson with you where the class as a whole has to identify a lot of objects, using only one another as a source of knowledge? When he taught that lesson to my class last year, he began by saying that he was certain that every student in the room knew something that he did not. We know things that you don't know, Ernst. Wouldn't you like to learn them?"

"We typically only take on two or three students a year," Ernst said, "and we only ever invite students who are new to the academy, except in extraordinary circumstances. Miss Hagan and Mister Knecht are in their third years, aren't they?"

"Sander and I are in our second years," I pointed out, "and you seemed terribly interested in having *me* join you."

"As I've said, extraordinary circumstances. Last year, Lennerd Tepperik was the captain of this chapter. He didn't think that our ranks ought to be opened to women, or to foreigners—or even to anyone who wasn't well-read. He had enough votes behind his argument to close the matter. Now he's a dragekadett in the dragonthede, and as far as I know, he's off on the western border in Runestung Hold."

"So put it to a vote, since you're very much a voting thede," I said, looking from one young man at the table to the next. I recognized Vinzent and Evind. I knew that the other young men, the third-year students, were Kam and Nils. I didn't know which was which. "Would you like us to return to our table over there while the five of you discuss it amongst yourselves?"

"That might be for the best, yes."

"Can I cast my vote?" Osvald asked, stepping forward from his place beside Sander. "You've said that I'm in no matter what, so I ought to be able to vote with the rest of you."

"You don't get to vote on matters until you've been initiated, Ozzie," Ernst said.

"Don't call me Ozzie."

"Stop behaving like a child, then."

"I am sixteen years old, and a dragoneer, and I'd have been here last year if Gretha hadn't had a fallow before producing Juniper's egg—"

"This is not the time or place for this discussion," Ernst said coldly.

"It seems that you've got a lot to think about," I said. "Frankly, I'm not sure that your little society is worth my time. If you were any kind of important, I'd have heard of you before, and your articles have nothing at all concerning direct action. It seems, to me, to be an exercise of young men gathering to puff one another up about what's wrong with the world and argue about the best way to change it, all to arrive at doing nothing at all. I have met with Jarl Joervarsson directly on two different occasions, and was a guest in his home from the ninth of May to the twenty-second. I told stories to his sons and had luncheon and tea with his wife.

"You seem to be operating under the impression that I should feel very privileged to be asked to join your group, that I should be jumping at the chance. But I think you've more to gain from my friendship than I have to gain from yours, in terms of making new connections to other parts of society. I think that each of us"—I gestured to my companions around me—"have more worthwhile things to say, individually, than you five do all together—because the five of you are all so very similar in your backgrounds, your experiences, your ideas.

"I have entertained this invitation because my friends seem to think that there's something worthwhile to be had in friendship with you. And I quite liked what Eskil Gerdasson had to say at the thynge in August; I *had* hoped that this chapter shared certain philosophies with him. If it doesn't, then it's not of any use to me. To any of us. So have us all, or none of us. Until you decide, I do believe that we're going to return to our table. Feel free to come and join us for further discussion once you've made a decision."

And before Ernst Gram or any of his followers could say a word, I turned on my heel and headed toward the food table to see what was on offer for dinner. The others followed.

THEN DINED WITH OSVALD

The dinner offerings tonight were roast beef, baked potatoes, cabbage rolls stuffed with a kind of savory bread pudding, and apple crumble. The six of us had time to eat and chat a bit about classes and the like before Ernst and his four followers came strutting up to our table. Again, half the dining hall seemed to be watching, very carefully pretending that they weren't.

"We've come to an agreement," Ernst said. He had an air about him that was trying—but failing—to achieve the kind of authority that Frau Kuiper or Jarl Joervarsson had when speaking. His voice was quieter when he continued, "The library, eight o'clock."

"We'll be there," I said, smiling. Ernst bowed slightly, in the way that was polite for a gentleman addressing a lady; then he and the others departed together back to their table. I couldn't fail to notice that Osvald had become attached to our group, not his brother's.

I still wasn't entirely sure that there was anything to this whole ordeal, but everyone at my table seemed very pleased to have Ernst invite us to his meeting, which couldn't *really* be so very secret. I was absolutely certain that the maids knew all about it, at least. I had enough various matters on my mind—my overtures to Theod, the prospect of spending time with Liberty, Kasaqua's conformation not fitting Anglish saddles, the utterly different attitude that Professor Schreiber had regarding skiltakraft as compared to Professor Ezel, everything that was going on back home . . . I didn't need more fuss and bother from a bunch of privileged young men who'd never had a real problem in their lives.

Osvald seemed to be in private conversation with Sander, and Sander seemed to be doing most of the talking through his tablet. Osvald read and answered glibly, only for Sander to write more. It seemed practiced, for them; something I'd never seen Sander do with any of the other students.

"So, Osvald, you and Sander were classmates at Schmidt?" Marta asked, always keen to pull the conversation back together when it wandered.

"Oh, yes," Osvald said, looking up from what he'd been reading, seeming to notice all of us for the first time since sitting down. "Same year, same quarters, all that. I expected to come to Kuiper's at the same time, but Gretha—our father's dragon—produced a fallow egg last year."

"A fallow egg?" I asked.

"Small, oddly shaped, nothing inside. When it was clear that it wasn't alive, Father had it blown hollow, and he keeps the shell in his study as an oddment."

"I've seen hens produce those," I said, considering. "It hadn't occurred to me that a dragon might."

"Her very first egg was fallow, too, but Father hadn't even been aware that she was carrying and didn't arrange for her to meet with a stud. That was long before any of us were born, when he was just a couple of years out of the academy himself. Every egg Gretha's had between then and now went elsewhere; there's detailed records and all. Four years ago, she produced the egg that hatched into Sidimund, and she ought to have produced an egg last year, but it came out fallow. It's lucky that she went into season this year, so I only had to wait another year for her to produce the egg that hatched into Juniper."

"How often do dragons produce eggs, typically? And at what age?" I asked. "The books I've read on the subject are a bit spare on details of breeding, and I imagine that it's going to become relevant for Kasaqua eventually."

"The breeding of dragons—at least breeding dragons along established bloodlines—can be a whole career. It's probably what I'm going to go into eventually, because I was lucky enough to bond with a female hatchling," Osvald said. "Ernst's Sidimund and my Juniper are both out of our father's dragon Gretha, but Sidimund is by Athelwulf, and Juniper is by Tyrstryke, because Athelwulf wasn't available at the critical time. Athelwulf is the more desirable sire of the two, but the fact that Juniper will be able to produce eggs of her own gives me the advantage in the balance, I think."

Which was mildly interesting, but did nothing to answer my questions at all.

"Bjalladreki dams typically start producing eggs at around five years of age, and will do so every two or three years until they're forty or so," Marta said with some confidence. "I learned as much as I could on the subject when Magnus was still in the egg and might have come out either way. His pedigree is respectable, but he's not likely to be sought out, especially as a stud."

"Gikka hatched in the spring of 1835, so she's eight years old now, and Dreyst was her first egg," Jadi said. "But I think that's a bit late, as dragons go?"

"It depends on the breed," Osvald said. "Kesseldraches are slow to mature, because they get so large, and it's not uncommon for them to be ten years old before they start producing eggs. I hope that Juniper starts sooner rather than later, though."

"Why's that?" I asked. Osvald gave me the sort of look that I'd grown used to receiving from Anglish people, as if he wasn't sure I was being serious.

"Because eggs belong to the dragoneer of the dam, generally, and eggs of sufficiently desirable parentage are highly sought after," he said, as if that ought to have been obvious. "As a second-born son, I've got to be realistic in how I'm going to make a living. My uncle is extensively connected in kesseldrache-rider circles, and I'd like to take up the trade, I think."

"It all seems rather . . . bloodless?" I said, considering. "I'm not sure that's the word I'm looking for. Cold, unfeeling. I confess I'd not given it a lot of thought until recently, but when Kasaqua begins producing eggs, I certainly won't even think of selling them. They'll be treated the way she was herself, nurtured in the meetinghouse and allowed to choose a partner from anyone in the village upon hatching."

"Well, that's a shame," Osvald said casually. "Yours is an exotic breed. If you can find a suitable sire for her, then her eggs would be highly desirable among the sorts of people who are trying to establish exotic lines here in Lindmarden."

"The idea of buying and selling dragons' eggs is exactly as repellent, to me and my people, as the idea of buying and selling *children* would be," I said, trying to sound diplomatic and not scornful. Osvald simply shrugged and looked to Jadi's side, where Dreyst was clearly trying to get Juniper's attention. Juniper, for her part, was exactly as stoic as Gerhard had been upon meeting Kasaqua, sitting at quiet attention with her eyes fixed on Osvald.

Looking to Jadi, Osvald said, "I'm not sure I'm familiar with your dragon's breed."

"He's a cross," Jadi said, looking at him like she expected a challenge. "His mother, my sister's dragon, Gikka—Gikhkayt—is a Pollish Złocisty. Papa had her egg imported, and she might be the only Złocisty in Lindmarden so far. We don't actually know who Dreyst's sire is; Gikka managed the whole affair herself. Our rabbi's son, who's the only one in Katshketeykh who knows from dragons, thinks that the father is probably a bjalladreki, but nobody's sure how Dreyst is going to turn out, with horns or spines or both. He looks a lot like Gikka did at this age, though—or at least I think so. Crosses usually take after their dams more than their sires, or so Anshel thinks."

"Anshel being?" I asked.

"The rabbi's son. Didn't I just say?"

"You didn't, not really," I said, and Jadi made a little hand-waving gesture that I didn't entirely understand.

"One of the principal concerns regarding Copper, when he chose me, was the fact that Herr Mahler had acquired the egg from a Berri Vaskosish dealer at great expense," Theod said. "I don't know if there are any other Akhari dragons anywhere in Lindmarden, though I understand from hearsay that they're not terribly uncommon in Berri Vaskos. There are more Kindah people down there, I think. It's a Kindah breed originally."

"Don't look now, but Ernst and the others just left the dining room," Osvald said. "Miss Wozniakowa and I will have to stop at the dragonhall to see that our charges are fed."

"I was planning to visit with Kasaqua, and Marta was planning to visit with Magnus."

The kitchen maids had begun clearing away the remainders from the food table, and most of the other students in the dining hall had already departed. A glance at the clock told me that it was just shy of seven. We all proceeded to the dragonhall together.

Osvald shared some classes with Jadi, and had an established friendship with Sander, so it wasn't terribly awkward for him to fold into our social circle; conversation was easy as we walked. He was able to explain to me that of the two third-year students, Kam was the shorter, yellow-haired one, and Nils was the taller, brown-haired one.

At the dragonhall, the hall lads were doling out buckets of

mashed roots, bones, and offal stall by stall, starting with the professors' dragons and then by year with fourth-years fed first. Kasaqua was impatient for her turn, turning in circles and pawing at the stall door. Marta politely asked that she be allowed to deliver Magnus his food herself, and while she was feeding him, Osvald pointed out Ernst's dragon to us. He was a half-grown male kesseldrache (already bigger than a horse, but only half as massive as Frau Kuiper's Gerhard), who regarded us imperiously. According to Osvald, he was a nearly perfect specimen of the breed, exhibiting ideal coloration and conformation and all. He compared and contrasted with his own hatchling, Juniper. Osvald seemed very knowledgeable about kesseldraches in particular, but none of the rest of us were bonded to kesseldraches.

When it came to the first-years' turns to have their dragons fed, Dreyst gorged himself on offal and turnips to the point that Jadi was obliged to carry him, because he refused to walk.

"You shouldn't let him eat so much," Osvald said disapprovingly, frowning at Jadi as she cradled Dreyst in her arms.

"What, I should let him starve?" she responded indignantly. "He's a growing baby!"

"If you let him get fat—"

"Mind your own dragon and don't worry about how I mind Dreyst," Jadi said, an air of finality in her voice.

"There's a reason that the Ministry of Dragons demands that dragoneers attend academies to learn how to care for dragons, to become licensed and all," Osvald insisted as we walked back to the school proper. "Bonding with a dragon *changes* people. Those who are irresolute or careless can easily be overpowered by their dragon's whims and desires. Dragons need discipline, to know that you as a dragoneer are a figure of firm authority—"

"Stop," Sander said. Osvald startled and looked at him; he was holding out his tablet.

Osvald took it and read it, then frowned and said, "Fine. But I'm not wrong."

Conversation had rather soured at that point, and we parted

company at the stairs—Marta and Jadi and me up to our room, the young men to their own quarters. Upstairs, Jadi deposited Dreyst onto her bed, where he promptly rolled over and demanded to have his belly rubbed.

Watching that, and remembering Kasaqua at that size, I couldn't help but feel a bit bad for Osvald's Juniper. She probably didn't get much petting at all.

SHE COMPARED SCHEDULES WITH HER CLASSMATES, AND MET WITH LIBERTY IN SECRET

I woke early on Wednesday morning, roused by the knowledge that Kasaqua had awakened and was unhappy to discover that she was still in her stall. She very much wanted me to wake up and come let her out. Jadi was already in the washroom, Dreyst sitting in front of the closed door with his tail thumping against the floor periodically. He glanced at me momentarily as I sat up and stretched, but went right back to staring at the door.

Marta was a lumpen mass of blankets huddled on her bed, no part of her visible. The tall clock indicated that it was just shy of six in the morning. I combed my hair and put it into a simple braid while I waited for my turn in the washroom, careful to be quiet; I didn't want to wake her.

"Good morning," I whispered to Jadi when she emerged from the washroom, clean and pressed and dressed in trousers. Dreyst did a wiggling little dance as she emerged, turning circles in his excitement.

"Good morning," she whispered in return, bending to pet him. "What classes do you have today?"

"I've got a directed study of al-jabr from eight to ten o'clock, but my afternoon has a free period."

"Oh, that's lucky; my free period isn't until Friday afternoon. I have husbandry in the morning, today, and skiltakraft in the afternoon. I think most of the first-year students do? I think they've arranged for our free period to be on Friday in deference to students who live nearby and might want to go home during the weekend. Do you have plans for your free period?"

"No, not really," I replied. "I didn't have any free periods at all last year. I think I had directed studies when most of the first-year students had a free period? I didn't pay much attention to anyone's schedule but my own, back then."

"I'm going to go to the library until the dining hall opens for breakfast; would you like to come?" she asked.

"Kasaqua's awake, so I'm going to the dragonhall," I said, shaking my head. "I'll see you at breakfast, though."

"All right, see you then," Jadi said.

I thought about my free period as I washed and got dressed. It was a novel idea; after ten o'clock on every Monday and Wednesday this term, the day would be entirely my own, and I'd have no one to answer to until the following morning's class. I could take a trip into the city, with that much time, if I could arrange train fare. Once Kasaqua had a proper saddle, it would be quite possible to forgo the train and simply ride her overland; Vastergot was something like five miles away, which was only an hour for a dragon at a brisk walk. But turning up with Kasaqua would very clearly identify me to any and all as "the nackie dragoneer from Kuiper's," and that might well be dangerous. I'd have to talk to Niquiat about his opinions regarding my reception in the city before trying anything.

I resolved to send Niquiat a telegram detailing my class schedule for this term; I could ask him to come and visit over the weekend, if he was able. *He* could still travel anonymously.

I went to the dragonhall directly; most of the dragons were still sleeping. Of course, Kasaqua *would* be an early riser in comparison with most of dragonkind. I let her out and spent most of an hour walking the grounds with her, letting her stretch out her legs and wings. Her wings were growing into their adult proportions, now, and she felt moved to flap them every so often—testing the way the muscles of her breast and shoulders moved in concert as her wings folded and extended and pressed against the air. She made me acutely aware that something at the base of her antlers felt itchy and strange, and that rubbing them against the wooden wall of her stall didn't help in the least. What *did* help was having me take firm hold of her antlers while she wrestled bodily against me, rather like playing tug-of-war with a dog. I tired of the game much more quickly than she did, to her frustration.

Kasaqua's antlers had first started growing around December of last year, when Kasaqua had been five months old, and they'd shed their velvet at the end of March and into April. That had itched abominably, too. I had no idea whether Nampeshiwe shed their antlers yearly in the way that deer did, but her mother had had a terribly impressive crown compared to Kasaqua's four dainty points. It was likely that her antlers would drop off sometime between now and December and grow back bigger and fuller. I had no practical way of communicating that to her, though.

At seven, I brought Kasaqua back to the dragonhall to receive her breakfast and went in to seek my own. Jadi was seated at a table with Sander, Theod, and Osvald, so I joined them.

"Is Marta still in bed?" I asked Jadi, pulling out a seat next to her.

"She was when I stopped back to get my books," Jadi said with a shrug.

"Most of the third-year class has Monday and Wednesday morning free," Theod said, sounding somewhat chagrined. "*I've* got a directed study of al-jabr, though."

"That's what I've got," I said. "At least we'll be classmates?"

"It wouldn't surprise me in the slightest to learn that Professor Nazari put both of us into a directed study so that you could catch me up to standard," Theod said. "After all, you managed to get me on track with skiltakraft when Professor Ezel couldn't. I have riding in the afternoon; I've heard that Mesman's going to be starting the third-year flight class on obstacles and flags."

"Marta will be in *that* class, I'm sure," Jadi said. "She's got to get up sometime, after all. When's your free period, if it's not this morning with the rest of your class?"

"Tuesday and Thursday morning," Theod answered. "With the fourth-year students."

It was a shame that we didn't have the same free period each week; that could have been time for us to spend together apart from others—away from the school, even. Away from prying eyes in general. I wondered, absently, if Liberty could somehow arrange to have a bit of time free on Monday and Wednesday afternoons. There was something absolutely infuriating about knowing that she was nearby but not being able to talk to her.

Theod and I proceeded up to the library after breakfast, not talking about much.

Professor Nazari—a Kindah man with animated manners, keen black eyes, and fast, thickly accented speech—was waiting for us when we arrived.

"Ah, excellent, very good, you're both here on time," he said brightly. "Now I must explain, neither of you are doing badly at al-jabr. You have been assigned this time and place to learn and practice advanced anglereckoning, because there would otherwise have been conflicts in your schedules this term. The second-year al-jabr class meets when you, Miss Anequs, will be in first-year lore with Professor Ibarra. The third-year class meets when you, Mister Knecht, will be second-year skiltakraft with Professor Schreiber. In the meantime, you, Miss Anequs, will be doing all the same work expected of the other second-year students, and you, Mister Knecht, will be doing all the work expected of third-year students."

He proceeded to give a lecture about the relationship of angles in a triangle, and how to work out the area of a triangle given limited information. Nothing of great note happened; I'd passed through anglereckoning last year, and al-jabr progressed quite naturally from those studies.

Theod and I both proceeded to the dragonhall after class. The first-year students were still bustling about, many of the hatchlings still wearing tack that they'd just received. I rather expected Jadi to join Theod and me, but she seemed to be engrossed in deep discussion with some young men from her class, Osvald among them. We took Kasaqua and Copper out and walked the trails until luncheon.

Theod had class in the afternoon, so I went up to my room to freshen up and found Liberty there changing the bedsheets. Properly changing them, not pretending like she had on Monday; there was a handcart full of soiled linens standing by the door.

"Hello!" I said, closing the door behind me. I had half a mind to shove a chair in front of it, to be sure that we wouldn't be intruded upon. But Marta and Jadi both had classes right now, so that wasn't likely. "Can I hug you?" I asked, glancing over my shoulder to make absolutely sure that the door was closed. That we were alone.

Liberty didn't answer; she simply stepped forward and embraced me.

"I missed you," I said into the hollow of her shoulder. The nape of her neck smelled like lavender.

"I missed you, too," she said back, as she pulled away to smile at me. "Sundays have been terribly dreary without our regular conversations. Talking with you is very different from talking with the other maids."

"I'm not sure how we're going to arrange things this year. I think Jadi will be understanding, but I know that Marta won't be. She's going to be away this weekend, though; I know that much."

"Well, on Saturday I have my salon; you'll come, won't you?"

"Yes, of course I'll come," I said. "I think I'll have to leave

Kasaqua in the dragonhall, though. She's big enough now that she can't be indoors in most places."

"In what little I've been able to observe in my time working here, most students keep their dragons at the dragonhall most of the time," Liberty said. "One doesn't generally see dragons in the mill district, unless it's a thanegard."

"I've noticed that, too," I said, frowning. "I have no idea how the rest of the students stand being away from their dragons so often. I'll have to ask Sander about it; he might have useful insights. Speaking of—do you know anything about the Disorder of the Grinning Teeth? They meet in the library after hours on Wednesday evenings?"

"Oh, you've fallen in with *that* lot?" Liberty asked in a tone that indicated great hilarity. "I don't know much personally, but the upstairs maids talk about them. They hang about in the library thinking that they're much more quiet than they are, getting tipped on meddyglyn and arguing about nonsense."

"Yes, that sounds about right," I agreed. "Everyone I asked seemed to think it was a good idea for me to become acquainted with them. It's all about making the correct social connections with the correct people—who I will probably never see or hear from again once I complete my education. Sander, especially, thought it would be a good idea."

"Well, I suppose he'd know better than anyone else who's who among the toff boys," Liberty said. "How's Theod? Did anything terribly interesting happen over the summer? Anything that you couldn't write out in a letter?"

I sighed, rolling my eyes in frustration.

"No! We kissed, but that's all. I talked to him about courting both of you. He's declared love for me on two separate occasions, and keeps talking about marriage, but I haven't been able to convince him to try anything . . . daring. I want arrange a meeting for the three of us, but I have no idea how to manage it with our different schedules. You two *ought* to meet each other."

"Well, I've got several hours free on Saturday," Liberty said sensibly. "Only part of it will be spent at the salon."

"All right. I'll see if I can contrive some way to get Theod to meet us afterward," I said.

"I don't know that I'll be able to find time to see you between now and then," Liberty said. "I've already spent longer than I ought to have changing these beds. There are several new maids this year, and I don't knew them well enough yet to know if they're safe. We'll have to be careful about being seen spending time together."

"I should let you go, then," I said, feeling disappointed. We'd hardly had time to talk at all.

"Saturday," she said, taking my hand and giving it an encouraging squeeze. I wanted her to stay, to sit and talk for hours about everything that had happened over the summer, and about Marta and Jadi and the DGT and everything. I very much wanted to lean forward and kiss her. But I didn't. We were *not* courting—not until she'd paid out her indenture.

"Saturday," I agreed.

And Liberty took her leave, taking the handcart of used bedsheets with her.

THE DISORDER OF THE GRINNING TEETH MET IN THE LIBRARY

That evening, at eight o'clock, I attended my first meeting with the DGT.

The school was hushed when we came back from the dragonhall, and the hallways absolutely empty as we made our way to the library. There were no lamps of any kind in the corridors, and everything felt very close and stifling in a way that it didn't during the day. I wasn't entirely certain that this was *allowed*—all of us assembling outside of our quarters after dark. I couldn't recall ever having been told about curfews or lights-out hours, but it might have been another of those things that I was just expected to already understand, like class schedules or rules of social engagement. The maid who'd found me in the library on Monday evening had certainly seemed to think it strange that I'd been there when she'd come to put the lights out. I hadn't paid much attention to the hour then, but evidently the lights were turned out in the library sometime between six and eight o'clock, because they'd already been doused for the night when we arrived.

The five members of the DGT were seated at the central table where I had my directed studies. They'd brought candles, which did a poor job of illuminating the space and made for a lot of flickering shadows. I had an oil lamp in my room—Marta and Jadi had them, too, on their bedside tables. Did the boys' accommodations not include such things? I'd never thought to ask.

"Hello—" I said, only to be interrupted by Ernst, who was sitting at the centermost position at the table, where the professor usually sat during a directed study.

"Initiates shall be silent until instructed to speak," he said, his voice ringing in the silence of the library. "Please be seated."

I gritted my teeth and resisted the urge to sigh, approximating a smile as I sat down opposite Ernst. I had thought that we'd dispensed with all of this nonsense during our conversation at dinner yesterday.

Theod sat to my right, Marta to my left. Sander sat beside Marta, with Osvald on his other side, and Jadi sat to Theod's right. Kam was right of Ernst, opposite Theod. Nils, on the other side, was opposite Marta. Evind sat beside Kam, and Vinzent beside Nils. No one was seated opposite Osvald. I glanced at Marta, wondering how she'd have arranged seating if she'd been in charge of assigning it. She seemed good at that kind of thing.

Ernst was bracketed by two of the several candles, and on the table in front of him was a bottle of dark liquid and a little cup made of ivory, or possibly bone. It was about twice the size of a sewing thimble and had unfamiliar text carved into it along the top and bottom edges. I couldn't read it, but I was reasonably sure that it was ancient Anglish or Norse.

"You have come here because you have been invited to join the Disorder of the Grinning Teeth," Ernst said, sounding not precisely practiced but . . . oratorial? "Before we open our confidence to you, you must take the oath and drink the elixir."

"The what?" I asked, raising an eyebrow, glancing at the bottle and then back at him.

"It unshackles the mind, and loosens the tongue, and brings

forth untold truths from the depth of the human soul," Ernst said, his tone very grave.

Kam interrupted then, saying, "It's just a kind of meddyglyn; don't worry."

Ernst shot him a *look*. Kam met his gaze, and for several seconds, a deeply uncomfortable silence filled the room. It was Ernst who looked away first, this time, turning his attention back to me.

"All of you, together, repeat after me," he ordered. "I solemnly pledge my commitment to the Disorder of the Grinning Teeth."

I glanced to Theod, who gave a minute nod, and to Marta, who seemed to be waiting for me to begin. In poorly coordinated unison, we repeated Ernst's words back to him.

Ernst went on, "I vow to pursue knowledge with unwavering dedication, to question and to challenge all presumptions, to introduce the unquiet thought, and to engage in thoughtful discourse."

We repeated that, too.

"With the privilege of membership comes the responsibility of confidence, to be judicious in the keeping of secrets from those that would do us harm."

Again, we repeated, and he continued.

"I pledge to never disclose to outsiders what is said by anyone in the confidence of the disorder, and should I break that trust, I hereby submit myself to Enki's wrath forever after."

Jadi hesitated, opening her mouth and then closing it again. Ernst's gaze turned to her expectantly, and in a very quiet voice, she asked, "This isn't a pledge *to* Enki, is it? I don't worship him. I can't. I'm Zhidi."

"If you think that Enki wants worship, you've absolutely misunderstood all of his lore—"

"Shut *up,* Kam!" Ernst growled.

"*You* shut up," Kam challenged, rising to his feet. "No one cares about the trappings and the rituals as much as you do. Lennerd certainly wouldn't have. If they each promise that what's said in the meetings stays in the meetings, that's good enough for me. If they break confidence and go off reporting what we say here to outsiders, it won't be Enki's wrath they'll need to worry about, it will be *mine.* If you don't like that, we'll start our own chapter without you."

"You can't do that," Ernst huffed, glaring up at him.

"Can't I? The articles lay out quite clearly how to go about starting a new chapter. If you're going to be an absolute ass about being the captain of the chapter, then maybe you just shouldn't be. You've had the title for all of three days and you're acting like it makes you jarl of the school. We're all supposed to be equals, Ernst. You're making a terrible impression on all of our new initiates, and I'm not standing for it."

"I believe that's *quite enough,* gentlemen," Marta said in a voice like cut glass. All of the young men's gazes turned to her, and Ernst's expression went from angry to stricken fast enough that I had to disguise a snort of laughter as a clearing of my throat. "Mister Hagelin, if you will kindly be seated?"

Kam sat down.

"I feel moved to express my profound discomfiture at the lamentable display of poor manners and rudeness exhibited by this assembly," Marta went on, in much the same tone. "I can only suppose that such barbarity is often overlooked in the roughsome sporting of *schoolboys,* and that our present company is not as far advanced from such habits as might be desired in *gentlemen.*" Something in the way she stressed the words made them sound like vile insults. "But there can be no excuse for squabbling among yourselves in the presence of esteemed guests, three of whom are ladies. It is very obvious by your habits that none of you are at all accustomed to pleasant discourse with ladies—one must suppose that you have not spent any significant portion of your time with your mothers or sisters, nor with any proper teacher of decorum. The most obvious mark of good breeding and good taste is a sensitive regard for the feelings of others, and it is abundantly clear that you have given absolutely no thought to our feelings. You've failed to provide adequate lighting, to arrange the room or think of the most amenable seating, to introduce yourselves politely and welcome us into your company. You have, in fact, made demands of us that presume superior rank on your own part. I had expected to meet with a group of young gentlemen tonight—scholars and philosophers, peers—but I find myself in a darkened library with a pack of boys playing at grave self-importance."

"I'm sorry, ma'am," Evind said, then sucked a breath through his teeth, as if he hadn't meant to say it.

There was a beat of silence so profound that I swore I could hear the ticking of someone's pocket watch.

I said, "Thank you very much, Miss Hagan. You've said that so much more eloquently than I could have."

Marta inclined her head gracefully, acknowledging my thanks.

"I propose this," I continued. "We begin again. No one is captain, because we are a circle of equals. All disputes henceforth will be settled by vote, and each person in this room will vote equally. We ought to establish some means of secret voting, I suppose—papers in a basket or something like. As a preventative against social pressures to vote in agreement with our close acquaintances."

"That sounds very reasonable," Kam said evenly. "I second the motion. Does anyone object?"

He turned his gaze to Ernst, challenge clear in his face. Ernst took a long, slow breath through his nose, but said nothing.

"Excellent," I said after a few moments of silence. "So, had this gone as planned from the jump, what topic would we have been discussing tonight?"

I was looking at Kam as I finished the question. Deliberately not at Ernst. I was rather done with anything that Ernst might have to say on any topic whatsoever.

"I think that we were going to talk about the inherent nature of humankind, and whether it's the same across all species of humanity," Vinzent said quietly.

And so, in a very shallow, halting sort of way that accomplished not much of anything, that was what we did until the clock chimed ten, at which point we proceeded back to our rooms.

It wasn't the most disastrous discourse I'd ever had, but there was much room for improvement in the future.

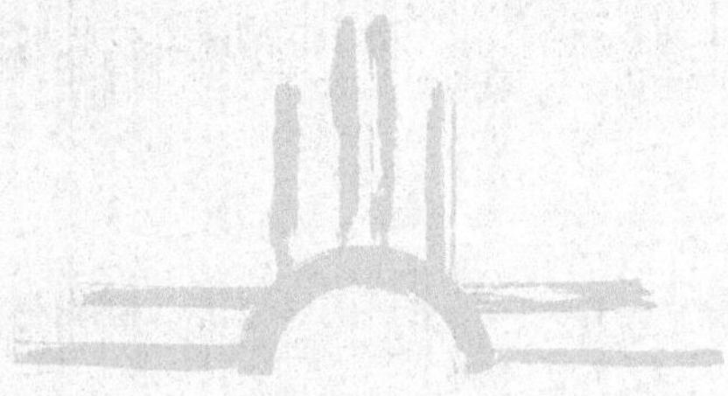

ANEQUS MET WITH A SADDLER

The following morning, I was awakened at six by the chiming of the clock. I was immediately aware that Kasaqua was already awake, and bored, and fretting that I was sleeping later than usual. I glanced at the window; the sky outside was overcast and slate gray, promising rain.

I muddled my way through washing and dressing, and together with Marta and Jadi proceeded down to breakfast, where there was coffee and oat porridge and toast with butter. I made polite small talk with everyone at the breakfast table about what classes everyone was going to and what the weather outside looked like. Evind and Vinzent seemed to have defected to our table from Ernst's, at least for breakfast. I didn't comment on it. Something was happening where Kasaqua was, and she wanted me to come and see it—nothing upsetting, just unusual and of interest. I proceeded to the dragonhall as soon as I finished eating.

There was a fully grown silberdrache sitting at attention just outside the dragonhall, wearing tack that I didn't recognize. It was a very pale example of the breed, white with subtle gray markings. The tack it was wearing was especially lovely: black leather with fancy knotwork patterns carved into it. The dragon watched me as I approached. I didn't like how appraising its gaze was, but it didn't have the sense of menace that the silberdraches on Naquipaug had. I gave it wide berth, entering the hall through one of the arches farthest from where it sat. The only fully grown silberdrache associated with the academy was Captain Einarsson's, so the presence of this dragon meant the presence of an unfamiliar rider somewhere nearby.

Professor Mesman was standing near Kasaqua's stall, talking to a man I'd never seen before. He was shorter than the professor, stout and pink-faced, with sharp gray eyes and dark hair slicked back. He was between forty and fifty years of age, if my guess was worth anything. He was wearing a leather apron with many pockets, some of which had tools poking out of them. Both men were looking at Kasaqua, but turned to me as I approached. Kasaqua, for her part, was standing with her chin resting on the door of her stall, wanting out but being terribly patient and a very good girl about it.

"Ah, Miss Anequs, I was hoping that you'd stop in before class," Professor Mesman said. "I've noticed that it is your habit to visit your dragon before the morning class period, which is good husbandry, as a rule. Careful, though; being too frequent with your affections and attention might cause your dragon to become fractious in winter, when you're not able to do so. Do make sure that your dragon has realistic expectations."

"I'll keep that in mind, professor," I said, trying not to frown.

If I could have had it my way, Kasaqua wouldn't be relegated to the dragonhall at all, at any time. She would always be by my side or waiting nearby if I had to go indoors to a place she didn't fit. It was plainly disconcerting how infrequently other students seemed to visit their dragons. I'd only had Theod to judge by, last year, and he visited Copper much more often than Marta visited Magnus or Sander visited Inga.

There was a beat of silence, and I looked to the man at the professor's side and then back to him, waiting for him to make an introduction in the Anglish fashion. He seemed to catch my meaning half a moment later when he said, "Yes, well . . . This is Mister Valteri Arnerson, an accomplished saddler and an associate of the academy and of the dragonthede. I'm sure you saw his dragon outside, but I'll let him make that introduction. Mister Arnerson, this is Miss Anequs of Mask Island. Mister Arnerson has come today, at the academy's request, to have a look at your dragon's conformation. It's uncommon for dragons to be put straight into custom tack, but yours *is* an exotic breed. You will be answering his questions and directing your dragon through the fitting process rather than joining the rest of your class in husbandry today."

"Thank you very much, sir, for coming on what I must presume to be quite short notice," I said to Mister Arnerson, dipping a curtsy—which felt strange to do, in trousers.

"No trouble at all," Mister Arnerson said, smiling. "To be honest, I've been hoping for an excuse to come have a close look at your dragon since reading about her in Captain Einarsson's report last year. I've never gotten a good look at one of the Markeslandi breed."

"I'll leave you to it, then," Professor Mesman said with a curt nod. "Hopefully you'll be able to join the riding lesson with the rest of the class this coming Tuesday."

"That might be a bit of a reach," Mister Arnerson said, looking thoughtful. "But I'll see what I can do."

Professor Mesman canted his head politely at each of us in turn, then strode off to the area of the dragonhall reserved for professors' dragons.

"Well, let's see how she moves—no tack yet; just take her out, and we'll make some loops around the flight field. She's not put off by other dragons, is she? Angharad will probably watch her the whole time."

"Angharad is your dragon?" I asked.

"Yes—sorry, I should have said. She's very even-tempered and calm, especially for a silberdrache."

"Kasaqua generally gets along well with other dragons," I said. "As long as yours doesn't loom or anything like that."

"Good, good—out we go, then. I'd like to see your dragon at a walk, a trot, and a full sprint without a rider, then at least a walk with you riding bareback—maybe a trot, too, if she's not too uncomfortable. I've heard that the nackies near the deep lakes ride these beasts without saddles, just padding, but I'm not sure of the veracity of those reports."

"Miss Wozniakowa mentioned that she knows of a man in Runestung Hold who's bonded to a dragon of the same breed as Kasaqua. I wonder if it would be helpful to seek his advice regarding saddling?"

"I'm not sure such a thing would be practical; your professor wants you participating in class as soon as can be managed," Mister Arnerson said, watching Kasaqua walk at an unhurried pace around the field's edge.

After a couple of loops, he said, "Have her speed up to a trot for a bit."

I used my whistle to bring Kasaqua to attention, and she had a moment of confusion; she wasn't in tack, and I never used the whistle unless it was time to work hard and be serious. She was never asked to be serious out of tack. She stopped short and looked at me, her ears back and her mane feathers flared. I had to repeat the whistle command asking her for speed, trying to fix the idea in my mind of her scrambling along at a trot. She seemed to understand then, and took off, looking back at me every so often as if to be sure that I was watching her, that I saw how well she was following directions that didn't even make sense.

"I can't say I've seen a gait quite like that before," Mister Arnerson said, looking puzzled.

"She moves very much the way a fisher moves—or a wolverine. Dragons with ancestors in Anglesland move more in the way that dogs or wolves do, from my own observations."

"I don't know that I've ever seen a fisher or a wolverine entire, just pelts," Mister Arnerson said with a chuckle. "So I can't really make much of that observation."

"A marten? A weasel? An otter?" I asked. He shook his head.

"My business is saddle-making, not natural philosophy. Can you have her speed up again into a full run? As fast as she's able to go?"

I blew three sharp notes on the whistle, and Kasaqua very enthusiastically picked up her pace, pelting around the field with her wings tucked tight against her body. Her gate was loping and bouncy, her back like a coiled spring. Mister Arnerson watched appraisingly until Kasaqua slowed down again, looping back to come and dramatically throw herself to the ground beside me shoulder-first, panting heavily and very pleased with herself.

"Can you have her stand at attention?" Mister Anerson asked after a few moments of staring at her fondly. "I'd like to take some measurements, then have you put her into tack."

I commanded her with the whistle again, and she flopped over, giving me a big-eyed pleading look, because she didn't want to stand at attention. She wanted to nap in the sun, and then hunt something. I repeated the whistle command, and she huffed, stretching expansively on the ground before getting back on her feet and standing like a good girl. She stayed still and performed poses, as she was instructed, while Mister Arnerson took his measurements and jotted them down in a little notebook, frowning thoughtfully the whole time.

I gave her a very thorough brushing down in her stall before putting her tack on. Others had arrived in the meantime, the rest of my class attending their own dragons in adjacent stalls.

Looking at the lay of the tack, I could see that even the saddle frame was overlong and stiff in a way that limited her range of motion. It didn't do much when she was at a walk, but it would certainly hamper her if she tried to run as she had just a few minutes earlier.

Freshened up and dressed in her best, Kasaqua and I returned to Mister Arnerson in the field, and he had me mount up without a saddle, the same way that Professor Mesman had on Tuesday. Kasaqua seemed more comfortable with the whole process this time, not the least bit surprised or unsure about having me on her back. The position I naturally settled into—seated in the hollow behind her shoulder blades, leaning a bit forward, my knees hooked over the bases of her wings—was comfortable and easy. If I were to design a saddle appropriate to Kasaqua, it wouldn't be a boat-shaped piece of wood and rawhide; her back wasn't shaped that way. The curve of her spine rose up behind me, keeping me forward by my own weight. I wasn't at all afraid of falling off, at least not at this pace. I scratched her behind the ears and urged her to pick up speed again, and at a trot . . . Well, the padded underlay did more than nothing, and she was very aware of my weight coming down on her spine. She slowed back to a walk without being told to. A walk was comfortable enough; she could carry me all day at this pace if I asked that of her.

"That's about what I expected," Mister Arnerson said, coming to walk alongside us, his gaze fixed at Kasaqua's shoulders. "The point of a saddle is to spread your weight and keep it off the dragon's spine, and especially off the wing muscles. Your dragon's uncommonly low in the withers. A hoop tree in the Vaskosish style might work—something low with a wide gullet, and quite short; she's got very little space between the withers and the wing bases."

The underlay was almost enough on its own, though it could do with a bit more padding directly under my rear and something stiff to either side. Saddle horns wouldn't go amiss, either, but those could easily be attached to the straps that fixed the saddle frame to the chest collar.

"I'll work something up for your class next Tuesday," Mister Arnerson promised, tucking his notebook back into one of the many pockets on his apron. "You can put her back up. Herr Mesman told me to tell you that you needn't wait for him. The rest of the class is trail riding today—"

He was interrupted by a distant peal of thunder, and we both looked up at the leaden sky.

"Though that might be cut short by circumstance," he said.

"Is it safe for me to keep riding her with just the saddle frame, so long as I don't let her go faster than a walk?" I asked.

"I think she'll let you know if you're making her sore," he said. "She doesn't seem like a reserved or long-suffering creature."

I laughed, and Kasaqua wondered what was funny. Herr Arnerson took his leave, and Kasaqua made several more loops of the flight field with me astride her, quickening her pace until it became too bouncy and then slowing again—feeling out what was possible and comfortable without a saddle.

I brought her back to the dragonhall as the first drops of rain began falling.

AND LEARNED ABOUT ANGLISH LORE

Kasaqua was not terribly upset at being put into her stall, because she'd run enough that she wanted to nap. It was pouring down rain by the time I finished putting her up, and I dashed back to the school wishing I'd worn a cape. My afternoon session of skiltakraft was largely uneventful, because Professor Schreiber had planned for us to practice skiltas out of doors, and that wasn't possible given the weather. We spent the period memorizing the structures and properties of various athers, comparing them to the skiltas that could produce them.

The following morning, I had lore with Professor Ibarra.

I'd been in directed studies with him last year, because I had not possessed any of the Anglish lore that was expected of a young woman of my age. I'd evidently stuffed enough of it into my head last year to perform well enough on examinations to land me in the general class of first-year students. Theod had shared the directed studies with me, which had made them bearable, but he'd done well enough to be placed in the *second*-year class. There was something annoying about that, something I couldn't quite put name to. He was a year ahead of me in his studies, and really properly belonged in third-year classes, so there was no reason for me to be upset that I was in first year and he in second, regarding lore. We were both of us behind, and in equal measure. He hadn't pulled ahead of me. It wouldn't be a terrible thing if he *did* pull ahead of me, either.

I arrived to Lecture Hall One quite early, to be sure of securing a good seat toward the front. Osvald Gram came and sat next to me, making quiet conversation with no real substance as the rest of the students arrived by twos and threes. Jadi came scampering in, the last student to arrive. She sat at my other side, looking slightly flushed, as if she'd been running. Professor Ibarra gave her a stern look—and then one to *me,* as if I were supposed to be Jadi's keeper or some such. I met his gaze evenly, challenging him to say something, and he looked away before I did. He rapped on his desk with the long stick that he used to point out notes on the blackboard, signaling that his lecture was about to commence. All the quiet conversations in the room stopped. The two hatchlings beside us—Jadi's and Osvald's—were sniffing at each other. Most of the other hatchlings in the hall were already settled. Looking around the room, I seemed to be the only student *without* a dragon at heel. Because I was a second-year student in a first-year class.

"Welcome, class, to Lore One," Professor Ibarra began. "Some of you might be wondering why you haven't been placed into separate classes for folklore and erelore, as I'm sure many of you were in primary school. The answer is simple: Folklore and erelore cannot be meaningfully separated, not before the modern era. What actually occurred in fargone eretide is wonderfully muddled with what occurrences we can suppose true or untrue by studying the leids, the sagas, and the many other stories that people have preserved across the generations. Now, it cannot have escaped your notice that I am, in fact, Vaskosish by birth."

He paused a moment, allowing several students to laugh nervously.

"I hasten to clarify that I am not in any way *Berri* Vaskosish—my family came to Lindmarden directly from Vaskosland in the years following the war between Lindmarden and Berri Vaskos, when the end of the trade embargo created new mercantile opportunities for people from the old world. I am the son of a cloth merchant, and not ashamed to say it. When Frau Kuiper was beating back the Berri Vaskosish along the banks of the Polvaara, with a young Leiknir Joervarsson under her command, I was a child playing with my fellows in a village square a dozen miles from the city of Ostagav. My family was privileged by fortune, and at the age of sixteen, I had the opportunity to stand before an egg, along with my brothers. When my dear Abiadura chose me, my father determined that we should travel to Lindmarden, that I should be educated in the ways of skiltakraft at High King's Academy in New Linvik. Ostagavia has a rich and storied erelore of dragoneering, but its academies of skiltakraft are outrageously expensive for anyone who is not a member of the royal lineage. It was at the High King's Academy that I first learned Anglish lore, and where I fell in love with it.

"Specifically, I fell in love with the way that time and place impact a story and its meaning—how different Anglish stories were from the Vaskosish ones that I'd grown up with; how by comparing fargone folklore to our knowledge of erelore, we can see the echoes of wars and overthrows and migrations and suchlike. The people who became the Anglish are originally of Norse stock—Anglesland having been previously peopled by Celtish, Saxish, Manksish, Brittonish, and Old Anglish savage tribes. The Anglish tribes welcomed and joined the Norse when they came to their shores, and through marriage became one people. With the might of Norseland behind them, they overthrew the other savage tribes. This we know from nonfictional accounts, diaries and ledgers, and official announcements and things. But, interestingly, by following the *stories* that people told and the figures that were in them, we can see the transformation of the nature and purpose and actions of various gods and heroes from time to time and place to place."

He turned to write on the chalkboard, narrating as he went.

"Imagine the following four people: An illiterate serfbound farmer in Norseland a thousand years ago. A moderately educated merchant in Anglesland a hundred years ago. A modern scholar in Tyskland last week. A student of erelore sitting in a class in Lindmarden today."

He turned back to us.

"If you ask each of them about who Fyra is and what she does, what she *means,* do you think you'll get the same answer from all four? No, of course not; you'll get very different answers! Here and now, we most commonly associate Fyra—and her handmaidens the Valkyrja, who we often regard as inseparable from her—with valor, honor, and bravery. Fyra means victory in battle and protection of the family, the clan, the hearth. But Fyra has many other associations in eretide. She is and has been the goddess of love, of beauty, of fertility, of sexual congress and childbearing, of war, of gold, of light, of fire, and of the sun. So why is it that the lore of Anglesland focuses on Fyra's prowess in battle? It is because for the people of Anglesland, the understanding of Fyra is colored by the understanding of the Celtish goddess Mor Rigan, a goddess of battle and death, the implacable reaper who comes for all mortals in the end. In Anglesland, the Anglish tribes' overthrow brought Norse ideas about Fyra, but the people who'd been overthrown turned those ideas over in minds that already knew of Mor Rigan, and the two became understood as one."

He reached to the top of the blackboard and pulled down a rolled-up map that was just like the one he'd laid out on the library table for Theod and me last year. With his long stick, he pointed to Vaskosland, just east of the center of the map.

"The Vaskosish gods seem to strike a middle balance between Ellanic ones"—he gestured toward Ellasland, which was between Vaskosland and Turksland—"and Anglish ones." He gestured broadly to Anglesland. "Vaskosish lore even includes some gods and heroes from Aprikish lore, and for good reason; note its proximity to Farth, Widnes, and Coptland. Coptland especially, because it was home to a great civilization in fargone eretide—the Kemet. Vaskosland sits in the middle of the civilized world, guarding the mouth of the midland sea. It is thus subject to the comings and goings of all seafaring explorers and traders from every land on the banks of the north sea *and* the midland. The city-nation of Barthelonia"—he pointed to a particular spot on Vaskosland, the stick making a sharp sound against the taut paper—"is by most estimations the richest city in the world, because it is the center of so many trade networks. All of these lands have very long sagas of erelore, whereas the erelore of the new world—North and South Markesland—is only quite recent, the lands having been found by Thorvald Eiriksson in the year 1574."

I couldn't keep in my exasperated sigh at the assertion that erelore didn't start here until 1574, when my people had been here living lives and telling stories since the beginning of time. If Professor Ibarra noticed, he made no indication.

"The ways that Ellanic, Vaskosish, Anglish, and Norse gods are so often mirrors of one another by different names points to some deeper truth about the nature of gods and mankind. Are Fyra and Athna the same goddess by different names, or different goddesses entirely? What of the many parallels of Joden and Jupiter? The parallels of Joden to the Celtish god Dagda? All three are said to wander the earth as they fancy, usually in the guise of old men, with the aim of provoking mankind to thought and action. Joden and Dagda each practice a kind of witskraft and are told to have brought forth the very concept of the written word by passing through a series of trials set by elder, more incomprehensible gods."

He paused to roll the map back up, revealing the blackboard once more.

"In this term of study, I'm going to ask you to read each of the assigned texts in great detail—to look closely at the text and pay attention to all the small and crafty ways that the author is trying to communicate the meaning of a story to you, the reader, who may live thousands of miles and hundreds of years away from place and time where the story was born. We will begin with the oldest of stories and move closer and closer to works of the present day, seeing how each story builds upon and reflects those that have come before. Comprehensive literacy is a relatively modern achievement of society, and for most of eretide, only certain classes of person would know how to read. These sages, often priests and witskrafters and very commonly dragoneers, would be expected to carry stories to people who could not read."

Eskil Gerdasson came immediately to mind; that seemed to be what he was about, at least from my limited experience with the man. I was still considering that when Professor Ibarra began calling students by name to come and receive copies of the first two texts we'd be reading for class, *Henrik's Chronicle* and *The Song of Osbeorht*. We were instructed to read both by next Friday's class, and to be prepared for a test and a discussion.

Jadi and Osvald both followed me when the class was dismissed. As soon as we were in the hallway, Jadi turned to me and said, "I've already read *Henrik's Chronicle*; learning the erelore of Anglesland was part of my studies along with the erelore of Poland and Tyskland and Norseland. I've heard of *The Song of Osbeorht* but I've never actually read it."

"I've never read either," I said.

"What *do* you read that's of any merit at all?" Osvald asked, his eyes narrowing a bit. "I read that article about you last year in the *Vastergot Gazette,* and you said that you read pennik novels and *Sybille Stosch,* of all things. Don't you think you're a little old for juvenile serials? What've you read that's actually for adults? That has actual bookcraft and cultural value?"

"I'm not sure that I understand what you're talking about," I said, making an active effort not to suck my teeth at him, because I was reasonably certain that he was insulting me with this line of questioning. "Can you name some examples of works that have bookcraft and cultural value?"

"The sort of things that you're given in primary school, for starters—the edda and the sagas, Ellanic philosophies, the plays of Vilhelm Speerman, *The Tales of Sigur Windtooth,* Arvald's *The Journey East.* One of my favorite modern authors is Rudhoff Rauchmann. Have you read *The Book of the Ancient Wood*?"

"No, I haven't," I said. "What's it about?"

"It's a collection of short stories, mostly beast fables, but really it's about the Norse overthrow of Anglesland and how society proceeded from the Dark Ages."

"I find it absolutely tiresome that I'm evidently supposed to know all about the erelore and folklore of a dozen different nations on the other side of the Great North Sea, but Anglish scholars aren't expected to know the least bit about nackie erelore or folklore! The only works I've seen that mention us at all are Emanuel Nordlund's *The Savage Peoples of North Markesland* and *Eiriksdottir's Leid.* The latter mostly details how many people Fyra Eiriksdottir's crew traded with or killed in battle as they ventured down the Runestung to the deep lakes."

"Well, to be fair, North Markesland doesn't have much erelore," Osvald said with a shrug. "Your people were wholly illiterate before Stafn Whitebeard discovered North Markesland in 1626—"

"We didn't have letters," I interrupted, folding my arms, "but that doesn't mean that we didn't have lore."

"That isn't the point," he huffed.

"What *is* the point, Osvald? What stories do you know about Crow? About Nampeshiwe and Nampeshiwe's Mother? What stories can you tell me about the hero Requeiska and his dragon, Nonoma? Do you know anything about Sequannit and Masquasup? About pukwadjisuk and nigummisuk?"

"No," Osvald said, frowning.

"Maybe you *ought* to, if I'm supposed to know all about Anglish lore. My people have been here since the beginning of time, and our lore is just as old and deep as yours. You're the newcomers here. I'm going to go visit Kasaqua at the dragonhall, and I think I'd prefer to do it alone. I'll see you at luncheon, I suppose."

"Can I come with you?" Jadi asked. "I want to hear more about nackie lore!"

"I'm not really in the mood," I said. "Ask again later."

Jadi nodded, and prevented Osvald from following me as I left, which I was exceedingly glad of.

SHE ATTENDED LIBERTY'S SALON

Friday afternoon's natural philosophy class was pleasant and engaging, though not particularly different from what I'd learned in the subject last year. I woke very early on Saturday morning, because I wanted to make sure Kasaqua got a decent run before breakfast; I'd be leaving her for several hours to attend Liberty's salon. Niquiat's reply to the telegram I'd sent him on Wednesday had been:

TO: ANEQUS
FROM: NIQUIAT

KEEP KASAQUA SAFE AT SCHOOL. MEET YOU SUNDAY NOON ON SCHOOL GROUNDS.

I had to presume that he'd explain in detail tomorrow; telegrams were paid for by the word. Apart from safety concerns, it was simply impractical to bring Kasaqua on the train and into the bustling city streets. A dragon always garnered attention, and a grown one much more than a hatchling.

Luckily, Kasaqua was growing accustomed to being stabled for long stretches of time. She didn't like it much, but her stall was comfortable and well-appointed, even if it was boring.

Breakfast was a quick and quiet affair; I ate alone. I'd slept alone, too; both of my roommates had departed yesterday afternoon. Marta had been collected by automotor to spend the weekend at home and hopefully have a meaningful conversation with her father. Jadi, as it turned out, had plans *every* Saturday with her cousins in the city. She wasn't terribly forthcoming as to what those plans were, and I hadn't wanted to pry. She'd very briefly introduced me to Herr and Frau Geller on Friday afternoon; I wasn't entirely clear on how she was related to them, because she just referred to them as "cousins." She'd left on the train with them.

It was just shy of seven-thirty in the morning when I met Liberty at the train station, and the train was due to arrive at seven forty-five. On Saturdays, it came through about once an hour. Liberty was wearing a smart day dress of brown-and-ginger-colored gingham. I was wearing the dress she'd made for me.

"I was afraid you weren't going to make it," she said, smiling as I joined her on the bench. "Something always seemed to come up for you on the first Saturday of the month last year."

"And I can't be sure that the same won't be true of every other month this year," I said ruefully. "But I'm here today!"

"I'm terribly glad that you are, because I *might* have let slip to Jenni that you were interested in coming, and she might have mentioned it to one or two people who've been following your story in the newspapers. There might be people there who will be excited to meet you."

"I'm not sure that bodes well," I said, a little hiccup of laughter escaping my throat. "People who are very excited to meet me without knowing anything about me have not, in my experience over the last year, been friendly or polite. Did I tell you about my tea party with Professor Tindra Brahe last year?"

"You did!" Liberty replied. "But I can vouch for these particular people. Everyone at the salon is a former resident of the Society for Friendless Girls."

"When I first met Theod, he was terribly standoffish, because he expected that I'd previously read about him in the newspaper. I didn't understand then, but I do now. People have all sorts of ideas and expectations about what The Nackie Dragoneer must be like."

"I'll bet," Liberty said, looking thoughtful. "But anyway, how's your first week been?"

"Well, I've got a free period on Monday and Wednesday afternoons this year, so that's a novelty—"

We continued talking about happenings at the school among the students and the staff as the train arrived and we boarded. We took the train right through the city center and into the mill district in the northwestern part of the city. It was the same train stop we'd gotten off at to visit Miss Jenni's shop, but that wasn't the direction we took. The streets here were all very narrow, most of the buildings three and four stories tall, with shops on the ground level, residences above.

Liberty led me expertly through the streets to a storefront with frosted glass windows. The sign above the door had red lettering on black, and read *Mendoza's Teas*. The sign on the door itself, with black text on white, read *Closed for Private Function, Invitation Only. Open to Public at Noon.*

Liberty had no hesitation at all in rapping on the door, and a voice from inside called, "Who's calling?"

"Liberty Braun and one guest," Liberty answered.

It occurred to me with a moment of shock that I hadn't been aware of Liberty's surname until this very moment. I hadn't known that she *had* one, and hadn't thought to ask, because Anglish people almost always introduced themselves by their first and last names, and Liberty hadn't. I lacked an Anglish surname—we didn't use them, among my people—and they'd assigned me one to facilitate that. Had Liberty's surname been assigned the same way? I'd have to ask her about it, later.

The door opened just a bit, revealing a man's face. Like Liberty, he was Blackfolkish. He looked at us appraisingly, then closed the door again. I heard the sound of a chain bolt being undone, and he opened the door and allowed us inside. I couldn't help but note that he was a very imposing man—over six feet tall and possessed of the kind of shoulders I associated with rowers.

It was something of a comfort, knowing that a very imposing man was sitting at the door, deciding who could and couldn't enter.

"Good morning, Miss Liberty," he said in a broad Vaskosish accent, closing the door behind us. "Who's your friend? Everybody's upstairs already. You're almost late."

"And you're almost polite," Liberty chided. "This is Miss Anequs, from the academy. Anequs, this is Jokin; he's Alazne's husband. They own this shop."

"A pleasure to meet you," I said, dipping my head politely, then letting my gaze sweep the room. There were a number of tables surrounded by chairs filling most of the space, and along one wall was a bar with a cash register. Behind the bar was a case filled top to bottom with glass jars. Liberty wasted no time in leading me across the room, to the door at the back, which opened to reveal a narrow staircase. I followed her up.

We arrived at a plain, serviceable room, where eight women were seated in folding chairs that had been arranged in a loose circle. I recognized Miss Jenni, but no one else. Everyone seemed to be Blackfolkish in whole or in part; one woman might have been partly nackie. The woman who rose from her seat as we entered was . . . eye-catching. She was an extremely beautiful woman of about fifty, plump and generously appointed, wearing the kind of day dress that Marta wore—rose-pink satin with many delicate lacy details and tiered ruffles. Her hair, pulled back in a complex array of braids, was dressed with a pair of feathered hairpins set with pearls. She had rows of pearls at her throat, as well, striking against the darkness of her skin. She looked elegant, poised, and self-possessed.

"Liberty!" she cooed as we entered, "I'm so glad that you were finally able to bring your friend! Come, come sit. You *must* introduce everyone, and you *must* begin with me."

The woman indicated a pair of vacant chairs to her left, and we took our seats. Liberty said, "Everyone, this is Miss Anequs of Masquapaug—which is the more proper name for Mask Island. Anequs, may I introduce Frau Tximeleta Azeria, who goes most often by Xixi. She's the founding member of our salon, and has done the most, financially speaking, for girls of the Society. We each owe her a great deal."

"A pleasure to meet you, ma'am," I said, nodding deference.

"The pleasure is all mine, I'm sure," she replied with a warm smile. There was a certain musical quality to her voice—not an accent, exactly, but something I didn't have a name for. "Miss Liberty has spoken of you with great esteem—particularly of the fact that you gifted her a *sewing machine*."

I felt myself flush under the praise, and looked down at my hands, folded in my lap. "My brother's part of a tinker's co-op in the cannery district," I said, by way of explanation. "He helped me repair it."

"You seem like a *very* useful person to know," Frau Xixi purred. "A dragoneer with a tinker brother."

Liberty cleared her throat, then said, "As to the rest of the introductions—you've met Miss Jenni already, at her shop. Moving left around the circle, we have Frau Alazne Mendoza; you met her husband downstairs. Beside her, Miss Kate Thyresdottir, who teaches reading at The Free People's School. Miss Martha Kirk, who works as a cook for a family uptown. Miss Annamari Haksel, a midwife. Miss Leine Braun, who does loomwork in a cotton mill. Miss Keira Braun, a maid of all work. Miss Sigune Braun, a merchant."

"We're none of us related, mind," Keira said. "Braun is just the surname given by the folkreckoners to any Black person who arrives in Lindmarden without one. Most of us here either came from Berri Vaskos directly or are the children of parents who did. Enthralled people in Berri Vaskos don't have surnames of their own."

"Not unless we take them for ourselves, at any rate," Frau Xixi mused. "I decided to be Tximeleta Azeria when I arrived here, and no one stopped me."

"I married into being a Mendoza," Frau Mendoza confessed. "Jokin brought the name with him."

"The Anglish are *very* fixated on surnames," I said, thoughtfully. "We don't use surnames at all, on the islands. Everyone knows everyone else, and any confusion is cleared up by mentioning one's relations. I'd be formally presented, for example, as Anequs, daughter of Chagoma and Aponakwe."

"Oh, that's terribly interesting!" Keira said, a note of longing in her voice. "I think that my father might have been one of your sort—a nackie, I mean—but I was sadly never able to know him. I'd lost both my parents by the time I was six, and was brought up almost entirely by the Society."

"I'm sorry for your loss," I said.

"Well, now that we're all here, shall we move on to business?" Frau Xixi said briskly, which had the effect of putting everyone in the room to attention. "I'll be taking on two more of-age girls in the next few months, and things have finally been squared away with poor little Sanna; I've got her studying under our cook, for now. That's about done me for the rest of the year, though, unless unexpected money comes in."

Liberty leaned close to me and explained, quietly, "Sanna's only twelve years old, and was posted as a maid in a great house.

She ran away from her posting because she was being mistreated. She turned up on Xixi's doorstep a couple of weeks ago; Xixi settled with the Society for three thousand marka to keep the matter from being brought to the moot. If Xixi hadn't stepped in, Sanna would have been caught out by the thanegards eventually and either turned back in to the custody of the Society or outright imprisoned. Xixi generally doesn't take on girls until they're at least sixteen."

I nodded, wondering just what profession Frau Xixi was in but not wanting to interrupt the discussion.

Frau Xixi, evidently noticing that Liberty was whispering to me, looked directly at me and asked, "Miss Anequs, if I might be so bold, what is your people's position on thralldom and indenture?"

"We don't practice such things on the islands," I said. "My great-uncle, my grandmother's brother, was made a debt-thrall and served for ten years aboard an Anglish merchant ship. He died still in debt."

"Then you'll understand better than most the terrible danger of falling into debt," Frau Xixi said gravely. "Thrand's Charter forbids the kind of life-debt thralldom commonly practiced in Berri Vaskos; people can be indentured, but they must be able to buy their freedom through work or go free after a certain number of years as dictated by their contract. In Berri Vaskos, there are no such protections. People can be bought and sold like cattle, and often are."

I brought my hands to my face, covering my mouth at the plain horror of that.

Frau Xixi continued, "My mother, may her soul rest well, was brought to Berri Vaskos from Vaskosland to work on a cotton farm. She was *owned,* body and soul, by the Vaskosish family who owned the farm. Because I was born her daughter, so was I. I was thirteen when my mother died, and I had nothing else holding me back, so I fled north and crossed the Polvaara during the war years. I don't remember exactly how I came into the keeping of the Society for Friendless Girls; I was young and confused and didn't speak a word of Anglish, and there were a precious lot of us fleeing Berri Vaskos. I was put onto a boat, and onto a train, and eventually delivered here to Vastergot and told that I owed the Society two thousand five hundred marka for the trouble of my keeping and passage. I spent five years working in a cotton mill to pay that debt. Practically all of the cotton that flows through the mills here in Lindmarden was grown and picked by enthralled people in Berri Vaskos, and you can be sure that *they'll* never see a pennik of the profit for their efforts."

I glanced down at the dress I was wearing, Liberty's gift. I had repaired a broken sewing machine and given it to Liberty, and she had used it to make me a dress, and it was a lovely dress that I was terribly glad to have. But I'd never given a thought to where the cloth and thread had come from. It had never occurred to me to think where calico *came* from—it came from shops! Machine-loomed cloth was smooth and long-wearing and so very easily gotten . . . and I'd never even for a moment considered cotton as a plant—something that someone had to grow and harvest. I ought to have. It was monstrous that I hadn't. I didn't even know what a cotton plant looked like, alive. Before the Anglish had come, my people had worn cloth-of-cattail, and cloth-of-nettle, and cloth-of-dogbane, and all manner of pelts and leathers. I had clothes like that; my dancing dress, and my sealskin cape, my raccoon-pelt muffler. They felt different than my calico dresses, holding a sacred import . . . because I knew their whole lore. My dancing dress was made from the skin of deer that my grandfather had hunted. We'd eaten its flesh, and made tools and ornaments from its bones and antlers and sinews, and leather from its skin. We'd *thanked* it.

I'd never thanked a cotton plant, or the person who'd grown it. I knew, abstractly, that calico came from the mill district. That people worked in mills for wages, just like Niquiat worked at the cannery.

What hands had picked the cotton that made my school uniforms?

Why hadn't I ever thought about it before?

I'd made plenty of cordage, as a child, but it was a pastime and a hobby and a craft, not a necessity. It had been a necessity just a few generations ago, when there'd been no shops to go to. When we'd all lived in the oldest ways.

"I can see you thinking," Frau Xixi said. Something about her voice reminded me of Grandma.

"Yes," I said, swallowing hard. "I am."

She smiled and said, "The goal of our salon is to offer comfort and aid to girls who find themselves in the same kinds of difficult circumstances that we have each found ourselves in. To have every girl we assist free and clear of her debt as quickly as possible, and to have her pleasantly situated all the while. Lindmarden prides in declaring itself a nation without poverty, where one will never see beggars on the streets, but that is because the people who might otherwise be begging are ushered away by the thanegards to places like the Society for Friendless Girls. The Society is ostensibly a charitable organization, and certainly they are a preventative against absolute poverty for girls with no one else to turn to—but let us not pretend that indenture is anything less than well-dressed thralldom. They will provide bed, board, and the most cursory of education to girls who've fallen on hard times, but they are less scrupulous than they might be in putting girls to work. They will post children as young as ten to positions in mills that have them scuttling between machines for twelve hours of the day without cease. All of the misses Braun are still paying their debts—contracts bought from the Society by proud citizens of Lindmarden like Elsie Brinkerhoff, who think that they are doing great and good things by offering positions. Do you understand, Miss Anequs? Our salon exists to try and ease the way for girls who are still *trapped*."

"Yes," I said, hesitantly. "I think I understand."

"I'll admit to somewhat ulterior motives for having invited you here, on Liberty's recommendation," Frau Xixi confessed. "For the last twenty years, Kuiper's Academy has routinely taken on girls from the Society, and it's a quite serviceable posting with few complaints. But we're always looking for new opportunities for placements, both for girls still under indenture and those who've worked through their debts. It's a very particular sort of girl who's interested in the work *my* girls do, after all; I will not allow anyone in my charge to be *pressed* into it the way we're so often pressed into cooking and cleaning and sewing and weaving and all that. My question for you, Miss Anequs, is whether or not your people might be amenable to providing positions—taking on apprentices for crafts and trades. If they might be, I hope that you'll be able to make introductions to the sort of people who could work on arranging such things."

"We don't deal much in coin on the islands, I'm afraid," I said. "But I don't know if that's entirely true of mainlanders. I could send a letter to the Confederation of the First People of Akashnet, making an introduction, though."

"That would be exceedingly helpful," Frau Xixi said. "And your brother's tinker co-op, is it accepting new members? I know that there are girls currently under the Society's care who'd be terribly interested in studying that sort of thing, and our salon might be able to help with dues—"

"Oh, certainly, I'll ask him! He's going to be visiting me tomorrow."

"That would be most excellent," Frau Xixi purred. "Now, has anyone got new business?"

The meeting proceeded for another hour, very efficient and congenial, everyone talking about the ups and downs of their work situations while Frau Xixi made notes in a little booklet. Liberty was due back at the Academy for one in the afternoon—her free period each Saturday was only six hours long—so we bid our goodbyes at the end of the meeting and got back on the train. It wasn't until we'd gotten off at the school's station and were walking back—when I was sure that Liberty and I were wholly alone and unlikely to be overheard by anyone—that I asked her, "What business is it that Frau Xixi in? She said that she's taking on two new girls this year, and you said that she typically only takes girls who are sixteen or older—"

"She's the matron of a house of pleasure," Liberty said plainly. "It's by far the best-paying sort of position that a Blackfolkish girl in a Friendless sort of situation might find, for those with the right temperament. Girls who choose that path can pay their debts off very quickly, spend a few years at it amassing a modest fortune to live off, then either retire to other work or become situated as companions for the kind of wealthy gentlemen who keep companions. It's not a path I'd have chosen, because I've no interest of that kind in men *at all,* but I can understand the draw."

I made a noncommittal noise, feeling my cheeks color at the thought. Of course I'd been aware, peripherally, that such things occurred; it came up sometimes in adventure and mystery novels. I'd never met anyone connected with the trade, though.

"You said at the meeting that your brother's visiting you tomorrow," Liberty said, changing the subject. "Are we still on for mending together in the girls' quarters? Your roommates are both away, aren't they?"

"Oh, Niquiat's not coming until noon, he said," I replied. "Yes, Jadi and Marta are both away now, but I'm not sure when Jadi's coming back; she didn't say if she meant to come back today or tomorrow, or at what time. I don't think that Jadi will be any sort of obstacle, anyway; she seems to have a different idea of what 'proper' is than Marta does. I mean . . . you met her, the other day. So we can still spend some time together in the morning, whether she's back or not. If you've the time just now, though, I'd like to arrange for you and I and Theod to all meet and talk. If you're game."

"I'm game," Liberty said, with a smile that made something inside me flutter.

"Excellent," I said, clearing my throat. "You don't have duties for another hour or so, right?"

"I don't, but I'd been hoping to get a bite to eat before it's my turn in the laundry."

"Would you like to come to the dragonhall with me to visit Kasaqua? I have a feeling that Theod might be there, and I'd really like all of us to talk together. Somewhere we won't be overheard. The trails, maybe."

Liberty gave me a sly sort of sidelong look, but smiled. "Should we be worried about being seen in one another's company at the dragonhall?" she asked. "I'll admit that I've actually very little experience with it; maids have little reason to ever go there."

"It's not likely to start untoward rumors, I don't think," I said thoughtfully. "Theod's friends with a lot of the lads who work there, and with Hallmaster Henkjan. Also it's not particularly close to a meal time or class, so I don't know if anyone will be about much."

"I'll trust your judgment," Liberty said. "But if anyone asks, I'm telling them that I asked to see your dragon because she's a rare breed. Lead the way."

THREE YOUNG PEOPLE SPOKE FRANKLY ON A COMPLICATED MATTER

Theod *was* at the dragonhall, as I'd expected; it was his most usual place any time he wasn't in class. Something like a quarter of stalls were empty, other students having taken their dragons elsewhere with them for the weekend, and the dragonhall was largely quiet. When we found Theod, he was seated on the floor of Copper's stall, utilizing Copper's bulk as a convenient sofa, his face very studious and frustrated as he stared at the book in his hands. He clambered to his feet as we approached, tucking the book away. Copper made a complaining noise, stretching and standing up with a glare of superlative annoyance.

"Anequs! Hello, I . . . uh . . . yes . . . I mean . . . can I help you ladies with anything?" he stammered, looking from Liberty to me and back with mild panic in his eyes. I bit my lip, resolute in my refusal to laugh. It really wasn't charitable at all to find his discomfort, his *seriousness,* amusing. If I told him that it was endearing and adorable, he'd probably huff about it.

"Mister Theod Knecht, please allow me to introduce Miss Liberty Braun. Liberty, this is Theod. I'm going to take Kasaqua for a walk along the trails, and Liberty is going to join me. I was wondering if you and Copper would like to come."

He closed his eyes and took a breath, and when he opened his eyes again, his face was the well-practiced, utterly serene blank that he could so suddenly affect. Copper nudged Theod's hip with his muzzle, making a noise of concern. From halfway across the hall, Kasaqua made an impatient noise of interest; she knew that I was here and wanted out.

"Tack?" Theod asked, glancing at Copper's tack hanging on the wall.

"Hadn't planned on it," I said. "We're walking, not riding."

Theod nodded, setting his jaw and swallowing.

"Yes," he said after a long moment. "I'd be delighted to join you."

He did not sound delighted.

Still, the span of five minutes saw me collecting Kasaqua and the lot of us heading out from the dragonhall, into the winding paths through the woods beyond.

The stretch of woods behind the flight field was roughly triangular—I knew because there was a framed map of the school and its grounds, as viewed from dragonback, in the library. Its far border was a stream that flowed from northwest to southeast, where it joined the river. There was farmland on the other side. The western border was the flight field and its flight course, and the southern border was defined by the train tracks. There were miles of winding paths all through the woods, some of them rocky and complicated. We took one of the least challenging ones, which I knew led to a small pond with a stretch of meadow. Kasaqua was very eager to play in the pond as soon as she realized the direction we were taking, running ahead and doubling back, goading Copper to chase her. None of us said much of anything until we were well out of earshot of the school, and I was the one to break the awkward silence.

"So . . . I'd like to love both of you," I said. "And I'd like all three of us to talk about that like sensible adults."

Theod flushed and coughed into his fist, half choking on his composure. Liberty was, as I'd expected, a bit more sensible. She surveilled the meadow and the pond, selecting a sunny spot on the bank to sit down, arranging her skirt expertly as she did so. I joined her, and Theod joined the two of us half a moment later.

"I've long come to terms with the fact that any woman I love is likely to have a husband," Liberty said, with diplomatic air. "It greatly reduces suspicion among society for at least one of a pair of women to be married. The two of you seem quite well suited—you're of the same social class, and of the same race, and of different sexes—which are the greatest requirements for good matches, according to society's rules."

"I don't care at all about Anglish society's rules," I said, frowning.

"I think you'll find that they care very much about *you,* though," Liberty said, sounding almost stern. "Being the only nackie dragoneers is going to keep the public eye on both of you for the rest of your lives, whether you like it or not. You are figures of public note. You've told me that love is much more free among your people—plural marriages, attachments between people of the same sex, all that kind of thing—but Anequs, you and I will *never* be able to have a marriage. The Ministry of Dragon Affairs would deem it immoral, and they'd take your dragon from you."

I looked to Kasaqua, who was already wading knee-deep in the water, stretching her wings out in the sunshine. She seemed to catch my pang of concern, glancing over her shoulder at me curiously. It was abominable that the Anglish should have the power, the *right,* to declare me an unfit companion to her for any reason at all, much less a reason so foolish as loving two people at once. Or for loving a woman.

"If the three of us built a household together, on Masquapaug—" I began, stubbornly, only for Liberty to interrupt.

"No. I want my *own* house. I've spent my entire life to this point with no place to call my own, no place to be alone with my thoughts. I want what Miss Jenni has—a flat above a shop that's mine and no one else's. I've thought quite a lot about this, since you mentioned that I'd be welcome on your island. You two can very easily have a perfectly respectable marriage—and probably ought to declare your intent to sooner rather than later. There's been speculation on the subject among the maids, ever since the Valkyrjafax ball last year, and I shouldn't have to tell you that there are people beyond the school speculating as well."

"You and Theod have both jumped immediately to marriage at the first mention of love!" I said, folding my arms. "I am sixteen years old, and you two are seventeen. Isn't that a bit young to be considering marriage?"

"Your cousin married at nineteen," Theod pointed out.

"That's old enough! Sixteen isn't," I insisted. "Besides, Mishona and Ashaquiat have been courting for years, and there's a child on the way."

"You didn't tell me about your cousin getting married, or about a child," Liberty said disapprovingly.

"I've barely been able to *find* you all week!" I countered. "There's been quite a lot going on, in case you hadn't noticed."

"There's always a lot of work to be done when the students first arrive, and I've barely been able to get five minutes to myself each day, so I'll apologize for not being readily available to you," Liberty countered, sounding not at all apologetic. "In any case, if I've understood in passing, your older cousin has recently gotten married and there's already a child on the way?"

"Yes," I replied. "I know I've talked to you about my cousin Mishona before, the drumsinger."

"You have, yes," Liberty said. "You hadn't mentioned that she was with child, though."

"She announced it at the wedding, in July, but she'd confided in me beforehand. The baby's expected in December."

"I take it that attitudes toward childbearing outside of marriage are, like many social customs, rather different among your people than they are among the Anglish?" Liberty asked.

"You have *no* idea," Theod said, shaking his head. "Ask her about her aunt Shanuckee sometime."

"I might just," Liberty said. "In any case, however, you ought to know that your cousin's situation would be *terribly* scandalous if society was aware. It's unlawful to engage in carnal congress outside of marriage; it's the sort of thing that leads to moot cases and holmgangs and blood feuds. It happens all the time, of course, but no one will ever admit to it. A young man is often forgiven for indiscretions, especially if he keeps them to women outside of society—"

"Like Frau Xixi's girls?" I ventured.

"Precisely. It's considered ill-mannered, and a young man might gain a poor reputation as a rake, but he wouldn't have much trouble in going on to a respectable marriage and a family and all. A young woman is never, *ever* forgiven if her reputation is damaged. If a young lady of Miss Hagan's social circle were to fall into a delicate condition without first being married, she would be forever ruined. A rush job of a wedding might save her, but otherwise? Her whole family would be shamed, cut from society, and never invited to any social occasion ever again. It would likely prevent any of her sisters from making suitable matches. She'd be disowned, or sent away to live with some distant relative in the countryside."

"I don't understand how the Anglish can be so awfully unfeeling," I said, shaking my head. "A child is a blessing in any circumstance at all."

"Well, you've told me that property passes from mother to daughter among your people," Liberty said, "so a woman might well be able to support herself and her child independently, if the child's father abandoned them. Given that Anglish property passes from father to son, a woman is most often dependent on her husband for support. In any case, you'd do well to formally announce your engagement and put to rest any speculation."

"This seems ridiculous, to me," I said, sighing through my nose. "Why should anyone outside of our families care at all about how we choose to conduct ourselves in personal matters?"

"I don't know if either of you pay attention to sensational papers, but they pay attention to you—to all dragoneers, really, and anyone of sufficient import and connection in society. There's word of an alliance forming between the Stafns and the Sørensens, for example—"

"Marta's friends mentioned that, back at her garden party in June," Theod said. "Ivar asked for Dagny Sørensen's hand?"

"Well, that's what the gossip columns have been saying," Liberty confirmed, "though no formal engagement has been announced in any of the major papers. Both of them are eighteen this year, I believe? They might be putting off a formal engagement until Mister Stafn completes his education. Until an engagement is formally declared, others are free to press their suit. Dagny Sørensen is a highly sought match, and I'm sure she quite enjoys leading on a whole flock of hopeful young suitors, but she'll have to choose one eventually. And there are obviously other young women who would wish to be pursued by Mister Stafn—"

"Obviously?" I asked, pulling a face. Ivar and Dagny were both thoroughly awful people, in my limited experience, and I couldn't imagine either of them being the object of anyone's affections.

"So I'll presume that you do *not* read sensational papers, then," Liberty said with a long-suffering sigh. "You two have been mentioned in certain columns, I assure you. The wisest course of action, should you wish to avoid that as much as possible, is to be as uninteresting as you can manage. People adore stories of scandal and ruin. Companionate engagements between well-matched parties make for poor gossip. Theod did a very good job of falling out of the news quickly, a couple of years ago."

"I was never aware that he'd been in the news at all, before I paired with Kasaqua," I said.

"That speaks more to the remoteness of Masquapaug than anything else," Theod said. "There were dozens of articles about the whole proceeding, when it was happening, and much speculation about my parentage and how I'd managed to connive my way into being chosen, whether Copper's breed had anything to do with it, and what ought to be done about me. You read Thane Stafn's editorial—he called the fact that Copper was allowed to bond with me a miscarriage of justice. It wasn't an uncommon sentiment, at the time. I was and still am exceedingly grateful to Frau Kuiper for her intervention in the matter. I made every effort to avoid further scandal—to do as I was told, to speak as little as possible to anyone at all, and to be forgotten."

I turned to Theod then, taking his hands in mine. Everyone had been so abominably *awful* to him when he'd done nothing wrong.

"I don't begin to understand why anyone, anywhere would care about the private lives of absolute strangers," I said.

"They don't have enough real obstacles in their lives," Liberty said. "The idle wives of rich men, in particular, make a lifework of vying for social position and renown. Anything that casts someone else down elevates them. So any romantic attachment that you and I form will have to be secret, at least from society. You and Theod will marry, with all the official announcements associated with a society wedding. You'll have to ask someone else how that sort of thing is managed; I'm sure Miss Hagan knows. I will have a modest dressmaker's shop on Masquapaug, with my own flat above, and we can visit frequently because that's what good friends do. No one will ever be given any reason to think that anything untoward is going on between us. Even if *you're* willing to heroically risk the ire of society for your principals, *I am not.*"

Theod loosed an enormous sigh at that and said, "*Thank you,*

Miss Braun. I've been thinking that, but haven't been able to put it into words—not even to myself." He turned to me, still holding my hands in his. "Anequs, I love you. I will go on loving you, no matter who else you love." He turned his gaze to Liberty and said, "Miss Braun, I do not consider you a rival, and bear you no ill will. I think that we're both in love with a wildly reckless hero, and that we ought to be joining forces to make her see reason."

"That seems agreeable to me, Mister Knecht," Liberty said, dipping a mocking curtsy. "I am not a great reader of novels, I'm afraid, so if there's some script about the appropriate way to declare love and propose partnership, I don't know it."

"I don't read novels either, generally," Theod confessed. "I've had a few passages read aloud to me, in the servant's quarters, but the housekeeper of the Mahler household disapproved of silly or frivolous writing. It was her opinion that we should only expose ourselves to 'improving lore,' which included the leids and sagas, Sudkalter's sermons, and relevant stories reported by newspapers that she considered reputable."

"Oh, Sudkalter's sermons are *so* tedious!" Liberty replied with a bark of laughter. "When I was living at the Society of Friendless Girls, the house matron would insist on reading a different one each night before bedtime!"

"That's worse," Theod said, pulling a face. "I'm so sorry."

Liberty giggled at that, and I felt a bit lost; I'd never heard of Sudkalter's sermons. Still, this introduction seemed to be going well. Liberty and Theod had things in common; that was good.

"Now that we're all of an agreement as to how to proceed, I really must get back—I'll barely have time to eat before taking up my afternoon duties," Liberty said. "We shouldn't be seen arriving together, I don't think; it might invite speculation. You'd do well to arrive separately, too, if you don't want to start rumors regarding possible impropriety. I'll see you tomorrow?"

"Tomorrow," I confirmed, nodding. "May I kiss you goodbye?"

Liberty offered a sly smile, but shook her head. "Not today," she said. "But sometime soon, yes."

I sighed wistfully, watching her go. I felt vaguely dizzy with elation, accomplished and hopeful that this, at least, might work happily for all three of us.

NIQUIAT CAME TO VISIT, WITH NEWS OF THE CITY

Jadi returned on Sunday morning, while Liberty and I were talking over mending. I explained Liberty's weekly visits, and Jadi didn't seem at all discomforted by the idea of spending time in friendly conversation with servants. She shared stories of a lovely visit with the Geller household. She explained, at last, that she had gone for something called "shabbat" at a Zhidish temple. Her people had their own neighborhood in the city, south of the cannery district, directly neighboring the Kindah quarter. From the way she described it, shabbat seemed to be something between a community meeting and a sacred ritual. Mostly she confided about how good it had felt to be among people of her own sort, even if they were distant relations that she didn't know well—to have songs, and games, and food, and conversation in her own language. That, at least, I could relate to quite well.

She'd been formally introduced to a number of people of her own age, as well, which had pleased her. The three of us conversed until luncheon, when I excused myself to go meet Niquiat at the station. Jadi and Liberty continued the conversation, which pleased me in a way I couldn't really put words to—that Jadi was willing to be friendly with Liberty, more than simply tolerating her out of politeness. That Liberty wasn't so concerned about getting in trouble because of it, the way she'd been last year.

I'd last seen Niquiat the second week of August, when he and Zhina had come to Masquapaug with newspapers and dispatches from Vastergot. Now it was the second week of September, and I had remarkably little idea of how things were in the city at large. I'd been in the city yesterday, but only on the train and at the salon, not about on the street.

My first impression of Niquiat, as he got off the train, was one of exhaustion. He seemed so *tired*.

"Hello, Chipmunk," he said, joining me on the platform and pulling me into a hug. He smelled like the cannery—more so than usual—and I had to wonder when he'd last laundered his clothes. Kasaqua, who'd been lying at my feet, got up and stretched and moved to sniff at him. He reached to pet her, and she ducked away, eyeing him with suspicion. He smelled *bad*.

"You don't look well," I said, standing back and looking him up and down.

"You're supposed to say 'hello' before you tell me how awful I look," he chided, offering a thin smile. "My landlord raised the rent, and I've been working double time to keep up. I *know* I can't keep on this way, before you say anything; I'm already looking for another building. There are even fewer places that'll rent to nackies now than there were before, and it's hard to spend time looking when I've got to spend so much time earning money. Rokiskwe left last week, no word of where he's gone, and I do not like the man who's renting the bed now. Come on, let's get off the platform and find someplace where we can sit down."

We ended up sitting in the shade at the trailhead behind the dragonhall, because it was reasonably out of the way without having to walk very far. Niquiat didn't seem up to walking very far. He seemed like he needed a good meal and a long nap.

"How've you been at school?" he asked, once we were situated. Kasaqua elected to lay down half a dozen yards away, where she could still see us without actually being in the shade.

"I'm doing well, all things considered. I have a free period every Monday and Wednesday afternoon for the autumn session. And I haven't been called to stand and be lectured at in Frau Kuiper's office even once yet."

"Well, that's something of an accomplishment, I suppose," he said with a chuckle. "You're only a week in, though. Plenty of time to accidentally upset someone, I'm sure."

"Professor Ezel's gone, and the new skiltakraft professor seems far more sensible about instruction," I said, considering. "Oh, and I've been pulled into a secret society of self-styled intellectuals. Marta and Sander both think it's an excellent social opportunity."

"Having rich and well-connected Anglish people on our side can't be anything but a good thing," Niquiat said. "They listen to each other more than they'll ever listen to nackies."

"Why did you tell me, in your telegram, to keep Kasaqua safe at school?" I asked.

"Because there are parts of the city where people might try to hurt her or you or both, if they identified you. You and Theod are in the news again, lately—now that the academy's back in session, I mean." He sighed, sounding weary. "There've been editorials and opinion columns and such—sorry I didn't bring any copies, but I'm strapped for coin. Your school's getting harsh criticism from the high-and-mighties who pulled their sons out and sent them to other posh schools farther off. Thirteen 'promising young dragoneers,' according to the papers, from 'the most established and influential families in the city.'"

"Marta says that the Grams and the Wilders are in that

category—old, established families. I hadn't worked out exactly how many students it was that withdrew, but I haven't been trying to do the scoring, either," I said. "I know we've got ninety-seven students this year, and thirty of them are first-years."

"I wouldn't know; I'm just going by what the papers and the general gossip on the street say. Germund Sørensen, Mathias Lindgren, and Thane Stafn have each written editorials in the *Vastergot Weekly Review* about why they've withdrawn their sons from Kuiper's. There've been articles about what it means for the academy to lose their support, and what that means for Varmarden Thede and Vastergot at large. Apart from your school, Varmarden's all farms and estates. Most of the rich folks have their old family estates in Varmarden or Estervall."

"How old and established can they possibly be if there were no Anglish people at all here before 1626?" I pointed out.

"Old enough by their own reckoning," Niquiat said with a shrug. "Or maybe just rich enough in Anglish coin."

"I'm going to have to study maplore about this, aren't I," I said, not at all enthused about the idea.

"Probably," Niquiat agreed. "The thanes are fighting amongst themselves along party lines. Svend Jespersen, the thane that the jarl replaced at the thynge in August? He's been writing essays, too. The new thane, Lingstadt, is in the Freemansthede—which is the same party the jarl's in. Jespersen was in the Eiriksthede, and his torgar for the islands was a Raven, and he mostly agreed with the Ravens' political aims. Of the five thanes, Authunsson, Lindgren, and Lingstadt are all Freeman. Jorborg Eidsson's in the Eiriksthede, and only Stafn's in the Ravens of Joden. The Ravens are *really* angry about it, accusing Jarl Joervarsson of interference, demanding an althynge for the landowners to vote for thanes. Jespersen's the third thane that's been replaced by torgar votes instead of landowner votes."

"There's supposed to be an althynge in 1845, isn't there?" I asked. "And we'll actually have votes in it this time, through the sachems?"

"There's ways to rally an althynge outside of schedule, I think, and that's what the Ravens of Joden are campaigning for. I don't know how most of it works. Sveni Audulfsson's been giving speeches in the Thane's Free Gardens, I've heard, but I haven't been to any of them. Valbrand Joervarsson—who's apparently the jarl's brother? He's been seen at the speeches, supporting Audulfsson, and there's a lot of gossip about that."

"I went with Liberty to her salon in the mill district, yesterday, but we didn't spend any appreciable time on the street. No one tried to talk to us, apart from the people we'd gone to meet."

"Don't know anything about the mill district, I'm afraid," Niquiat said with a shrug.

"I spent some time with Liberty today, too, catching up on this and that," I continued. "Her salon's all made up of girls who are or used to be in the Vastergot Society for Friendless Girls. They wanted to know if your tinker co-op is accepting new members."

"I don't know how much longer the co-op's going to keep operating, to be honest. Jorgen and Strida are talking about moving to Runestung Hold, and if they go, there's no way that Zhina and Ekaitz and me can keep paying the rent on the workshop. I've actually been exchanging letters with Auntie Shanuckee about setting up a shop on her family farmstead. The house where Shanuckee and Father grew up has been standing empty since Shanuckee and her children went to live with Mamisashquee and her husband. There've been arguments with Anglish people from Nack Port about it being 'unimproved land' that no one's living on; the treaty of 1825 has a whole section about where the Anglish are allowed to settle new farmsteads. If I build a business on that land, it counts as 'improvement' under Anglish law, and our family would have a stronger claim against squatters. It'll be years yet before either of Shanuckee's girls are old enough to marry and take up the old farmstead."

"Mother would be happy to have you that much closer," I said. "So would the rest of us."

"Vastergot's getting less safe," Niquiat said. "Zhina said she's game to come with me in a new co-op, if we found one, but her family's probably not going to like that much, because she'll be farther from them. I don't know if there's already any kind of enginekrafter operating out of Nack Port, either—I'll have to find that out."

"Which is easier said than done, now that Nack Port is closed to anyone but the Anglish," I said.

"Exactly. And there's still the problem of shipping in supplies; we wouldn't have ready access to the junkman by the docks. Most of what we have to work with are things that have been thrown away. I don't know that Nack Port has enough people who'd be casting off the kind of junk we can salvage engine parts from."

"You know, once I've got Kasaqua making athers, I might be able to pull in a significant income by selling them to the right sorts of people," I said. "Zhina seemed very interested in having a source of strahlendstone, if I remember correctly, and she can't be the only one. Sander's looking at athermaching as a career, so it must pull in the kind of money that the Anglish consider a good income. Professor Ezel didn't ever do practical work, at least not with first-year students, but I'm reasonably sure that Professor Schreiber is going to have us actually crafting athers this term."

"Money would certainly help," Niquiat said with a bark of laughter. "I won't say no to you funding our venture, should you happen to come into a flush of markas."

"I'll keep you in mind," I said. "Have you eaten luncheon yet? I don't think anyone would complain about you joining me in the dining hall, if you haven't. We might even run into some of my classmates who might like to be introduced to you."

"I won't say no to a free meal," Niquiat said, climbing to his feet. "Does that mean you have to put Kasaqua into a stall or some such, though? I can't imagine they let her inside, as big as she is now."

"She's getting used to it," I said. "And I haven't eaten luncheon yet."

"Well, then," Niquiat said, offering me a hand and pulling me to my feet, "lead the way."

ANEQUS RECEIVED A SADDLE

On Monday morning, I had my directed study of second-year al-jabr with Theod. I slipped up to my room afterward, to write some letters—to Mother, and to the sachem, and to the Confederation of the First People of Akashnet. As I dropped them off in the mail room before luncheon, Frau Brinkerhoff intercepted me to *gently remind me* that the dining hall and its provender was intended for students of the academy, not for guests. So someone had evidently made note of Niquiat joining me for luncheon on Sunday. I assured Frau Brinkerhoff that I didn't intend to make a habit of having my brother visit, and also that I'd been told last term that I was allowed to have guests on school grounds when class was not in session. She made some polite and demure comments about how *of course* it was acceptable to have guests, and my brother was welcome, but that the dining hall was not a public house. There were certain standards of decorum to be maintained, and I ought to consider the impression that my actions made on others.

I told her that I would consider more carefully in the future.

Marta returned from her visit home sometime in the middle of the morning, joining us for luncheon. I arrived somewhat late, owing to my conversation with Frau Brinkerhoff. The table that I'd come to consider "ours"—the one that I'd shared with Marta and Sander and Theod last year—had become a somewhat crowded affair. Jadi made five, and Osvald six, and following our general acceptance to the DGT, Evind and Vinzent had evidently joined our group to make eight. Ernst, Kam, and Nils remained steadfastly at their old table, which was probably for the best, because a single table couldn't have comfortably supported more than eight.

Marta, for her part, seemed in significantly better spirits than she had before going home for the weekend, but I hadn't had a chance to converse with her about it. I sat down with my plate, the conversation at the table already ongoing.

"What class has everyone got for afternoon?" Jadi asked. "I know Osvald and I have skiltakraft."

"I've got a free period," I said. "I think all of the second-year students do?"

Sander nodded affirmation, glancing to Evind and Vinzent.

"Yeah," Vinzent said. "Have you got plans for it?"

"I was going to go to the library and catch up on some reading," I said carefully. I wanted to avoid being invited to any sort of group activity. "I've got a lot of studying to do if I'm to keep up with you DGT lot, regarding philosophy."

"Ah, yeah, I suppose you would," Vinzent said, with a twinge of disappointment.

"I believe that Theod and I both have husbandry," Marta offered. "On the flight course."

"Oh, I can't *wait* until Dreyst can fly." Jadi sighed wistfully, poking at her food. "I've been aloft with Dynah, on Gikka, but Dreyst will be too big for that by the winter recess. It tires her out, carrying two riders and a hatchling."

"Are you going home for the winter recess?" I asked.

"It's not decided yet; I might just stay with the Gellers. Dynah's going to come visit, either way."

Conversation proceeded pleasantly through luncheon, with nothing much of interest said. Class schedules, plans for the following weekend, things like that.

I spent my afternoon session walking the trails with Kasaqua and then in the library, looking up some of the philosophers that the DGT had mentioned: Broadman Aristonson's *Politeia* and *Republic,* Frankle Speck's *Leiter des Intellekts,* and Johan Russert's *Diskurs über Ungleichheit.* Each of those works seemed to presume that the reader was familiar with the earlier ones, and they were all opaque and tedious in their wording and turns of phrase. Broadman had very firm opinions about the nature of mankind—that there were kinds of people, distinct from birth, some suited to leadership, some suited to war, and some suited to "base work" like farming and crafting. He posed that society's job ought to be to winnow the people and sort them into their "proper" places. The other two referenced that treatise a lot. Speck's work was the most interesting of the three, because he seemed to approach everything through the same principals of natural philosophy that Professor Ulfar taught—but he also had frankly chilling ideas about nature and how it was mankind's destiny to conquer and tame it.

On Tuesday morning, I had husbandry again with Professor Mesman. I woke early, dressed to ride, and reported to the dragonhall while most of the class was still taking breakfast. Once again, Valteri Arnerson's dragon, Angharad, was resting outside of the dragonhall. I was thus wholly unsurprised to find Mister Arnerson standing near Kasaqua's stall, carrying a saddle. Professor Mesman wasn't in evidence.

"Good morning," he said as I approached. "It's a bit of a rush job, but I think this saddle will be serviceable. You can report any issues back to me, and we'll work on them when she grows out of this one and needs a new one anyway."

"Morning," I replied, opening Kasaqua's stall and gesturing

for Mister Arnerson to join me inside as I brushed Kasaqua down and began putting her into tack. I left off the saddle frame, because I knew it was too long and too stiff. Mister Arnerson didn't comment on that, but simply handed me the rather odd-looking saddle. It was very plain, made of smooth brown leather devoid of any ornamentation or stitching that wasn't strictly structural. It was much rounder and deeper in the seat than the standard-issue saddles, a great deal shorter front to back, and wider and more U-shaped in the gullet, compared to the standard saddles' V-shape. When I set it on Kasaqua's back, on top of the quilted underlay, she put her ears back—not because she was particularly upset, but because it was a new sensation, different than the previous saddle or the saddle frame. It wasn't the immediate rejection that she'd had with the standard saddle, which was a good sign. The sides of the saddle tree laid properly, resting flush against her ribs just above where the wingleather joined her body, and once the cinches were tightened, it didn't gap in the middle or rock back and forth. Once I was sure that everything was laying the way it should, I stepped back to let Mister Arnerson take a look.

"Oh, that's much better," he said, more to himself than to me, as he checked the tightness of the straps and ran his fingers all around the edges to check for gapping. "Get some stirrups on and see if you can mount up with her standing; she's not particularly long-legged like some Vaskosish breeds, so you ought to be able to get on without her lying down and without a mounting block."

I attached the stirrups as instructed. Then, with only *slight* trepidation, I took hold of the saddle horn nearest me, set my foot into the stirrup, and swung myself bodily upward and over, missing the opposite stirrup at first and having to hunt for it with my foot. I'd made the stirrup billets too short; this saddle had me sitting farther back, my knees still hooking over Kasaqua's wing joints, but at a different angle than without the saddle. Mister Arnerson was good enough to help me lengthen them, and once he'd done so, I sat . . . comfortably. The saddle seemed unpleasantly stiff under me, but that might have been because it was very new.

Other students began arriving at the dragonhall, tacking up their own mounts.

"Let's see what your professor's got to say," Mister Arnerson said, walking out of the stall and gesturing for me to follow. I urged Kasaqua on, and she was quite enthused with the idea of going out and stretching her legs.

Professor Mesman was standing by Kostbar at the back of the dragonhall, near the row of chairs. Several of my classmates were standing nearby with their dragons, and they turned to look as Kasaqua and I approached at a walk, Mister Arnerson keeping pace.

"Ah, excellent," the professor said, blowing his whistle to keep Kostbar standing at attention while he came to inspect the new saddle and the way I set in it.

"Your knee is still turned out more than is ideal, but I think that's something you can work on through practice, and you're not hunched forward the way you were bareback. Take a few laps around the field at a walk, then at a trot, making note of anything that feels off."

I instructed Kasaqua to follow the professor's directions, while the professor and Mister Arnerson spoke quietly together. The saddle was a very marked improvement on either standard Anglish saddles or bareback riding, but there was something *off* about it that I couldn't quite put words to; something alien or uncomfortable, having to do with stiffness and a feeling of detachment from Kasaqua. It was not the kind of saddle my ancestors would have used to ride Nampeshiwe . . . I didn't know what a proper Nampeshiwe's saddle would look like or how it would differ from this saddle, only that it *would* in some way.

But this would serve, for now.

I'd have to go about finding out what the original people of the deep lakes did, regarding tack and saddling. Kasaqua was not an Anglish dragon, or a Vaskosish one, and there had to be tried and tested traditions regarding Nampeshiwe in places where the Anglish hadn't set foot.

I'd have to ask Jadi, later, to ask Dynah about the possibility of introducing me to the neighbors she'd mentioned at the garden party—the Howden-noshawnee. Not *my* people, not the traditions we'd lost, but closer to them than anything the Anglish might come up with.

In any case, by the time I'd rounded the field half a dozen times, alternating between a walk and a trot—Kasaqua still wasn't entirely comfortable at a run, even with the new saddle—the rest of my classmates had finished tacking and reported for class.

I was allowed to join them in trail riding for the first time, that class period.

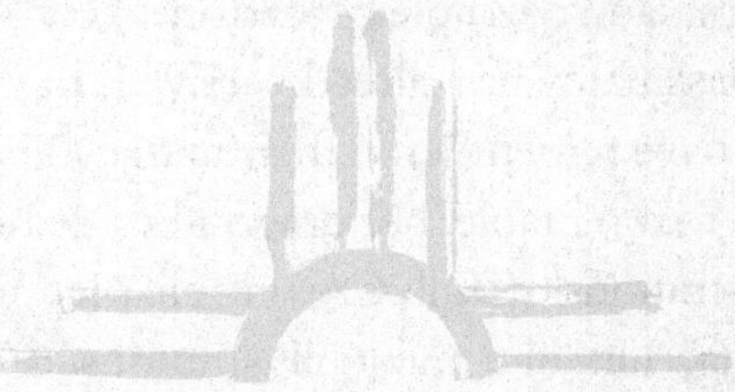

AND PRACTICED THE CREATION OF ATHERS

That afternoon, I had skiltakraft.

Professor Schreiber had told us at the end of Thursday's class that if the weather was fine on Tuesday, we'd be meeting at the far end of the flight field—and that we ought to bring our dragons with us, but that they needn't be in tack.

I knew the place she'd indicated; it was where Frau Kuiper had administered the practical portion of my skiltakraft examination in May. There was a wide, shallow, bowl-shaped hollow of sandy soil there that was ideal for scratching skiltas into. It was also well away from any buildings or overhanging trees. Professor Ezel hadn't seen fit to bring first-year students there, and I couldn't help but wonder whether or not Professor Schreiber did; I'd have to ask Jadi.

There were five of us who all had second-year skiltakraft together: Theod, Sander, Evind, Vinzent, and me. Since we all took luncheon together, we all reported at once to the dragonhall to gather our charges before proceeding to the field.

Kasaqua was *very* curious as to what we were about as we made our way to the flight field; she'd absolutely have been game for more riding. She'd carried me on her back for the fullness of the morning class period, which was longer than I'd ever ridden her before, but she wasn't especially tired.

Professor Schreiber had set up a little folding table in the center of the sandpit, and a couple of cartons were set on it. Several other of our classmates had already arrived, but no one I knew well enough to have remembered their names. The professor was standing by the folding table, her dragon beside her.

I'd seen illustrations of fully grown velikolepni in my book on dragonreckoning, but like most illustrations of dragons, they hadn't really captured the truth of the living creature. This dragon was a bit darker than Inga in coloration. Where Inga was cream-and-wheat-colored shading to gold, this dragon was gold all over that shaded to a tawny brown. It was a smallish dragon, for being fully grown—from nose to tail, it was only fifteen feet long, where Kasaqua's mother had been twenty, and kesseldraches and silberdraches were more like thirty. Its ears were smaller than those of most breeds, its conformation fine in an almost dainty way—more like a fox than a wolf. It carried a three-tiered crown of golden-brown horns, each set progressively larger and more curved. The barbles around its mouth and above its eyes, looking like those of a catfish, were unique to the breed—at least as far as I knew.

There were twenty-five students in this class—all twenty-four of the second-year students, and Theod. Copper looked a bit out of place, a full year ahead of any of the other dragons in growth and conformation. Theod had his stoic face on about it.

Once all of the students and their dragons had arrived, Professor Schreiber said brightly, "Good afternoon! For those who have not otherwise been introduced, this is my dragon, Hans. He is a velikolepni—a breed perfected by the wandering people of Roveland. Roveland and Russland are largely inhospitable places; thus, it has been important to them that their dragons be able to frequently and reliably produce useful athers from base materials such as air, water, stone, soil, and wood. A velikolepni is not a particularly imposing creature, but will be able to continue breathing onto skiltas long after most other breeds have exhausted themselves. The breed is thus favored by athermachers and professors of skiltakraft. Now, please collect a pair of goggles and a half-pint jar of water from the table, then take a place around the edge of the sandpit, forming a circle. Try to keep at least six feet apart from one another—it's important that your dragon is able to easily discern your skilta from anyone else's."

When we'd each gathered our supplies and returned to our places, Professor Schreiber reached into the other carton and pulled out a palm-sized ball of pale wood, followed by some short wooden sticks.

"Motes are represented to us most often as points or circles on a page, but it's helpful to consider them in three dimensions; they are *spheres.* Motes are so small that we will never see them, not with any lenses than can be crafted by man. Yet we're able to know their forms, because they show themselves in their behavior—they obey natural laws that can be easily observed. For example, vetna can form one attachment with other motes—it possesses only one place for other motes to attach to."

She turned the ball so that we could see that there was a small hole drilled into it.

"In contrast, stiksna can make two attachments."

She took a second ball from the carton, this one painted red, and showed us that it had a hole drilled on either side, like a bead. They weren't drilled all the way through, though; I couldn't see light passing from the other side.

"Zurfni can make three attachments, and kolfni can make four."

Two other balls—blue and black, respectively—with three and four holes.

"If you can remember the word 'VeSZK' and can count to four, you will know everything you need to know to do the overwhelming majority of practical skiltakraft. Think on the simplest compound athers: Water is made from one mote of stiksna and two motes of vetna."

She used the little sticks, stuck into the holes drilled on each ball, to attach a single red ball to two white ones.

"As you can see, in water, every point of attachment on all three motes is filled—no place remains for anything to attach. This means that water is very stable, very comfortable being water. It occurs abundantly in the world with no particular effort made by anyone but the authors of creation, who undoubtedly made the rules that motes abide. But, have a look at this situation—"

She took a kolfni mote, and attached a single vetna mote to it.

"This ather retains three points of attachment that are unfulfilled—it is uncomfortable, unstable. It longs to attach to something else, to fill those empty points of attachment."

She filled each of the holes with sticks, but attached nothing to the other ends, leaving them to stick out in an awkward, unbalanced-looking fashion.

"In this state, it's called a kolbind—kolfni *bound* to, in this case, vetna. The vetna is well contented, but the kolfni is seeking further connections. You will not find free kolbinds outside of an active skilta, because left to its own devices, it will always find something else to complete it. Today, we will be producing spirit of vinegar. It is made from kolfni, vetna, and stiksna in this arrangement."

She took a few moments to attach the other motes, making a specific shape with the little wooden pieces.

"This mote of kolfni is attached at all four of its points; twice to vetna and once to another kolfni, which is itself attached to two motes of stiksna, with one of the attachments being doubled. The singular attachment leaves the stiksna's other point of attachment free to join with a mote of vetna. To create this compound ather, we will first gather our materials—in common practice, all of the materials needed to make spirit of vinegar can be gleaned directly from ordinary air. If we were to divide a measure of quite typical air into one hundred parts and sort them by kind, seventy-seven parts would be pure zurfni, twenty-one parts would be pure stiksna, one part will be suspended water—who can tell me the structure of water?" She turned around, looking at everyone in the circle.

"Two parts vetna to one part stiksna, ma'am," someone standing at the other side of the circle called out.

"Correct! Of the remaining one part, one-half part will be smothering air, which is . . . ?"

"One mote of kolfni and two motes of stiksna," another voice answered.

"Also correct! The last half part of the air will be dross. Now, because having twenty-five of you attempt to pull half a pint of water out of the air at once would leave the air unbearably dry, I've provided water to start with. We will be pulling kolfni from the air by breaking smothering air into its motes, then combining the vetna, stiksna, and kolfni into the arrangement that makes spirit of vinegar. What's left in the jar should be nearly pure, much more concentrated than vinegar intended for the kitchen or laundry. Who among you can tell me what a säure is?"

"Something that turns mossdye red," one of my classmates said. "The opposite of a base."

"Correct, but imprecise. To be perfectly accurate, a säure is any compound ather containing vetna that can mingle with base compounds to form salts. Essigsäure—spirit of vinegar—is one of the commonest used in athermaching. In coming weeks, we will also be crafting salzsäure—spirit of salt; safflesäure—spirit of saffle; saltpetersäure—spirit of zurfni; and kohlensäure—spirit of kolfni. You will begin by drawing the skilta for vetna, and within it drawing the figures for stiksna and kolfni at half size. I will be walking around the circle making note of your progress, and I will show you how to join the figures in the way that gives the skilta its order."

She began walking slowly from student to student, watching as we drew figures in the sand. I was concentrating on the positions of the motes on the wooden model, which she'd left sitting on the table—four motes of vetna, two of kolfni, two of stiksna.

"Your dragons' part in the creation and manipulation of athers is simply to breathe exactly where and only where you indicate, at the time—"

There was a *very* loud popping sound somewhere to my left, not at all unlike the sound of the gun that had been turned on me in May. Screaming followed immediately—a young man and a dragon. Several of the dragons had bolted at the noise and were being chased by their student companions. Vinzent was sitting on the grass, scrubbing at his face with his arm, a pair of goggles clutched in his hand. His dragon—a young silberdrache—was dancing from foot to foot with his wings flared, making distressed noises. A sweetish smell pervaded the air, faintly similar to ether.

Professor Schreiber's voice rang clearly above the sudden commotion. "EVERYONE, TO THE DRAGONHALL—IMMEDIATELY!"

Without hesitation, I mounted up on Kasaqua, and through force of will alone, made her understand that we needed to be *away* from here, that we needed to go back to the dragonhall with great haste. I was peripherally aware of others following me: Theod on Copper, Sander running alongside Inga. I hushed Kasaqua to a stop when we arrived at the dragonhall—and the field just behind it, where Professor Mesman held classes. It was only a few hundred yards from the sandpit, but it felt much farther. Kasaqua's sides were heaving with the effort of sprinting as I dismounted.

"What happened?" Theod asked. I turned to find him close at my side, looking back toward the sandpit, one hand stroking Copper's neck.

"I have no idea," I said, looking around for Sander and sighting him; he was kneeling on the ground nearby, with Inga's head in his lap.

Professor Schreiber arrived some minutes later, leading Vinzent's dragon with a length of rope. The dragon wasn't being particularly cooperative, digging his heels into the ground and trying to look back toward the sandpit.

"Whoever was closest to Mister Wilder, check yourselves and your dragons over for injury; there were shards of glass when the jar exploded," Professor Schreiber barked with authority. "Mister Wilder has been put into the care of Frau Brinkerhoff. He's very lucky not to have lost an eye. What you have just seen is a display of what can happen when one behaves carelessly or rashly with a skilta—even a quite simple one."

"What happened, though?" Evind asked. He'd been standing right beside Vinzent, but didn't seem to be hurt.

"Mister Wilder decided for some reason to instruct his dragon to activate the skilta he'd drawn before I'd examined its soundness," Professor Schreiber practically spat, obviously furious. "Given the smell, I can only conclude that he produced not vinegar, but an air of rusted ether—composed of two parts kolfni, one part vetna, and one part stiksna in a particular arrangement. Let this be a lesson to all of you: Skiltakraft is a dangerous business. It must be done correctly, or the outcome can be quite catastrophic. The jar, filled far beyond its capacity, exploded. The air of rusted ether was released. It is unwholesome to breathe, and readily catches fire, which is why I had you evacuate the field. Good show, by the way, to those of you who maintained composure and control of your dragons."

"Is Vinzent going to be all right?" Evind asked, his eyes wide and his face open in a way that made him look much younger than he usually did.

"I don't know, Mister Skovgaard," Professor Schreiber answered, her blue eyes flinty. "All we can do now is keep him in our thoughts and pray for Fyra's mercy." In a louder voice, she called, "You will take the next few minutes to calm your charges and place them back into their stalls. I have obviously overestimated the class's competence and readiness for practical work. When your dragons are situated, report to the skiltakraft laboratory."

With that, she led Vinzent's dragon into the dragonhall, her own Hans walking at heel on her opposite side.

There was nothing for any of us to do but put our dragons away and report to the laboratory.

SHE STUDIED SKILTAKRAFT WITH SANDER

One of the first things that Professor Ezel had ever said to me was: "*There is no room for mistakes in skiltakraft. It is done correctly, or it isn't. If you do it incorrectly, there are consequences.*"

My mind kept supplying images of Sakewa's burns, of Birning Svenisson's death, as I brushed Kasaqua down. Professor Schreiber's grim face; Vinzent's scream.

The breath of dragons was dangerous because it was powerful. *The shapeless medicine of a dragon's breath is change.* That phrase was literal; a dragon's breath tore the very stuff of creation apart, changed it into something new. Vinzent had been in that same class with me, had heard Professor Ezel say all the same aggressively dire things, and had loosed a dragon's breath on an unsound skilta anyway.

And there'd been consequences.

Kasaqua made a concerned crooning noise, her flank rumbling under my hand. I took a long breath, deliberately turning my mind from such things, focusing on brushing her down. On being calm. Kasaqua was still absolutely aware that something was wrong, that something bad had happened or was happening. She did *not* want to be put back into her stall. I didn't want to put her back into her stall.

I walked to the skiltakraft laboratory, swallowing hard around the lump in my throat.

The clock in the main hall indicated that it was half past two; there was still half an hour of class left when we assembled in the skiltakraft laboratory. The professor waited until all twenty-four of us were present before launching into a vehement lecture.

"I had not considered the possibility that a class of second-year students, who have passed first-year skiltakraft under *Reinhard Ezel* of all people, would hold any individual careless enough to craft a directionless skilta and the blind arrogance to activate it with the breath of a dragon. When Professor Ezel had you do practical work last year, didn't he impress upon you the importance of safely proceeding step by step?"

We didn't deserve such vitriol, because none of *us* had done anything wrong. Vinzent had, and he was elsewhere now because of it. I raised my hand. Professor Schreiber looked at me expectantly.

"Professor Ezel didn't do practical work with the first-year class, ma'am," I informed her. "I'd never activated a skilta at all before my examination in May."

There was a general murmur of agreement among my classmates.

"In all of your first year of study, you did no practical work? None of you?" Professor Schreiber asked, frowning, looking around the room.

"All of our work was done on paper, ma'am," another student said.

"I . . . see," she said, her frown deepening. "This class will meet again on Tuesday, here in the lab. I very obviously need to give a lecture on safe practices before we attempt practical work again. I hadn't been aware that Professor Ezel's teaching practices had changed so much in recent years. I suggest you take some time between now and our next meeting to familiarize yourself with the various potentially dangerous compound athers that can be assembled from just vetna, kolfni, and stiksna. If you wish to impress, outline dangerous compounds that can be assembled from any three of the known athers and draw diagrams of the skiltas that would produce those compounds. Class is dismissed."

I met Sander and Theod in the hallway. Sander had already written something on his tablet, and handed it to me as soon as he joined us. It read: *I'm going to the library to work on diagrams of dangerous compounds, would you like to join me?*

The quiet of the library and the methodical work of drawing skiltas would be soothing, and what else was I going to do between now and dinner, anyway?

"I'd love to," I said, handing the tablet to Theod. He read it, then frowned as he handed it back to Sander.

"I'm going to take Copper out for a trail ride," he said. "He's still upset by what happened in class. Aren't your dragons upset?"

I closed my eyes, concentrating on my bond with Kasaqua, on the part of me that was aware of her wants and needs.

"Kasaqua's asleep," I said. "I had husbandry for first period—we rode the trails all morning."

Theod looked at me then, something unreadable in his eyes. He was trying to tell me something, but I hadn't the slightest idea what. The moment stretched painfully, shattering when Sander coughed into his fist.

"I suppose I'll see you at dinner, then," Theod said, closing his eyes and turning from us. I felt like I'd failed a test as I watched him walk away.

It wasn't at all fair that I kept coming up against tests without warning. Theod needed study even more than I did; he really ought to have joined us.

I set my jaw and sighed through my nose, turning back to Sander.

At the library, we chose one of the small tables at the back. Sander had been writing as we walked, and pushed a list in front of me as we sat down.

V+K Combustive Airs: KV4, swamp gas. KV3V3, air of alcohol. KV3KV2KV3, third combustive air. KV3KV2KV2KV3, fourth combustive air. KV3KV2KV2KV2KV3, fifth combustive air. KV3(KV2)4KV3, sixth combustive air. KV3(KV2)5KV3, seventh combustive air. KV3(KV2)6KV3, eighth combustive air. KV3(KV2)7KV3, ninth combustive air. KV3(KV2)8KV3, tenth combustive air. I'm going to draw the diagrams of these in order, you should too and then we can compare.

There was clearly a pattern to the list, but it didn't entirely make sense to me. Maybe the pattern would be clearer once I saw them as atheric diagrams and not just formulas. I set the tablet between us on the table, where either of us could easily refer to it, and laid out my paper and ink. Somewhere out of sight, a clock chimed three. By the time it chimed four, I'd filled dozens of pages with atheric diagrams and corresponding skiltas. More than once, I'd taken the time to draw them with curving, swooping lines of the kind that would be used in dance rather than the straight lines that made the spiky star-shapes that appeared in all the textbooks; they were easier for me to follow the direction of. I did them on separate pages, not the ones I intended to compare with Sander's work.

I'd gotten by last year almost entirely on memorization; Professor Ezel hadn't explained that different kinds of motes had different numbers of potential points of attachment. Knowing that made a lot of the texts I'd read make more sense. The diagram for rusted ether was roughly triangular: a mote of stiksna at the top, joined to two motes of kolfni, which were joined to each other, with two motes of vetna attached to each kolfni. I drew the butterfly-shaped diagram for air of alcohol and compared it to the diagram for rusted ether; the former looked like the latter, with one mote of stiksna attached to the kolfni motes. It might have been easier if I had a set of those wooden balls and sticks that the professor had shown us in class. I leafed through my stack of papers, pushing some to the side, uncovering the sketches I'd done of curved dance skiltas. Sander's gaze landed on the page, and I saw him stop, like a clockwork toy that needed to be wound up again. The quill he'd been holding hovered halfway between the inkpot and the page. His eyes widened a bit; he wasn't even breathing.

"Are you quite all right, Sander?" I asked, rearranging my papers to cover those notes. That spurred him back into action. He was shaking his head, reaching for his tablet, writing furiously. He put it in front of me, then turned and scurried out of the library, leaving his tablet behind. I'd *never* seen him leave his tablet behind, not without duress.

The tablet said: *Wait here dont go anywhere Im getting a thing in my room just wait*

He returned a while later, looking flushed, having obviously run all the way to his room and back. He had a little wooden case tucked under his arm, and he put it onto the table in front of me with a forcible thump, snatching the tablet up again. I tentatively moved to open the case, looking to Sander to see if that's what he wanted. He wasn't looking at me; he was engrossed in writing again.

Inside the box were a series of brass gears. All of them had little pointed teeth on their margins. Some of the larger ones were hollow, and toothed on the inside edge, as well. The largest one, a ring, was the size of a dinner plate. The smallest was the size of a pennik coin. Some of the smaller ones were shapes other than circles—oblongs, egg shapes, five- and six-sided shapes with rounded corners. They had words and numbers stamped on them, and the solid ones had holes drilled in them at marked intervals with labels. The lid of the box was lined with a sheet of cork, and a box of narrow wax pencils in several colors. Sander made a throaty, urgent sound that made me look up. He was holding the tablet out to me.

"Windenbilds skiltas the way you draw skiltas look it's important," he said, all in a rush.

I read what he'd written: *This is a windenbildmacher; it's a toy more than anything. I've had sets like this since I was small, and being interested in windenbilds was one of the things that made my father think I might be suited as a dragoneer. Watch, I'll show you how it works.*

When I looked up, he'd laid a piece of paper on the cork-lined lid of the box and tacked the biggest gear down on top of it with push pins. He selected one of the smaller gears and carefully laid it into the hollow center of the bigger gear, meshing the teeth together. He shook a wax pencil out of the box, not seeming to pay much attention to what color it was, and lined it up with one of the drilled holes in the smaller gear. As I watched, he moved in a precise and obviously practiced way to run the inner gear along the outer, drawing a swooping line. As he rolled the gear around and around the circle, the offset hole meant that the line progressed into a flower shape . . . quite similar to my dance skiltas. The line met itself after twelve rounds of the circle, making a twelve-petaled flower shape.

"Sindle!" Sander said, followed by a strangled little laugh. He set the pencil aside and removed the tacks so he could hand the paper to me. I took another piece of paper and drew a skilta for pure sindle in the traditional way, marking the motes and joining them with straight lines. The two, viewed one next to the other, were clearly different versions of the same thing. They didn't mirror each other, but they . . . rhymed?

It felt important, the same way my realization about the dancing had felt important.

With these tools and a bit of forethought, one could easily draw absolutely flawless skiltas.

Sander pulled the windenbild toward himself, and with another colored pencil, marked the outermost curves of the twelve petals, then drew straight lines over the top of the curved ones: a traditional skilta in blue atop a flower skilta in red.

"I feel like we should keep this a secret until we've tested it," I said.

Sander frowned, picking up his tablet and writing, *Surely we should bring this to Professor Schreiber's attention. This has the potential to change the way skiltakraft is taught and practiced.*

"I don't know if Professor Schreiber can be trusted, not yet," I said. "This is the sort of discovery that could make you thousands of markas and more. If she claims to have come up with it, who'll believe that it was you? She's a professor, and you're a second-year student."

And you. What inspired you to draw a skilta that way, with curved lines?

I bit my lip, considering. Sander was a friend, but he was still Anglish. I didn't want to talk about my people's dances with him . . . he'd want to *study* that. My mind raced for some other answer that would put him off, and landed squarely on the strange engine that Niquiat's tinker co-op had rescued from a junk pile.

"Remember my brother's co-op?"

Sander nodded.

"I saw a piece of some kind of engine; Zhina thinks it's from Shiang-Gang originally. It had a skilta on it like this, with curved lines. Several skiltas, actually, more complicated than I know how to read. But I find them easier to draw by hand than trying to make perfectly straight lines."

I should very much like to have a look at that, if your brother's still got it, Sander wrote.

"I can work on arranging that," I said. "Just promise me that you won't tell anyone about this, not until we've got a better handle on it. I don't want anyone stealing this discovery from us. From you, really—"

Sander made a negative sound, writing on his tablet, *It's as much your discovery as mine; you'd have worked it out yourself if you'd seen a windenbildmacher set before. We should study this together.*

"Agreed," I said. He thrust his hand at me, grinning, and I shook it.

We had a secret.

AND MET AGAIN WITH THE DGT

Vinzent joined our table at dinner that night, his left cheek and forehead plastered with gauze; he'd been hit by shards of glass when the jar had exploded. Professor Schreiber had been right; he was *very* lucky not to have lost an eye. His goggles had been in his hand, not on his face, where they belonged.

He was sullen and quiet all through dinner, and none of us said anything on the subject. I rather wanted to ask what in the world he'd been thinking, but it seemed rude, so I remained silent.

On the evening of Wednesday the thirteenth, after dinner, the DGT met again in the library. Ernst, Nils, and Kam were already installed there when the rest of us arrived. I hadn't been paying attention to when they'd left the dining hall, but I hadn't seen them at the dragonhall when we all joined Jadi and Osvald. It was only the first-year students who had to bring their dragons to be fed; Kasaqua was fed in her stall, whether I visited her or not. Had those three even visited their dragons? It struck me again how terrible it seemed to spend so little time with one's dragon. I had no idea how they could stand it, or why they'd want to.

No one, not even Ernst, made any complaints this time about us being a group of eleven.

"Good evening, everyone," he said as we entered and took our seats—roughly the same seats as last time, I noticed. "Hopefully this meeting will go more smoothly than the last. We have a topic for this meeting that I was only made aware of this very afternoon; Eskil Gerdasson's had a letter to the people of Vastergot published in the *Vastergot Gazette,* a direct response to a speech that Sveni Audulfsson gave on Monday at the Thane's Free Gardens. Before I read it, we will partake of the elixir."

All of the extant members of the group were in agreement that "partaking of the elixir" was a critically important step at the beginning of a proper meeting. The little cup was, Evind had informed us at dinner, made of mammoth tooth and inscribed with an old norse prayer for *hugur.* It was a word he insisted meant something different from and more than just "thought," but which he couldn't explain in a satisfying way.

The elixir was a *very* sharp spirit. It was bitter and tasted of hummingbird mint. The cup held a spare mouthful, and no one insisted that I had to take more than that. Once we'd all taken a drink, Ernst capped the bottle and set it aside. He spread the newspaper on the table and read aloud.

On Jarldom, Kingship, and the Future of Lindmarden—
By Eskil Gerdasson, a landless bastard.

I am not a citizen of Vastergot. I'm not even a citizen of Lindmarden, nor am I likely to ever become one. I am a visitor from Anglesland, blown across the Great North Sea by the winds of fate—just the same way that Stafn Whitebeard and his sons arrived at the Fishhook Headland in 1628. I am thus an impartial observer of this young nation as it comes of age. You celebrated two hundred years in the year 1828, and the whole of the world took notice.

Lindmarden is a bountiful nation, flush with land and goods, and in just two hundred years it has become as rich and influential as many of the nations of the old world. You have the lumber, the coal, the iron, the granite and marble, the grain, the whale oil, the fish. You have men with the cunning and grit to turn these resources into money and power. The kings of the old world talk about Lindmarden, and mostly say fine things.

According to the 1840 folkscoring, there are 7,234,876 citizens of Lindmarden. 2,411,625 live in New Linvik and its outlands, directly under High King Yngvarr Silvertooth. 1,205,812 live in Runestung Hold, under Jarl Rikkert Halfhand. That means that 3,617,439 citizens live in Vaster's Hold, under Jarl Leiknir Joervarsson. Half of them live inside the city limits of Vastergot.

According to Thrand's Charter, there should be one torgar for every thousand landless citizens, so Vaster's Hold ought to have 3,618 torgars. It doesn't. Vastergot ought to have 1,809 torgars. Arjan Stafn is the thane of the city of Vastergot, and when I looked into it, I could find only 135 torgars reporting to him.

Vastergot and its outlands have just five thanes. I'm sure this was a wise delegation of powers when Vaster Stafn was jarl, and Vastergot was a town of 10,000 people. But two hundred and more years have passed since then.

I attended a thynge this past August on Nack Island, where Jarl Joervarsson appointed four new torgars to represent the landless people of Nack and Mask islands. This is nothing more than what the law says those people are owed, yet there are so many people who are so very angry about it.

Through all of eretide, mankind has wrestled with two

natures: innangard—order, civility, and lawfulness; and utangard—chaos, wilderness, and lawlessness. Joden oversees innangard. His brother, Enki, oversees utangard. In this way, balance is maintained.

There are certain persons who believe that storied tradition is the only way to maintain innangard; people who look to the sagas and the leids and see in them the one true way that all people must be, forever and ever. Herr Sveni Audulfsson, the petty king of the Ravens of Joden, wants all of us to know that he is a very powerful man with strong ideals. He wants you to believe that he has a plan for a more perfect Vastergot, Lindmarden, Markesland, and The World. He would have you believe that your great city is in a state of decay, and has been since 1836, when Leiknir Joervarsson was elected to the position of jarl. He and his people much preferred Kjeld Niklasson, who cared about the concerns of the smallfolk only so much as any thrallmaster cares for his thralls. Did it please you, oh people of Vastergot, to be thralls? To have your sons thrown into the slavering mouth of war with Berri Vaskos? Leiknir Joervarsson fought at the siege of the Polvaara, and so did Niklasson. Sveni Audulfsson cannot claim the same.

High King Yngvarr Silvertooth is a man of eighty, and long has he wrestled blind and toothless Elli, who defeats all men in the end. It is not unwise to consider who will sit the high king's throne when he either chooses to step down, or takes his leave for Valhalya. We will have an althynge in January of 1845; this is the law. The Ravens of Joden are demanding one this coming January, two years ahead of the natural order, because they are so terribly upset that we have a jarl who actually does the work of a jarl.

I urge you, landless people of Vastergot, to find out who your torgar is if you don't already happen to know.

Write him a letter, visit him at the moot, shake his hand and tell him what concerns you, as a citizen. If every household sought to make its wishes and desires known to its assigned torgar, it might illustrate just how woefully lacking the common people are in representation.

Sveni Audulfsson shouts in the Thane's Gardens, and Joden watches, and Enki grins.

Think on that.

When he'd finished, Ernst paused, looking around the table at each of us.

"So, what questions does this raise?" he asked.

Jadi spoke up immediately, before anyone else could. "Herr Gerdasson said that the Ravens of Joden look to the leids and sagas as the means by which the law should be established. Why? Which leids and sagas, and why those ones?"

"Well, given that they call themselves the Ravens of Joden, I'm willing to bet it's the edda and the sagas of Joden, and the saga of the Volesungs, and Sigur's Leid, and Brynhild's Leid—you know, the wisdom words!" Kam replied to her, looking a bit puzzled.

"I *don't* know; I'm not Anglish," Jadi said, with an obviously feigned look of incomprehension. "I'm Zhidish. What if I've never heard these stories? Can't you tell me what's good about them?"

"I haven't heard most of them, either," I pointed out. "They're not part of the lore I was brought up on."

"Well, it's not really entirely your fault that you've been denied a proper education, given my understanding of nackies and their lack of civilization—" Nils began, only to be interrupted by Sander knocking on the table. He was looking at Nils crossly, and handed his tablet to Marta, who read aloud: *Anequs has not been denied a proper education. She simply received a very different one. I'd wager she knows more facts about more things, generally, than you do.*

Marta paused then, looking up and meeting Nils's gaze as she handed the tablet back to Sander. "I, for my part, quite agree," she said.

"I'm sorry; I've said it wrong. I didn't mean to question your intelligence!" Nils said quickly, throwing up his hands. "We wouldn't have invited you to join our conversations if we thought you were stupid, after all."

"Oh, what a glowing compliment," I said, folding my arms. "I'm ever so pleased to be judged 'intelligent' by your estimations."

"Enough sniping at each other," Ernst said sternly. "I believe Miss Wozniakowa posed a question. What's good about the wisdom words, as a body of work? Why ought people study them?"

"Because they outline the truths that Joden learned and wanted mankind to know," Osvald said. His voice took on a quality that let me know he was reciting from memory when he continued, "Joden hanged himself on the world tree for nine days and nights after drinking Hrothvitnir's milk, and each of those days, he was granted wisdom about a virtue of man—truth is better than lies, bravery is better than cowardice, honor is better than dishonor, loyalty is better than betrayal, discipline is better than negligence, self-reliance is better than dependence, industry is better than idleness, battle is better than surrender, and generosity is better than stinginess—especially to one's lessers."

"And what if we, as participating members of mankind, disagree on any of those points?" Jadi asked with a sly grin. I rather liked how bold she was being in her questions.

I'd spent a year among the Anglish being told that they were good and right, that they were the keepers of civilization, and that their ways were obviously superior to those of my people . . . and I hadn't bothered wasting my breath on trying to convince them otherwise. Marta was well-meaning, but very much saw me as a project—an ignorant savage in need of improvement. Professor Ibarra openly stated that there was no lore in this part of the world before the year 1574, and Osvald had insisted the same after class. None of them had invited me to share my views and opinions; I'd had to voice them unasked or leave them unsaid. Theod had very much taken to heart all the awful things he'd been told about his parents and the people of Naquipaug at large. I hadn't bothered trying to find out what most of my classmates thought they knew about my people; I hadn't seen it as worthwhile.

Jadzia Wozniakowa did not, evidently, feel any hesitation in arguing her points. Maybe there was something to that, at least here and now.

"No one can possibly argue that lying and cowardice and dishonor and betrayal and negligence and dependence and surrender and idleness and stinginess are better than their opposites," Osvald insisted with a frown, staring at her.

"I'd argue that those pairs of ideas aren't the only options," I said. "Where does prudence fall on a scale of bravery to cowardice? How can anyone live without some measure of dependence—of reliance on others? I spent this week reading Aristonson and Speck and Russert to try to catch myself up to the things that all of you suppose that you know. I disagree strongly with *all* of them about what constitutes virtue, and what the nature of mankind is."

"Men are inherently driven by self-interest," Vinzent said. "Every man wants to gain personal happiness and achieve comfort and pleasure in life—and it's the right of every man to seek them! Goodness and wickedness are determined by *how* a man goes about achieving happiness."

"What makes some things good and other things wicked, though?" Jadi pressed.

"Well, what do *you* suppose makes some things good and others wicked?" Osvald demanded.

"Ah, that's one of those questions we could sit and argue about for weeks, if we want," Jadi crowed, laughing. "I don't think that battle is better than surrender, for example—I think the best thing is understanding and compromise. That's what you meant by the pairs not being everything, right, Anequs? There are third roads to take. I say it's better to live peacefully than to go to war, if war can be avoided. I think Gerdasson would agree with me, too—look what he said about the slavering maw of war devouring people's sons."

"I think that attitudes toward battle, and glory gained in battle, are really more the purview of men than of women, generally," Nils said.

"Oh, and would you say that to Frau Kuiper?" Marta asked, her voice sharp.

"I *said* generally. She's the exception, not the rule," Nils insisted. "Most women will never go to war, and so shouldn't have opinions about it. Do you plan to go to war, Miss Hagan?"

"No, but I'm likely to have a husband and perhaps sons, someday. I shouldn't like to lose them in senseless battle," she said.

"What makes a battle senseless, though?" Ernst asked. "In Joden's saga, he says that all men will die, that wealth and property will die, that the only thing that doesn't die is fame of one who's earned it. The point of a good life is to create a legacy—a name for yourself that will go on after you've died. No one goes to Valhalya whose name isn't on the lips of his fellows."

"Which is dependence," I said. "A wholly self-reliant man can't gain fame."

"Well, when Joden walked among men, most of the fame he's talking about came from raiding and overthrowing and suchlike," Kam said.

"How is raiding and overthrowing different from murder and theft?" I asked, leaning forward just a bit. "I've read Emanuel Nordlund's *The Savage Peoples of North Markesland,* and he makes much of the 'idleness' of the Naquisit. Arjan Stafn accused in his letter last year that we make no progress or innovation, do nothing to improve the lands on which we live, accumulate no wealth, and generally exist without ambition. Earlier, Osvald said that industry is better than idleness. I'd like to challenge that. I don't think there's virtue in labor for the sake of labor, in endlessly harvesting beyond one's needs. If I've understood the argument that he made, the Naquisit of the 1740s ought to have been laboring at every hour of every day to accumulate goods to sell and thus become wealthy. Herr Gerdasson said in his letter that we—Lindmarden—have all the things. The lumber, the coal, the iron, all of that. Do you suppose it's just chance that we have these things? That we haven't spent all of time judiciously using what we need and making sure there's plenty left over?

"Nordlund expressed bald astonishment at the fact that any time a group of Naquisit people deliberated to fell a tree, they'd plant another in its place—usually of the same kind, or of another useful kind that would make the forest stronger for its presence, like a chestnut for a hickory tree. But if you fell a tree for its wood and bark, that means you don't have a living tree anymore. You have a responsibility to replace what you've taken. I don't think that Nordlund understood the Naquisit half as well as he thought he did, and the immense popularity of his book seems to have put a lot of stupid and wrongheaded ideas into the heads of scholars who develop their opinions without ever having visited the islands."

"That's an interesting observation, Miss Anequs—" Ernst began. At the front of the library, the clock softly chimed. Everyone went silent, listening. It chimed ten times.

We all had classes to go to tomorrow morning at eight o'clock. Well, except for whichever year had their free period tomorrow morning. Theod had mentioned sharing his free period with the fourth-year class.

Theod hadn't said a single word during this meeting. I could tell, though, by the look in his eyes, that he'd been listening.

"We ought to pick this up again next week," Ernst said. "This has been one of the more interesting conversations that our chapter's ever had."

"I told you that it would be better if we just invited the lot of them," Kam said.

"Yes, yes, you were right and I was wrong," Ernst replied, rolling his eyes. "In any case, good night, everyone. You've given all of us some interesting things to think about."

And with that, he stood and started putting out candles. All the young men departed downstairs to their rooms, and Jadi and Marta and I up to ours.

MARTA EXTENDED AN INVITATION

On Thursday, I had husbandry in the morning and kept on working with Kasaqua on gaits until luncheon. Skiltakraft that afternoon was very boring—a harsh lecture about safety that had obviously been prompted by Vinzent's mistake on Tuesday.

On Friday, Jadi departed for her weekend with the Gellers after our shared lore lesson.

Luncheon having ended, Marta and I were alone in our room, preparing for our afternoon sessions—I had natural philosophy, and she had lore. Quite without preamble, she asked me, "Do you have any plans for Saturday?"

She said it with a kind of very deliberate casualness, but there was a spark of urgency in her eyes that made me pause.

"It's Theod's birthday, this Saturday. Why do you ask?" I replied carefully, setting down the satchel I'd been putting books into.

"It's just that I've received a telegram; Frau Brinkerhoff informed me after the morning session—"

"And you didn't mention it at luncheon?" I asked.

"Our table at luncheon is no longer . . . intimate," Marta said, sounding frustrated. "Anyway, Father sent word. Frau Morris and her children arrived yesterday and are settling in at Sjokliffheim. I thought it would be good of me to introduce Mathilda to other young women of my acquaintance. I've sent word to Lisbet, too, but she hasn't replied yet. It would be a casual gathering, just luncheon and tea; it wouldn't even be an overnight stay. Mister Otterlo would pick us up in the morning and return us in the evening."

"Why invite me but not Jadi?" I asked, looking at her sidelong.

"Miss Wozniakowa has made clear that she is not and will never be available for Saturday engagements," Marta said. "There's no point inviting her to something that she'd have to decline, and it would be rude to make a gathering known to her that she couldn't possibly attend. Treating others as you'd prefer to be treated and treating others the way they'd prefer to be treated are different things, I think."

"I can see the sense in that, but I'm not sure I'd agree. I don't know how *her* people feel about that kind of thing, and it seems unkind to not invite her if you don't know how she feels about invitations that she must turn down."

Marta frowned at that, then shook her head and went on. "I think you're a very good judge of character, Anequs," she said, like it was a confession. "You don't hesitate to make your assessments known, or to question and challenge . . . anything! I'd like you and Lisbet to be there, because I want to know what you each think of Mathilda."

"She's not going to be *my* sister," I said. "Your own estimations of her seem much more important than mine or Lisbet's."

"I don't know if I can trust my own estimations," Marta said. "I've spent most of my life trying to impress Dagny Sørensen and pining after Niklas, after all. I've known Lisbet for years and never even tried to befriend Sander. I flew into hysterics when I learned about Papa remarrying, and you were so frightfully *sensible* about the whole affair. Having listened to you both times at the meetings of the DGT . . . I value your opinions."

The admission came as a shock to me, and I had to wonder when that had changed for her, because when Marta and I had met a year ago, she had very obviously not valued my opinions at all. She'd approached me as a *project,* a social inferior in need of improvement. A savage in need of civilizing. I was happy to learn that her attitude had changed, toward me, but this was the first time she'd communicated any such thing to me.

I sighed.

"Yes, I'll come with you tomorrow to meet Mathilda, so long as we're back in a timely fashion after luncheon so that I can still spend some time with Theod," I said. "Will Sander be coming?"

"No, this is exclusively a girls' party," she said with conviction. "I haven't even begun to work out *how* I'm going to be politely introduced to Iain; Mathilda is closer to my age, and a girl, and knowing her first will probably smooth things along. We're probably going to talk about dresses for Valkyrjafax—as my stepsister, Mathilda will, of course, be invited to our ball here, and will need to be appropriately outfitted. Your measurements haven't changed significantly from last year, have they? I'm sure my seamstress—"

"Can't I just wear the bronze taffeta again?" I asked, my brow furrowing.

Marta looked absolutely horrified at the suggestion.

"You've had *lichtbilds* taken of you in that dress. Of course you can't be seen in it again!"

"Ever?" I asked, incredulous.

"Not at the same event! Not at any ball, really," Marta said, looking absolutely appalled. "You can certainly wear it to evening functions at home, among friends and family. If we were having a dinner party instead of a luncheon, it would be suitable for our gathering tomorrow. But you've very famously worn it to the Valkyrjafax ball last year; you can't wear it to the same ball this year. It would give the impression that you only own one dress—"

"I *do* only own one dress like that," I said. "I know that the yellow dress that I wore to Fyrafax and to your garden party isn't at all suitable for Valkyrjafax, because it's a springtime dress, but the taffeta is an autumn dress, and—"

"The society papers will tear you apart if you wear that dress again to a public function," Marta said with an air of finality. "Public opinion matters, even if you'd like to pretend that it doesn't."

I blew a sigh through my teeth, because she probably wasn't wrong about that.

"My friends and family do not generally have the sort of functions that I'd wear a ball gown to, Marta," I said. "It's been packed away for a year, and I've had no occasion to wear it. Would you like it back? I understand that such gowns are very dear—"

"I'm going to presume that you do not *mean* to give insult," she said severely, crossing her arms and glaring at me.

"Where I come from, when you find yourself in possession of something that is of no further use to you, but which might be very useful to someone else, you give it away. As a child, practically all of my clothing passed to me from Mishona and other older cousins, and when I'd outgrown it, it passed on to Sakewa, or to other girls. None of them will have use for a bronze taffeta ball gown!"

"I gave it to you," Marta said. "What you do with it is your business, not my own. I will not take it back."

"Would it be rude of me to give it to someone else?" I asked. "Am I supposed to just . . . keep it packed away? If so, for how long? What do *you* do with dresses that cannot serve you anymore?"

Marta frowned again and looked thoughtful for a moment, then answered, "I'm reasonably certain that they go to charity; our housekeeper manages all that."

"So would it be socially appropriate for me to give the dress to a charitable cause, if I know that I won't have occasion to wear it again?"

"I suppose," Marta said, sounding fretful.

"What should I wear tomorrow? For luncheon with you and Lisbet and Mathilda?"

"You don't have a proper tea gown," Marta observed, worrying at her lip with her teeth thoughtfully for a moment. "The day dress with the stripes might suit; that one looks very well on you."

She wasn't wrong about that; the dress Liberty had made for me was the smartest and most flattering dress that I owned. Liberty would know what to do about the taffeta ball gown; Miss Jenni might be able to sell it in her shop. I had no idea how much such a dress could fetch, secondhand, but any amount of money could be put toward her paying off her debt and get her that much closer to freedom.

"All right," I said. "I've got to get to class. I'll go with you tomorrow to meet Mathilda, and I'll wear my striped dress. Will we be having breakfast as usual, or dining at Sjokliffheim?"

"Breakfast here, luncheon there," Marta said. "Thank you, Anequs. For coming with me. It means a lot. I don't have many friends."

I smiled at her and went back to packing my satchel, saying nothing of the fact that she might have more friends if she was more willing to treat everyone she met as an equal.

Maybe it was time to invite her to sit and talk with Liberty and me on Sunday mornings.

ANEQUS VISITED SJOKLIFFHEIM, AND MET NEW PEOPLE

The following morning, after breakfast—where we explained our plans for the day to Theod and Sander—Mister Otterlo arrived in the automotor to take us to Marta's house. Knowing that we'd be gone most of the day, I insisted quite firmly on visiting Kasaqua at the dragonhall before we departed. Marta thought it was unnecessary—that I was coddling her unduly, and that it was rude to make Mister Otterlo wait.

"If we'd had more time to plan, we might have ridden the dragons overland to your house and avoided taking Mister Otterlo's time at all," I said, trying not to sound snappish.

"That would have taken *forever,*" Marta lamented. "Magnus covers five miles an hour at a walk, and ten at a brisk trot, and I can't imagine Kasaqua's any faster. The automotor is twice that fast and a bit more."

"Oh, no, two hours instead of one!" I said with mocking severity. "Copper is already too large for a horse stall, and Kasaqua will probably be too large by winter recess; Theod and I are going to have to travel overland to the docks in Catchnet to get home. I've already worked it out—by pacing between walk and trot, we ought to make it in four or five hours."

"Besides the time, we'd have had to dress for riding and would have needed to wash and change before meeting Frau Morris and her children, and it would have been awkward," Marta insisted. I rolled my eyes and sighed dramatically, but didn't challenge her further on the subject.

Traveling by automotor was bracing, speeding along between twenty and thirty miles an hour with the wind catching my hair, more akin to sailing than anything else. By the time we'd discarded our goggles and wrappers, everyone at the house had already been informed of our arrival. We joined them in the front parlor: Marta's father and three strangers—presumably Frau Morris and her children. Her father rose as we entered, coming forward to draw Marta into a hug. He released her after a moment and turned, his hand perched on her shoulder as he faced the others.

"Janet, I'm delighted to introduce my daughter, Marta, currently enrolled at Kuiper's Academy, and her schoolmate, Miss Anequs. Girls, allow me to introduce Frau Janet Morris and her children—Mister Iain Morris and Miss Mathilda Morris, lately of Scotsland."

I dipped a polite curtsy, noting from the corner of my eye that Marta was doing the same, which meant I'd guessed correctly about the proper response to that kind of introduction.

Frau Morris was a stately woman between forty and fifty years of age, tall and stout with very pale skin. Her dark hair, pulled back with a pair of combs, was shot through with silver. Marta had already told me that Iain was twenty and Mathilda eighteen—the same ages as several of our classmates. Both had the same dark hair as their mother. Iain was broad-shouldered and stocky; Mathilda, shorter and plump. While Frau Morris and Iain were looking at Marta, Mathilda was looking at *me* with a disconcerting level of interest. Her eyes were very green.

"Greetings, Marta, Anequs," Frau Morris said, inclining her head slightly at each of us in turn. "Please, come sit."

She had a very distinctive accent, broad in the vowels and lilting in cadence. It was quite different from the Anglish that I was used to.

"We're still waiting on one member of this party, aren't we?" Frau Morris asked, looking to Marta's father.

"Miss Lisbet Jansen, yes," he replied. "I'm sure she'll be along presently. Now Iain, if you'll join me in my office, we can leave the ladies to their own devices. I've got some plans I'd like your opinions about."

Within a few moments, Marta and I were seated opposite Frau and Mathilda Morris, the low table between us set with tea and cakes and bread and jam. Frau Morris took up something from just beside her; it quickly resolved into some kind of knitting that I wasn't familiar with, something worked with just one hooked needle. Mathilda was still staring at me, unblinking. It reminded me of the way that Niquiat looked at engines and clockwork things—fascination with an *object.* It was distinctly uncomfortable to be the focus of such scrutiny.

"I've never met a native before," she said at last, sounding flustered. Her accent was the same as her mother's, and she spoke very quickly; I had to pay close attention to understand her. "I've read all of J. Goodlove Barrelman's *Longrifle* stories, and Emanuel Nordlund's accounts of his time on Nack Island, and *The Captivity and Restoration of Frau Hrodland.* I've read the interviews of you and the other native dragoneer that were published in some local paper—they were reprinted in the *New Linvik Quarterly,* which is the only periodical from Markesland that they keep in regular circulation at the Library of Glascau. Both of you seem very articulate in your command of the Anglish language, and—"

"Mathilda," Frau Morris said, a warning tone in her voice. Mathilda immediately went silent and turned quite pink, looking down at her hands in her lap. If I hadn't known that she was eighteen, I'd have guessed her younger than I was—more like Jadi's age.

"You say that as if you're surprised that Theod and I speak articulately," I said, raising my eyebrows. "I learned Anglish from the cradleboard, right along with Masquisit, and as far as I know, Anglish is the only language that Theod has command of. I've never heard of the *Longrifle* stories, or anything about *Frau Hrodland,* I'm afraid."

Marta glanced at me, something slightly frantic in her eyes. This was not going well, as first introductions went. There was tense silence for a few moments; then, Marta turned to Mathilda and asked, "So, you like adventure novels?"

"Oh, yes, very much so!" Mathilda said, brightening a bit, glancing at her mother as if for approval. Frau Morris had turned her attention back to her needlework, though, and didn't meet her daughter's gaze. "I'm very fond of historical and philosophical romances."

"Have you read any Johanna Lindemann?" Marta asked. Mathilda's smile faltered just slightly, disappointment in her eyes.

"Lindemann's not really to my taste," she said carefully. "Love stories aren't . . . I mean . . . I like stories about distant places and times, about people who think and act very differently than normal everyday people. I like to read explorers' accounts: Björn Ironside's accounts of his raids in Tuscanland and Aprika, and Karsten Niebuhr's accounts of his travels across the Arabish dryland. Marco Niccolosson's accounts of the far east, and Gartzea's journey up the Great Serpent River in South Markesland. And of course, *Fyra's Leid,* and the *Longrifle* stories, which are all about the exploration of North Markesland. I still can't quite believe that I'm actually *here,* even when I've got an actual native sitting opposite me—and a very famous personage, at that! You must have had a *fascinating* life before becoming a dragoneer, living on a remote island far from civilization."

I might have said something about Masquapaug not being all that far from civilization, having a post and telegraph office and regular ferry service, but a young woman in servants' clothes appeared in the doorway to announce Lisbet Jansen's arrival. She had someone else with her—a woman of forty or so, in a plain but serviceable day dress—who was *not* announced. I remembered one of the girls from Lisbet's school—Saskia, perhaps—saying something about needing to have chaperones to leave the school grounds; I had no idea what that meant about the unnamed woman's place in society.

Marta rose to meet and embrace Lisbet, taking her hand and guiding her over to our little gathering, going through formal introductions in the Anglish style, ending with, "Lisbet and I have been friends since primary school; her brother, Sander, is one of our classmates at Kuiper's."

"So he's a dragoneer, too?" Mathilda asked, wide-eyed.

"He is!" Lisbet answered cheerfully, taking a seat on Marta's other side. "His dragon, Inga, is a velikolepni."

"I'm afraid I don't know much about dragon breeds," Mathilda confessed. "What sort of dragon is yours, Marta?"

"Magnus is a bjalladreki," Marta said, a strange timbre in her voice—disappointment, or self-consciousness, or something like that. "The breed's general utility has made them quite the most common sort of dragon in Lindmarden."

"Well, I don't think that *any* dragon can really be called common," Mathilda said. "I've never seen any dragon that's not a silberdrache, and even then, I've never been able to get close. Your dragon will be living here while you're in residence?"

"Yes," Marta said, glancing at the doorway that her father and Iain had left through. "Papa and I need to talk more about the building of the dragonhall, I think. We've been housing Magnus in the stable, when he's here, but he's getting entirely too large for that sort of patched-up solution."

"I should very much like to meet your dragons, wherever such a thing might be possible," Mathilda said, unhidden longing in her voice.

"Speaking of that," Marta said, "I wanted to formally invite you to our school's Valkyrjafax ball, at the end of October. The school is very much in want of young ladies at such functions, because the students are overwhelmingly young men. We have three women students this year, in a student body of ninety-seven. Students are encouraged to invite their sisters and acquaintances to make up the numbers. It will be a lovely opportunity for you to meet others of my social circle."

"Oh, Ma, please say I can go!" Mathilda asked, sucking in a breath and holding it at she looked to her mother. Frau Morris looked up, unsmiling, eyes thoughtful.

"This event is well-chaperoned, I presume?" she asked, looking to Marta.

"Of course, ma'am," Marta answered. "Lisbet joined us last year, and several other girls from Vígsteinnsdottir's Academy for Young Ladies."

"We had a lovely time," Lisbet said, nodding. "The professors are generally in attendance, and the parents of some students. You might like to come yourself, ma'am, as a chaperone—it would be an opportunity to become better acquainted with your social peers here in Lindmarden. If you have a calling card, I'll happily pass it to my mother. I'm sure she'd love to meet you."

Lisbet did not sound entirely sincere in that assertion, but then, I'd *met* her mother. I didn't know much about the social circles of women of Marta and Lisbet's class, but Frau Jansen was not someone I'd recommend as a friend or acquaintance.

"Well, that's certainly something to look into," Frau Morris said, turning her attention back to her needlework.

Marta excused herself for a moment to fetch a stack of magazines with watercolor plates of all the newest ball gown fashions. Off-the-shoulder dresses were evidently very much in favor this season, as were tiered, layered skirts with decorated hems. One of the magazines came with a booklet of fabric swatches: silks and satins and taffetas. I was thumbing through it while the other three girls discussed details of bodice construction and what style would flatter Mathilda best—and what was most fashionable this season in New Linvik, and in Glascau and Lunden. I came upon a swatch of red fabric that shifted color in the light, flashing from the color of ripe cranberries to the color of black cherries and back—something in how it had been woven. It was a smooth, crisp fabric—a taffeta of some kind. The label affixed to the bottom corner said *Shot Silk—RedBlack no.17*.

"Marta," I said, catching her attention, holding the fabric swatch out toward her, "I want a dress made of *this*."

Marta's eyebrows went up as she took the fabric from me; then she frowned.

"Well, it's a *very* strong color," she said, hesitantly. She frowned and looked thoughtful, looking from me to the fabric and back. "But then, you've a strong complexion. Come over by the window, stand in the light, hold it up to your face."

The four of us made a procession first to the window and then to a shadowy corner lit only by a gas lamp.

"I think it would look very becoming on you," Lisbet announced, glancing from me to Mathilda to Marta, as if she expected someone to challenge her. "And dresses for Valkyrjafax can afford to be very bold, can't they? Mother always insists on putting me in demure shades, but that shouldn't limit anyone else. You wore apple green last year, Marta, and it was beautiful!"

"Well, I'll tell you what, I'll talk to Papa later, and I'm sure he'll approve of having my seamstress make you a dress so that your mother has no say in it at all, this year!" Marta insisted. "You can make it up to me someday when you've got a household of your own, if you like."

Marta had never indicated to me that I should or would be able to "make up" for either of the dresses she'd gifted me, or the one she was about to gift me. I had to wonder what that meant to her, regarding Lisbet. Anglish matters of money continued to elude me, by and large.

The four of us continued conversing about dresses and about

the Valkyrjafax ball all through luncheon, Marta taking detailed notes to pass along to her seamstress all the while. Mathilda, it was decided, would have to have something in a green shade that flattered her eyes. Lisbet looked very well in purple, but purple wasn't really a Valkyrjafax color, though blue could be. Marta set her heart on another of the shot silk swatches—a rose-pink shade that reflected gold.

After luncheon, a carriage came to collect Lisbet and her chaperone and take them back to Vígsteinnsdottir's Academy. Marta's father and Iain returned, and we said our goodbyes and joined Mister Otterlo in the carriage house to be escorted back to school.

As we were putting on our goggles and wrappers, Marta asked, "So what do you make of Mathilda and her mother?"

"Mathilda seems well-meaning," I said, thoughtfully. "She's obviously an avid reader, though I get the sense that she's spent more time between the pages of books than she has out and about in the world. She was entirely too interested in me—or her *idea* of me? Still, she doesn't seem like a bad sort, not mean-spirited or anything. I can't say much about Frau Morris at all—she was so quiet the whole time."

"Well, that's to be expected; she was there as a chaperone. I doubt she has much interest in the society of girls of our age. In the telegram that Papa sent, he explained that Mathilda's never been out in society before. Her late father's illness began several years ago, when she was much too young to think about such things, and it's rather left her behind. Coming to Lindmarden can be something of a fresh start for all three of them, but especially for her. She really ought to be out meeting suitable young men, trying to make a good match, to secure her future."

"You might have told me that before," I said, only mildly annoyed.

"I didn't want your opinion to be biased by the knowledge," Marta said. "I wanted to know your true first impression."

"Well, you've gotten it," I said. "She seems a decent sort, and I wouldn't mind spending more time with her. I'll have to look up some of those books she mentioned, I think, to get a better idea of where she gets her notions about me and my people. I've never even heard of the *Longrifle* stories, or *Frau Hrodland's Captivity and Restoration*. Who's Frau Hrodland, by the way?"

"We had to read about her in primary school," Marta said, distaste creeping into her voice. "Back in Sigur Windtooth's time, she was very famously carried away as a prisoner by the Lenni-lenni people when they raided her settlement, and was held among them for three years. She was able to keep a detailed journal of the experience. As to the *Longrifle* stories, I've never read them, but I've read many criticisms of them. J. Goodlove Barrelman has no formal education in literature, and it shows very plainly in the writing. The stories are all extremely fanciful and romantic, lacking substance or purpose."

"Well, then, I'll certainly have to look them up now," I said, grinning.

Marta frowned, and Mister Otterlo informed us that the automotor was ready. We climbed aboard, and the noise of the engine and the wind prevented further conversation for the duration of the ride back to school.

THEN SPENT THE EVENING WITH THEOD

Marta and I parted ways when we arrived, she to our shared room, and me to the dragonhall. The clock in the main hall read half past four. Kasaqua hadn't been out all day, and I could feel her annoyance and frustration. Besides, the dragonhall was the likeliest place for Theod to be.

I found him in Copper's stall, reading as he leaned against Copper's side.

"Happy birthday," I said, making him look up with a startled expression that softened when he realized it was me. "I'm going to take Kasaqua out for a walk before we lose the light; would you like to come?"

"Of course," he said, smiling and tucking the book away. "How was your visit to Marta's?"

I recounted the events of the day, and my impressions of Mathilda and Frau Morris, as I got Kasaqua out of her stall. We didn't bother with tack; the dragons weren't on duty.

The soft crunch of dry leaves beneath our feet was a counterpoint to our conversation as Theod and I walked deeper into the woods. The path was flanked by ferns and overhanging branches that filtered the late-afternoon sunlight, casting dappled shadows across the forest floor. The leaves above were a mix of summer green and the red-gold of autumn. The air smelled of fallen leaves and the last of summer's warmth.

I glanced over at Theod, noting how he seemed a little lighter today, his shoulders less tense than usual. We followed the gentle path to the pond, as we had with Liberty.

"But that's enough about Marta and her family," I said, as we settled down beside the water. "What did you do today?"

"Henkjan took me out to luncheon in the city; a pub he knows. We had smörgåsbord sandwiches and beer, and sang some songs. He, uh . . ." Theod coughed, looking mildly embarrassed. "He gave me a book."

"Oh?"

Theod reached into his jacket, where he'd tucked the book earlier. It was a small volume, handily sized for a large pocket, bound in plain brown paper. On the cover, the title was printed just slightly off-level: *A Young Man's Guide to Love and Marriage.*

There was no author cited.

Theod let out a soft, nervous chuckle, looking at me and clearly waiting for some response on my part. I thumbed the book open and was mildly surprised to find that the first two pages were a pair of quite detailed illustrations labeled "Man and Woman in a State of Nature." The woman was holding a cup in her left hand, the man a spear in his right, and they were holding hands. They were entirely naked.

"Dare I ask what kind of book this is?" I asked, glancing up at Theod, who looked absolutely mortified.

"Turn the page, look at the table of contents," he said, looking down at his boots.

Within, the title appeared again, followed by a list of chapters:

DIFFERENCES OF THE SEXES
THE RELATION OF MARRIAGE
THE PROPER PLACE OF A HUSBAND, AND OF A WIFE
PURITY AND FIDELITY; THE CONSEQUENCES OF INDISCRETION
THE YOUNG WIFE AND MOTHERHOOD
THE NATURE OF WOMAN WHEN SHE IS WITH CHILD
THE CHANGES WHICH PRECEDE, ATTEND AND FOLLOW CHILDBIRTH
PRESERVING PERFECT HAPPINESS IN A HOUSEHOLD

"Henkjan gave you this book?" I asked, raising an eyebrow.

"He said something about my being eighteen now, and that he's seen me spending a lot of time with *you,* and knowing that I've never had a father to tell me certain things. He was stumbling through it, and he shoved the book into my hands and changed the subject very quickly thereafter. I didn't want to ruin it by telling him that I've gotten talks about the mechanics of . . . physical love. How babies come to be, and that."

I continued thumbing through the pages; under the chapter heading for DIFFERENCES OF THE SEXES, there was a quotation rendered in bold text, which I read aloud.

"'It is well known that woman's sexual inclinations are much less impetuous than man's. In fact, it is not uncommon for a wife to possess no great passion at all—merely a wish to perform her duties as a wife and mother.'" I couldn't help laughing out loud at that, which made Kasaqua come bounding over to see. "I can attest, as a woman possessed of certain inclinations, that *that* is absolute nonsense!" I said as soon as I was able to stop laughing. "I think Henkjan meant well, but this book sounds like it's full of ridiculous ideas. I dare say it's even worse than the *Guide to Perfect Comportment* that Marta gave me! Did he really think this would be helpful?"

Kasaqua butted her nose against my hands, curious as to what was causing my amusement. I scratched behind her ears, then looked back at Theod. "What do *you* think about this book?"

He shrugged, looking slightly more comfortable now that my laughter had broken the tension. "Henkjan's heart was in the right place, I suppose. He's been . . . well, something of a father figure to me since I arrived at the school. I think he was trying to help, in his own way."

I flipped through a few more pages, still occasionally snorting with laughter. When I turned to the chapter heading about PURITY AND FIDELITY; THE CONSEQUENCES OF INDISCRETION, it had subheadings listed Powers of the Genital Organs at Rest, Powers of the Genital Organs when Excited, Powers of the Genital Organs in Action, and Deleterious Effects of Misuse of the Genital Organs. Turning to that last claim curiously, I found another quote rendered in bold text:

" 'Misuse of the Genital Organs, that most loathsome and debasing of practices, does not merely tarnish the body and mind, but corrupts the very essence of one's being. It is the secret plague that unleashes a torrent of diseases upon the body of the unfortunate who partakes—weakening the heart, destroying the strength of the limbs, and withering the vital energies. It befouls the imagination, turning the mind toward every unwholesome desire, twisting it to inevitable moral decay. The loss of strength from the loss of one's vital essence is so profound that even the simple act of standing becomes an insurmountable challenge. Furthermore, the victim becomes increasingly prone to melancholy, fits of rage, and an irreversible despondency that may lead to insanity. Those who indulge in this vile act are cursed to suffer from a perpetual state of nervous agitation—trembling hands, pallor, waxen skin, loss of hair, loss of teeth, and premature old age.'

"I can't imagine anyone actually believing some of these statements. 'The proper place of a wife is first and foremost to provide comfort to her husband'? Absolutely ridiculous."

"I'm glad you find it so amusing," Theod said, but there was a smile playing at the corners of his mouth. "Though I'm not entirely sure what to do with this book now."

Kasaqua, sensing our playful mood, nudged Copper and then took off into the underbrush, looking back over her shoulder as if to invite him to chase her. The light was growing fainter, casting long shadows through the trees.

"We could always use it to start a fire," I suggested mischievously, holding up the book. "Or perhaps we could read the most absurd passages to each other and mock them? Listen to this: 'It is clear that a woman, in the exercise of her marital duties, should never allow herself to feel the base inclination to enjoy the act for her own pleasure. Her duty is purely for the continuation of the species. To desire intimacy for one's own gratification is a vice most unbecoming.'"

Theod laughed—a genuine, full laugh that I rarely heard from him. "I think Henkjan would be mortified if he knew we were laughing at this."

"Well," I said, snapping the book shut and handing it back to him with an exaggerated dramatic flourish, "we can't let such profound wisdom go to waste! I propose we keep this as our secret source of hilarity. Imagine us years from now, pulling this out at the most inappropriate moments to read the most absurd passages."

Theod's laugh was softer now, but no less genuine. "You'd do exactly that, wouldn't you? Interrupting some serious diplomatic meeting at the jarl's court to dramatically read about 'the base inclinations' of marriage."

"Henkjan meant well," I said. "He cares about you." I watched Theod's expression shift—that vulnerability he rarely showed, quickly masked by a formal seriousness that wasn't totally unlike his blank "servant" face.

"Well," he replied, "at least he didn't give me a comportment guide like the one Marta gave you. I'm sure that would have been even more unbearable."

The forest was growing darker, early twilight settling around us. Theod stepped closer, reaching to brush a stray hair away from my face. There was something in the way he looked at me—a softness, a warmth. For a moment, we were perfectly still. Then he leaned in, and I met him halfway, our lips meeting in a gentle, tender kiss. It was soft, brief—more a whisper of affection than a passionate embrace.

"We should head back," I murmured as we parted. "It's getting dark, and the dragons will be waiting for their evening feeding."

Theod nodded, a slight flush on his cheeks. Kasaqua bounded ahead, Copper following more sedately, as we made our way back through the deepening twilight.

SHE CONVERSED WITH FRIENDS

The next morning was Sunday; Jadi was still away at the Gellers'. Marta seemed loath to get out of bed, making complaining noises as I went about the business of washing and dressing.

"I'm going to the dragonhall to visit with Kasaqua. After breakfast, Liberty is going to be coming up to sit and chat over mending," I said in her direction. "You'll probably want to be up and dressed by then."

Marta made another grumbling noise and turned over, pulling the covers over her head.

"I was hoping you'd join us today. Jadi joined us last week, and we had a lovely time."

"I've got little enough in common with Miss Wozniakowa, and nothing at all in common with your servant friend," Marta grumbled, turning over again to glare at me from her nest of blankets. The way she'd said "servant" sounded . . . strange. Not precisely an insult, but something like it. I frowned at her.

"I think you'd be very surprised to learn how much the two of you have in common, actually," I said, crossing my arms. "You seem to be laboring under some illusion that because Liberty is a servant, she's some different species of person."

"She occupies an entirely different part of society," Marta replied.

"*I* occupy an entirely different part of society than you," I said. "If I'd grown up in the city, I might well be working as a laundress or seamstress or something like that. Do you still feel that you have so little in common with *me* that we can't converse?"

"You know I don't; I've told you that," Marta grumbled, sitting up and grinding a fist into her eye. "But—"

"Liberty is very interested in and knowledgeable about fashion and its history. I bet you'd have a lot to talk about if you were even a little bit game."

Marta huffed, hauled herself out of bed, and trudged her way to the washroom.

But she *did* join us, after breakfast. So did Jadi, when she arrived back from the Gellers' on the morning train.

Nine in the morning saw the four of us occupying all of the stuffed leather chairs in the front part of the room. Liberty was working on mending, me on beadwork, Marta on ribbon embroidery, and Jadi on tatting lace. Dreyst curled up at Jadi's feet, sleeping.

Liberty seemed . . . *not entirely enthused* by Marta's presence. Something was strange and quiet about her, the same kind of quiet blankness that Theod so often slipped into. Like the woman who'd served as Lisbet's chaperone, yesterday. I didn't know how to broach the subject, how to shake her out of that and get her to be the same Liberty she was when Marta wasn't around. She hadn't acted like this with Jadi; I had to wonder what made Marta and Jadi different in Liberty's estimations.

Jadi was explaining to us her newly finalized plans for October.

"I'm going to be away for a bit to stay with the Gellers; it's the High Holy Days soon."

"The . . . what?" Liberty asked, not looking up from the button she was replacing on the cuff of a uniform shirt.

"Zhidish holidays," Jadi said. "Dynah had a *lot* of trouble about this when she went here, and our father had to come and talk to them in person, but it's all sorted now. I've already talked about it with Frau Kuiper, and it's arranged with the Ministry of Dragon Affairs and all. Dreyst can come with me for the whole thing, I mean; that's the part the ministry cares about."

"How long will you be away? What will you do about your studies?" Marta asked, frowning a bit.

"I'll be leaving Friday afternoon next week, like usual, but then Rosh Hashanah starts on Sunday the twenty-fourth and ends on Tuesday the twenty-sixth. I'll be coming back on Tuesday and will probably make my afternoon class, but not my morning one."

"What's it a holiday about? Is it a harvest holiday, like Valkyrjafax?" Liberty asked, her voice very soft and . . . different. High? Sweet? It was the same way she'd spoken the very first time we'd met, in the library on my first day at the academy.

"Rosh Hashanah is new year—Zhidish people keep a different calendar than the Anglish one that everyone uses," Jadi explained. "I'll be here for the rest of that week, but then gone again next Friday—Yom Kippur is from October third into the fourth, and that's the holiest day of the year for us. After that, Sukkot is Sunday the eighth through Sunday the fifteenth. That's what I *really* wanted to talk to you about, because I wanted to invite all of you to the end of Sukkot, so I can introduce you properly to the Gellers and everyone. I told them all about the DGT when I visited over the weekend. The second meeting was much nicer than the first, and it reminded me of Shavuot, so I had a lot more to say about it this time around."

Jadi did not strike me as someone who was ever in want of something to say, no matter what the situation. The thought made me smile.

"Sukkot is a lot of fun," she continued. "It's a street festival where every family sets up a sukkah—a little booth—in front of their house. You take meals there, and go from booth to booth to visit and talk and all."

"And it's on Sunday the eighth, you said?"

"No, sorry; I said it wrong, maybe. It *starts* on Sunday the eighth, at sunset. It goes all week long, until sunset on Sunday the fifteenth. I'm inviting you to the fourteenth or fifteenth, in the daytime. I'm going to invite everyone at our lunch table—you don't have to all go at the same time, if you don't want. You don't have to come at all, I guess, but I'd be happy if you did."

Liberty did look up from her mending then, her hands resting poised in her lap. She fixed Jadi with a keen, penetrating gaze and asked, "To be entirely clear, are you inviting *me,* or just Marta and Anequs?"

"Yes, I'm inviting *you,* didn't I just say?" Jadi said, sounding a bit puzzled, looking to me for a moment as if I had some secret knowledge before looking back to Liberty.

There was a brittle moment of silence before Liberty said, "As a Blackfolkish woman and an indentured servant, it behooves me to make sure of things like this. I can never take for granted that I'm actually part of any group, except at my monthly salon. In my experience, most Anglish people regard most Blackfolkish people as a kind of animated furniture."

"Well, *I* certainly don't think that," Marta said, her tone performatively horrified. "It seems to me a very mean thing to paint all Anglish people with the same brush, simply because you've had what I presume to be rather horrible experiences with rude or unkind people who happen to be Anglish. If . . ."

Her words dwindled to silence when she realized that the three of us, Liberty and Jadi and me, were all staring at her, unsmiling. Her eyes went wide and pained, and I sighed through my nose.

"Marta, I would like all of us sitting here to be *friends,*" I said. "Think of this gathering as the ladies' auxiliary of the DGT, if that helps you frame it in your mind. If you don't want to be grouped into Liberty's understanding of how Anglish people behave, you'll have to prove yourself different from the common mode in some way. She's not wrong about the attitudes that the students and staff generally seem to have, regarding the servants."

"That's not at all fair, Anequs," Marta protested, frowning. "I *know* you've been reading Broadman Aristonson, so you ought to have a good understanding about the natural equalities and inequalities of mankind. It is entirely natural for people to seek society with people of their own kind—"

"What kind are you that's different from Liberty?" Jadi asked, leaning forward in her chair. "Is it the same kind or a different kind than me, or Anequs?"

Marta turned very pink, her eyes huge and wet—as if she might burst into tears at any moment.

"If I'd known that I would be accused of . . . of I don't even know what . . . I would not have agreed to join you three," she stammered, breathing hard.

"Oh, stop it. You're not as fragile as you're pretending to be, and none of us will be impressed by tears," I said. "You're free to leave, if you like."

"This is my room!" Marta snapped back, "I shouldn't have to be the one to leave!"

"I probably should just go—" Liberty began, quietly.

"No, Liberty, don't," I interrupted, reaching out to put my hand on the arm of her chair. "This is my room and Jadi's room as much as it is Marta's, and we outvote her two to one."

"I'm a third-year student, which means I've got preference of seniority," Marta insisted. "I know that you have high-minded ideals, Anequs, and that you come from . . . unconventional roots. But it's ultimately unkind to pretend that everyone is perfectly equal. Liberty is *not* one of our classmates and does not share our station. It's cruel to lead her on."

Liberty took a sharp breath in and let it out very slowly, her eyes closed.

"I think you ought to answer Jadi's question, Marta," I said, turning to her and fixing her with my gaze. "What do you mean by 'kind' when you say it's natural for people to seek society with people of their own kind?"

"I mean that you've made both of us terribly uncomfortable by trying to force us together," Marta said, glaring back at me. "Liberty is a servant, and obviously an industrious and congenial one. We are very lucky to have her, and greatly appreciative of her good work. But she's not a dragoneer, and not a scholar. Not . . . not a member of society! I'm sure she wants as little to do with me as I want to do with her; it cannot possibly be comfortable for her to be dragged before her betters as some kind of performance—"

"How exactly are you better than her, Marta?" I asked.

"I mean *social* betters, Anequs, and you know that! You're painting me to be some sort of monster, but you're the one who's been terribly rude by forcing us into this situation."

"The three of us had no difficulty having pleasant conversation last week," I said, gesturing broadly to Jadi and Liberty and myself. "Do you think I've been comfortably at ease every time I've been asked to pretend at being an Anglish lady for your elation, or Frau Kuiper's, or whomever's? I allowed myself to be dragged to Sjokliffheim yesterday as some kind of performance to your future stepmother and stepsister, to play the fascinating and exotic savage, to be evidence of how worldly and cultured *you* are—"

"That's not fair!" Marta practically shouted, tossing her embroidery aside and rising to her feet. "Nothing will ever be good enough for you, will it? You've got to press and wheedle and challenge and disagree with anything anyone says! I've half a mind to send a telegram to Papa and tell him to cancel the order for your dress, since you seem not at all grateful to be uplifted to any kind of social position."

She glared at me, clearly expecting some kind of dramatic reaction on my part. I remained sitting, looking up at her, holding her gaze. I was, in fact, slightly bewildered that she thought the threat of denying me her charity—which I had never asked for—

would upset me. I was supposed to scramble at an apology, or something like that. It was clearly what she expected.

"All right," I said, after a long and tense moment of silence. "If you don't want to buy me a silk gown with your father's money, that's fine."

The color drained from Marta's face, and her mouth opened slightly, then closed again. She swallowed thickly, and without saying anything else, strode over to the door and took her leave. The door slammed in her wake loudly enough that everyone on this floor had certainly heard it. A long beat of silence followed as I looked to Liberty and Jadi. Liberty was looking down at her hands, her face studiously blank. Jadi was frowning.

"I'm going to go talk to her," Jadi said, carefully setting her lace down on the table.

"Thank you," I said, watching her go. "You'll probably have better luck than I would."

Jadi's departure, with Dreyst scrambling along at her heels, left Liberty and me quite alone. I was about to say something conciliatory, but Liberty looked up at me with anger flashing in her eyes.

"You might have *told* me that Miss Hagan was going to be present," she said, her voice cold and flat. "I'd have made a polite excuse."

"I didn't expect it to go so horribly wrong," I said. "I'd thought . . . I'd hoped that Marta was coming around. She was game about joining the DGT with me. Which, by the way, I've been meaning to invite you to—"

"Absolutely not," Liberty responded instantly, looking even angrier. "You don't understand at all, do you? You and Miss Hagan and Miss Wozniakowa can all get on because you're all dragoneers. You and I can get on because we're both women of *work,* who don't come from money and don't enjoy a place as women of society."

"Jadi's a society lady, and neither you nor she seemed uncomfortable talking last week," I said.

"I'm not at all sure what to make of Miss Wozniakowa, to be quite honest; I think her people might have a somewhat different attitude about servants than is common among the Anglish. And she's younger than any of us, not yet fretting about her future. Anequs, Marta Hagan is the kind of person who hires people like me to do her laundry. Or, rather, she's the kind of person who hires a housekeeper to manage affairs like that without ever having a single thought in her head about it. She's not entirely at fault; I ought to have kept my mouth shut apart from saying thank you to Miss Wozniakowa's invitation. It's not as if I'll be able to attend, so there was no point in being prickly about being politely invited."

"Why shouldn't you attend?" I asked, frowning.

"Because I have just six hours away from my duties each week, Anequs!" she said in a tone that somehow sounded like shouting, despite being quite soft. "I have Saturday mornings to myself, and that's all. I can only manage to come here and sit with you on Sundays because I can do mending at the same time, and *that's* been washed down the drain today; I'm woefully behind. I ought to go back downstairs and hope that Miss Hagan doesn't think of saying anything about my behavior to Frau Brinkerhoff. You ought to go find her and make up with her, because you'll be in a terrible fix if she doesn't buy you a new dress for Valkyrjafax. You *can't* wear the one you've got, I hope you know that, and I certainly haven't got the time or the money to make you anything of the kind, if that's what you were hoping—"

"I do not care *at all* about Valkyrjafax," I said. "And I wouldn't impose upon you. Marta told me that I can't wear the bronze taffeta dress again to any public function, which means that it's of no use to me whatsoever. Do you want it? I'm sure you could make something lovely with the fabric, or see if Miss Jenni can't sell it secondhand—"

"You can't be serious," Liberty said, her face going blank . . . going *shuttered.*

"Why can't I?" I demanded, frowning. "I wouldn't begin to know what to do with it, not like you will."

"That dress has got to have six yards of silk—taffeta like that can sell for fifteen marka a yard. I've no doubt that it cost *someone* an excess of a hundred marka to have that dress made for you."

"I asked Marta what I ought to do with it, since I can't wear it again to any public function, which is the only kind of function I'd ever need that kind of a dress for. She said that her old dresses go to charity, and that her housekeeper handles that sort of thing. If the proper thing for me to do is to give it away—because it's doing no one any good at all sitting in my wardrobe—then I can think of no one who will make better use of it than you."

"What you ought to do is sell it and use the money to buy a new dress for the ball," Liberty said.

"I don't care at all about the ball!" I said, folding my arms. "If Marta decides not to outfit me, then I just won't go."

"You can't just not go to the ball. You're one of only three young women at the academy," Liberty insisted, in a very matter-of-fact tone. "Everyone will notice if you don't go, and everyone will speculate, and it will cause no end of trouble."

"Then I'll pen a treatise about the absolute stupidity of spending a hundred marka on a silk gown to be worn once and only once. I'm sure *some* paper will be willing to publish it, just because it'll have been written by The Nackie Dragoneer. If there's going to be talk and rumors and whatnot about my deciding not to play along this year, I'll give them something to talk about."

"You really do mean it, don't you?" Liberty asked, narrowing her eyes and looking at me sidelong. "Do you mean to make yourself into a philosopher, then?"

"I still have no idea what that means, really—it's what Herr Gerdasson is, isn't it? Of all the fully realized dragoneers I've met, he's the most interesting."

"You would say that," Liberty said, with a tight little bark of laughter. "Fine. If you're set on giving me the dress, I'd be an idiot to refuse. If I plan this correctly, with this unexpected windfall, I might be able to pay off my debt by the winter recess. I'll want some money to put by, though, before leaving this post. I wouldn't want to impose on anyone's charity."

I wanted to tell her that she was welcome to come live on Masquapaug for free—but I thought better on it before I opened my mouth. It wasn't the right time to talk about things like that. I stepped over to my wardrobe and took the dress out. It was a very lovely dress, and someone had obviously put a lot of work into the making of it, and it seemed a shameful waste that it was just sitting here doing no one any good.

"You're sure that Miss Hagan won't be upset at you for giving this away? More upset than she already is, I mean?" Liberty asked as I handed the dress over to her.

"I asked her if she wanted it back, and she was insulted that I'd suggest such a thing," I said. "She said to give it to charity. I'm giving it to someone who'll know better than me how to put it toward the greatest good, which is precisely what she does when she hands her castoffs to her housekeeper. Marta's got no good reason to be mad at my giving you the dress—she might well be upset, but it won't be for a good reason."

"I'll have to find somewhere to put it by for a week, since I won't be able to see Miss Jenni before next Saturday," Liberty said. "Thank you. I really do appreciate this, and I understand what you're trying to do, getting Miss Hagan and I to talk, but I don't think that's going to work, and it would be more comfortable for both of us if you didn't try it again. If she's going to be around, I would prefer not to be present in the future."

"I'm sorry," I said. "I thought . . . I thought it would be like last weekend."

"You think better of people than they deserve, I think," Liberty said, looking at me fondly. The way her gaze softened made something go melty and strange in my belly. I very much wanted to embrace her, to kiss her.

But I only bid her good day and watched her take her leave, the dress tucked into a neat bundle on top of her basket of things to be mended. I ought to have gone to find Marta and Jadi, to try and make up with Marta . . . but I went to the dragonhall instead. It was the likeliest place for Theod to be.

AND LEARNED SOME UNCOMFORTABLE TRUTHS

I found Theod in Copper's stall; Copper was lying down, and Theod was resting against his bulk, reading a book. He looked up at me as I entered and said, "You look upset. What happened?"

"I've made rather a mess of things with Marta," I answered. "If I get Kasaqua out, do you want to walk the trails with me and talk a bit?"

"Of course," he said, tucking his book into a satchel and thumping Copper on the shoulder to wake him before climbing to his feet. Five minutes saw the four of us walking away from the flight field, toward the woods and its network of paths. I caught him up on the disastrous attempt at my Sunday morning social circle.

"I tried to introduce Marta and Liberty and . . . well, I suppose I tried to force them to converse as equals," I said with a sigh. "It went poorly."

Theod was quiet for a long moment before asking, "How did Liberty take it?"

"She was angry with me and said I should have warned her that Marta would be there—that she'd have made a polite excuse not to come." I ran my fingers through Kasaqua's feathers. "I thought . . . I don't know what I thought. Maybe that if Marta just had an opportunity to actually *talk* with Liberty, she'd see . . ."

"That Liberty is a person worthy of respect?" Theod's voice was gentle, but there was an edge of something harder underneath.

"Marta's just—"

"Comfortable," Theod finished for me. "She's comfortable with things as they are, as they've always been for her. You're asking her to be *uncomfortable,* to question everything she knows about her place in the world. You fall into a complicated place where you're her equal as a student and a dragoneer, but you're Liberty's equal as a poor person who knows what work is. You've thoroughly rejected Marta's attempts to elevate you to a position in society. She probably thinks you're trying to lower her position to your own level."

"I don't see that there's any 'level' distinctions to be made!" I said, knowing that it sounded petulant, even as the words left my mouth. "Marta makes much about 'social betters' and 'social inferiors,' and it's all absolute nonsense. I understand why Marta responded poorly, but Liberty being angry about it . . . I didn't expect that. She said she's only got six hours to herself every week, and she doesn't want to spend any time she doesn't have to with Marta."

"Can you blame her? It's exhausting, having to play nice for the gentry. You just *don't,* and you take the consequences as they come, and that's one of the amazing things that I love about you—but Liberty and I were raised to be servants. We were trained up in how to say: 'Yes ma'am, yes sir, right away, as you say, I'll have it done, thank you sir, that's very kind' and to be beneath notice when we're not being immediately useful. The only time you get to turn it off is when there aren't any toffs around—when you're with people of your own kind. People who don't have the power to blacken your name and prevent you from working. That's what it's really about, in the end. If a person like Marta complains to Frau Brinkerhoff that Liberty was rude to her, Liberty would be sent packing to a worse job than the one she's got. Better to avoid the possibility by having as little to do with people like Marta as possible."

"It makes sense when you put it that way," I admitted.

"You're right that it's nonsense, but it's nonsense that has real power over people's lives."

We walked in silence for a moment, the dragons ambling to either side of us on the shaded path. Finally, I asked, "How do you manage it? Being caught between the two worlds like this?"

Theod gave a bark of humorless laughter and said, "Not very gracefully, most of the time. I've got more protection than Liberty does; being a dragoneer means that minor social infractions can go overlooked. Frau Kuiper's patronage . . . I mean, you've seen it. But it's still . . ." He trailed off, considering his words. "It's still exhausting sometimes. Watching you throw it all to the wind, saying exactly what you think to everyone regardless of their station . . . I envy that. But I worry for you, too."

"Worry for me?" I asked.

"You've made powerful connections who protect you—Frau Kuiper, chiefly, and through her the jarl himself. But you've made powerful enemies, too. Sveni Audulfsson's out for you, *because* Birning Svenisson shot you, which he did because the Ravens of Joden are scared at the prospect of nackies having dragons. You've made it very clear in every interview and statement that you plan to go home to Masquapaug with Kasaqua when this is all over. When it was me in the spotlight, I was exactly as grateful and dutiful and conveniently contained as could be managed. I was Frau Kuiper's pet project, never expecting to leave the school."

He stopped walking and turned to face me. "I don't want you to change. Your fierce honesty, your refusal to accept arbitrary rules—it's part of who you are. But please be careful, Anequs. Not everyone is as understanding of your . . . directness as Liberty and I are."

The concern in his eyes made my chest tight. I stepped closer, drawn to his warmth, to the steady certainty of his presence. "I'll try to be more mindful," I promised. "I don't want to make things harder for either of you."

Theod smiled, reaching up to brush a stray hair from my face that had come free from my braids. "That's all anyone can ask. Now, shall we head back? It's almost time for luncheon, and if we're both missing, people will talk."

I nodded, grateful that he'd helped me understand what I'd inadvertently put Liberty through. We turned back, heading toward the school. I didn't especially delight in the thought of having to face Marta again. I stopped at my room after departing the dragonhall but before going to luncheon. Jadi was there with Dreyst, and Marta wasn't, for which I was very glad.

Jadi fixed her gaze on me as soon as I stepped through the door, and she said, "I've talked to Marta. She's being ridiculous, of course, but she's also genuinely hurt that you'd choose Liberty over her. She wanted you to chase after her when she slammed the door and ran away."

"I wasn't choosing anyone over anyone. I was trying to—"

"I know what you were trying to do," Jadi interrupted, holding up a hand. "And you're not wrong. Marta's exactly the sort of sheltered rich girl who needs her horizons broadened. But you went about it all wrong."

"Did I?" I asked, bristling slightly. She was probably right, but also it was hardly her business to correct me. To insert herself between Marta and me.

Jadi leaned forward, her eyes intent. "You tried to just push Marta and Liberty together without preparing either of them, like trying to teach someone to swim by throwing them in the ocean."

"Some people learn to swim that way," I said. "My mother carried me into the ocean before I could walk."

"Oh, sure, some people learn to swim that way—and some people drown." Jadi's voice was sharp, but not unkind. "I agree with you about Liberty; the way most Anglish people treat servants is shameful. But Marta's never had to think about any of it before. She's barely left her father's estate and places just like it, except to attend school."

"So what do you suggest?" I asked, sinking down into one of the overstuffed leather chairs at the front of the room. Jadi crossed the room to join me, but didn't sit.

"Let me go get her, and we'll talk. Just the three of us. I've convinced her that you weren't trying to humiliate her, which is more than nothing." Jadi rolled her eyes. "She's sitting in the library right now reading one of those novels where the heroine is terribly put upon by the world and not appreciated at all for how good and kind and charitable she is. Not even a Johanna Lindemann novel; one of the inferior knock-off types."

"Do you think she's actually going to withdraw her offer of a dress for Valkyrjafax? I need to start making plans, if she is."

"No," Jadi said with a slight smile. "I talked her out of that, at least. Pointed out it would make her look petty and spiteful. I asked her what Sander and all the boys in the DGT would think if they learned about that, and that made her reconsider."

"You appealed to what others might think of her," I said, frowning. "She shouldn't care so much about what others think of her."

"If you want to actually change Marta's mind about anything, you need to be more subtle about it."

"I'm not very good at subtle," I said.

"I've noticed," Jadi said, smiling in a way that showed off all her teeth. "It's one of the things I like about you; you say what you mean. But it doesn't always serve among people who are in the habit of *not* saying what they mean. Will you let me help? I think I can get her to make peace, at least. But you'll have to be willing to meet her halfway."

"What does meeting her halfway mean, exactly?" I asked, frowning.

"It means apologizing for springing Liberty on her without warning. It means acknowledging that you could have handled things better—" Jadi held up a hand as I started to protest. "I'm not saying you have to apologize for your principles; you're not wrong that we all ought to be able to talk around a table together because we're all just girls about the same age, and we all live here for the time being. It's just . . . you need to say sorry for how you went about it."

"And what about Liberty?" I asked, slumping back against the chair. "She was cross at me, too. I went and talked to Theod about it, and I think I know better now why she was cross, but—"

"One thing at a time," Jadi said firmly. "First, we need to mend things between you and Marta. Then maybe, very slowly, we can work on shaking all of the nonsense out of her head. But it has to be careful and slow, and so very, very *polite* and *appropriate,* if you want it to work on a girl like Marta."

"That's more or less what Theod said," I admitted.

"Theod is wise, then," Jadi said with a small smile. "So, will you let me arrange this? I promise to be on your side if Marta starts spouting nonsense about 'natural inequalities' again."

"All right," I said, dragging my hands across my face. "But I won't pretend to agree with her views just to keep the peace."

"I would never ask you to," Jadi said, standing up. "Just . . . try to remember that she's not cruel on purpose. Sometimes people can surprise you, if you give them the chance."

"Did I show you the etiquette book that she gave me when we first met?" I said, looking at Jadi sidelong.

"You didn't," she said, giggling, "but save it for later. We can laugh at it together sometime. I'll go get Marta."

"Thank you, Jadi," I said. "Really . . . I want you to know how glad I am that you're willing to play mediator between Marta and I."

"Helping people fight well is one of my very favorite things to do," Jadi said, grinning. "You should see me sometimes with my brother and my sister. Stay right here; I'll be back in just a minute."

She did return just a minute later, Marta following with her arms crossed around the book she was holding, a frown on her face. She sat down heavily in the chair opposite me, not precisely looking at me while she did.

"I'm not a monster," she insisted in a sullen tone.

"I'm sorry that I painted you as one," I said. "I didn't mean to."

"Did you mean what you said about my making you 'play the savage' to impress Mathilda? You have to know that's not what I meant, and if you really felt that way, I'd feel positively awful—"

"I don't think you were thinking about it that way on purpose," I said carefully, "but that's what it felt like because of the way Mathilda looked at me. I don't think she meant it that way, either. No one meant to give any offense. It rankled, regardless. Are you going to cancel the dress of red-black shot silk?"

"No, I'm not going to cancel the dress. I was just angry, is all, because I felt like you were accusing me of being monstrous. I don't see why it's such an effort for you to at least show a little gratitude, though! I'm trying to give you a gift, and you're acting like it's an inconvenience. Like you wouldn't even care if I withdrew my offer."

"I never asked you for it, Marta. I never asked you for anything," I said, trying to keep my voice even. "I'm not going to stand here and beg for a silk gown, or pretend that I'd be dismayed to be denied one."

Marta's expression hardened. "Well, I'm offering it, because you'll need it. I don't want you to end up embarrassed or disgraced because you don't know how to dress properly or behave correctly—"

Dreyst made a little chirping noise of concern, and Jadi stepped forward slightly and touched Marta's arm.

"Marta," she said, her voice calm but firm, "is this really about the dress?"

"Of course it's about the dress!" Marta replied, though her voice was less certain now. She was silent for a moment, considering. "It's about doing the right thing, about making sure Anequs doesn't ruin her chances. About helping her fit in, even if she doesn't see it that way."

"I don't need your help to fit in," I said, "and I don't need anyone's pity, either. I don't need you to be my savior, Marta."

Marta's lips pressed together, and for a moment, she looked as though she might argue again, but then she exhaled sharply and turned to Jadi.

"I'm trying," she said, the frustration now laced with something softer—perhaps the smallest hint of doubt. "I'm trying to make this easier for her, and I feel like she doesn't appreciate it at all."

"You can't force someone to be grateful," Jadi said, "especially if they don't feel like they need what's being offered. That's not how gratitude works."

"I'm not *ungrateful,*" I said, trying very hard to make my tone gentle. "But it's not just about the dress; it's about what it represents. When I accept gifts from you, I'm not free to make my own choices—my own mistakes."

"You wear the dress that Liberty got for you all the time," Marta said, looking down at the book, now sitting in her lap. There was a hint of jealousy in her voice, and it occurred to me that maybe that's what this was *really* about. That I preferred Liberty's company and sense and thrift and skill to Marta's . . . everything.

"The dress that Liberty made for me suits me. It's a dress for a person of the class and station that I am, instead of the one you'd like me to pretend to be."

Marta's eyes flicked away for a moment, and she pursed her

lips, as if weighing her words carefully. When she spoke again, it was quieter, though still edged with frustration.

"I just thought . . . you needed it. I thought that you'd be happy, or at least grateful. You should be. It's not as if I'm asking for anything in return. I don't want to be made out to be some kind of villain for trying to help."

I was trying to figure out what to say to that when Jadi said, "Marta, Anequs isn't saying she doesn't appreciate your gesture. She's saying that she doesn't want to feel like she owes you something. It's important that you understand that."

There was a long, tense silence in the room.

Finally, Marta asked, "So . . . was I wrong to offer you a dress in the first place? Last year, I mean? Should I stop doing that?"

"I won't say that it hasn't been a help, having you outfit me," I said. "If you hadn't, I'd have to be in Frau Brinkerhoff's office explaining that I don't own appropriate clothes for the kind of functions that everyone seems to think I have to attend here. If you decide to withdraw your charity, though, I'm not going to fall all over myself about it. I'm not ashamed of who I am—of not being a rich society lady who can afford a dress that's meant to be worn in public just once. I won't be your charity case, Marta. I won't be beholden to you for something I didn't ask for."

Marta blinked, clearly taken aback, and seemed to struggle with the words before finally nodding stiffly.

"Fine," she said, though there was still a touch of dissatisfaction in her voice. "I'll keep the order for the dress. Just . . . don't act like I'm the bad one here. Like I've done something wrong. I've been trying to *help*."

"I understand that. I'm just saying that gratitude isn't something you can demand. I don't want to owe you anything. I don't want to feel like I'm picking over coals just because I didn't express gratitude the way you expected."

Jadi gave smile and an encouraging nod. "It's a start," she said. "We've still got a long way to go, but it's a start."

"I suppose it is," Marta said, glancing briefly at me before looking down again. "But just remember . . . not everyone gets the chance to wear a ball gown like that. You looked lovely in it, and I'm sure you'll look lovely in this year's dress, too."

"Thank you," I said after a long moment, because she clearly intended for that to be complimentary.

"There now, all friends again," Jadi said brightly. "Let's go down to luncheon before the tables are all picked over; I'm starving."

And so we did, and went downstairs to join the young men at our increasingly crowded luncheon table.

THE ACADEMY HOSTED A GUEST

The following morning was Monday, which meant my directed study of al-jabr followed by a free period in the afternoon. I woke before either of my roommates, which was quickly proving to be the common course of events. Dreyst, who was tucked up into a loaf with his feet beneath him and his tail and wings curled in tightly, watched me with sleepy curiosity from his perch on the foot of Jadi's bed as I washed and dressed. I met Theod at the dragonhall, and we took Kasaqua and Copper for several turns around the flight field while I told him about Jadi helping me make up with Marta.

Breakfast was chatty and amiable. Jadi presented her invitation to Sukkot festivities on the fourteenth and fifteenth of October to everyone else at the table, and questions about Zhidish holidays dominated the conversation. Theod and I worked on al-jabr and anglereckoning until luncheon.

In the middle of luncheon, though, Professor Ibarra appeared at the head of the room and called for attention. When the room had quieted, he said, "I have an announcement to make. It has come to my attention that Herr Eskil Gerdasson, the famous lore-keeper and orator, is presently visiting Vastergot. He has agreed to come and give a lecture. It will be held on Wednesday, the twentieth, at eight o'clock in the evening, in the great lecture hall. All students and faculty are invited to attend."

By unanimous decision, our Wednesday meeting of the DGT was cancelled in favor of going to see Herr Gerdasson speak.

I spent the afternoon session riding Kasaqua along the trails. We found a stand of fox grapes growing between two boulders at the crest of a particularly rocky and unwelcoming path, and I had a handful, popping the flesh free from the musky skins—but the vines were young and the grapes very sour, even though they were ripe. Kasaqua was terribly pleased to gorge herself on them, not at all put off by their sour bite.

On Tuesday, it rained miserably all day long, and so both husbandry and skilatakraft lessons were held indoors. On Wednesday, I spent the afternoon period with Sander in the library, working with his windenbildmacher set. Mostly just playing with it, on my part, but *he* was working very diligently on a chart of which holes on which gears could be applied to which athers.

After dinner, when I went to visit with Kasaqua while Jadi and Osvald and all the other first-year students brought their charges to be fed, the dragonhall was abuzz with activity. Herr Gerdasson's dragon, Tamsyn, was lying on the grass just outside the dragonhall. She had her head right down on the ground between her forefeet, and a swarm of hatchlings was gathered around her face. Her mouth was wide open in a grin and was making a low crooning noise at the lot of them. I was put immediately in mind of Mamisashquee telling stories to a gang of attentive children, and couldn't help grinning.

The lecture hall was full to capacity, the same way it was when class assignments were handed out on the first day—all of the professors were present, as well, and Fraus Kuiper and Brinkerhoff. Professor Ulfar perched in his ambulatory chair at the top of the room, nearest the entrance, and most of the rest of the professors occupied that row. First-year students got the front row, closest to the lecture stage, because that was the row with a wide space in front of it for hatchling dragons to sit. Ernst had evidently been one of the very first people to arrive and had claimed seats in the second row, center, for every member of the DGT besides Jadi and Osvald, who sat right in front of us with Dreyst and Juniper. There was a lot of chatter, hushed conversations, and speculation. Many students had brought notebooks and wax pens.

I sat between Theod and Sander, with Marta on Sander's other side and Jadi next to Theod. When the clock chimed eight, Herr Gerdasson strode onto the stage, twirling his distaff around his hand as he walked. He was wearing a vividly purple suit, the lapels thickly embroidered with flowers and glittering beads. His yellow hair was in two plaits that hung over his shoulders, and he had purple aster flowers tucked into the braids. His eyes were outlined in black, presumably the same sort of thing that Marta had worn and offered to put on me for the Valkyrjafax ball last year—but the way he was wearing it was considerably bolder than the way Marta had, with sharp black lines forming extended points at the corners of his eyes.

He used his distaff to rap on the desk three times and called, in a clear, even voice that rang out across the hall, "Everybody shut up, I'm going to talk now!"

All of the murmurs and chatter in the room ceased, though some giggles and throat-clearing persisted.

Herr Gerdasson began, "Well, look at all of your bright young faces, so eager to take up your careers as dragoneers! Especially all of you in the first row with your hatchlings; I remember when Tamsyn was that little! Sort of. It was many years ago, you understand."

There was a murmur of laughter from the audience at that,

and he continued. "I suppose your teachers have filled your heads with all sorts of proper things about discipline and responsibility and the sacred trust between dragoneer and dragon—and they're not wrong! But they're not entirely right, either. You see, the thing that none of your teachers will tell you—because they're all far too respectable—is that dragons are gloriously, wonderfully *impossible* creatures. I'm sure that all of you already have stories of your dragons' unexpected antics, and most of your dragons are hardly even out of the shell."

He gestured broadly to the front row of students and the hatchlings at their feet.

"The first thing you need to know about being a dragoneer is that you haven't just paired with a mighty steed and a powerful engine of skiltakraft; you've paired with the most peculiar friend you'll ever have in your life. Tamsyn and I have traveled from Old Anglesland to Tyskland, from the icy shores of Norseland to the warm stones of Frankland, and let me tell you—she's gotten me into just as much trouble as I've gotten her into! Dragons have personalities as distinct as any human's. Some are morning creatures; some won't budge before noon without a bucket of fish and a good scratch under the chin. Some love the rain; others will sulk for days if they get their wings wet."

He paused again, waiting for the murmur of laughter to quiet.

"My Tamsyn? She's convinced she's a scholar! Sits and listens whenever anyone's telling stories, then wants to go see every place she's heard about. Or maybe just every place in general; it's hard to tell. But here's the real secret—the thing that makes being a dragoneer different from any other calling in the world: You're not just learning to work with your dragon, you're learning to see the world through their eyes, too. And let me tell you, there's nothing quite like seeing the world from above, through the eyes of a creature that was born to own the sky. Now, some folk will tell you that certain bloodlines of dragons are better than others, that a dragon with a perfect pedigree is in some way superior to an unplanned cross of unknown parentage. Nonsense! Complete and utter nonsense! I myself am of unknown parentage—"

He had to pause for a moment, because Frau Brinkerhoff had a sudden coughing fit. I wonder if she'd choked on the revelation that Herr Gerdasson's parentage was "unknown" . . . which seemed strange to me, given that—from what I knew of the Norselandish style of surnames—his name implied that his mother had been a woman named Gerda.

"—and Tamsyn, for those who have not seen her, is a *ruddy* silberdrache—red as blood and rust where breeders of distinction would insist she ought to be silver and gray," he continued. "There's some who say that ruddy silberdraches only bond with people likely to become skalds and bards and that sort of thing, but I'm not sure if it isn't the other way around—that only people with that kind of temperament welcome a dragon who hatches out the 'wrong' color. It's not about the breeding; it's about the bond. I've seen silberdraches too timid to fly in a stiff breeze, and I've seen the scrappiest little greenback outfly a storm."

"Greenback" wasn't a breed that I was familiar with; I wondered where in the world they might be from. They hadn't been mentioned in any of the books I'd read on the subject of dragon-reckoning.

"Remember this, if nothing else," Herr Gerdasson continued. "Your dragon isn't just some magnificent beast to be controlled. They're your companion in making trouble—er, I mean, in *facing life's challenges.* They're your partner in questioning the way things are, and imagining how they could be. And sometimes, just sometimes, they're the wiser one of the pair. So yes, learn your lessons. Master your skills. But don't ever let anyone tell you there's only one right way to be a dragoneer. The real art of it isn't in following every rule. It's in figuring out which rules matter and which ones are just getting in the way of you and your dragon becoming who you're meant to be."

He stopped for a moment, bowing and making a flourish with

his distaff, and there was applause from the audience. When they'd quieted, the lecture continued, moving easily from subject to subject; he was an engaging speaker.

After some time and much oration, he asked, "Now, then! Who has a properly rude question for me? Those are always the most interesting ones!"

Jadi raised her hand, and as soon as Herr Gerdasson looked at her, she asked, "What's that thing you're carrying?"

"It's a distaff!" he answered cheerfully. "It's a tool used to hold wool or flax when you're spinning, but it's also a symbol of seitherkraft, and of the god Enki. There are some who say that because spinning and weaving are women's works, the distaff is a feminine symbol. Others say that because of the way a distaff is *shaped,* it's a masculine symbol—and some distaves are more obvious about that than mine. It makes sense, then, for it to be a symbol of Enki, who changes his shape as suits him and who has been both the mother and father of gods and monsters. *I* carry this distaff as a mark of my office as a seitherman, so anyone can know that I am one from ten paces away and decide accordingly if they want to turn tail and run. Also it can be useful for knocking sense into the head of someone who needs it, sometimes."

He rapped sharply on the desk with the head of the distaff to illustrate the point.

"What's a seitherman?" another student asked; I didn't see who. His accent was Vaskosish, though. It occurred to me that I had no idea what the gods of Vaskosland were named, or what they were like. Professor Ibarra had mentioned some in passing, I was sure, but I couldn't recall anything just now.

"A seitherman is a devotee of Enki—the clever one, the shapeshifter, the solver of problems! Enki is the god of change, and the mother of all dragons. For what is a dragon if not change made flesh? They can transform athers and compounds and such, but they can also change the very way a society functions! A message that would take weeks by horse can be delivered in days, sometimes even *hours.* A town that would have been isolated by winter snows can be reached year-round. Take Tamsyn and me, for instance. According to 'proper' society, dragons should be used for very serious and official business—military purposes, or the affairs of the wealthy like racing and breeding and whatever, like dogs and horses. But do you know what Tamsyn and I do? We travel from stead to stead, gathering stories, spreading ideas, and yes—sometimes making delicious trouble! Tamsyn has sat through more philosophical debates than most scholars, has helped smuggle banned books across borders, has carried messages between lovers whose families forbade their marriage. Was any of that 'proper' use of a dragon's abilities? Perhaps not. Was it *right*? Absolutely! Because that's what Enki teaches us—that progress doesn't come from following the old ways blindly, but from asking 'why not do it differently?'

"Let me tell you something they won't teach you in your regular lessons: Being a dragoneer puts you in a unique position to *question* things. When you're up there in the sky, looking down at all the artificial boundaries mankind has drawn on the earth, you start to realize how arbitrary many of our 'sacred traditions' really are. Oh, they'll tell you that, as dragoneers, you have a duty to uphold the established order. And yes, you do have duties—but they are first to your dragon, then to your conscience, and only after *that* to whatever authority claims to command you. Remember, your dragons aren't just tools—they're thinking, feeling beings who *chose* to partner with you. You want to know what real responsibility looks like? It's not about blindly following orders. It's about looking at a situation from all angles—like a dragon surveying the ground below—and asking yourself, 'What's the *clever* solution here? What has no one else thought of?' Sometimes the most responsible thing you can do is cause a bit of chaos. Shake things up. Make people *think*. Who else has a question?"

"Isn't Enki the god of madness, and chaos, and destruction, and lies?" another voice asked; someone higher up in the hall, nearer the professors. "Why would anyone devote themselves to such a god?"

"Enki is all that and more!" Herr Gerdasson said, grinning to show off all of his teeth, his eyes wide and glittering. "Clever Enki teaches us that sometimes the most valuable thing we can do is be a bit 'utangard'—wild, unexpected, *free*! Destruction is very often the only path to new creation. Every really good story is a pack of lies. Take it from someone who's spent years living by the hospitality of others—the world needs both those who maintain order and those who question it. As dragoneers, you'll have the privilege of choosing which role you'll play. Sometimes you might even play both—helping maintain peace one day and challenging unjust laws the next. And if someone tells you that's not how things are done because it's not the way your ancestors would have done it? Well, you can tell them that the dead are *dead,* and they don't get a say anymore in whatever the living decide to do! The future of dragoneering belongs to you young people, who can dare to imagine new possibilities. With a dragon by your side, you have the power to help make those changes happen. So yes, learn your flight patterns. Master your landing techniques. But also learn to think for yourself, to question what you're told, and most importantly—to listen to your dragon. Sometimes they have a better grasp of what's right than all the learned scholars in their fancy halls. Now, all those questions were far too civilized. Hasn't anybody got a question for me that would make your regular teachers *faint*?"

"Is it true that you were run out of the High King of Frankland's court for engaging in unlawful congress with one of the queen's maids?" Ernst asked.

Above us, Frau Kuiper very loudly cleared her throat and said in a warning tone, "Mister Gram"—but Herr Gerdasson cut her off with a bark of loud, ringing laughter.

"See, *that's* the kind of impertinent question the lot of you ought to be asking—the kind of questions that make people frown and growl and choke and go red-faced," Herr Gerdasson said, with another hearty peal of laughter. "As to the question itself, I was . . . politely encouraged to take my leave of the Franklandish court for a lot of different reasons. For the record, though? It wasn't a maid."

There was a quiet murmur of speculation at that revelation, which was interrupted when Kam asked, "In your letter to the people of Vastergot, published in the *Vastergot Gazette,* you warned about the rising influence of the Ravens of Joden. As dragoneers, what role should we play in preventing groups like them from gaining more power?"

"Ah, now there's a properly *dangerous* question!" Gerdasson said, his eyes glittering as he twirled his distaff. "Men like Sveni Audulfsson appear now and again across eretide in the lore of every land. You're all familiar with the erelore of Wicked King Henrik, aren't you? My fellow skald Vilhelm Speerman wrote a bunch of rather good plays about him. Rikkard the Hunchback, as well. What about Ivan the Terrible, of Russland? Vlad the third, of Wallachia? And those are just the ones we know to be *actually real.* In folklore, we see Gwyrlass the Unworthy, Oddlief the Glutton, Koschei the Deathless. Men who will do anything and everything to have their own way. They tell people who are afraid of change that change can be prevented, that anything going wrong is the fault of *those other people.* Now, what happens to those kinds of men in stories, and often in eretide? They're overthrown!"

He rapped his distaff sharply on the desk.

"Your duty as dragoneers isn't to any party or even to the crown; it's to the truth you see with your own eyes. So use those eyes well. Watch who your torgars really serve; find out who they are and if there are enough of them. Know the smallfolk who live in your neighborhood, and find out what they care about. Carry messages for those who need their voices heard, and don't be afraid to tell anyone to shut up when they've been talking too long—"

The clock at the back of the hall chimed ten, and when it had finished, Herr Gerdasson said, "Exactly like that! I believe that'll be the end of my rambling for tonight; most of you have classes in the morning, don't you? Off you go, and think about what I've said. Think about questions you've been afraid to ask, and then *ask them.* If someone tells you that asking questions makes you utangard?" His grin turned fierce. "Well, sometimes a bit of chaos is exactly what justice requires."

There was applause from the audience, and Professor Ibarra rose and gave a short speech thanking Herr Gerdasson for his time and wisdom. We were all dismissed, and proceeded in a more or less quiet and more or less orderly fashion to our rooms.

I had a lot that I needed to think about.

NEWS CAME FROM THE CITY

The next morning, the dining hall buzzed with animated conversation, clusters of students gesturing with half-eaten toast and leaning across tables to voice their opinions.

"I can't believe he actually answered Ernst's question about the Franklandish court," Nils said, stirring his porridge. "Most visiting speakers would have just ignored it, or gotten horribly offended."

"There've been visiting speakers before?" I asked, setting down my plate and taking my seat. I glanced at Theod for confirmation, and he shrugged.

"None last year, but the year before that, there was a natural philosopher who came to lecture about her expedition to some southern islands off Berri Vaskos," he said. "I, uh . . . I didn't go to it."

I nodded sympathetically; Theod's first year here wasn't something he talked about much. It hadn't been easy for him.

"What about what he said about off-color dragons?" Osvald asked. "I've never heard anyone challenge breeding standards like that before. My uncle would have a fit. He's always going on about bloodlines and proper pedigrees."

"Uncle Otto wouldn't care about silberdrache standards," Ernst said. "Just kesseldrache ones."

"Still," Osvald pressed.

"What I don't understand," Kam interjected, setting down his cup, "is why he didn't give a clearer answer about the Ravens of Joden. All that talk about folklore and wicked kings—it felt like he was dancing around the real issue."

"Wasn't that his point, though?" Jadi asked. "About how sometimes being indirect is the clever solution? He told us to watch them carefully and help people speak up against them."

"Professor Mesman didn't look too pleased during all the bits about questioning authority," Ernst observed with a grin. "Did you see his face when Gerdasson started talking about dragoneers having a duty to their conscience before their commanders?"

"Thank the gods that Professor Ezel isn't here anymore; he'd have had a *fit,*" Evind said.

"Ugh, I can imagine!" I said, shaking my head. "I'm more interested in Herr Gerdasson's point about dragons changing society, though. We spend so much time in our lessons learning about what dragons can do *physically*—riding and flight and skiltakraft. We don't much discuss their impact on how people live, and think, and connect with each other."

"That's because you don't pay attention in your lore classes," Marta said, her tone chiding. I glared at her over my porridge, and she looked very deliberately unbothered.

"What I mean is that our people—nackies, I mean—used to have dragons. Then they didn't, and that changed how life was on the islands for a couple of hundred years," I said. "Just speed of travel—a canoe with strong paddlers can get from Masquapaug to Naquipaug in about an hour, and that's in clear weather. Copper can make the trip in ten minutes, give or take. Jadi, Dynah was explaining that the two of you took two days to get here from Runestung Hold. How long would it have taken if you hadn't been able to fly?"

"I don't know if it even *could* be done overland," Jadi said, looking thoughtful, absently scratching Dreyst's head. "A lot of the way is just wilderness, with no roads of any kind. When Dynah first came here, she and our father and Gikka traveled by boat down the Shademuck River. Our journey this year was much faster, even with Gikka carrying both of us and Dreyst."

"What struck me was his point about seeing the world from above making you question boundaries," Theod said. "I've noticed that myself, now that I've got words to put to the feeling. When you're up there with your dragon, all the property lines and border markers everyone fights about just . . . aren't there. They aren't *real.* You just fly right over them."

Our conversation was cut short by the need for us to get to morning classes—Sander, Vinzent, Evind, and I all had husbandry. Professor Mesman was sure to have more than a few things to say about Herr Gerdasson's lecture. I had skiltakraft in the afternoon, where Professor Schreiber was very animated in her praise for the lecture. On Friday, I had lore in the morning, and Professor Ibarra gave us a reading list of the stories that Herr Gerdasson had cited: Kings Henrik and Rikkard, Gwyrlass the Unworthy, Oddlief the Glutton. It didn't escape my notice that he seemed to only focus on the ones from Anglesland. I had natural philosophy in the afternoon, and then the Gellers arrived to take Jadi for her weekly visit to their home. Marta was visiting home for the weekend, as well, which left the room free for Liberty and me to talk over mending on Sunday morning. I was only a little surprised to learn that she and several of the other serving staff had listened to Herr Gerdasson's lecture from in the hallway.

Marta returned late Sunday afternoon, but Jadi didn't because of one of the holidays she'd mentioned, the one that ran from the twenty-fourth to the twenty-sixth.

On Monday morning, which was the twenty-fifth, I washed, dressed, and proceeded to the dragonhall to visit with Kasaqua before breakfast, but I found a tangle of people and dragons already waiting there. Frau Kuiper was standing outside the dragonhall with Gerhard tacked and ready, talking to Hallmaster Henkjan. Captain Einarsson was standing opposite them with his huge, ill-tempered silberdrache. There were two other silberdraches just behind him, ridden by men wearing the black-and-red livery of the dragonthede. Frau Kuiper noticed my approach before anyone else—because of course she did.

"Miss Anequs, what are you doing out here?" she demanded tersely, her eyes hard.

"I came to visit with Kasaqua. I usually do, before breakfast."

Frau Kuiper looked to Henkjan, who nodded. She frowned and looked back to me, saying, "That won't be possible today, I'm afraid. Go back inside. There's going to be an official announcement to the student body before breakfast is served."

"What's happened?" I asked, gazing past all of them, trying to see into the dragonhall. Kasaqua was awake, and curious about the general activity—the presence of strange people and dragons. She wanted to come out. "Why can't I see Kasaqua?"

"This has nothing to do with you, Miss Anequs. For once. Go back inside and wait for the announcement."

I wanted to argue, but something grave in her eyes, in the hard line of her mouth, brought me up short. Something was very, *very* wrong.

I proceeded to the dining hall without complaint, finding it entirely empty. I was too early; breakfast was served between seven o'clock and eight o'clock, and it wasn't quite half past six yet. I considered going to the library, or back to my room—if there was going to be an important announcement, then Marta ought to be here for it. Marta had a free period on Monday mornings and was likely as not to lay about in bed until ten in the morning if no one woke her. I was still considering when Sander arrived, Osvald and Juniper just behind. His eyebrows rose as he saw me, and they came to join me at the table. Sander was already writing on his tablet as he sat down, and he slid it across the table to me as soon as he was finished.

You're not usually here this early, why today?

"I tried to go visit Kasaqua, like I do most mornings, but Frau Kuiper and Hallmaster Henkjan are out there with Captain Einarsson and some thanegards. They wouldn't let me into the dragonhall. I was told to come back inside and wait for an announcement of some kind."

Sander looked a bit troubled and took the tablet back to write, *The staff usually start to put out breakfast a few minutes before seven, and I like to be done eating before it gets crowded.*

"Frau Kuiper said the announcement would be before breakfast," I said. "I think they're trying to get all of the students together in one place for it."

Other students began filtering in by twos and threes. The clock at the far end of the room chimed seven, but no one arrived from the kitchens to lay food on the serving tables. Theod joined Sander and me just before Marta did. She seemed to only be half awake, and mumbled something about letting her miss breakfast and the indignities of being roused by a maid.

"What's going on?" Theod asked as he sat down, his gaze moving over the empty serving tables.

"Breakfast is being delayed because there's going to be an announcement," I said. "That's all I know, and I only know that much because I ran into Frau Kuiper outside the dragonhall. Captain Einarsson is here with a couple of soldiers of the dragonthede."

"*Soldiers*? Not thanegards or jarls' guards?" Theod asked.

"Thanegards wear those gray coats with the brass buttons, and the jarl's men wear blue. The men outside were wearing black and red, like Captain Einarsson," I said. "And they're riding silberdraches. Frau Kuiper had Gerhard at the ready, too."

At ten past seven, Captain Einarsson appeared at the head of the room, looking very pale and grave. He had a handbell, which he rang until the room quieted and everyone's attention was turned to him.

"Students of Kuiper's Academy," he began, his voice ringing out across the hushed dining hall, "there has been a . . . significant incident . . . in Vastergot. Following a gathering in the public gardens last night, a large gang of armed men rioted through the cannery district. The thanegards have been able to put the riot down, but there are many people injured, and there have been several confirmed deaths. We have word from the thanegards that some kind of explosive was utilized, and that the riot may have involved one or more dragoneers. There are fires still being checked. Until further notice, all students are restricted to academy grounds. All incoming and outgoing communications will be carefully monitored until further notice."

Cold dread pooled in my stomach, making me feel sick and faint; Niquiat lived in the cannery district. Theod's hand found mine under the table, his fingers cold and his grip tight.

"Niquiat," I whispered, turning to Theod. "Do you think—"

"We'll find out," he said quietly.

"We understand that those of you who have family in the city will wish to communicate with them as quickly as possible," Captain Einarsson continued. "To that end, anyone who wishes to send a telegram may report to the mail room at eight o'clock to form an orderly line. Frau Brinkerhoff has been attending the school's telegraph, and all incoming messages will be delivered directly to students at their rooms; there's no need to hang about the mail room waiting for word. For those sending outgoing messages, we ask that no message exceeds fifty words and that students with siblings in attendance confer with one another to ensure that only one message is sent to each household. Classes will be suspended for the day, and we are asking all students to remain indoors for the time being—in your rooms, the library, or here in the dining hall. While I'm certain that many of you are concerned, rest assured that the well-being of your dragons has already been secured. I have personally selected a pair of officers of the dragonthede to safeguard the dragonhall. Those of you whose dragons are capable of flight may be called upon to meet with me later in the day; we may need to arrange a flying watch."

A heavy silence fell over the hall as the captain finished speaking. The usual morning chatter was replaced by urgent whispers and the scraping of chairs as students moved to sit with their siblings or closest friends. Osvald left us to join Ernst.

Sander was already writing on his tablet, his normally neat script slightly rushed. *Do you think this has anything to do with the Ravens of Joden? Sveni Audulfsson's been giving speeches in the Thane's Free Gardens.*

"What do you think they mean about dragoneers being involved?" Theod asked, looking at me uncertainly. "I can't imagine that anyone in the dragonthede—"

"I can," I replied, frowning. "Otrygg Otryggsson was a jarl's guard, once. How many dragoneers are there in Vastergot? How many of them are members of the Ravens?"

"We don't know anything for certain yet," Theod interrupted, though his expression was troubled. "Let's wait until we hear more details before speculating."

I needed to see Kasaqua. I could feel her concern—she had picked up on my distress and was trying to understand what had me so upset. I tried to convey reassurance to her, to let her know that everything was all right. It was hard, because everything *wasn't* all right.

I needed to send a telegram to Niquiat.

The kitchen staff began bringing out breakfast, though few students seemed interested in eating. No one was forming a line at the serving tables.

"I'm going to the mail room to send a telegram to Niquiat at the co-op. I'll send another home to Masquapaug, if I'm allowed," I said, then considered. "Jadi's people in the city aren't in the cannery district, are they?"

No one at the table knew where, exactly, the Zhidish quarter of the city was. Miss Jenni's shop was in the mill district, and Mendoza's Teas, where Liberty's salon met. How far had the riot spread? What counted as the cannery district by Anglish estimations?

Sander tapped on the cover of his tablet with a fingernail, getting my attention before sliding the tablet in front of me. *I expect that the servants and staff are more likely to have friends and family in the cannery district than most of the students are.*

I read the words aloud for everyone else's benefit.

"Let me go with you to the mail room," Theod said, rising and offering a hand to help me up. "You send word to Niquiat, and I'll send word to my aunt on Naquipaug—she can let everyone on the islands know."

We left the dining hall, finding the corridors already busy. As we walked, I could hear fragments of worried conversations.

". . . said they had *bombs* . . ."

". . . can't believe dragoneers would . . ."

". . . my cousin owns a factory there, right next to . . ."

The line for the mail room already stretched down the hall, and most of the people waiting weren't students. As Sander had said, they were maids, and men from the dragonhall. Many had papers clutched in their hands, messages already composed.

"What do you think will happen now?" Theod asked quietly as we joined the line. "If dragoneers really were involved, I mean . . ."

"Then Captain Einarsson and the Ministry of Dragon Affairs will hunt them down," I replied. "The dragonthede takes oathbreaking very seriously. Look what happened to Otrygg Otryggsson."

"It took months and months for it to happen, though," Theod countered.

I thought about Niquiat, about his co-op, and the cannery, and Haddir's, and that little pub on the waterfront where we'd gone to see Ekaitz's cousin play. The cannery district was the only part of Vastergot where I'd seen other nackies at all. It was the poorest part of the city, and where most of the people who weren't Anglish lived. It couldn't possibly be a coincidence that it was where the Ravens of Joden had turned their hands to violence.

A young man—one of the dragonhall workers—emerged from the mail room carrying a basket full of little cards. Telegrams. Presumably those that had been received, incoming missives from students' families. He walked away toward the young men's quarters.

"Are they really going to read all of our messages?" I asked, watching him disappear around the corner with his basket of telegrams. "There must be hundreds."

"They have to," Theod said quietly. "If dragoneers are involved, the ministry will want to know who's saying what. Most of the students come from established dragoneering families. There might be students who are related to whichever dragoneers were in the riot."

I thought about the conversations I'd overheard, the careful way some of my classmates spoke about "preserving our heritage" and "those who ought not be allowed the command of dragons." Had any of our classmates known that this was coming? Had they supported it? How many of the students had traveled home over the weekend, and how many were still at home? Marta and all the other third-year students, apart from Theod, had their free period on Monday and Wednesday mornings.

Another maid emerged from the mail room, clutching a telegram and crying. Her friend wrapped an arm around her shoulders and led her away. I couldn't tell if she was crying from relief or from grief.

The line moved forward again. Through the open door of the mail room, I could see Frau Brinkerhoff at the telegraph, her face drawn with concentration. Behind her, a stack of message cards was growing steadily higher. Messages were coming in faster than they were going out. A maid arrived behind her, and without looking, Frau Brinkerhoff handed her a spare handful of telegrams—

not enough to warrant a basket. She nodded and turned, looking at the card in her hand, then looking up at me. Our gazes locked for a moment, and she came toward me, holding out one of the telegrams. Handing it to me.

"Thank you," I said, my throat feeling tight, but she was already walking away toward the stairs. Toward the room that Marta and Jadi and I shared.

I looked down at the telegram in my hand, which read:

TO: ANEQUS
FROM: NIQUIAT

SAFE AT ZHINAS. CO-OP BURNED. EKAITZ DEAD. STAY AT SCHOOL.

I leaned against the wall, feeling slightly faint. I was marginally aware of Theod saying something to me, and I pushed the telegram into his hand. I didn't have it in me to say anything out loud. Niquiat was safe. Niquiat was *safe.*

Everything else could wait a moment.

A GROUP OF FRIENDS DISCUSSED ITS IMPLICATIONS

By nine in the morning, when classes would have begun, all of the professors had joined the gathered students in the main hall and dining hall. I didn't know where most of the servants were—if they were gathered somewhere below, or if they were expected to go about their work as usual. Food certainly appeared as usual from the kitchens. I didn't know where Liberty was, or whether she had people she cared about in the cannery district. There was no way for me to find out, and it was *maddening.*

Couriers on dragonback, Einarsson's men—different from the ones standing guard at the dragonhall—delivered us updates as they were posted. Professor Ibarra, as the loudest and clearest orator, had been chosen to read any and all arriving bulletins aloud to the room.

Jarl Joervarsson's response to the night's events came swiftly. He called an emergency thanesmoot and made an official statement in the palace's great hall.

According to the *Vastergot Gazette,* the jarl had said:

Yesterday, in the Thane's Free Gardens, members of the political thede known as the Ravens of Joden held a rally, headed by their wroughtthane Sveni Audulfsson. The thede has been loudly complaining about this and that for years, lamenting what they call "the downfall of society." Lately, they have been calling for an althynge to be held outside of schedule, because they do not approve of the appointment of new torgars—the people who are meant to listen to you and report your concerns to the thane. Yesterday, Sveni Audulfsson gave a speech to a crowd of some thousand people that was so venomous and filled with invective that Thane Arjan Stafn and his torgars felt it prudent to have the thanegards disperse the gathering. Instead of departing peacefully back to their homes, the crowd turned upon the thanegards with violence and, having forced them to fall back, proceeded to rage berserk through the streets from the Free Gardens down into the cannery district and the harbor. There has been much loss of life, much land and property laid to rack and ruin. There are *still* brave men putting out fires and searching collapsed buildings for survivors.

I am here before you today to say that there will be no tolerance for the kind of mindless savagery shown last night by citizens of Vastergot to their own people. *This ends today.* Word has already been sent to every torgar in the city, and I want the names of every known member of the Ravens of Joden. We will search their homes, their businesses, their meeting halls. Anyone who has aided or sheltered the men who did this will answer for the deaths our city has suffered.

People of Lindmarden, we are better than this. Let it be known that every district will be protected. Every citizen—Anglish and otherwise, whether born here or newly arrived—will be defended. I have called upon the thanegards of Vastergot, Varmarden, Skaldstead, Estervall, and Catchnet.

I have called upon the dragonthede, headed by Captain Johan Einarsson. I have called for aid from Runestung Hold to the north and Kingstead Hold to the south. My men will swiftly see to the restoration of law and order. You will see them in the streets, setting things to rights. If you have done nothing wrong, you have nothing to fear from them and their renewed vigilance. You should welcome them. It is your duty as citizens of Vastergot and of Lindmarden to obey them and assist them in whatever way you can.

I knew more than I cared to know about what the renewed vigilance of thanegards meant; it meant occupation and surveillance of the same kind we were seeing on the islands. It did not escape my notice that Sveni Audulfsson had been allowed to draw a crowd of hundreds *repeatedly*—this hadn't been his first speech—while Sachem Wompinottomak's meeting back in June had been immediately deemed "an unlawful assembly" and "a prelude to violence."

Osvald came back to our table, Ernst with him. Kam, Nils, Evind, and Vinzent all joined us as soon as he did. I noticed that other students—and *professors*—were taking note of our assembly, but no one else approached. We were left to hold court at our own table.

"Father's telegram this morning demanded to know if I was 'keeping appropriate company,'" Kam said to Ernst as they both sat down. "I haven't sent a reply; I figure I've got the excuse that the school's got just one telegraph, and everyone wants to use it. He didn't even ask if I was safe."

"I'm sure the school sent out a blanket message to all the families' households that everyone is *safe,*" Marta said. I glanced at her, then at Theod. Theod met my gaze knowingly. I very much doubted that such a message had been sent to Masquapaug or Naquipaug, even if it had been sent to other families. We hadn't been turned away by Frau Brinkerhoff when seeking to send a telegram, like some of the other students had.

"This is exactly what happens when people take philosophy too seriously," she continued, smoothing her skirts and glancing at me. Meeting my eyes for just a moment longer than was polite. "Turning political discourse into violence—it's *unconscionable.* None of it can possibly matter enough to warrant riots."

"They're rabble-rousers who don't understand how governance works," Ernst scoffed. "They can't just call an althynge whenever people are upset. Otherwise, we'd have a new jarl every few months."

"Well, their attempt to murder Jarl Joervarsson failed last year," I began, only to be interrupted by Vinzent.

"That was one man's action! The Ravens of Joden as a thede formally condemned Birning Svenisson's actions as not representative of the thede's beliefs and goals."

"Birning Svenisson was Sveni Audulfsson's *son,*" I said. "At the thynge on Naquipaug—"

"Where?" Vinzent asked.

"Nack Island," Theod supplied.

I blew a sigh through my teeth and continued. "At the thynge on *Nack Island* in August, Audulfsson said that his son was not a patient man, and that he acted rashly. He never said that Birning was *wrong* to try and kill the jarl. I think he's more upset that he failed."

"The jarl's response concerns me more than the riot, frankly," Nils said. "Searching homes? Making lists of members? That's not justice—that's persecution. He can't outlaw a political thede out of existence."

"It's necessary," Ernst argued. "We can't have gangs of berserkers burning down the city."

"But the precedent it sets!" Nils insisted. "The Freemansthede being in power and stomping out the Ravens of Joden seems well and good now, but what if the Eiriksthede or even the Ravens themselves come into power at the next althynge?"

"I'm frankly surprised that Thane Stafn even tried to have the crowd disperse. Isn't he a Raven himself?" Kam asked. "He pulled

Ivar out of the school and sent him all the way to New Linvik over Frau Kuiper's politics, after all."

"And good riddance to him," Evind said.

"Thane Stafn is officially a member of the Eiriksthede, like my father," Kam said. "Most of his torgars are members of the Ravens, though—or they were. I can't see them being allowed to stay torgars, given the jarl's speech."

"It's because the jarl declared that he'd be appointing a pack of new torgars to shore up the numbers," Evind said. "It's *supposed* to be a torgar for every thousand smallfolk, so Stafn should have something like two thousand of them reporting to him."

"He has a hundred and thirty-five," Marta said. I looked to see that she was reading directly off Sander's tablet, which made sense. I wouldn't have expected Marta to know how many torgars reported to Thane Stafn, but Sander cared about that kind of thing.

"And if the jarl is going to appoint eighteen hundred new ones, most of them aren't going to be Ravens or even Eiriksthede; they're going to be Freemansthede. Like the jarl," Nils concluded.

"Like anyone who's got a lick of sense," Ernst insisted.

"Our father says that every man thinks the Freemansthede sounds fine until he inherits and has to manage accounts and taxes and such," Osvald said.

"He says that because he thinks I spend too much time on philosophy," Ernst replied sourly.

"They're not wrong to see that as a *political overthrow* is what I mean," Nils said. "The jarl *is* eliminating people who disagree with him and using new appointments to stack votes against the ones he can't dismiss."

"No thane can possibly listen to the wants and needs of two thousand torgars. The thedes ought to be broken up into districts that each have their own thane, to keep things manageable," Ernst said. "I'll bet you anything that's what Joervarsson's really after—public support of adding more thanes to the council. He'll want to get the idea in everyone's heads before the next althynge."

"And the Ravens want an althynge to happen *before* that idea gets in people's heads," Kam said, thoughtfully.

"The jarl said: 'If you've done nothing wrong, you have nothing to fear,'" I pointed out. "From what I've seen, that's what people say before they start deciding *what* you've done wrong. Who gets to decide? The same people who already hold all the power? How often is anyone appointed torgar who isn't Anglish?"

"The jarl appointed *two* nackie torgars, one from each island, and they voted in a new thane of Catchnet because Jespersen's been a useless old barnacle for years and years," Ernst insisted. "It was the kind of victory for the Freemansthede that'll go down in eretide. We should draft a statement. As the DGT, we should take a position—"

"Are you *mad*?" Kam interrupted. "That's exactly what we *shouldn't* do. We're just students. Leave statements to people like Gerdasson."

"But if we believe in introducing the unquiet thought—" Ernst began.

"There's a difference between philosophical discourse and getting ourselves disinherited," Kam interrupted sharply. "Or worse."

Marta cleared her throat. "I believe we should all be very careful about what we say regarding these events. Even in confidence."

"Are you suggesting we shouldn't discuss it?" Vinzent challenged.

"I'm suggesting we remember our pledge of discretion," Marta replied. "Especially now."

"So, what, we do nothing?" Theod asked, frowning at her. "Let's not pretend that it's some sad coincidence that the cannery district is where the berserkers headed; that's where most of the people who aren't Anglish live. It's where the nackies and Vaskosish and Kindah and Blackfolkish people live."

"Everyone always blames the foreigners, as if the natives never cause trouble," Osvald said.

"The Anglish aren't natives to Lindmarden," I said, setting my jaw. "The nackies are."

"I'm sorry, you're right," Osvald apologized quickly. "You know what I *meant,* though, don't you?"

"I do," I said. "But according to the erelore that Professor Ibarra has put in front of me, Vaster's Hall, on Vaster's Hill, was finished in the year 1650. That's when it was declared a city and not just a steading. Before that, the hill was called Maswachu: the Great Blue Hill. The Maswachuisit people lived there. Before Catchnet was Catchnet, it was Akashnette, and the Akashneisit people lived there. Before Gannet Cove, there was Naregannsette, and the Naregannisit lived there. You're *newcomers,* all of you. We ought to find out what the Confederation of the First People of Akashnet has to say about this. I know that there are a lot of nackies in the cannery district . . . or at least there were, until last night."

"The Ravens are entirely Anglish," Evind pointed out. "That's part of their whole philosophy. They're entirely up their own arses about being the descendants of Brave Viking Norsemen."

"Which makes it worse," Nils added. "Joden forfend Lindmarden should differ from Anglesland in any way! They don't like that we have torgars at all, really; they think that the smallfolk have no business voting. But crushing them out through political force won't change their minds about that."

"I wonder how many of the people who went berserk really understand that," Kam said. "They must have mostly been smallfolk, or we'd have heard names by now. I wonder if they know that they're spilling blood for a cause that will turn them back into thralls."

"Most smallfolkish people don't know what's good for them; that's why we have torgars in the first place," Evind said. "Votemanship is good until it becomes rabble-rule."

"Whatever happened to 'In a more perfect world, there wouldn't need to be torgars or thanes or jarls or kings'?" I asked.

"We don't live in a more perfect world is what," Evind said. "A lot of the poor smallfolk can't even *read.* Of course they don't know what's good for them."

There was a sour sort of silence for a moment, and Sander started writing on his tablet. A moment later, Marta read aloud, "So what do we *do*?"

"We keep meeting," Ernst said. "We keep talking, and thinking, and we remember everything we see and hear."

"And maybe," Evind added softly, "we make sure that we know who we can trust—for when the time comes that talking isn't enough."

" 'The unquiet thought cannot be killed,' " Ernst said, and it sounded very much like some quote he was reciting. " 'It can only be buried, and it grows stronger in the dark.' "

"Like a turnip," Osvald said with a snort. Sander laughed. No one else did.

"I think that it's very important that we maintain a standard of decorum," Marta said carefully, glancing toward the doorway. Toward the dragonhall. "We cannot allow ourselves to credit this kind of savagery or seem to desire retribution. *We are dragoneers;* any of you might be called up into the dragonthede to fight for the jarl. Regardless of who the jarl happens to be."

"Except you ladies," Kam said, gesturing broadly to Marta and me. "You're safe."

"Who else here has been shot?" I asked, glaring at him and then looking around the table. Theod was fixing me with an absolutely adoring gaze when I met his eyes, and I had to look down to keep from reacting.

"I didn't mean—" Kam faltered.

"I'm sure you didn't," I said.

"Are we really just going to go about our normal routines?" Vinzent demanded. "While people are being killed in the street?"

"What would you have us do?" Marta asked. "Storm the thanegard barracks?"

"We could write letters," Osvald suggested. "To the papers, anonymously—"

"The papers wouldn't publish them if we did," Ernst said.

Sander scratched down something quickly, and Marta read, "There are other ways to spread words."

Professor Ibarra appeared at the front of the room then, ringing a handbell for silence. When we'd become sufficiently quiet, he said in a voice that rang clear through the dining hall, "Attention, students of Kuiper's Academy of Natural Philosophy and Skiltakraft. We are deeply saddened by the tragic events that have taken place in the city yesterday and through the night. Our condolences go out to all those affected by this devastating situation. We understand that many of you may be feeling unsettled or anxious following this news. Please know that the safety and well-being of you and your dragons are our top priorities.

"Our school grounds remain secure, and we are in close communication with the jarl and his representatives to monitor the situation closely. Classes will resume as scheduled tomorrow, and the school grounds will be opened to typical movement, but we continue to ask that no student leave the school grounds without informing and receiving express permission from Frau Kuiper or, if she is not available, from Frau Brinkerhoff. Until tomorrow, we ask that you remain indoors. We are still taking account of students who were not present on school grounds during these tragic events. You will be relieved to learn that we've heard from most of your classmates who were visiting home for the weekend, and they have assured us of their safety and intention to return later today. We would like to encourage students to return to their rooms, at this time, to facilitate the delivery of messages."

I frowned, not liking at all the fact that we were being dispersed—that we were being *confined.* I wanted very much to go and visit with Kasaqua. If the school grounds had been deemed safe, I could think of no reason that I shouldn't be allowed to visit the dragonhall. It was only a small comfort that Kasaqua didn't seem particularly upset about anything; she was curious as to what had me worried, but she had no special complaints of her own apart from her nearly ever-present desire to be out of her stall and at my side.

As Marta and I proceeded up to our room, I considered the potential benefits and consequences of simply refusing to obey and visiting Kasaqua anyway. Through the bond we shared, she helpfully informed me that she was entirely capable of getting out of her stall by herself; she stayed there when I asked it of her because she was a good girl, but she understood the simple latch that held the stall door closed. I tried to convey to her in no uncertain terms that she should *not*. That I was *fine*.

I considered, fleetingly, the possibility of Theod and I simply going home until all of this was settled—classes and the ministry and everything else be damned.

THE DAY PROCEEDED

After luncheon, Liberty arrived at our room, bearing letters. I had to resist, with great difficulty, the urge to embrace her; Marta was watching.

"Are you well? Have you heard from anyone in the city? Miss Jenni, the rest of the women at your salon?"

"Nothing yet," she said, shaking her head. "What I've been able to work out from hearsay is that the mill district was mostly spared; nothing but shouting and a few broken windows. It wasn't until they got to the cannery district that the rioters started setting fires."

"Well, please let me know if you hear anything, and if there's anything that I can do."

"I don't think that there's anything that any of us can do except weather the storm," Liberty said, her mouth a thin line. "But thank you."

She handed me the letters and took her leave. The look she gave me made it clear that she'd rather have stayed.

Marta and I received a letter from the Gellers, informing us that Jadi was safe, and that she'd be returned to the school as planned on Wednesday morning. Marta received a letter from her father, asking after her safety and assuring her of the safety of everyone in her household. I received a letter from Niquiat that read:

Dear Anequs,

I hardly know how to write this letter. My hands are still shaking, and I keep having to stop to wipe my eyes. Everything is gone. Everything. I'm safe, and as well as I can be given the circumstances. I'm staying with Zhina's family for the time being, but we're leaving tomorrow—I'm going home. There's nothing for me here anymore.

The workshop was burned to the ground; we managed to take the Shiang-Gangish engine and the plans we made from it, but very little else. Ekaitz went back inside trying to save his tools and some rare parts when the roof caved in; he's dead. I keep thinking about how we were laughing together just yesterday morning. He was telling me about a girl that his cousin introduced him to, how much he fancied her. Ekaitz was just nineteen years old—and now he's dead.

The cannery where I worked is a burned-out shell. The building where I was staying is just a pile of charred bricks. I don't know what happened to Bjarni, or Tarvo, or Rokiskwe. I haven't even tried to find out. I don't even know how to try.

I watched everything that I've spent the last few years working for turn to smoke last night. There was a dragon, Anequs—one of the huge green bear-dragons that the dragonthede favors. When I read the jarl's speech about "mindless savagery," I wanted to scream. These were our neighbors, people we knew, people we traded with! I recognized faces in that gang, men who worked at the cannery, at the docks. People who brought things to the co-op to be mended just last week were marching with the gang and throwing torches through windows last night. They were screaming things like "skrælings and nithings have no place in Lindmarden" and "garbage in the streets must be burned."

The thanegards are everywhere now, nosing through the ruins and asking questions of survivors. I've seen them drag people away, people I know had nothing to do with this. They say they'll find everyone responsible, but will that bring Ekaitz back? Will it rebuild our street? Will it give me back the years of work I've lost? Jorgen and Strida have gone to stay with Jorgen's parents in Runestung Hold. The enginekrafters co-op is well and truly dissolved.

I wish I could tell you something more hopeful, but for now, all I can do is promise that I am alive. Please send this letter on to Mother, after you've read it—I didn't have enough money for postage for two letters and I know that your school has a mail room. I will write again as soon as I can, though I fear I may not have the means to send a letter often. Don't worry about me, I will find my way through this. Keep safe, I love you.

Niquiat

I'd only met Ekaitz a handful of times, at the co-op and at Haddir's. I didn't know much about him other than he'd been charming and flirtatious, and that he was Niquiat's friend. And now he was dead.

I wondered if Haddir's had been burned down; if Haddir himself was safe. I wondered a lot of things—too many to pick apart one from the other. There was a roaring in my head, and I wanted more than anything to go home and explain all of this to Mother and Grandma while Mother braided my hair and unbraided it and braided it again. I wanted to see Niquiat, and hug him, and never let go.

I wanted to show this letter to Theod before I sent it on to Mother.

I did the next best thing and copied it down, word for word. I wrote my own letter to Mother and everyone else back home and folded it together with Niquiat's before sealing it up and taking it to the mail room.

Frau Brinkerhoff was there, looking pinched and tired, with dark circles beneath her eyes. Professors Schreiber and Ulfar were there, as well, Professor Ulfar's chair backed into a corner with all its legs tucked in and under as far as they'd go. They were reading letters from a basket on the little table between them, eyes darting quickly along written lines. As I watched, Professor Schreiber finished the one she was reading, folded it up and stuffed it back into its envelope, and dropped it into a carton at her feet that had been marked SEND.

There was a carton beside it that said DON'T SEND.

She immediately selected another letter from the basket, opened it, and began reading.

"Add any outgoing correspondence to the basket," Frau Brinkerhoff said wearily, barely glancing up at me. "The contents will be looked at before it's sent anywhere. If there's anything objectionable, you might be asked to rewrite the letter—nothing at all is going out until tomorrow morning."

"Thank you, ma'am," I said, trying not to let anger touch my voice. What business did they have regarding anything at all that I wanted to say to my family? What counted as "objectionable"?

I dropped my letter into the basket, watching it settle among the others. Some of the envelopes were tear-stained, others crumpled from having been clutched too tightly. As I turned to leave, Professor Ulfar made a soft sound of distress. He pushed a letter across the table to Professor Schreiber, who read it quickly. Her lips pressed into a thin line, and she shook her head, adding it to the DON'T SEND carton without comment.

I left wondering whose words had just been intercepted, what news deemed too dangerous to share. I wondered again if any of my classmates had known this was coming—if they had family or friends who'd been part of the berserker gang.

I went back to my room, because—for the moment, at least—I wasn't supposed to go anywhere else.

CLASSES RESUMED

I barely slept at all, a thousand thoughts in my mind each clamoring for attention. As soon as the edge of the sky started to brighten, I got up and made my way to the dragonhall. Hallmaster Henkjan was standing at the entrance with a man in a dragonthede uniform. There was a silberdrache stretched out on the grass, soundly asleep, with its head resting on its crossed forelegs. In the blue light of dawn, it looked white, almost luminous. Both Henkjan and the soldier were cradling cups that steamed in the cold morning air. Henkjan noticed me first, and his face fell into something equal parts annoyed and resigned.

"Morning, miss," he said evenly.

"Good morning, Hallmaster Henkjan," I said. "I've come to visit with Kasaqua."

"I warned you a couple of weeks ago that your dragon would have to get used to being stabled," he said. "Seems I ought to have warned you that *you* need to get used to that, too."

"If you don't let me in to see her, she's likely to come out to see me," I said.

"And if she did, that would be a breach of control on your part," he said sternly, frowning. "Your dragon ought to know better."

"I have husbandry at nine o'clock, anyway," I argued.

"It's not gone six yet," Henkjan argued right back.

"I want to practice tacking and run some drills with her," I said, raising my chin a bit. "I haven't slept all night. She's been restless, because I've been upset—because *berserkers rioted through the city and one of my brother's friends is dead.* I haven't been able to settle my own mind, so how can she be expected to settle hers? I am going to spend some time with my dragon, and no one is going to stop me. Do you really want to make this into a fight and a scene? I'll go get Professor Mesman if I have to."

Henkjan and the soldier exchanged glances. The soldier shrugged slightly and took another sip from his cup. The silberdrache on the lawn twitched an ear but didn't wake.

"You know full well Mesman won't be awake at this hour," Henkjan said, but his voice had lost some of its edge. He studied my face for a long moment, then sighed. "I suppose he'd side with you if he was, in the name of study and that. But, mind, stay where we can see you. No rambling off along the trails, and absolutely no leaving school grounds—"

"We'll behave, I promise," I said quickly.

He made an assenting kind of noise and stepped aside. As I passed him, he added quietly, "I am sorry about your brother's friend, miss."

The familiar smell of the dragonhall—hay and leather, the particular mineral scent of dragon, and just a hint of blood and offal—enveloped me like an embrace as I entered. Most of the dragons were still sleeping, but I could hear Kasaqua stirring in her stall before I reached it. She had her head up, waiting for me, her eyes gleaming in the dim light. She stood as I entered the stall and pressed against my hand when I stroked her neck and shoulder, a low rumble of concern vibrating through her throat. Of course she'd felt my distress all night. Of course she'd been waiting.

I got her tacked. She waited patiently as I fumbled with buckles and straps, occasionally nudging me gently with her nose and huffing when I took too long with a particular fastening. We made our way out to the practice yard, where the pre-dawn light was painting everything in shades of gray and blue. She matched her pace to mine, her warmth beside me both familiar and desperately needed. I didn't really want to run drills. I just needed to move, to do something other than lie in bed thinking about Niquiat's letter, about Ekaitz, about the Ravens of Joden. Kasaqua made a soft questioning sound, sensing my continued unease. I reached up to scratch the spot behind her jaw that she loved. Kasaqua curved her neck around me and extended a wing above my head, creating a shelter of sorts with her body. I leaned against her, feeling the steady rhythm of her breathing.

The sky was growing lighter. Soon, other students would be waking up—going to breakfast, preparing for classes, acting like everything was normal. But for now, it was just Kasaqua and I, walking circles in the flight field while the silberdrache slept on the lawn and Henkjan pretended not to watch us too closely.

Kasaqua noticed something and made a chirping noise, turning her head. I followed her gaze and saw Theod crossing the field between the school and the dragonhall, approaching Henkjan and the soldier.

A few minutes later, he and Copper joined us; he hadn't bothered putting Copper's tack on. He didn't have husbandry today.

Theod and I walked in silence for a while, Kasaqua and Copper flanking us like protective bulwarks in the growing dawn light.

"I got a letter from my brother yesterday," I said quietly. "About the riots."

Theod glanced at me but didn't interrupt.

"Everything's gone. The co-op, the cannery, even the building he was living in—all burned to the ground." I swallowed hard. "His friend Ekaitz . . . he went back into the burning workshop to try to save some tools. The roof collapsed. He was only nineteen."

Kasaqua pressed closer to my side and made a low, concerned sound.

"He said there was a dragon," I continued, my voice bitter. "A kesseldrache, from the way he described it. It wasn't strangers doing this; it was people from the neighborhood. People my brother knew, people who'd come to their workshop before." I kicked at a loose stone on the ground. "They were screaming about 'skrælings' and 'nithings' having no place in Lindmarden. About burning garbage in the streets."

"Anequs . . ." Theod started, then seemed at a loss for words.

"Niquiat's staying with Zhina's family for now, but he's planning to go home as soon as he can afford the fare. The enginekrafters co-op is finished."

We'd stopped walking. Kasaqua curved her neck around me again, creating that sheltering space with her wing. I closed my eyes, squeezing out a pair of tears that made me scrub at my face with the cuff of my shirt.

"I should be there," I whispered. "I should be going home with him, welcoming him back."

"You're where you need to be for Kasaqua," Theod said, stroking Copper's neck. "Skiltakraft lessons and testing and all that is going to be all the more important now. We'll need to be able to defend ourselves—against other dragons, maybe. Against other dragoneers."

I sighed, because he was right—and I didn't want him to be.

The morning light was brighter now, the first pale rays of dawn creeping across the flight field. I took a deep breath and wiped my face again, pushing the ache of Niquiat's letter down into the pit of my stomach. I couldn't afford to fall apart; I had class.

"Do you plan to come in for breakfast?" Theod asked. I shook my head.

"I'm not hungry, and I'd rather spend the time with Kasaqua," I said. "I really ought to do some drills before class. I'll see you at luncheon?"

"All right," he said. He looked like he wanted to say something else, but then glanced back over his shoulder to where Henkjan and the soldier were both watching us, and said nothing.

I led Kasaqua through walking and trotting and running, grounded by the strength and power of her beneath me. When my other classmates began to arrive after breakfast, I walked her back to the place where class met.

Professor Mesman told us that we'd just be riding the trails today; that we all needed to simply spend time with our dragons without thinking overmuch about unfortunate events in the city. Ekaitz was dead, and Niquiat's whole life had burned down, and to the professor and my classmates, it was all just "unfortunate events." Kasaqua was happy to push herself, out on the trails, choosing paths that required jumping and climbing.

We were both hungry and sore by the time class ended, and both glad of it.

ANEQUS AND HER CLASSMATES DISCUSSED THE PRACTICALITIES OF SKILTAKRAFT

That afternoon, I had skiltakraft with Professor Schreiber—and with Theod and Sander and Vinzent and Evind. If the professor had noted the five of us pushing two desks together, she'd decided not to comment upon it.

Today we were back on fundamental principles, outlining how many points of attachment each of the known athers possessed. The little ball-and-stick models were being handed around, illustrating the possible points of attachment. Vetna, brinesna, grunesna, kalisna, and silber could each form exactly one attachment. Stiksna, sindle, saffle, limesna, spelter, quicksilber, and strahlendstone could form two. Zurfni and pospor could form three; kolfni and zan, four; arsen and nebsalve, five. Then there were the queer athers, which could exist in more than one state—kessel could have one or two, geld could have one or three, isen could have two or three, blassgeld could have two or four, and ulfram could have anywhere from two to six, though six was by far the most common.

"Professor Schreiber," one of my classmates—not someone I knew well, a young Vaskosish man—began, making the professor turn around, "I was wondering . . . is there any application of skiltakraft that we could . . . use in a more practical way? Martial applications, for instance?"

"*Martial* applications?" The professor asked, frowning and furrowing her brow. "Could you clarify what you mean by that, Mister Ituarte?"

"Well . . . weapons, defenses," he clarified, his voice sounding a bit more uncertain. "Clouds of poisonous airs, things that explode or burn or whatever."

"I understand your enthusiasm, but I must remind you that skiltakraft—particularly the fantastical version you've described—is governed by laws that require a deep understanding of fundamentals. I'm sure you've studied minglinglore, and may be under the impression that it's all about mixing athers together to create explosions or potions. But I'm here to teach you *why* certain reactions happen, and, more importantly, the concerns regarding safety and philosophical rectitude that come with manipulating athers."

"We know the safety principles, Professor," Evind said, looking sidelong at Vinzent, who had his eyes studiously down, gazing at the notes in front of him. He wasn't wearing bandages anymore, and it was clear from the way the wounds on his face were healing that he was going to have scars. "We want to know how to apply this knowledge in real-world, practical ways. What's the point of all this learning if we can't do anything to defend ourselves should we come under attack?"

It was something I'd been wondering myself; Professor Schreiber's carefully constructed lecture on atheric principles seemed fragile against the raw reality of dragons reducing buildings in the cannery district to ash and wind. To Kasaqua, breathing a stretch of beach into black glass, turning Birning Svenisson to ash between her jaws.

"I understand your concerns, given the recent terrible events, but you have nothing to fear—you are students, not soldiers. You are many years away from being asked to go into battle, if ever you are, though I certainly hope you are not. The goal of your education is *not* to rush ahead to the applications that seem flashy or immediate. It is to understand *why* certain athers react the way they do under certain circumstances, why those reactions are *predictable,* and how to make sense of the world on the level of motes. You can't leap into complex operations until you've learned the building blocks of atherlore."

Evind leaned forward, challenging, "What good are pure principles when your family is threatened?"

"Do you have reason to believe that your family is threatened, Mister Skovgaard?" Professor Schreiber asked, folding her arms and glaring at him.

"Mine is," I said.

The professor's gaze moved to me, her mouth forming a thin line. "Miss Anequs—"

"Professor," I pressed, "I don't know if this is true of anyone else, but I know people who have been directly impacted by the riots this past weekend. My brother lived in the cannery district, and his home and workplace have both been destroyed. One of his friends was killed. I don't know anything about Mister Ituarte's situation in life, but I know that's a Vaskosish name, and that the Ravens of Joden are eager to mete out violence to anyone who isn't Anglish."

Professor Schreiber's expression shifted, caught between scholarly distance and genuine concern—torn between her commitment to academic principles and the very real danger that some of us were in. The other students watched, waiting. Professor Ezel would never have tolerated such a statement from me—he'd have shouted and sent me from the room. He'd have devised some way of punishing me for daring to talk back. But Professor Ezel wasn't here, and Professor Schreiber was. She hesitated, a flicker of uncertainty crossing her face, as she looked at me and then to the young Vaskosish student—Mister Ituarte.

"I . . . I understand your concern, Miss Anequs," Professor Schreiber finally said, her voice quieter, almost reluctant. She stepped away from the board, moving closer to where we sat. "It is true that many of us have been affected by the . . . unrest . . . in the city. No one is immune to the consequences of the world outside these walls. But that's precisely why we need to be careful about how we channel our anger, our fear, our desire for action. Skiltakraft is not a weapon to be wielded recklessly."

"You *are* teaching us how to wield it, though, aren't you?" Evind asked, his voice sharp with frustration. "You're showing us the rules, the structure, the philosophy behind it. But what do we do when the world doesn't follow those rules? What happens when the safety principles break down because the world outside doesn't care about those principles?"

The professor stiffened at Evind's tone, but instead of responding harshly, she sighed. She folded her hands behind her back and looked down at her feet as she made a circuit around the classroom, passing in front of each of the desks in the circle.

"You're not wrong," she said at length, when she'd reached the front of the room again. "The world is unpredictable. Unforgiving. But we, as dragoneers, must have command of the principles of skiltakraft, or we will lose control over it. You've seen what happens when people who don't understand the complexities of athers try to manipulate them." Her gaze shifted to Vinzent, who flinched slightly. "What happened last Tuesday was tragic. It was a direct consequence of ignorance, a desire for mastery where none existed. I am *teaching* you, Mister Skovgaard," she said quietly, "but teaching takes time. Mastery of skiltakraft doesn't happen overnight. If you apply it incorrectly—if you wield the athers with only a glimmer of understanding—the consequences could be far worse than anything the Ravens of Joden could do. I'm not asking you to sit idly by, but I *am* asking you to think carefully about the path forward. If you seek power without understanding, you'll lose yourself in it. That, more than anything else, is what I'm trying to protect you from—the temptation of easy answers, the allure of force without wisdom."

"Some of us are at more immediate danger than others, Professor," I said.

"I don't doubt that, Miss Anequs," she replied, "but that isn't something within the purview of this class. Let us return to the material. For now, we will focus on the fundamentals. You're not *wrong,* Miss Anequs, Mister Ituarte . . . all of you. The world is changing, and I won't ignore that reality." She turned her eyes to Vinzent, who was sitting still, his hands clenched tightly in his lap. "If you want to understand how to use skiltakraft *wisely* in the world as it is now, then you must understand why we value the process of learning—not as an abstract ideal, but as a way to protect you when the world insists on taking shortcuts."

We all sat in silence for a moment, a mix of tension and acceptance in the air. Eventually, Professor Schreiber turned back to the chalkboard, her voice returning to its usual measured tone. "Once you've become familiar with how many points of attachment are possible for each ather, it's possible to predict the responses of multiple athers. . . . I'm sure that at some point in your studies of natural philosophy, you've seen what happens when aerated salt—rising soda used in baking—is mixed with spirit of vinegar. Who can tell me what happens?"

There was a long, uncomfortable silence. Professor Ezel had not often asked questions in class, and when he had, he'd always stated exactly who he was asking. More than once, he'd asked Sander to answer something, then refused to read anything Sander had written down to instead demand that he "spit the words out."

I broke the silence by saying, "Aerated salt, added to spirit of vinegar, produces a great deal of foam that falls very quickly. What's left behind is salty water."

"*Close* to correct, Miss Anequs," she replied. "What is left behind in the container after the kolfni and skitsna have fled into the air is water and salt of essig—that being the Tysklandish word for vinegar. If the water is driven out of it by boiling, or by a skilta's process, you will be left with a fine white powder that has many practical uses—but it is not table salt. As to what's really happening when we perform this simplest of athermaching: Aerated salt is made from brinesna, vetna, kolfni, and stiksna, in this arrangement."

She paused to fiddle with a set of balls and sticks, assembling a compound ather. The center was a mote of kolfni, surrounded by three motes of stiksna. The centermost stiksna was attached with a *black* stick, the others with plain wood-colored sticks. The left stiksna attached to a mote of vetna, the right to brinesna, which was represented by a yellow-colored ball with just one hole in it. She passed it to the student at her left.

"Keep that going around the room until everyone's had a chance to look at it," she ordered. Turning back to the class at large, she said, "You'll notice that the attachment between the kolfni and one of its stiksnas is black. Can anyone hazard a guess as to why?"

Sander raised his hand. Everyone stopped and watched to see how Professor Schreiber would proceed.

"Yes, Mister Jansen?" she asked expectantly.

Sander tapped the paper in front of him—he'd been writing notes. He'd already drawn a version of the model that was being passed around the room, using circles and lines, and he'd drawn the stiksna that didn't have a second mote attached to it as attached to the kolfni with two lines. Which suddenly made sense to me, the realization feeling somehow electric, exhilarating. If kolfni possessed four points of attachment, but only three motes attached to it, then of course it would want to attach to something twice, and stiksna had two possible points of attachment, so if they could be swung round to both face the same way, they could both attach to the kolfni . . .

Professor Schreiber walked to our desk and looked at the notes that Sander was pointing to, and her face lit up.

"Yes, exactly," she said, "Mister Jansen here has drawn a model of rising soda in two dimensions. Do you mind if I pass this around the class for everyone to have a look at?"

Sander nodded, looking positively elated.

Professor Schreiber plucked the page from his desk and handed it to Theod, who nodded thanks but had just the slightest bit of panic in his eyes. He seemed to calm when Professor Schreiber moved away from us, and handed the paper off to Evind immediately. I'd have to wait for it to come all the way back around the circle if I wanted to study it more carefully.

Professor Schreiber busied herself with assembling another model of wooden sticks and balls as both the first model and Sander's drawing passed around the room, and after everyone had seen it, she asked, "Who can tell me what's special about the attachment of the lonely stiksna to the kolfni?"

"It's attached twice," someone said. I didn't know him by name, but he was a few desks to the right of us.

"Correct, Mister Engle!" she said with a smile. She went on to explain what I'd realized, seeing Sander's drawing—that two motes could attach together twice, or even three times. A double attachment was represented with a black stick; a triple attachment, with a red one.

She continued in that fashion for the remainder of class, demonstrating the ways in which athers predictably behaved under certain circumstances. When the clock struck three, we were dismissed with assignments to practice and the promise that if we all displayed a solid understanding of the principles, we'd be trying practical work again next week.

In the hallway, Evind leaned against the wall and groaned theatrically.

"I hate how she just put down the question of martial applications with frippery about fundamentals and philosophies and insistences that we're not soldiers. Most of us are probably *going* to be soldiers sooner than later, and Anequs has already seen battle, of a sort—"

"I wouldn't call what Kasaqua did to Birning Svenisson 'battle,'" I said.

"He shot you, and your dragon killed him," Evind said. "That's practically a holmgang."

"I'd prefer not to talk about it," I said. "I think the professor's right in that we need to understand what skiltakraft *is* and how athers behave before we focus on what it can *do*."

Evind glanced at Vinzent, who glared back at him.

"If you want to say something, say something," Vinzent challenged.

Before Evind could say anything, I interrupted, "What I'd really like to know more about is how skiltakraft is practiced by other people elsewhere in the world. I know the Kindah people have a different way of doing it, and that they call it thaumaturgy. Back when our people had dragons—"

"Nackies had dragons?" Vinzent asked, tilting his head.

"Yes, we had dragons," I said, looking hard at him, because he ought to have known that. "Emanuel Nordlund mentions native dragons in *The Savage Peoples of North Markesland,* and his time on Naquipaug was around 1750," I said. "My grandmother was born before our people reckoned years according to Anglish calendars, but she tells that when *her* grandmother was a little girl, there were still Nampeshiwe—dragons like Kasaqua—on the islands. There are a lot of stories with dragons in them, and their breath was used to do all kinds of things."

"That's fascinating," Evind said, leaning forward. "I never knew about nackie dragons. Were they all like yours?"

"I don't know," I replied, thinking back to my grandmother's stories. "The stories say they helped our people in many ways—digging up plots for gardens, hunting whales, protecting us from enemies. But when the great dying came . . ." I trailed off, not wanting to delve too deeply into that.

We walked in silence for a moment, each lost in our own thoughts.

"Still," Evind said as we reached the entrance hall, "I hope she shows us some practical applications soon. Understanding is good, but . . ." He glanced out the window at the dragonhall and the flight field.

"But sometimes you need more than understanding," I finished for him. "I know. But maybe understanding is where we have to start."

As we proceeded to luncheon, I couldn't help but wonder what my grandmother's grandmother would think of me learning skiltakraft in an Anglish academy, using models and principles so different from the ways our people once shaped dragons' breath. I thought about Niquiat and Zhina trying to understand the Shiangish engine. Perhaps, I thought, that was its own kind of attachment point—a way of connecting different ways of knowing, different ways of *being* in the world. I wanted to know more about how everyone else did skiltakraft, and how we'd done it two hundred years ago.

I wanted better teachers than the ones I had.

A STRANGER CAME FROM THE NORTH

On Wednesday morning, I had my directed study of al-jabr in the library with professor Nazari, while Theod worked on his anglereckoning. He had husbandry and thus flight classes in the afternoon, while I had a free period with the rest of the second-year class. I stayed with him in the library after the allotted class time, walking him through the lesson he'd just had after the professor had left, because he understood it better when I explained it.

I was abruptly aware that something was happening at the dragonhall, something that demanded my *immediate* attention. Theod's head jerked up, and our eyes met; he must have felt something similar from Copper. I nodded, and we left all of our books and papers exactly where they were, hurrying out of the library and toward the dragonhall. We were at the top of the stairs when Professor Schreiber found us. She looked just a bit frantic, her cheeks pink and her eyes wide.

"There you are!" she said, breathless. "Miss Anequs, Mister Knecht, you are wanted immediately at the dragonhall. Your dragon, Miss Anequs, has somehow gotten out of her stall—"

She said more, but I wasn't really listening as we tripped down the stairs and out the front doors.

There were a number of dragons gathered in the space between the dragonhall and the school proper. A dozen students were hanging on the margins of the tangle, some with their dragons and some without. The first-year class had husbandry on Monday and Wednesday mornings, and a lot of them seemed to be present. I saw Osvald and Juniper, but not Jadi or Dreyst. Hallmaster Henkjan was standing with a broom in his hand, looking harried. Frau Kuiper and Gerhard stood beside Captain Einarsson and his silberdrache. Several other soldiers of the dragonthede with their own silberdraches and kesseldraches flanked them, and in the center of the crowd . . . a Nampeshiwe. Kasaqua was standing before it, her wings flared, her tail shivering in excitement.

It was the only fully grown Nampeshiwe I'd ever seen, apart from Kasaqua's mother—and I'd only seen her fleetingly, at a distance. This dragon was darker, more tawny than golden. The feathers of its mane were chestnut-colored, with black quills. Where Kasaqua's feathers were confined to the crown of her head and the back of her neck, this dragon's mane came together at the front and formed a beard like a blue heron's—the feathers were very long and fine, and they shone with a bronze iridescence, like turkey feathers. Its antlers came to at least a dozen points. Like Kasaqua and her mother, this dragon had brown-black markings on its face—on its muzzle, around its eyes and cheeks, and onto the backs of its ears. They were different from Kasaqua's markings, and hers were different than her mother's had been—perhaps the markings were wholly unique to each individual? It was leaning forward to touch its nose with Kasaqua's, making a low crooning noise that I could feel in my bones.

Standing at the Nampeshiwe's side, facing Frau Kuiper and Captain Einarsson, was a nackie woman. She was around my mother's age, forty or so. Shorter than Frau Kuiper. Her skin was brown and weather-lined, her hair dark with gray scattered here and there, done up in two braids. She was wearing dark canvas trousers and a calico blouse, and over it a long buckskin coat with fringes at the shoulders and hem, embroidered with beads and quillwork.

"I've got a writ of passage," the woman was saying, holding her hands out in an appeasing gesture. "Signed and stamped by Rikkert Halfhand himself."

Kasaqua realized I'd arrived, and turned her head to look at me over her shoulder. She made an encouraging call, telling me that I ought to come and see. Frau Kuiper followed Kasaqua's gaze, looking past her to Theod and me.

"Ah, good, you've found them," she said, nodding curtly at Professor Schreiber.

"We were in the library, ma'am," I said. "What's . . ."

"This is *far* more fuss than it needs to be," the woman said, handing a letter to Frau Kuiper.

"We apprehended this dragon and the woman riding it several miles north of here, traveling over unimproved forest and farmland," Captain Einarsson announced. "She claims to have come from Runestung Hold, and that she was making her way to the academy. We thought it prudent to escort her."

"And much obliged for that," the woman said, offering a thin smile that didn't reach her eyes.

Frau Kuiper handed the letter to Captain Einarsson, who gazed at it critically.

"Frau . . . *Flies,*" he said, as if the name sat wrong in his mouth, "I hope you understand the gravity of arriving, unannounced, with unknown intentions, on a strange dragon of unknown provenance—"

"I came on behalf of the Haudenoshownee Confederation . . .

Rikesband is the word you use, I think? Not sure how I was meant to be announced, besides coming here and announcing myself. I thought that Jarl Halfhand and Jarl Joervarsson had all this hammered out already."

"I'm afraid they do not," Captain Einarsson said. "If Jarl Joervarsson had any knowledge of your arrival, it was not conveyed to me or anyone else at the Ministry of Dragon Affairs."

"My apologies then, for any failing on my part," Frau Flies said. "But as I said, this is all much more fuss than it needs to be. I come in peace, I promise. I came to talk to these two young folks here, in fact, if my guess is right." She nodded toward Theod and me.

"Frau Flies," Frau Kuiper began, only for her to interrupt.

"Just Sadsong. I'm not *Frau* anything. I only even have a surname on there because you Anglish get all persnickety about it on paperwork. I go by a lot of names, and you probably can't say *any* of them right, so you can call me Sadsong. I picked 'Flies' as a surname because it's what I do—Sadsong Flies. Pleased to meet you."

"This is most irregular," Frau Kuiper said, taking a breath and tugging on the hem of her coat. "But your writ does seem to be genuine. Captain, if you concur—"

"I will want to speak to Jarl Joervarsson directly," he said, thrusting the letter back at Sadsong. "I very strongly suggest that you and your dragon remain here, at the academy's dragonhall, for the time being. If you go elsewhere in Vaster's Hold, you may be detained by thanegards."

"Well, that *was* the plan," she said, patting the dragon's flank. "Eatsfeathers here's been on the wing for two days, on and off, and wouldn't mind a big meal and a long nap."

Eatsfeathers, which was evidently the Nampeshiwe's name, made a rumbling sound of agreement at Sadsong's words, shifting his weight from one foreleg to the other. Now that I looked more closely, I could see the weariness in his posture—particularly in the way he'd folded his wings.

"Very well," Frau Kuiper said, straightening her shoulders. "We shall arrange accommodation for you and your dragon, for the time being. Miss Anequs, please ensure that *your* dragon returns to her stall; we'll have to investigate later just how she was able to get out. Mister Knecht, you may join Miss Anequs."

Kasaqua showed no intention of returning to her stall. She kept glancing between me and Eatsfeathers, her tail twitching. I could feel her curiosity humming through our bond. She wanted to know more about this newcomer, this dragon that was *like her* in a way that none of the other dragons at the academy were.

"If I might suggest," Sadsong said, a hint of amusement coloring her voice, "perhaps we could let them visit a while longer? Seems to me they've got some catching up to do, and the little one's excited."

She gestured broadly at the two Nampeshiwe, engaged in a back-and-forth where Kasaqua leaned in to sniff at Eatsfeathers, and he reeled back just a bit.

Captain Einarsson's expression remained stern, but Frau Kuiper's features softened slightly as she watched the dragons. "I suppose that would be acceptable. Under supervision, of course."

"Of course," Sadsong agreed. "And while *they* get acquainted, I could have a word with these young folks? It's been a long flight, and I could use a walk. Eatsfeathers wants his tack off, too."

Frau Kuiper hesitated, then nodded.

"I'll have Hallmaster Henkjan chaperone; I've obviously got some telegrams to send, and I'm sure you, Captain, will want to report to the jarl directly. Hallmaster, if you could assign an appropriate stall?"

"Yes, ma'am," Henkjan said, nodding. "It would help if the rest of this lot could move along, though."

He looked over his shoulder at the audience of students, some with their dragons, standing at the periphery.

"Quite right, Hallmaster," Frau Kuiper said, frowning, as if just noticing the crowd of students. Her voice was somewhat louder when she said, "I'm sure the rest of you have other places that you could be. The dining hall should be opening for luncheon soon. Along now, everyone; no need to stand about gawping like fish." Lowering her voice again, she turned to us and said, "Miss Anequs and Mister Knecht, you will join Hallmaster Henkjan and Frau Sadsong."

Frau Kuiper handed Gerhard off to one of the hall lads with instructions to take off his tack and brush him down. Inside of five minutes, the hallmaster had shown Sadsong and Eatsfeathers to one of the stalls at the end, where the professors' dragons were quartered. They were somewhat larger than the stalls allotted to students' dragons.

"You ought to go get your dragon out from whichever of these cells he's stashed in," Sadsong said, nodding toward Theod. "And once this big lummox is set, we can take a walk around the field."

"Yes, ma'am," Theod said, nodding sharply. His face had gone studiously blank at some point, retreating to his "servant" role. Henkjan stood half a dozen paces away, instructing some of the hall lads, but I had no doubt that he was keeping eyes and ears on us.

"That was *entirely* more to-do than I thought it was going to be," Sadsong said, shaking her head. "I don't think we did introductions properly, but you're Anequs, aren't you?"

"Yes, I'm Anequs, and this is Kasaqua. Theod's dragon is Copper."

"Sadsong Flies, and this here is Eatsfeathers," she said, patting his flank. Pleased to meet you. Been meaning to since the middle of last year, when the two of you were interviewed by the newspaper, but things are sticky up north because of the schism and all."

"The schism?" I asked.

"Between the Haudenoshownee Confederation and the Konossioni; the Kanienkeha are divided about the newcomers—the Anglish and whoever else," Sadsong said, working at ring-and-toggle ties to take a set of saddlebags off of Eatsfeathers and set them on the floor. "Out west, the Wapashneepee—the whitewater folks—have basically declared war, and they'll kill a pale man on sight more often than they won't. We—the Haudenoshownee, I mean—have been trading with the pale folks since before they started settling. I know Rikkert Halfhand; he's not a bad man, but he's a *stubborn* cuss, and I wouldn't want him for an enemy."

I remembered Captain Einarsson and Jarl Joervarsson talking about the Hudden-seeonnee Rikesband and the Kannon-seeonnee Rikesband. If I was recalling correctly, the captain had said that the Hudden-seeonnee were helpful in 'pushing back' the Kannon-seeonnee. I had to presume that the 'Konossioni' that Sadsong was talking about were the same people.

Theod returned, with Copper at heel. Copper seemed interested in Eatsfeathers, but not excited in the same way that Kasaqua was. Copper positioned himself between Theod and the rest of us, standing at attention.

"I'm afraid I don't know much about any of the people north of us," I said. "Until last year, I'd never been farther inland than Catchnet. There's been a lot to learn since I've become Nampeshiweisit."

"I don't speak whatever it is you're speaking any better than I expect you speak Kanienkeha, so it's probably simplest if we try and keep to Anglish as much as we can, to stay on the same page."

"Oh, I'm sorry," I said, feeling my face flush. "In my language, Masquisit, the kind of dragon that Kasaqua and Eatsfeathers are is called Nampeshiwe, and dragoneers are Nampeshiweisit. I don't think the word 'dragoneer' means quite the same thing, which is why I hesitate to use it."

"In Kanienkeha, Eatsfeathers is called a Misigennebeg, and I'm his Misigennebegka. I reckon you're right about 'dragoneer' being a different kind of thing. Hold on a second; let me get this off him."

She paused, patting Eatsfeathers's shoulder twice. He obediently laid down, and she lifted the saddle off his back. Kasaqua dropped into a play-bow and stomped her front feet, but Eatsfeathers only yawned in response.

The saddle that Sadsong set down was quite unlike the Anglish saddles I'd become used to. It was *woven,* like a basket, from fine strips of wood. The back was higher than any Anglish saddle I'd seen, the back cantle curving out into two horns. I could imagine how they'd hug the rider's lower back. There were no saddle horns at all on the front; it rose into a sort of curving shield shape that was flat across the top.

"That's beautiful," I said, studying the saddle's craftsmanship. "I've never seen anything like it."

The woven wood strips seemed to be laid over a piece of buckskin, and there was a hinged part in the middle where the woven base—which was in two parts—was laced together with buckskin strips. It would be able to fit into the curve of a Nampeshiwe's back where it rose up sharply. Sadsong smiled, running her hand along one of the curved back horns. "Made this one myself; black ash splints—they're strong but flexible. Takes a while to weave one, but they last for years if you take care of them. Lighter than Anglish saddles, too, which matters on a long flight. What kind of saddle have you got for her? I've looked at Anglish saddles before, can't see that they'd work on our dragons—Anglish breeds have stiffer, straighter backs."

"I can show you how I get Kasaqua kitted out in tack from start to finish, if you like, and I'd appreciate any advice that you have. I've only just started riding her in the second week of September. The standard saddle didn't fit her at all, and the school had to have one made."

Sadsong finished getting Eatsfeathers's tack off entirely, setting each piece neatly aside. All of it was markedly softer than Anglish tack—made from buckskin instead of cowhide leather. The front edge of the saddle had quillwork in red and black, and the top edge had leather braid sewn across it—it would provide grip in a different way than Anglish saddle horns did.

Henkjan came back to check on us and brought a bucket of roots and offal with him. Kasaqua was immediately interested; it wasn't a time of day that she usually got fed. Eatsfeathers made a warning chuffing noise at her, and her ears went back, her feathers flattening, but she was conciliatory, deferring to Eatsfeathers in a way she never had to any Anglish dragon.

"Come on, then," Sadsong said, gesturing toward the stall door. "Show me how you get her ready for riding."

Kasaqua didn't want to leave Eatsfeathers's side . . . but Eatsfeathers made a dismissive noise at her and, having devoured everything in the bucket, curled up with obvious intentions of sleeping. Kasaqua didn't think it was fair; it rankled. I whistled for her to come to heel, and she did so with annoyed reluctance.

As we walked, I noticed Theod hanging back uncertainly, Copper still positioned protectively beside him. Sadsong must have noticed, too, because she turned to him with a gentle smile.

"You're welcome to join us, if you like. Copper seems well-trained in the Anglish way, so it might be interesting for you to see some differences."

I gathered my tack while Sadsong examined the stall setup, her eyes lingering on the Anglish-style mounting block and the heavy iron rings set into the walls. She didn't comment, but the gaze she cast on everything was very critical.

"First, there's the underlay," I began, holding up the piece of quilted felt, "then the saddle frame—"

Sadsong took the stiff piece of leather from me, turning it over in her hands, frowning.

"We don't use anything this rigid; this is too long and doesn't have enough bend."

"That's what I've been thinking, too," I said, showing her the cinches next. As I demonstrated each piece of Kasaqua's tack, Sadsong identified how Eatsfeathers's tack differed. Hers seemed better suited to a Nampeshiwe's body—lighter, more flexible, working with the Nampeshiwe's bouncy, weasel-like gait.

"And here's the saddle they made for her," I said, lifting the modified Anglish design. "It's better than the standard one, but . . ."

"But it's still fighting against the shape of her," Sadsong finished, running her hand along the stiff underside of the saddle tree, knocking on it with her knuckles. "Tell you what. If you can get permission from your professors, I could teach you how to make a *proper* Misigennebeg saddle. It's the wrong time of year for black ash splints, and I don't know that black ash even grows this far south, but I'm sure there's someone nearby who weaves baskets, and we ought to be able to lay hands on *something* that'll suit. The weaving takes time to learn, but you seem like a careful worker. We'll talk about the ceremony of harvesting an ash tree in a good way some time in the future."

"I'd like that very much," I said, feeling my heart flutter a little at the thought, "though I'm not sure how the academy would feel about it—and Professor Mesman in particular. He's the professor of husbandry, riding, and flight."

"Let me worry about your professors," she said, a hint of steel entering her voice. "It's time they learned there's more than one way to work with dragons. I'm sure your professor is a perfect expert about *Anglish* dragons, but our dragons are a different kind of creature. The thing about Anglish dragons is they've been bred to be what they are, like dogs or horses. But Misigennebegs, or Nampeshiwe—they're still wild things that *choose* to be with us. You can't force them into Anglish ways any more than you could force a wolf to be a sheepdog."

Sadsong ran her hand along the edge of my saddle and continued, "The saddle's just the beginning. There's a whole way of *being* with them that the Anglish don't understand. The whistles you use—they're good for what they are, but Misigennebegs have their own language. They speak to each other, and to us, if we learn to listen."

To demonstrate, she made a soft trilling sound in her throat. Kasaqua's head snapped around, her feathers rising in interest.

"See? She knows what that means, even though she's never

heard it before. It's in her blood, like the way she moves, the way she hunts. These things don't need to be taught; they need to be *remembered*."

I thought about the way Kasaqua had deferred to Eatsfeathers over the food, how naturally she had responded to his authority. "She's never acted like this with other dragons," I said. "She usually just . . . does what she wants."

Sadsong laughed. "Of course she does! She's young, and she's only been around dragons who don't speak her language. It would be like putting a wolf pup in with a litter of puppies. It wouldn't learn how to be a proper wolf."

From his spot near the wall, Theod cleared his throat softly. "Begging your pardon, but . . . how do you learn their language? The proper way, I mean?"

Sadsong's expression softened as she looked at him. "First, you have to forget everything the Anglish taught you about dragons being servants or beasts of burden. A Misigennebeg is a friend who chooses to share their life with you—and I think any dragon is, really. The language comes from that understanding, first and foremost."

She turned back to me. "Your Kasaqua, she's chosen you. But she's trying to speak a language she wasn't born to. Let me show you both how to listen to what she's really saying. I don't know what kind of dragon it is you've got there, young man—"

"Copper is an Akhari. It's a Kindah breed," Theod said.

Sadsong shrugged and said, "Well, that's outside of my knowledge, then. But you're welcome to whatever talks me and Miss Anequs have. Might do you good." Sadsong settled onto a hay bale, her movements fluid and unhurried. Kasaqua inched closer, drawn by something in the woman's posture that I couldn't quite read. She looked around, as if to make sure that no one was especially paying attention to us.

"You two know the story of Requeiska and the hurricane? Do they tell that one down here?"

"I know it," I said.

"I've never heard it," Theod admitted, looking down at his feet.

Sadsong made another of those soft trilling sounds, and Kasaqua lay down at her feet, ears pricked forward with interest. Even Copper lifted his head, though he stayed close to Theod.

"Well, then," Sadsong said, "how about you tell me the version that you know, and I'll see if it squares with the version I know?"

"All right," I said, sitting down on another bale of hay opposite her and beckoning Theod over to join me. When he sat down, I began.

THIS IS THE STORY THAT ANEQUS TOLD

In the days long past, not so very long after the first people lived, there was a great hero named Requeiska. He was a Nampeshiweisit, and his Nampeshiwe—named Nonoma—was as brilliant as the sky at sunset. One day, at the time of year when summer becomes autumn, there came a queer wind from the southeast. The ocean swelled, waves lapping greedily higher and higher up the beach. The air grew thin, and many people could feel it as a dull aching in their heads and a slow tiredness in their bones. They knew that a storm was coming.

Requeiska climbed onto Nonoma's sun-bright back, and together they flew southeastward over the ocean, though the wind and rain were fierce and biting. Higher and higher they flew, above even the clouds—for Nonoma was strong and skilled in ways that no Nampeshiwe hatched today can match. From this high place, far out over the water, they could see the great whirling storm. A hurricane.

Requeiska scratched his chin and grinned, saying, "Well, now, the Southeast Wind has sent us a dancer, but she's come without a partner! It would be rude not to join in—let's go invite everyone. I think I know just who would love to dance with the hurricane."

He flew back home to Masquapaug and called out to the people there, "Southeast Wind has sent us a dancer—we must hold a fitting dance. I'm off to invite the other guest of honor!"

Now, in those days, there were many Nampeshiwe and Nampeshiweisit living on the islands—and on the mainland, too. Requeiska visited each village and steading and called everyone to come to the top of the great temple hill on Slipstone Island, where they assembled in a circle around the four stones there. Then he flew away into the north, to visit the icy waters east of the great island Ikkarumikluak, where the seal hunters live—you might know it as Vinberland. Such a journey would take a long time, today, but Nonoma was faster than any Nampeshiwe alive, and so they were able to get there before the sun set.

Requeiska called out to the cold waters of the north sea and said, "Hey, we're going to have a dance on Slipstone Island! A hurricane from the southeast is coming to visit us, and she is so beautiful that you would not believe it! You should come and dance with her! Follow me!"

In the meantime, all the people and their dragons were assembling—a hundred dragons, or a thousand, or maybe more than that circled the island. They flew from north to east to south to west, in accordance with tradition, which was exactly opposite the way the hurricane was spinning, because hurricanes are fickle things that do not care about doing things the proper way. So many Nampeshiwe were there that they rivaled the hurricane's greatness.

As the storm approached, Requeiska returned with the cold current from the north following him. He called into the hurricane, "No, no, you're spinning all wrong! That's last season's dance. Here, let us show you the new way! We have invited another guest, and he is so handsome that you would not believe it!"

The people on the ground began a great dance that the Nampeshiwe watched from above, a shape and a form for their breath to follow. All together, they loosed their breath into the circle of dancers. The north sea current flowed around the eastern side of Slipstone Island, moving to meet the hurricane as she came. Each breath of the many Nampeshiwe created whirlpools that spun counter to Hurricane's dance.

Hurricane, not wanting to appear foolish, began to follow the lead of the people, and the Nampeshiwe, and the terribly strong and handsome north sea current—with whom she was, of course, quite taken. Farther and farther out to sea Hurricane and Current danced. Finally, far from shore, Current said something that no one else heard that persuaded Hurricane to follow him beneath the waves. Her winds scattered across the ocean, becoming nothing more than brisk breezes and gentle rain.

That's why even today, when storm clouds gather and the wind begins to spin, the people know to call upon Nampeshiwe and Nampeshiweisit to dance with cleverness and beauty, to turn hurricanes away from the shore and back out to sea, where they are best suited. And if you watch the waves carefully, you might see a cold riptide ready to dance with the next storm that forgets its manners.

ARRANGEMENTS WERE MADE

After the story, which Sadsong said was a lot like the version she'd heard, we walked around the flight field for a while, talking about how I'd come to bond with Kasaqua and how I'd come to be at the school. Theod explained his situation, too, though he was very glib about it. Sadsong said it was a shame what'd been done to him, being taken away from his family and raised by the Anglish, and he seemed *embarrassed* about it; that was something we'd have to talk about later, he and I. We talked about the riot, and the political climate in the city, and the moot back in August, and our families back home.

We brought Kasaqua and Copper back to the dragonhall, then went to take luncheon, the three of us sitting tucked away in a corner at a different table than our usual one. We were late, and the dining hall wasn't as crowded as usual, but there were still a lot of stares and whispers. I was absolutely certain that there would be a lot of questions as soon as my classmates could corner me and demand answers without it being horribly impolite.

As far as I knew, we were still going to have a meeting of the DGT in the library after dinner. I briefly considered inviting Sadsong to it, but decided I'd save that for next week.

After luncheon, we went right back to the dragonhall. Theod had husbandry for the afternoon period, and Sadsong wanted to be introduced to Professor Mesman. Theod was still getting Copper into his tack when the professor joined us.

"Ah, Miss Anequs, Mister Knecht," Professor Mesman began, "I was hoping to find you here." He turned his attention to Sadsong, inclining his head politely. "And you must be the visitor that everyone's all abuzz about. I'm Professor Mesman; I teach dragon husbandry, as well as riding and flight techniques here at the academy."

"Sadsong. *Just* Sadsong," she replied, extending a hand. "Pleased to meet you."

Professor Mesman paused for a moment longer than was polite before shaking her hand, and Sadsong said, "Seems your folks know their business. Eatsfeathers settled in nicely, and he's not bothered by the food or the accommodations. Mind you, he's used to letting himself in and out as he pleases from any kind of shelter; if he wants to laze in the sun, he's *going* to."

"It is customary at this dragonhall to bar the stall doors when a dragon's been put up," Professor Mesman said disapprovingly. "Miss Anequs, I understand that your dragon managed somehow to get out of her stall when Frau Sadsong first arrived?"

"Yes, sir. I'm sorry; she was terribly excited. She didn't cause any harm to anyone; she just wanted to see Eatsfeathers."

"Be that as it may, there is the matter of how she managed to do it," the professor pressed.

"I expect she just lifted the latch," I said, a bit confused. "She's watched me open and close the door hundreds of times; she understands the mechanism of a bar latch."

"Do you think that you could persuade her to do it again? To demonstrate the technique?"

"Certainly, though I'm not sure it's the best idea to encourage her if this is something you don't want her doing. I've tried to impress on her that it's important for her to stay in her stall when she's put there."

Theod stayed in Copper's stall to finish getting him ready for class, while the professor and Sadsong followed me to Kasaqua's stall. I called her name, and for a moment she was very confused—I fixed in my mind the idea of her sliding a forefoot through the gap between the stall door and the wall, trying to convey *permission*—that this was something I wanted her to do.

She lifted the latch with no trouble at all and nosed the door open, coming to join us in the corridor with a little trilling sound of greeting. Professor Mesman looked . . . disturbed.

"My guess, by the look on your face, is that Anglish dragons can't do that?" Sadsong asked with a wry smile.

"That's an uncommon show of both intelligence and dexterity on the part of your dragon," Professor Mesman said to me. He looked to Sadsong and asked, "I take this to mean that *your* dragon could also easily walk out of his stall on a whim?"

"He can and he will, whenever the fancy strikes him," Sadsong said. "He's *not* invested in you thinking he's a good boy. He won't do any harm, mind, not unless I tell him to, but he's not a beast that you can just put in a cage."

"That's a somewhat troubling attitude, Frau Sadsong," Professor Mesman said after a long pause. He turned his attention back to me and asked, "That's something your dragon worked out on her own? You didn't train her to do that, or some similar trick?"

"No, sir," I said. "She's always been able to do that; she's just chosen not to until this morning, because she wants to be good. I suppose Sadsong's arrival—or, probably more Eatsfeathers's arrival—seemed important enough for her to disregard the general rules of appropriate behavior."

"She came out of her den to greet an elder is what she did," Sadsong said. "I wouldn't expect anything less."

"I . . . see," Professor Mesman said. "In any case, I have a class to teach. Miss Anequs, what class do you have for the afternoon period?"

"Monday and Wednesday afternoons are my free period, sir," I answered. "I was actually going to ask for your approval to take on a directed study under Sadsong. She has particular knowledge of Kasaqua's breed that would probably help tremendously. You should see her tack. It's different from Anglish tack, and I think it would suit Kasaqua's conformation much better."

He frowned for a long moment, looking at Sadsong, and at Kasaqua—who was sitting up at heel now, patiently attentive—and then at me.

"I'll want regular reports on your progress, and once your dragon is flying, any sessions involving actual flight will need to be supervised," he said after a bit of silence. He turned to Sadsong. "And I should very much like to have a discussion with you about comparative techniques in both husbandry and instruction. Perhaps over tea, on Friday afternoon? I won't be able to carve out time before then, I'm afraid."

"Make it coffee," Sadsong said, "and you've got yourself a deal."

"Very well," Professor Mesman said. "I really must get to my class now—though I expect that quite a lot of time will be wasted explaining your presence and that of your dragon."

"I wouldn't call that wasted time, but I'm not you," Sadsong said with a shrug. Turning back to me, she said, "Come on, then. If we're going to do this 'directed study' properly, I should show you how Eatsfeathers's tack *works*. It's going to take some doing to make a set for Kasaqua, but the principles are the same."

We spent the afternoon in Eatsfeathers's stall, where Sadsong had stowed her equipment. By the time the husbandry students began returning, we had a rough pattern laid out for Kasaqua's new tack.

"We'll need to source materials—you folks on the islands have proper buckskin, I'll bet," Sadsong said, rolling up our sketches. "Need to smooth everything over with those ministry fellows before I get you to introduce me to your folks, though. Maybe by Saturday?"

"Maybe," I said, doubting that it would happen that quickly.

We were intercepted outside the dragonhall by Frau Kuiper and Frau Brinkerhoff.

"Ah, Frau Sadsong, excellent—this is Frau Brinkerhoff, our house matron here at the academy. I would appreciate it if you could join us in my office to discuss your stay with us," Frau Kuiper said. "Miss Anequs, I believe that you're much desired in the dining hall by your usual group of associates. Miss Wozniakowa has returned safely, and has already joined them. I trust that you will endeavor to prevent sensationalism as much as possible?"

"Yes, ma'am." Turning to Sadsong, I said, "Have a good evening; I'm sure we'll talk again soon. I've got husbandry in the morning and skiltakraft in the afternoon, tomorrow. I'm sure that Professor Schreiber will be very interested in meeting you as soon as it's reasonable."

"I will see that all of the professors and staff are made aware of Frau Sadsong," Frau Kuiper said.

"I'm going to need for you to stop putting 'Frau' in front of my name, whenever that's convenient," Sadsong said, with hard eyes and a thin smile. "Other than that, I'd be happy to say my hellos to whomsoever you think I ought to."

I proceeded to the dining hall. Jadi was sitting at our usual table, talking with Marta and Sander and Theod and Osvald. Dreyst was sitting in her lap, even though he was getting too big for that to be comfortable or practical. Juniper was lying at the foot of Osvald's chair, looking forlorn.

"We barricaded in our temple, doused all the lights, and sat quietly in the basement," she was saying as I sat down. "We were lucky; they didn't come there. The rioting and the fires all happened around Center Street and Cannery Street and all the little streets down to the harbor. The Kindah quarter overlaps some with the cannery district, and the Zhidish quarter overlaps with the Kindah quarter, but not in the same places. The Zhidish quarter is basically just Woodward Road and the little side streets off it, and plenty of Anglish people live there, too."

"But you could hear it?" Marta asked, her eyes wide.

"The screaming, yes," Jadi said. "And we could smell the smoke. Herr Geller went up to look from the window a few times. He said he could see the fires a few streets over. Someone came and knocked on the temple door around midnight. We were all terrified. But it was just the matron from the boarding house next door, asking if we could take in some of her lodgers, because she was worried about her building catching fire if the wind changed."

"Did you?" Theod asked. "Take them in, I mean?"

"Yes. We let them in through the side door—several little old ladies who all worked at the same laundry off Cannery Street; we knew them as neighbors. They stayed until morning. Their building didn't burn down."

"I'm just glad that you're safe," Marta said. "It must have been so awful."

"It was worse for other people," Jadi said, looking down.

"Does this mean that your holiday thing in a couple of weeks is canceled?" Osvald asked.

"Of course it's not!" Jadi said, sounding slightly indignant. "We're just going to be extra careful about it. Dynah's going to come down and stay for a while; it will be nice for everyone to see how Gikka has grown. With Gikka and Dreyst both there, I can't imagine that anyone would be stupid enough to threaten us. No one in the cannery district had dragons to protect them. If they had, then maybe the riot wouldn't have happened in the first place."

"They say there was a dragoneer among the berserkers, though," Osvald insisted. "Someone with command of their own dragon might not be put off by the threat of dragons—"

"The ministry will find out if that bit's true, and if it is, they'll find out who it was," Marta said, clearly trying to sound sensible and sure but not quite succeeding.

"I think it will depend entirely on who the dragoneer was and who they know, politically," Osvald said. "And that's if there was even a dragon there at all—"

"My brother *saw it,*" I insisted. "He described a kesseldrache."

"There aren't that many kesseldraches in Lindmarden," Osvald said, sounding troubled. "The breed suffered terrible losses during the war with Berri Vaskos . . ."

"Well, then, it shouldn't be too hard for them to find out who it was—unless someone somewhere has made it their business for that dragoneer to not be found," Theod said. I caught his gaze across the table; we were both thinking the same thing. The ministry might have found it useful to make an example of Otrygg Otryggson, but he'd threatened *the academy.* That was a rather different thing than attacking the cannery district. *Skrælings and nithings have no place in Lindmarden* was not an unpopular sentiment among some people.

"How many dragoneers are there in Lindmarden, anyway?" I asked. "I've never seen anyone with a dragon out and about in the city, apart from thanegards."

"The Ministry of Dragon Affairs keeps records of every dragon that's hatched in Vaster's Hold," Osvald said, "but I don't think they're generally available to the public. There's a memorial plaque somewhere in the Ministry offices that has the names of all the dragons that fell in the war with Berri Vaskos, and their riders; Uncle Otto brought me to see it once. I remember thinking it was a lot of them. I know that a lot of dragoneers who graduate from the academy join the dragonthede, and anyone who wants to go into racing moves to New Linvik, because there's practically no racing society here."

"Only because no one has gone to the trouble of founding a racing club," Marta said. "There are certainly enough riders of bjalladrekis to support one, and they're the best racing breed."

Sander wrote something on his tablet and slid it to Osvald, who read aloud, "Kuiper's Academy has been open and taking in students since 1830. Before that, the only academy of skiltakraft in Lindmarden was High King's Academy in New Linvik, and that was founded way back in the 1640s sometime."

It came as a revelation to me that this school had been founded so recently; for some reason, I'd thought it much older and more established than that. Finding that it had been built within my lifetime . . . what had the academy's grounds been like before? Had the train station come before, or after?

"So if Kuiper's turns out twenty or so new dragoneers every year . . ." I considered aloud.

"That's only recently," Osvald said. "Back when it was founded, there weren't as many students in each class. Frau Schreiber was one of *eight* students who completed their education in 1833. There's a list of every graduate the academy's ever had, in records in the library."

"Dynah finished up here in '40, and there were sixteen in her class," Jadi offered.

"So the number of dragoneers in Lindmarden must be in the hundreds, at least," I said, calculating mentally. "Ernst is due to finish this year, isn't he?"

"Yes," Osvald confirmed.

"And there are how many students in the fourth-year class?"

"Twenty-one," Jadi said, shifting slightly as Dreyst adjusted his position on her lap. "Some of them might stay on for a fifth year, though, if they need to. Dynah stayed on for an extra year to perfect her skiltakraft."

"But many move elsewhere, like Osvald said," Marta pointed

out. "Kerstin Linna, who roomed with me in my first year, went to Tyskland to finish her education."

"There's the racing circuit in New Linvik, a different dragonthede in every hold, and seeking fortune abroad. Only a fraction of dragoneers stay in the city."

"And of those," Theod added quietly, "how many might sympathize with the Ravens of Joden and the rioters?"

An uncomfortable silence fell over the table. I pushed the food around on my plate, my appetite suddenly diminished.

"Well, I, for one, am looking forward to your holiday celebration, Jadi," Marta finally said, breaking the tension. "Will there be special foods?"

Jadi's face brightened. "Oh, yes! Stuffed cabbage rolls, and tzimmes—which is a stewed fruit dish with carrots—and apple cake. And there's a special bread we bake with candied citron pressed into patterns on top."

"That sounds delicious," I said, grateful for the change in topic. "I do hope that we're still allowed to go. As far as I know, we're still under orders to remain on school grounds, aren't we?"

"Oh, Herr Geller had *words* with Frau Kuiper when they brought me back!" Jadi said, her voice conspiratorial. "*I'm* certainly still going, because if the academy tried to keep me or Dreyst from Sukkot, Papa would pull me right out of this school and find some other way for me to gain an education. Maybe back in Polland, if it came to that. I don't know if anyone else will be allowed to come join me, though, with everything that's happened."

"Are we still meeting tonight?" Theod asked in a very quiet voice, glancing over to the table where Ernst was sitting with Kam and Nils and Vinzent and Evind. "The DGT, I mean?"

"Yes," Osvald said. "The library, eight o'clock." Juniper whined softly from under the table, and Osvald reached down to scratch behind her ears. "They're going to want to know about that nackie woman and her dragon."

"And I promise I'll catch everyone up," I said, glancing at the clock against the far wall. It was, somehow, already almost seven.

We all proceeded to the dragonhall together to see to the feeding of our charges.

AUTUMN CAME

Sadsong sat in on both of my classes on Thursday, observing quietly and taking notes. Professor Schreiber was far more enthused with her presence than Professor Mesman was, and kept needling her for comments and questions, but she was *very* close-mouthed on the topic of skiltakraft and how it was practiced among her people. On Friday, after lore with Professor Ibarra, I received a letter—they were still being delivered directly to students' rooms, to limit crowding in the mail room. It had been opened and stuffed awkwardly back into its envelope, and I wondered which of the professors had read it and approved of its contents as "suitable." Opening it, I recognized my mother's handwriting instantly.

Dear Anequs,

I hope this letter finds you well. Niquiat and Zhina arrived safely on Tuesday morning, along with your letter. I hope to have this reply on the morning ferry, so I do hope you'll receive it sometime on Friday. Zhina's sleeping in your bed; I know you won't mind. Sigoskwe and Sakewa are very excited to have Niquiat at home, even under these terrible circumstances. I'm happy to have him home, too; he's sick in his heart from everything that's happened. I think it would help him to see you; the two of you were always close.

Something is happening on Naquipaug; there are dragons flying overhead most days, now—the gray-and-white sort—but the thanegards at their new outpost won't tell us anything. I miss you terribly and would like to see that you're safe. Please come home when you can.

All my love,
Your mother

Frau Kuiper's office was on the third floor, at the end of the hall, behind a pair of very imposing doors. Frau Brinkerhoff's office was just to the left of it, and all of the other professors except for Professor Ulfar had offices along the same hallway. I noticed as I was passing that Professor Schreiber didn't have a brass plaque with her name engraved on it like all the other professors did; the door that had been Professor Ezel's office last year instead had a card with her name neatly printed on it, hanging in a simple wooden frame.

I knocked on Frau Kuiper's door and received no answer. I tried a second time before turning to Frau Brinkerhoff's door; no luck there, either. Neither of them were in their offices, which meant I'd have to go hunting for them elsewhere. I had no idea where to seek out Frau Kuiper, but Frau Brinkerhoff was most likely in the mail room, manning the telegraph. I didn't know if anyone else at the school even knew how to operate the machine, or decipher the tatkraftish pulses that traveled along the wires to and from written words.

She looked grim when I arrived at the mail room, sitting pale and drawn at her desk. Frau Brinkerhoff had the kind of wrinkles around her eyes that made her look like she was smiling, even when she wasn't, but she didn't look like she was smiling right now. She looked very, very tired.

"Is there something that you need, Miss Anequs?" she asked, looking up at me as I entered.

"Yes, ma'am. Sorry to be a bother, but Professor Ibarra said that no student is to leave the school grounds without informing and receiving express permission from Frau Kuiper or yourself. I checked at her office, but she's not there—"

"Frau Kuiper is presently attending Jarl Joervarsson's court in an advisory role, assisting Captain Einarsson," Frau Brinkerhoff said with a sigh. "There's no reason for you to leave school grounds."

"My mother wants me to come home for the weekend. I'd like to introduce Sadsong to my family and people—"

"The recent events in the city are precisely why we can't have students tripping about hither and thither through the city," she interrupted crossly. "Until everything is sorted—"

"My brother's flat burned down. One of his friends was killed," I said. "He's gone back home, and Mother wants me to talk with him. *I* want to talk with him."

"I'm afraid that will be quite impossible," Frau Brinkerhoff insisted. "Your dragon is particularly remarkable in appearance, and you are a person of some note in the public consciousness. There are individuals in the jarls' court who are particularly interested in your location and that of your dragon—"

"If any of the other students' parents sent a letter requesting that they come home, would they be allowed to go? With their dragons?" I asked.

"That's . . . a delicate matter, I'm afraid," she said, sounding pained. "Most of the other students come from established dragoneering families. They have dragonhalls on their family estates.

Many of the fathers of our other students fought in the war. You, and Mister Knecht, are in a unique position—"

"And so is Sadsong, I take it?" I said, folding my arms.

Frau Brinkerhoff's mouth formed a thin line. She set down her pen and folded her hands on the desk before her.

"Miss Anequs, I appreciate your concern for your family. Truly, I do. But you must understand that the current situation in the city is precarious. Every dragon housed at this academy's dragonhall is, in the eyes of the law, associated with the school. We are responsible for their welfare *and* for any harm that they might do out in the wider world. I'm sure that you've heard, by now, the rumors that a dragon and thus a dragoneer were present in the gang of berserkers who rioted through the cannery district on Sunday night into Monday—"

"It's not just a rumor; my brother saw the dragon and described a kesseldrache."

"A kesseldrache that was almost certainly housed and educated at this very academy sometime within the last dozen years. A rider who was approved by both this institution and the Ministry of Dragon Affairs as possessed of sufficient intelligence, knowledge, skill, and moral character as to be trusted with the command of a dragon."

"Which speaks more to the ministry's inability to correctly judge that rider's character than anything else," I said. "I don't understand why that should prevent me from taking Kasaqua home for the weekend as I did on several different occasions last year."

"Your failure to understand is not something that I have the wherewithal to address at this time, Miss Anequs," she said, sounding both weary and annoyed. "All dragons *will* remain on school grounds until Captain Einarsson approves otherwise. Dragons that leave school grounds will be detained by the Ministry of Dragon Affairs, as Frau Sadsong's dragon was. She is *very* lucky to be accommodated here, because the ministry would have been well within their rights to imprison her and her dragon at the thanegards' barracks."

"So no one will be allowed to leave school grounds," I said, trying to make my frustration evident.

"No *dragon* will be allowed to leave campus, no. Not even the students from established dragoneering families will be allowed to remove their charges elsewhere, for the time being. Karina was quite clear on this matter before she departed for court. What our students choose to do regarding that fact is their own prerogative."

"Are you suggesting that I . . . leave Kasaqua here? Go home without her?" I demanded.

"I am suggesting nothing whatsoever," Frau Brinkerhoff said. "The conclusions that you draw are entirely your own. The school's purview is first and foremost *dragons.* We have neither the right nor the ability to detain citizens of Lindmarden by force. You may take your leave at any time, but your dragon will remain here."

I sighed and uncrossed my arms, letting them fall to my sides. She didn't understand; she wasn't a dragoneer. She didn't have a reason to care.

"How long will this restriction last?" I asked.

"That depends entirely on how quickly the situation in the city is resolved," she said. She picked up her pen again, a clear signal that our conversation was drawing to a close. "My suggestion to you is that you write to your mother explaining the circumstances. I'm certain she'll understand."

"And Niquiat? My brother needs me."

Her expression softened slightly, and she said, "I'm truly sorry about what happened to your brother and his friend. But putting yourself, your dragon, and this academy as an institution at risk won't help him or anyone else. The best thing that you can do right now is to focus on your studies and remain *safe.* Perhaps you might write to your brother directly. Sometimes putting thoughts to paper can be more meaningful than spoken words. Any letters that you write will, of course, be reviewed. You needn't worry about postage, however; we'll manage that."

I did not thank her as I left.

I attended natural philosophy with Professor Ulfar, and wrote letters to Mother and to Niquiat, and presented them to Frau Brinkerhoff unsealed and ready for inspection. I knew they wouldn't reach Masquapaug until Tuesday at the earliest; the ferry only ran on Tuesday and Friday.

Dynah arrived after luncheon on Friday to collect Jadi, escorted by a pair of Captain Einarsson's soldiers. She reported that they were intercepting any dragon on the wing, now. Jadi was allowed to join the Geller family for the duration of the Zhidi holidays, *and* was allowed to bring Dreyst with her. I tried very hard not to be resentful about it; she was being allowed a dispensation that no one else was because she had people to argue on her behalf that Frau Kuiper cared about offending. I had to wonder if, despite Frau Brinkerhoff's assertions, any of the other students' families might be able to pluck them out of the academy and take them home. Did Marta's father have that kind of pull? Did Ernst and Osvald's family?

My family certainly didn't have such powers.

I spent the entirety of Saturday with Theod and Sadsong, never going out of sight of the dragonhall. Sunday was the first of October. Marta excused herself to the library in the morning, leaving Liberty and me to our weekly sewing circle. We mostly talked about Sadsong, and about my frustration with Kasaqua being trapped here. Liberty was, as ever, pragmatic about everything that was happening. She wanted to know if I'd be able to attend her salon on the seventh. I told her that I'd have to petition Frau Brinkerhoff for train fare; there had been no discussion of provisional funds for me this year as there'd been last year.

When I asked on Monday, I was told that students were still being *asked* to remain on school grounds, and that I would not be provided funds to assist me in denying that request.

If I was going to go anywhere, it would have to be on foot.

ANEQUS SHARED A QUIET MOMENT WITH LIBERTY

I didn't go to Liberty's salon on the seventh. Liberty did, though; the proscription against leaving school grounds only applied to students and their dragons, not to staff. Under the pretense of taking Kasaqua on a constitutional walk, and assuring Henkjan that I would *not* be leaving the academy's grounds, I was able to go to the train station to meet Liberty when she returned.

She was wearing the same dark green calico dress that she'd been wearing the first time we'd met at the station. She looked mildly surprised to see me there, waiting for her.

"What are you doing here?" she asked.

"I wanted to make sure you got back to school safely," I said. "And I was hoping we could walk together and chat a bit. I know you've got to get back to your duties in the afternoon, but you still have an hour and a half before that, don't you?"

"I suppose that's true," she said, looking around as if to

make sure that we were alone, as the train pulled away from the platform. I watched some tension melt from her shoulders and neck when she'd made sure that no one was watching us.

Kasaqua came bounding over, dropping into a play-bow before Liberty, which made her smile. Liberty's smile never failed to be dazzling.

"Was everyone at the salon all right?" I asked gently, once she'd scratched Kasaqua behind the ears and fallen into step beside me as we walked back along the path that led to the school.

She paused, a long breath escaping her.

"No one's dead, if that's what you mean," she said, her voice distant. "The salon was quieter than usual. Tensions are still high in the city. There've been a number of arrests, and thanegards on every corner—dragonthede, too, in busy places like the downtown station. They've been detaining anyone they find suspicious for whatever reason, keeping them for however long they like. A pair of guards came to talk to Frau Xixi about the men who visit her establishment. No one knows if they'll get caught up in whatever it is the thanegards are doing, but they've been paying special attention to anyone who isn't Anglish."

"Do you think they'll cancel next month's gathering?" I asked.

"They might; the idea was discussed in passing," she said. "It will depend entirely on the climate of the city in the next few weeks. Mendoza's is safer than some other places, I think, because the thanegards know that it's a frequent meeting spot for Freemansthede supporters. Ravens and their ilk wouldn't give business to Blackfolkish proprietors, after all."

"Would you be up for walking the trails a bit before heading back to the school?"

"Won't someone be missing you and your dragon?" she asked, frowning.

"I told Hallmaster Henkjan that I was taking Kasaqua out to stretch her legs; I think as long as I have her back at the dragonhall by the time luncheon is being served, it will be fine. Out on the trails it can be just us; no one will find us there."

"Unless some other student decides that they want to take their dragon out for a constitutional walk," Liberty said, folding her arms.

"Kasaqua will warn us if anyone's coming," I countered. After a long moment, Liberty nodded, and together we veered off the trail and into the woods.

The dry crunch of leaves from two weeks ago had been replaced by the soft squelch of damp earth beneath our boots. The trees had shed most of their summer green, leaving the branches adorned with vibrant hues of scarlet, russet, and gold. The light rain from yesterday had left the ground slick, turning the fallen leaves into a slippery, glossy carpet. A cool mist hung between the trees, the forest cloaked in a soft veil. The air smelled richer now—earthier, the scent of wet foliage and decaying leaves mingling with rain-soaked wood and moss.

Liberty spoke, her voice cutting through the quiet. "I took the dress to Miss Jenni this morning, by the way," she said, turning her head slightly to meet my gaze. "She'll try to sell it for me, though I won't get any money until she's found a buyer. It's a bit of a waiting game. Once it's sold, I'll get a portion of the sale price. I don't know how much demand there's going to be for fall ball gowns now, though; I don't know if folks are still going to have big celebrations of Valkyrjafax with everything that's going on in the city."

"So, I just gave away a hundred markas worth of dress," I said, half-joking, half-serious. "And you're going to get a *portion* of the sale price, eventually?"

Liberty snorted, a sound I hadn't expected from her. "Eventually." She nudged me with her elbow. "But don't worry. When it sells, I'll be able to pay off my debts, even after Miss Jenni takes her consignment portion."

I smiled despite myself, relieved that she wasn't too bothered by the uncertainty of it all. "I hope you're right. You deserve better than this, Liberty."

"I know," she said, her tone quiet but earnest. "But this is what I've got, right now. Honestly, I'm getting by. I've got a roof over my head and regular meals and pleasant company, which is more than a lot of people can say."

The steady rhythm of our steps was comforting, familiar, the woods a refuge from the outside world. Kasaqua trotted ahead, moving with an easy grace despite the mud and slick leaves, occasionally glancing back to make sure we were following.

"Hallmaster Henkjan got Theod a book for his birthday, did I tell you?"

Liberty stopped, her eyebrows raised. "No, you didn't! What book?"

I dropped my voice to a conspiratorial whisper. "It's called *A Young Man's Guide to Love and Marriage.*"

Her face took on a knowing sort of look, and she asked, "Wait, is it one of those 'instructions for good health' kind of books? *Henkjan* gave it to him?"

"Apparently, because he's eighteen now, it's Henkjan's idea of a 'fatherly' gift. It's full of the most ridiculous claims—you wouldn't believe it."

"I spent a few years at the Society for Friendless Girls," she said. "There's no claim that any pamphlet or magazine could make on the subjects of marriage and physical love that I haven't seen before."

"One chapter's about the proper place of a wife and the *duty* of marital intimacy . . . it insists that women don't feel passion like men do. That the act of love is simply about duty. *Duty!*"

Liberty burst out laughing, her face lighting up with genuine amusement. "I'm sure that for some Anglish girls married off to advantageous suitors, it is. Think about *The Sisters Baumgärtner.* Would Dorothea have been so keen to jump into Torsten's bed if her bedroom activities with her husband were anything but an unpleasant duty?"

"I suppose that makes sense, in light of that," I conceded. "But it gets worse—there's a whole section about *the consequences of misuse of the genital organs.* It talks about how one act of 'indiscretion' will lead to *melancholy, madness,* and an irreversible *decline in your vital energies*!"

Liberty stifled her laughter with a hand over her mouth. When she stopped giggling, she said, "Oh, *that's* fascinating. What did Theod have to say about the matter?"

"He didn't say anything about it; he was too preoccupied with trying not to die of embarrassment. But I had to laugh, and I couldn't stop!"

Liberty's laughter subsided, but she kept smiling as we continued walking, side by side. There was an ease between us now, the tension of the past weeks slipping away, replaced by something lighter. Her hand slipped into mine, warm, firm with a dressmaker's calluses.

The soft rustling of the trees seemed to echo our easy conversation, and for a moment, everything felt simple.

"I should be getting back to my duties," Liberty said after a few minutes, a touch of regret in her voice as she looked upward, gauging the quality of the afternoon light.

"May I kiss you?" I asked. Her dark gaze held mine for a few agonizingly long seconds, and then she smiled and stepped closer, pulling me gently into a kiss. It was brief—just a brush of lips—but it felt like a promise, like a tiny rebellion against the world and everything happening in it. Slow and unsure at first, but it deepened as soon as she let me in. I could feel her—her breath, her heart, everything that had been held back between us. I didn't care if it was wrong in Anglish estimations. All I cared about, in this moment, was her.

When we finally pulled apart, it felt like the world was still—like the forest was holding its breath with us. But then, as always, the moment slipped away too quickly. Liberty stepped back, her expression soft but guarded. "I have to go," she said, her voice almost apologetic. "I've got duties. You know I can't stay."

I nodded, a thousand things unsaid caught in my throat. They came out as, "I know."

The look in her eyes told me that she knew, too. So we walked back to the dragonhall together.

PREPARATIONS WERE MADE

Friday the thirteenth was Niquiat's birthday. When I told Frau Brinkerhoff, she allowed me to send him a telegram and acted as if that were terribly magnanimous of her. I asked if he'd be allowed to visit, and while he *would* have been, he didn't have the money for train and ferry fare both ways.

On Saturday the fourteenth, the dresses that Marta'd had commissioned for Valkyrjafax were delivered—her gold-shot rose pink and my black-shot red. At her insistence, we spent much of Saturday morning modeling the dresses and trying out hairstyles. The red dress was absolutely *striking* on me, and standing in it before the mirror, I felt . . . powerful. Warsome. The bronze dress last year had looked well on, and had complemented my coloring, but this dress was something else entirely. This was a dress that made declarations.

"It will be lovely to have something to take our minds off all this political nonsense," Marta said, facing her dressing mirror but meeting my eyes through the reflection. "I've been writing back and forth with Lisbet, and with Mathilda. They had tea last weekend, the two of them, and it's lovely to see them getting along. Mathilda speculates that Lisbet is quite taken with Iain, but Lisbet has mentioned nothing of the sort in her letters, so I'm not sure. It's a shame that we can't invite him to join us for the ball, but the proportion of young men to young ladies is already so skewed, we couldn't *possibly* add another gentleman to compete for the ladies' attention."

I found that I cared even less for Valkyrjafax this year than I had last year, which I confided to Sadsong and Theod when we went walking with our dragons that afternoon.

"I'm going to make it my business to bump elbows with all of the professors and parents," Sadsong said. "I haven't got anything at all appropriate to wear to that kind of thing, and no one's talked to me about it, but I want to see if they'll have the nerve to make me leave if I just turn up in riding leathers."

That was something I hadn't considered . . . the possibility of not just failing at or disregarding social rules, but breaking them on purpose, brazenly. What would have happened if Marta had decided to withdraw her offer of a dress and, rather than not attending at all, I'd shown up in one of my day dresses? Or if I'd shown up in the buckskin dress I wore to *proper* dances?

I'd have to keep that possibility in mind for next year. It was the sort of audacious disobedience that Herr Gerdasson would approve of; I could imagine him laughing and congratulating me.

I decided, against Marta's objections, to wear my hair in a distinctly Masquisit style on the evening of Valkyrjafax.

Jadi came back on the evening of Sunday the fifteenth with a basket of apple tarts and little sweet buns studded with candied fruit to share with everyone, since none of us had been able to visit her in the city while she'd been away. She'd acquired a dress for the occasion while she was away: a golden-yellow satin affair with embroidery on the bodice—some of it in gold thread—that she explained was a distinctly Pollish style.

I attended my classes, completed my assignments, and wrote my papers. I attended meetings of the DGT. I wrote home about everything that Sadsong was teaching me and inquired about the possibility of having saddle-making supplies shipped to the school. It was a considerable expense, but provisioning a dragoneer was the sort of thing that the whole village could rally behind. There was talk among my fellow students that *surely* travel restrictions would be lifted after the ball. After all, so many people were being allowed to *visit* the school grounds—sisters and cousins of students, mostly, to make up the numbers of ladies.

On Friday the twenty-seventh, classes were suspended. Our dragons were fed earlier in the day, around luncheon, and then shut up in the dragonhall. Dreyst, being small enough that he was still able to be indoors, was confined to our room. He'd seemed terribly forlorn about it, and I felt for him; last year, Kasaqua had at least had Magnus for company. Dreyst was left entirely alone. Jadi spent a long while consoling him in a language that I didn't understand.

At sunset, we all assembled outside of the school for the same rite I'd witnessed last year—oaths to the Valkyrja and to Fyra, the skiltas to make mead, and the burning of the straw horse.

Lisbet Jansen had arrived not with her mother, but with Frau Morris and Mathilda. Frau Jansen was, Lisbet reported, "indisposed"—and she would say no more on the subject. Both Jansen siblings seemed much more comfortable without Frau Jansen present. No one attempted to take Sander's tablet from him.

Hartvig Ravnsson was no longer a student at the academy, and so Bergitte Ravnsdottir was not invited to this ball. Annetta Virtanen and Saskia Britsch, however, still had brothers in attendance to invite and chaperone them. I was introduced to quite a few more people this year than I had been last year, mainly owing to my new association with the young men of the DGT. Osvald and Ernst had a younger sister named Lena, which came as a surprise to me, because neither of them had *ever* mentioned her. She was newly fourteen and just back from primary school, and this was the first proper ball she'd ever been to. She attached herself to Jadi's side immediately, as the young woman closest to her own age. Marta and Lisbet and I left them to it, joining Saskia and Annetta. I also met Vinzent's sister, Alma, and Nils's cousin Dagmær—who insisted that we must call her Dagga. Both had been present at last year's ball. Neither had been introduced to me on that occasion.

They made a performance of lamenting it.

This year, Theod asked me to join him in the first dance—the Vermillion Waltz—without having to be hunted down. In fact, my dance card was entirely filled within the half hour before the ballroom opened. The opening waltz and a later tanz with Theod, a polka with Sander, and dances with Evind and Vinzent and Osvald.

The bell rang three times, alerting us that the ballroom had been opened, and I allowed Theod to take my arm and lead me to the dance floor.

THE FESTIVITIES OF VALKYRJAFAX WERE INTERRUPTED

Theod and I danced to the Vermillion Waltz, then took refreshment in the form of spiced cider and apple cake. I danced a polka with Evind, and chatted with the other girls on the subject of our classmates' dancing skills. Sander and I were in the middle of the Drunken Dragon Polka when I suddenly became aware that *something wrong and bad and frightening* was happening at the dragonhall. I stumbled to a halt mid-swing, another pair of dancers crashing into me. I managed not to fall, but did scramble forward in a very undignified way. The music came to a discordant stop, replaced by gasps and shouts and noises of complaint. When I straightened up, I realized that more than half of the dancers were looking toward the main entrance, and the dragonhall beyond. From outside, I heard the deep, trumpeting call of a dragon. Then a crash and a groan: the sound of the main hall's huge double doors being thrown open.

By unanimous and unspoken agreement, everyone abandoned

the dance floor and rushed to the main hall, where most of the professors and chaperones were already gathered. Theod found me; Sander joined Marta and Lisbet. There was a great deal more pushing and jostling than could possibly be called civilized as we all crowded through the door, and when I finally got an unobstructed view, it was to see Jarl Joervarsson standing just inside in the wide-open doorway. He was carrying a child—a boy. One of his sons, I realized. I'd told stories to the jarl's boys during my convalescence at the palace, back in May. There was a bleeding gash on the jarl's forehead, and blood streaming down one side of his face. Jarl Joervarsson's eyes swept the room, glassy and haunted. The boy in his arms was sobbing, his face pressed against his father's shoulder. Blood matted the jarl's yellow hair, and his fine clothing was torn and bloodstained.

"The palace, the dragonthede barracks. They've killed the dragons," he said, his voice carrying across the hushed and breathless hall. "All the men of the dragonthede who were loyal to me—*their* dragons. Slaughtered in their stalls."

I gasped, joining the collective sounds of dismay that filled the hall. The hall erupted into chaos, students and guests talking, shouting, crying out in shock. Frau Kuiper came forward, the crowd parting around her. She was wearing a dark blue ball gown, which did not suit her nearly as well as her usual coat and trousers. She raised her hands and called out, her voice commanding and implacable, "Everyone, calm yourselves!" Turning back to the jarl, she demanded, "Who?"

The jarl put his son down, but the boy stayed close to his father's side, scrubbing at his face with the back on one hand.

"Sveni Audulfsson and his traitors," the jarl said. "They've taken the palace, murdered my advisors. Thane Lingstadt and Thane Authunsson are dead. The Ravens have infiltrated the dragonthede."

"Where's Heidi?" Frau Kuiper asked. That was the jarl's wife.

"Safe," the jarl said. "Agnar's with her, and her maids. Karl, though . . . my oldest . . ." He stopped, and for a moment, something fragile and terrified flickered in his eyes. Then it was gone, replaced by a steely resolve. "I came here because you're one of the few people that I know I can trust, Karina."

"Yes, of course," Frau Kuiper said. "You came on dragonback?"

"Einarsson's dragon, and those of his personal guard," the jarl said. "This was no gang of berserkers. This was organized, planned. They waited until we were in the middle of our own Valkyrjafax celebration and all struck together. Men of the dragonthede, men whom I *trusted.* They turned on their brothers, killing specific dragons. We've maybe a dozen surviving dragons whose dragoneers are loyal to me. I don't know how many dragoneers have defected to Audulfsson's cause."

"Our dragons," I called, my heart racing. "The dragonhall!"

"The dragonhall is secure," Captain Einarsson said, stepping in through the main doors. He had a pistol in his hand, and two soldiers flanking him. "I've posted my remaining loyal men around the perimeter; broke up the peasant-revel that the servants were having outside and told them to go to their quarters and wait there. The school grounds ought to be secure—for the moment, at least."

Liberty was probably safe, then, if the staff had been informed and ordered inside.

"How many dragons do you have with you, Leiknir?" Frau Kuiper asked.

"Seven here, a few more still on patrol," the jarl replied. "The rest have been killed, or turned traitor. I don't know who's which yet."

"How many do we *know* are under Audulfsson's command?" she pressed.

"At least twenty," the jarl said grimly. "Perhaps more."

A ripple of fear passed through the gathering. I did the mental calculation. Frau Kuiper's Gerhard, Professor Ibarra's Abiadura,

Professor Mesman's Kostbar, Professor Nazari's Zati, Professor Schreiber's Hans, Captain Einarsson's silberdrache, plus seven more with the jarl. Sadsong's Eatsfeathers. Thirty first-year students and twenty-four second-year students—myself included—whose dragons weren't capable of flight yet. Twenty-two third-year and twenty-one fourth-year students whose dragons *were* capable of flight. Dragoneers with wildly varying skill at skiltakraft.

Every single dragon—all hundred and eleven of them—was capable of loosing at least one breath that could reduce whatever it touched to ash and wind. Kasaqua had been able to melt stone and sand when she was just a few days old.

Kasaqua made me aware, through our bond, that she was coming to find me. I *needed* to go out to her. I heard shouting from the dragonhall, too far away to understand what was being said. I thought I heard Henkjan's voice. Sadsong appeared beside me, her face set with determination. She was dressed in her riding leathers, a sharp contrast to everyone else's formal attire. A strangled little laugh escaped my throat, seeing her. But nothing was funny.

"I'm going out to my dragon now," she said, nothing remotely hesitant or questioning in her voice. "Before he breaks something."

"Frau Sadsong—" Captain Einarsson admonished, only to be silenced by a booming roar and a scream from outside. Sadsong shoved her way past the captain. After exchanging a glance with Theod, in which he seemed to be trying to convey "Don't!" with his eyes, I followed in her wake.

Eatsfeathers and Kasaqua were both outside of the dragonhall already; he was in front of her, bellowing at Henkjan, who was trying in vain to herd him back into the dragonhall by brandishing a broom. Kasaqua's head shot up when she saw me, and she nosed her way past Eatsfeathers and ran to my side, putting her head on my shoulder.

Behind me, the crowd was spilling out of the main hall and onto the lawn.

"This is *entirely* unacceptable," Frau Kuiper shouted, her voice ringing out in the cool night air. "Everybody stop, at once!"

"Frau Kuiper, permission to go to the dragonhall?" a voice called from the crowd. I turned to see Ernst Gram. "We need to prepare our dragons. Even hatchlings can help defend from the ground; they ought to be let out of the students' quarters."

"If they've infiltrated the dragonthede and slaughtered dragons, it stands to reason that they may be targeting the academy next," someone else said.

"Agreed," said the jarl, his hand resting protectively on his son's shoulder. "We flew a circuitous route to avoid pursuit, but they'll have deduced where we've gone. We have perhaps an hour before they arrive in force. Maybe less."

Frau Kuiper studied him for a moment, then nodded.

"All right," she said. Her gaze hardened as she surveyed the crowd, and her voice rang out in command when she said, "All students should prepare their dragons—but not alone. Professors, please proceed to the dragonhall and secure your own charges. We'll divide the students into groups and send them to prepare their dragons in turn. No student is to be left unattended until we can determine loyalties." Her gaze swung around to Sadsong and me, each standing by our dragons now. "Anyone who attempts to leave school grounds will be presumed disloyal. Guests, I ask that you return to the ballroom. Professor Ulfar, if you could help to secure and fortify that position?"

"Yes, ma'am," Professor Ulfar called from somewhere beyond the doorway, his voice crisp.

"How can we possibly know who to trust?" another student called out. "Anyone here might be colluding with the Ravens!"

"We start with the obvious," Captain Einarsson said grimly. He stepped forward, pistol still in hand. "Everyone with family ties to the Ravens of Joden, step forward now."

A terrible silence fell over the crowd as we all looked at one another. Kam Hagelin stepped forward, his chin raised defiantly.

"*Fuck* my father," he said. "I don't know if he's allied himself with the Ravens, and I don't care. I am my own man, and my loyalty is to Jarl Joervarsson."

He dropped to one knee and bowed his head to the jarl. Ernst stepped up behind him and did the same, and Osvald followed after a moment of hesitation. Other students followed suit, kneeling or just bowing their heads as space permitted. When the jarl looked at me, I nodded.

"We need to fortify," Frau Kuiper declared. "The younger dragons can be positioned around the perimeter. Mesman, the third- and fourth-years should prepare for aerial defense—"

Professor Mesman stepped forward. "I'll coordinate the defensive positions with Captain Einarsson."

"What about skiltakraft?" someone asked. "Those of us with stronger abilities could form an outer defense."

"Good," Frau Kuiper said, nodding. "Professor Schreiber, organize those with the strongest skiltakraft abilities. Focus on defensive measures—reinforcement, concealment, early warning."

The night that had begun with music and celebration now hung heavy with the promise of violence. I was still wearing a ball gown. Behind me, in the dragonhall, I could hear the restless cries of dragons sensing the change in the air, calling out in confusion and alarm.

Somewhere beyond the horizon, enemies were already winging their way toward us.

They would not find us unready.

THE BATTLE LINES WERE DRAWN

Theod was called to Professor Mesman's group, and I was called to Professor Schreiber's. I embraced him and *kissed* him before we parted, not caring at all who noticed; if it was shocking or improper, no one said anything about it. Marta embraced first Lisbet and then Sander before disappearing to put Magnus into flight tack. All of the non-dragoneer party guests, Lisbet and Mathilda among them, were bustled into the ballroom. They would be barricading it from within with tables and chairs. The first-year students, captained by Frau Brinkerhoff and Jarl Joervarsson himself, were positioned in the main hall with their young dragons at heel as a last line of defense in case the rest of us failed and the Ravens' forces managed to breach the school proper. The staff were alerted of the coming threat, and a number of the young men from the dragonhall joined in the defense, despite not having dragons of their own. They took up whatever weapons they could lay hands on in the form of shovels and garden forks, kitchen knives and fire irons. They added something like thirty or forty fighters to our forces. Frau Brinkerhoff manned the telegraph and immediately began contacting every dragoneer within twenty miles; Dynah Wozniakowa arrived on her dragon Gikka within half an hour. She immediately joined Mesman's group with the other flyers.

Outside, the sky was overcast and starless, the night impenetrably black beyond the flickering light of the candle lamps that lined the path. The wind was chill and damp, still smelling of bonfire smoke. I was mildly surprised to find that Sander and I were the only second-year students in Professor Schreiber's group—hand-selected from all the other students for being especially proficient in skiltakraft. There were fourteen students, and together with the professor, we were in command of ten bjalladrekis, three silberdraches, two velikolepnis, and one Nampeshiwe. Apart from Sander and Nils, I didn't know any of the students well. We were stationed at the sandpit opposite the dragonhall, and Professor Schreiber set us to the task of making flasks of säure and flamestuff, pulling the necessary athers from the air, soil, and grass. She inspected each of our skiltas with great care by the light of a kerosene lamp, and no one attempted to activate one without her approval.

We were each able to craft two or three items before our dragons needed to rest and recover their breath. The velikolepnis were much faster to recover than other breeds, able to activate more skiltas in quick succession. Inga was able to activate eight skiltas before faltering. Hans, being a fully grown velikolepni, was able to activate *ten.*

The products of our efforts were given directly to Frau Kuiper, who meted them out to the professors and upper-class students.

Scouts on the wing returned harrowing news. The Ravens had commandeered a train. Several hundred men and at least a dozen dragons were massing near the train station, and some had pistols and rifles.

Frau Kuiper stood before the assembled students, professors, and staff. Her face was illuminated by lamplight, casting deep shadows across her weathered features. Gerhard loomed behind her, a living silhouette against the night sky. She raised her hand, and an immediate hush fell over the gathered defenders.

"Students of the Academy, dragonriders and companions alike, tonight we face a darkness greater than the moonless sky above us. The Ravens of Joden are coming for our jarl, for our dragons, and for the future we represent. I see fear in your eyes. *Good.* Only fools feel no fear on the eve of battle. But in your eyes, I also see determination. I see the fire that marks a true dragoneer. Each of you was chosen by your charge because something in you burns brighter than others—a capacity for courage, for sacrifice, for love of these magnificent creatures who share their lives and magic with us. Remember your training. Remember that what we do here tonight is not just for ourselves. Every skilta you activate, every defensive position you hold, every moment you stand your ground, protects not just Jarl Joervarsson, but the very basis of votemanship and fairness. Sveni Audulfsson would make himself your king and crush you beneath his boot. We will not allow it. Those of you crafting säure and flamestuff—your work gives us weapons. Those taking to the sky—you are our eyes, and our swift might. Those standing guard within—they are our last hope, should we falter. Look to your dragons, look to your companions. We fight not just for our own lives, but for theirs. These men have slaughtered dragons this night, and we will not allow them to slaughter more. Stand fast. Trust your dragons. Trust each other. For the Academy! For our dragons!"

She raised her hand, and the gathered dragons lifted their heads in unison, a chorus of haunting cries echoing across the grounds, vibrating with a cadence I could feel in my bones.

From the distance, toward the train station, came the answering cry of other dragons.

Out of the darkness, a voice called—a full-voiced man amplified by a shouting horn:

"We've come in the name of the Wroughtjarl of Vastergot, Sveni Audulfsson! We have taken the royal palace, and we have the fealty of the dragonthede and the thanegards. Deliver to us Leiknir Joervarsson, Karina Kuiper, the savages, and their dragons—and the rest of you will be spared. Fail to deliver them to us, and there will be no quarter! Repeat, there will be no quarter!"

Frau Kuiper's voice pierced the darkness like a blade. "We have more than one hundred dragons in our ranks, and reinforcements on the way. If you value your lives, turn back now. If you think to face us, hope that the gods will grant you mercy—for we will not."

Her words were punctuated by Gerhard's bellow of fury as he leaped into flight. There was a thunderous flapping of wings as the rest of the flyers joined him aloft.

The first shots rang out from the darkness—rifles cracking in the night. I couldn't help but flinch and duck, feeling Kasaqua's sudden alarm, because she remembered what gunfire sounded like. Everything around me seemed to sharpen, my heart hammering with rage and terror in equal measures.

"Now!" Frau Kuiper screamed, her voice distant.

As one, the flyers hurled their flasks downward toward the advancing line of men. Glass shattered, and safflesäure splashed to burn wherever it landed. Flamestuff pooled on the ground and ignited in waves of brilliant fire, engulfing the first line of advancing men. The flight field was filled with flickering illumination, blue-white flashes above punctuating each release of dragon breath. Without the shaping of a skilta, the breath rent everything it touched to its principal athers.

A gust of hot air blew back at us, bringing a stench like burning hair. *The shapeless medicine of a dragon's breath is change.* The world changed around me as I clung to Kasaqua's side.

Light flashed, and I saw a bjalladreki tumbling from the air, one of its wings grotesquely torn by the claws of another dragon.

Rider and dragon both plummeted, screaming, into the trees beyond the flight field with a horrible crashing noise.

Light flashed, and I saw Gerhard launching himself to meet another kesseldrache. The two collided in midair, talons locked together, spinning through the sky as Gerhard's hind feet raked across the other dragon's belly.

Light flashed, and I saw a silberdrache with a blood-covered face loose a breath at a young kesseldrache, fallen to ash without even a chance to scream.

Light flashed, and I saw Captain Einarsson's silberdrache dive through a cloud of ash that had once been a man, her silver scales gleaming with reflected firelight as she banked sharply to avoid rifle fire from below.

Light flashed. Light flashed. Light flashed.

A tremendous roar split the air as Mesman's falterdrache unleashed his breath directly into the center of the advancing line. The world seemed to pause for a heartbeat as a section of the field simply ceased to be—men, dragons, weapons, and earth reduced to swirling motes. In the darkness that followed, I heard Kostbar make a piercing cry that stopped too suddenly.

The Ravens were advancing in waves, moving in the darkness between flashes of dragonfire. The air was beginning to thicken with ash and smoke, obscuring everything, making me cough and blink through watering eyes. I could hear shouted commands cutting through the horrible roar of battle.

"Mister Jansen, to me!" Professor Schreiber screamed. Inga darted past me, Sander astride her bareback, hunched low to her neck. Kasaqua pressed closer to me, her sides heaving with anxiety and eagerness. I could feel her desire to join the fight properly, to protect me, to unleash her breath upon our enemies.

The Ravens pushed forward across the field, and now I could see their faces in the intermittent light—grim, determined men with blood on their faces and fire in their eyes. These weren't just rabble; these were true believers in whatever cause Sveni Audulfsson represented. Suddenly, the sky above us darkened further as a massive form descended toward us—a kesseldrache, its riders in the black uniform of the dragonthede.

"Run!" Professor Schreiber screamed, hauling herself up onto Hans's back. "Scatter!"

I hauled myself up onto Kasaqua's back, hooking my knees over her wing joints, burying my hands in her mane.

"Found the little savage bitch and her dragon! Here!" the man's voice called, close enough for me to actually make out the words. Kasaqua leaped mightily, and the kesseldrache's breath scoured the ground where we had been. I could feel the heat and wind of it at my back through the silk gown I still wore.

"Alive if you can . . ." a voice screamed somewhere behind us. "Audulfsson . . . son . . . reward!"

A silberdrache landed heavily in our path, its rider leveling a pistol at us. Everything seemed to sharpen and brighten as Kasaqua and I became one creature—a creature that needed to make the bad thing in front of us *not be.* A pistol—that was a pistol—*pistols hurt bang loud pain! Breathe in, scream out, unmake it and keep running.*

We were one creature that leaped into the air and extended our wings.

It hurt in our shoulders arms hands fingerbones, because we were too heavy, but we were strong it was important, we were going to hurt ourselves, the badloud everything was going to hurt us, away away away!

Another dragon screamed from the other way, behind the academy, and *that was Tamsyn; we knew her voice*! We landed clumsily and *scraped our feet scrabbling in the grass feetpads hands hurt* and staggered to a halt beside the wall of the dragonhall, because *den safe closed hide,* but stopped because others were coming.

Tamsyn's cry sounded again, closer this time, joined by other dragon voices, unfamiliar but strong. I fought to make us two again, to drag myself back into my body. The intense oneness of our selves had saved us, but now I needed to think clearly. Kasaqua shuddered beneath me, her breathing labored from the brief, desperate flight.

Several dragons were sweeping in from the northwest, silhouetted against the smoke-filled night. Leading them was the unmistakable ruddy-scaled form of Tamsyn, with Herr Gerdasson astride her back. Behind him flew at least eight other dragons—all full-grown, all with experienced riders. Frau Brinkerhoff's telegrams had reached their targets.

"Reinforcements!" I called to anyone who could hear me. "From the northwest!"

Tamsyn banked sharply, then dove toward a cluster of Ravens' dragons that had been harassing Professor Mesman's group. Her breath flashed blinding blue-white, like lightning, and two dragons and their riders became ashes.

The other reinforcement dragons spread out in a practiced formation, creating a protective arc over the academy grounds.

"Enki's Fire!" Herr Gerdasson bellowed, and the arc of dragons all swooped in unison. I heard the popping, smashing volley of flasks they'd thrown . . . and then the battlefield was illuminated as bright as day, exposing the Ravens' positions. The enemy forces hesitated, suddenly visible and vulnerable without the cover of darkness.

"Fall back, children!" Herr Gerdasson's voice boomed across the grounds. "Get to the dragonhall! We will hold the perimeter!"

I urged Kasaqua toward the nearest dragonhall entrance, her legs trembling with exhaustion. Our brief flight had drained her more than I realized. I could feel her confusion and elation. She had never flown before tonight, hadn't really known she could, until desperation drove us.

As we staggered into the dragonhall, I saw Sander and Inga racing toward us. Sander's face was streaked with soot, but his eyes were alive with a fierce determination I had never seen in him before.

"You flew! Isawyouyouflewyouflew!" he shouted, all in a rush.

"I know!" I called back, half-laughing, half-sobbing from the sheer impossibility of it. "She wasn't supposed to be able to yet!"

Before he could respond, Professor Schreiber appeared astride Hans, her hair wild around her face.

"Inside, all of you!" she shouted. "The perimeter defense is re-forming. Reinforcements have arrived."

We hurried into the dragonhall, which was crowded with people and dragons. Stall doors had been taken off their hinges to make barriers. Captain Einarsson stood at the far end of the hall, barking orders. His dragon was lying down in her stall, growling in obvious pain; the leather of one wing was hanging in shreds. Blood pooled on the hay-strewn floor beneath her.

"Gerdasson has arrived with eight riders from the northern outposts," Einarsson was saying. "Two more groups are on their way from the west and south."

I slid off Kasaqua's back, and my legs nearly buckled as I hit the ground; I hadn't realized how tightly I'd been gripping her with my thighs and calves.

As I leaned against Kasaqua's side for support, the guards parted to allow someone entry. Theod staggered in, supporting himself against the harness-ring at Copper's shoulder. Copper limped slightly, a long gash visible across the flesh of his shoulder and wing joint. The harness strap was hanging loose, having been severed.

"Theod!" I called out, pushing myself upright despite the aching in my thighs.

His face was streaked with ash and sweat, but his eyes lit up when he saw me.

"Anequs!" he called. "You're alive, thank the gods."

We met in the middle of the hall, embracing fiercely. He was shaking, or I was shaking—or we both were. Our foreheads pressed together; our breath mingled. *We were both alive.* We stood there for what felt like a long time, the walls of the dragonhall barely muffling the roars and screams outside.

"Copper's shoulder—" I began when I could move again, pulling back to look at him over Theod's shoulder.

"Just a flesh wound. He'll be all right," Theod said, his voice tight with concern. He was trying to convince me of something that he wasn't sure about. He glanced at Kasaqua, who was watching us with bright, alert eyes.

"Is she—did I hear right? Did she fly?" he asked.

"Yes," I said, still hardly believing it myself. "Not far, and not particularly well, but she flew."

Captain Einarsson's voice cut through our reunion. "They're retreating! The Ravens are falling back to the train station."

A ragged cheer went up from those gathered in the dragonhall, quickly hushed as the captain raised his hand.

"Don't celebrate yet," he warned. "They're regrouping, not surrendering. We have reports that—"

The guards parted again, admitting a stranger I'd never seen before. He was a tall man with a weathered face and a gray-and-white beard, wearing the leather flying jacket of a courier dragoneer.

Behind him limped an adult bjalladreki with a deep gash across its chest, carefully making its way into the hall.

"Captain Einarsson," the man called, his voice rough with exhaustion. "Courier Haglund, northern outpost."

Einarsson strode forward to meet him. "Report, Haglund."

"The reinforcements from the west will be here within the hour—sixteen riders, mostly garrison dragonthede who refused to join Audulfsson's coup." Haglund paused to wipe blood from his brow. "And the southern party is thirty minutes behind them. But there's something else you should know."

A pair of hall lads rushed to help the injured bjalladreki, guiding it to an empty stall. Several students had pushed forward, anxiously scanning Haglund's face.

"My father—" one began.

"Is Torgar Alvenholm with you?" another demanded. Josef Alvenholm.

Haglund held up his hand, and they went quiet.

"Many of your fathers are among the reinforcements," he said, nodding. "They rode out the moment word reached them. Torgar Alvenholm is with us, yes."

"The rest of the dragonthede? The thanegards?" Captain Einarsson asked, stepping forward.

"Taken, as the Ravens claimed," Haglund said with a look of pain.

Silence fell over the hall as the implications of his words sank in.

"Audulfsson's declared himself Wroughtjarl of Vastergot 'until order is restored.' He says they'll have an althynge."

Murmurs rippled through the gathered students and staff. Outside, the sounds of battle had faded to occasional distant shouts and the beating of dragon wings as our forces pursued the retreating Ravens.

Captain Einarsson looked around at all of us—students in torn ballroom finery, professors with weapons in hand, dragons with wounds being tended to, the barricaded doors and the floor marked with blood and worse.

"Then I fear," he said grimly, his eyes reflecting the first pale light of day filtering through the high window on the east wall, "as of sunrise, we are officially at war."

Moniquill Blackgoose is the bestselling author of *To Shape a Dragon's Breath,* which has won both the Nebula and Lodestar Awards. She began writing science fiction and fantasy when she was twelve and hasn't stopped writing since. She is an enrolled member of the Seaconke Wampanoag Tribe and a lineal descendant of Ousamequin Massasoit. She is an avid costumer and an active member of the steampunk community. She has blogged, essayed, and discussed extensively across many platforms the depictions of indigenous and indigenous-coded characters in sci-fi and fantasy.

ABOUT THE TYPE

This book was set in Garamond, a typeface originally designed by the Parisian type cutter Claude Garamond (c. 1500–61). This version of Garamond was modeled on a 1592 specimen sheet from the Egenolff-Berner foundry, which was produced from types assumed to have been brought to Frankfurt by the punch cutter Jacques Sabon (c. 1520–80).

Claude Garamond's distinguished romans and italics first appeared in *Opera Ciceronis* in 1543–44. The Garamond types are clear, open, and elegant.

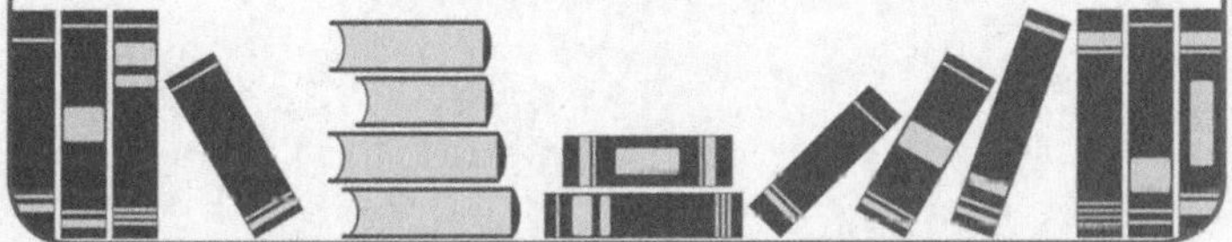